I0675679

THE PLAYGROUND BOOK 1

THE JESTER,
THE HEDONIST

CASSANDRA LEUTHOLD

The Jester, the Hedonist
Copyright © 2018 Cassandra Leuthold
All rights reserved.

Published by Green Hill Press
South Bend, IN

ISBN-10: 1-947367-03-X
ISBN-13: 978-1-947367-03-6

This story is a work of fiction. Names, characters, and events are products of the author's imagination or are used fictitiously. Any resemblance to actual events or persons, living or dead, is coincidental.

Cover design by Deranged Doctor Design

The Jester, the Hedonist

Chapter One

Fawn strode down the hallway, every step landing hard but steady on her thin two-inch heels. She barely caught glimpses of her assistant, Chloe, trying to keep up behind her left shoulder.

Chloe's plastic glasses, black on the outside and red-pink on the inside, slid out of place. She pushed them up to the bridge of her delicate nose. She stumbled on her taller chunky heels but righted herself. Her high-shine auburn hair dusted her collar bones where her lilac blouse gaped open to expose them. She rebalanced her notepad over her forearm as well, scribbling with her bejeweled pen. "Move Thursday's meeting to Friday. Got it. What about the letterhead?"

Fawn answered on autopilot as she turned into her sunlit office. "Keep it. I can't afford to spend time on it now."

Chloe made another note. She tapped her pen against the notepad. "We've had several more offers to redesign the company logo. Any interest in starting there?"

Fawn shook her head. She circled her glass-top, metal-legged desk and dropped into her plush orange chair. Her charcoal-grey suit jacket hung over the chair's back. "Little changes aren't going to do it. If I want Better Mind to stay relevant and ahead of the competition, I need bigger ideas than redrawing what already works."

"Okay."

Fawn looked away as Chloe jotted down her decisions on the notepad and gazed out the far bank of windows at the distant faded-blue sky. Fawn plucked at the striped cuffs of her bright-pink blouse. "What's next?"

"Janet called to say she read the *Times* interview. I told her you were in a meeting with upper management, so she left a message that she was proud of you and she'd like to do lunch. She understood, of course, that you're busy."

"Busy trying to keep her baby alive and thriving." Fawn

trailed her attention across the items on her desk, from her matte-silver laptop to the collection of shiny metal-framed photographs. She'd bought the laptop to give herself an edge in multitasking and staying on top of her responsibilities. The photos, minus their fancy frames, Fawn had displayed in every cubicle and office she'd ever worked in. Years had passed since Fawn first set foot in Better Mind's fourteenth-floor rooms, fresh out of college, sporting flats and excited about putting motivational videos together for various big-name clients. The photos had survived the trek to the fifteenth floor when Janet Mercer promoted Fawn to her mastermind team, even though Fawn dropped the box of her belongings when she saw her new office.

Fawn picked up a picture of herself and her sister, Tara. How differently their lives played out remained one of their family's biggest understatements. For every career success Fawn reached, Tara seemed to counter with personal success. Fawn came to work at Better Mind. Tara got married. Fawn got promoted. Tara had twins. Janet asked Fawn to take over company operations after her retirement, and Fawn gladly accepted.

Tara bought a house.

Fawn frowned at the photograph. It was one of her all-time favorite shots, but its age taunted her today. Fawn and Tara basked in brilliant sunlight, Fawn topped with a black mortarboard dangling a white tassel. Tara stood with her arm around Fawn, her round chin tossed up under her grin. Fawn had always considered it a look of pride and defiance, as if to say, *Nobody better mess with my big sister out in that world.*

The last time Fawn saw Tara's dress from that day, yellow tulips on blue, it was in a heap of clothes Tara tossed out of her closet. "You want any of this?" Tara griped over her shoulder, reaching for another dress on a hanger. "None of this fits me after the kids."

Fawn, seated on the edge of Tara's bed, had folded her arms over her fit belly and rejected the offer.

Fawn set the photograph, one her father had eagerly

snapped, back in place. On its left, the siblings' parents beamed together at the lake while the sun set in crimson and fuchsia beyond its waves. To the graduation's right sat the newest comer to the collection, Fawn's nephews in green helmets racing down the sidewalk on blue bicycles with training wheels. Fawn grumbled at it. "This picture's practically ancient. I should really make a point to bring a recent one." Tara and their parents certainly provided Fawn with enough of them.

Chloe's voice spiked with urgency. "Do you want me to write that down for you?"

Fawn's adrenaline from the morning's nonstop meetings flagged, and she rested back against the chair's upholstery. "No."

Her parents looked so happy up at the lake. Euphoric, even. And how relieved and invincible had Fawn felt when she took that diploma in her hands? Could she even relive a part of that enthusiasm and freedom now? The twins smiled with open mouths as if their neighborhood sidewalk was the world's most thrilling roller coaster.

Chloe's tone picked up some edge. "Fawn?"

Fawn scooted her chair in and sat up. She calculated by the flat, firmness of Chloe's question how many times she'd already asked it. At least three. And by the rumbling that quivered along the right side of Fawn's stomach, she knew what Chloe's real question was. "No time for lunch. Grab me a power bar from the lounge and run down to the café for a green smoothie. I have a one o'clock, right?"

"With Demetria."

Fawn forced a weak smile and brought up her calendar on the laptop's screen. "Haven't I spent enough time with my VP today?"

Chloe tipped her head to one side and adopted a bright smile. "You'll be glad to know you're meeting with the website design team at two."

Acute, dull pain radiated through Fawn's stomach. She laid her hand over it. "Discussing?"

Chloe flipped back several pages in her notepad. "The color scheme."

"Not important," Fawn groaned.

"And if we should change where we get our stock images from."

Fawn raised her index finger. "That needs to be considered. All right. Get me the quick lunch and the smoothie." Fawn wobbled getting to her feet. She smoothed the wrinkles out of her knee-length black pencil skirt. "If I asked for a coffee, what number would that be for me today?"

"Number three."

Fawn's stomach ached. She waved her hand in front of her. "Just the smoothie."

"Green."

"Extra green."

Chloe made a note. "Got it. Anything else?"

"The strength to get through this day."

Chloe chuckled and raced off on her wide high heels.

Fawn jogged around her desk and called after Chloe down the hallway. "And some fruit if you can find some."

Chloe turned around and speed-walked backwards. "What kind?"

"Like an apple or something."

Chloe nodded and spun around. A bell dinged at the end of the corridor, and Chloe dashed for the parting elevator doors.

Fawn groaned at her twisting stomach and ducked back into her office. She settled into her orange chair for another, deeper look at her day's calendar on the laptop. "Website team at two. Marketing at three. Four, I talk to the new director of sales."

Fawn scrolled through the rest of her itinerary. She drooped back from the laptop against her chair. "Once again, I'll be lucky to get out of the building by six-thirty."

Fast-paced footfalls in the hallway made Fawn look to the door in anticipation.

Chloe rushed in. Her notepad flopped up and down under a

crinkling power bar in one hand. She extended her other hand to Fawn across the desk.

Fawn squinted at the flat, plastic-wrapped item Chloe offered her. "What's that?"

"Kiwi-lime dried-fruit bar. It was the closest thing the lounge had to an apple. It says it's made from real fruit."

Fawn sighed and took it. She tore the wrapper open and chewed off a bite. "My smoothie?"

"I'm running down for it now." Chloe tossed the power bar on the desk and took her cell phone out of the back pocket of her black dress pants. "I placed the order in the elevator."

"Good. Get the extra—"

"Green. I will." Chloe sprinted out of the office.

Fawn ate half the fruit bar before skimming part of the wrapper in passing interest. "All the fruit with only half the water." She cleared her throat and wandered over to the windows across the room.

The city played out its day a hundred and fifty feet below her. A bus hummed by, followed by a line of standard-issue cars, over-sized pickup trucks, and immaculate SUV's. People strolled the sidewalks, some hung with purses, others lugging weighted backpacks. A group of five thirty-somethings dressed in suits walked into the restaurant across the street.

Footsteps on the carpet pulled Fawn away from the view. Anticipating her assistant, she raised her fruit bar to wrestle another bite free with her teeth. When she saw Monica paused inside the doorway, Fawn lowered her lunch substitute. "I thought you were Chloe."

Monica propped a hand on her slender hip. Her sleeveless purple dress swayed just above her knees. Her lips slid into a sideways smirk of disapproval as she sauntered over. "No, not Chloe."

"Or maybe Janet, returning to replace me after talking me into replacing her."

Monica reached for the fruit bar. "I'm not either of them

because they encourage you to eat this way. Where's your lunch?"

"This is it. Part of it."

"The rest of it?"

Fawn pointed the fruit bar at the desk. "By my laptop and the smoothie Chloe's bringing me from the café."

Monica folded her tanned, freckled arms. "I didn't realize the fifteenth floor had such serious sanctions against food resembling food. Do you remember having lunch down on the fourteenth? Those club sandwiches we could barely fit our hands around? The pickles the size of your arm?"

Fawn smirked. "Your arms, maybe."

Monica gave Fawn's shoulder a gentle push. "Yours are still all muscle from hitting the gym so hard to get over the stress of this place."

"Funny, isn't it?" Fawn gazed out the window at the meandering passersby and steady traffic crawl. "Better Mind makes motivational videos with some of the best technology and psychology in the world. But the longer I run it, the worse I feel."

Monica's grey eyes widened, and she relaxed her arms at her sides. "How bad is it?"

Fawn shrugged and ate the rest of her fruit bar. She moved to the trash can beside her desk and dropped the empty wrapper in. "You just caught me at a bad time."

Monica rubbed her palms together and caught up to Fawn. "How about eating a real lunch? I bet you'd feel ten times better."

Fawn collapsed into her chair and picked up the power bar. "Can't. I only have room in my schedule for one real meal a day." She turned her laptop to show Monica the calendar.

Monica gave it the briefest of glances, unimpressed. "Have dinner with me, then. Cooked by a real person. You know they're still doing that now."

"I just saw a bunch of people going into Enzo's across the street."

"Why can't that be you?"

Fawn patted the top of her laptop screen.

"Right." Monica held her arms out and bowed down to the laptop. "The almighty evidence."

Fawn chuckled and opened her power bar wrapper.

Chloe careened into the office and set a clear plastic cup on Fawn's desk. An acid-green concoction filled it almost to the lid. "One smoothie, extra green."

Fawn pinched the straw and stirred it in circles through the mixture.

Monica covered her face with her hands and pretended to sob. "That used to be a salad. A salad!" She hunched her shoulders forward as she dragged her feet to the door, clad in flat-soled boots. In an instant, she straightened up and flipped her long, straight black hair over her shoulder. It shuddered down her back to her waist. "Seriously. Dinner. With me. Tonight. No rescheduling. What time do you get out of this fancy prison cell?"

Fawn set her hand on her laptop to face its screen toward her.

Monica pursed her thin lips.

Fawn hesitated. "I'll meet you at eight."

"Where?" Monica shot her hips to one side and leaned against the doorway.

"The place with the onion rings."

Monica showed her pearly teeth in an aggravated smile. "That's probably a bar or a fast-food place you're thinking of. You know what?" She clasped her hands together. "It's summer, not that you'd know it from this air-conditioned winter paradise. We're going to Smuckey's, and we're sitting on the patio, and we're enjoying the evening breeze and leaving all of this calendar business here in the clouds. Okay?"

Fawn's heart relaxed. "Sounds good."

Monica waved with undulations of her fingers and wandered off down the hall.

Chloe rifled through her notepad with crashes and crinkles of the pages. "I bumped into Lars downstairs. He wants to talk to you about the packaging for the boxes when clients purchase the physical product."

Fawn's mind loaded the series of logical follow-up questions into single file. But her heart danced ahead to sitting down with Monica for a chat, a chicken sandwich, and a tall glass of red wine. She prompted Chloe with a simple, "Mm-hmm."

Chloe beat a tattoo on her notepad with her pen. "Okay. He says what we have now is outdated. It's wasteful, when it should be green."

"Like my smoothie." Fawn flicked her eyebrows up at the blend in the clear cup.

"Yeah. Ha. He means good for the environment. So many big companies consider their impact now."

"We do."

"But it's not always front-facing, I guess."

Fawn mulled her smoothie over like it held something strange and potentially inedible. "What else?"

"He'll go over it with you in the meeting. But he did mention the extra paperwork and plastic wrap is confusing, overwhelming, and…" Chloe squinted at her notes. "Oh, it says frustrating."

"That's not good." Fawn longed for those past, leisurely lunch breaks packed with jokes and actual cuisine. She forced herself to take a long sip of the smoothie. She'd need every ounce of its calories, vitamins, and chlorophyll to power through the next eight hours.

"No, it's bad. When can we fit him into the calendar? He sounded kind of urgent about it."

"Well, we don't want to irritate our customers before they've even introduced our videos to their employees." Fawn scooted her chair up to the laptop. She sucked smoothie up through the straw just as Monica passed by the glass panes flanking Fawn's office doors.

Monica frowned at Fawn, shook her head, and kept walking.

Fawn put the smoothie cup aside. "Let me get through the rest of today's meetings. Then I'll find a time for Lars."

Chloe stood perfectly still for a long second. Laughter

bubbled out of her mouth, and she laid a hand flat against her chest. "I thought you meant that. You got me good."

Fawn suffered a crooked grin. "Just testing you. We'll squeeze him in at the end of the week."

~

Outdoor security lights streamed lemon-yellow beams into Fawn's dim bedroom. She left the dresser and nightstand lamps off. She steadied her hand on the dresser's wooden corner and pried her high heels off. They tumbled to the carpet with padded thuds.

Fawn blinked her dry eyes several times, trying to focus her mind. "Going out to Smuckey's with Monica. What do I wear?"

Fawn's overworked fingers fumbled with the hook-and-eye clasp on the back of her skirt. She fought with it until thin metal snapped and freed her way to the small, elongated zipper pull. She wriggled out of the skirt and peeled her pantyhose off. She wadded it into a ball and whipped it across the room. "Evil. Whoever invented you is not my friend."

Blowing a breath upward to blast her wispy bangs out of her eyes, Fawn went to her closet and wrenched the door open. As usual, it scooted across the surface of the beige carpet. Fawn yanked on it harder until she could see the full contents of her closet. She tapped her foot as dress after blouse presented itself. "If I show up in any of this, it's going to look like a business dinner."

Dark-blue denim promised something different. Fawn lifted the garment down into full view on its hanger. The sleeveless denim dress nipped in sharply at the waist, and the last time Fawn had worn it, it had fallen several inches short of her knees. "Not trying to get laid here." She smacked the hanger's open loop back in place on the metal pole.

The six months since Fawn had found herself in a romantic situation — any at all — widened like a chasm inside her chest. The increasingly familiar pain crept into her stomach, and Fawn fought tears. "Not crying over you again. This is between Monica and me."

She forced the closet door toward closed. It snagged halfway there, and Fawn gave up. She moved over to the dresser beside it and started opening drawers. "What do I want to wear?"

Like magnets, the obvious options pulled Fawn to them. She held them up, a baggy t-shirt and drawstring cotton pants. She put them on and flicked the light switch by the room's entrance.

Fawn blinked hard at her reflection haunting the mirror like a haggard apparition. She stared at herself, hardly recognizing who had once been energetic and eager to be a part of the world. Ruddy exhaustion rimmed her eyelids. Her eyeliner might've stayed mostly in place for the last fourteen hours, but its matte black was almost matched by the bruise-like crescents under her eyes. Her concealer could barely keep up with her schedule.

Fawn held the t-shirt's extra material out from her sides. The name of her high school and its burly, snarling mascot graced her chest. "I've finally become *that* girl. Fourteen years out of high school, and this is the best casual outfit I can find. I can't go out like this."

The pink of her pants caught her attention and shocked her. Rainbow-graced clouds floated across the pastel background. "I thought these were khakis."

Fawn scratched her head. She wanted to change out of her way-too-casual clothes, but she couldn't make herself move. "Okay, nearest acceptable compromise."

Fawn wrestled herself out of her t-shirt and pajama pants. She dug up a pair of black yoga pants that clung to her butt and an old peasant top that looked brand-new because she rarely wore it. Re-dressed and somewhat pleased, Fawn moseyed out into the main room of her apartment. Two cream-colored couches staked out a living room by the front door to her far left. A boxy pine-wood table served as the grounding feature of a plain, low-key dining area just to her left. A single nail head jutted out of the opposite wall, left by the previous occupant and still awaiting the decor of Fawn's choice. Fawn stopped by the table and its full set of chairs.

"Six chairs," she muttered. She swept her hand over the top of the closest upholstered chair back. "Who am I kidding?"

The pain in Fawn's stomach radiated a little further out. She rested her palm over it and wandered into the kitchen at the back of the apartment. "Maybe a little snack will calm this down before I attempt to sell some bold-faced lies to my best friend."

Fawn opened the refrigerator and leaned down to get a better look at its contents. The new angle didn't make any new food appear. A carton of almond milk and a half-full plastic basket of strawberries sat on the top shelf. With a flutter of hope and interest, Fawn retrieved the strawberries. White, hairy mold greeted her from the topmost berries, which had darkened from scarlet to crimson.

"Gross." Fawn tossed the carton at the garbage can beyond the end of the counter. It sank inside and thumped against the bottom. "That was lucky."

Fawn returned to the fridge and rubbed her stomach. "Let's see."

The middle shelf held a wilted salad with sagging tomatoes inside a plastic shell. Fawn crinkled her nose. Three pieces of pizza sat stacked on a plate covered with plastic wrap. The refrigerator door cradled half a dozen eggs and a jumbo jar of crunchy peanut butter.

Fawn set the jar on the counter and lowered a box of crackers from a cabinet. Grabbing a knife from its drawer, she made and ate a succession of small sandwiches. When the pain in her stomach subsided, Fawn put her snacks away and brushed crumbs off her palms. She tied her sneakers on and snatched her purse from the bedroom.

She drove over to Smuckey's in her slick, sleek SUV. Its overstuffed seating and countless touch-pad controls comforted her. She let the CD in the player do its thing, and she started to relax. "That's right. Everything's not so bad."

She parked at Smuckey's. The parking lot was fuller than she expected. "Are we even gonna get a seat on the patio?"

Instantly, Fawn spotted Monica. Despite Monica's tall, thin stature and curtain of dark hair, floodlights illuminated her in the remaining strands of day. Monica lingered by the front doors, scanning the area with casual turns of her head. Unlike Fawn's thrown-together outfit, Monica looked effortlessly chic in a flowing turquoise tank top and almost-black blue jeans.

Fawn had always been able to find Monica quickly, even in thick, unruly crowds. Rock concerts, political rallies, and the one time they participated in a city race had all proven no match for their friendship. That relieved her, too.

Pain poked the side of Fawn's stomach, and she winced. Grabbing her purse, she climbed out of her SUV and made a beeline for Monica on the sidewalk. "Did the patio fill up already?" A line of interlocking, seven-foot bushes obscured the view of the patio. Fawn tried to peer through the branches and needles.

Monica bucked her chin up. A grin spread across her face. "I've been here for twenty minutes. I got us a table."

"You're a life saver."

Monica led Fawn through the restaurant dining room toward the doors to the patio. A waitress smiled at them from a neighboring table. Monica pointed to Fawn. "I found my friend."

The waitress curled the top page back on her notepad. "Good. I'll be right with you."

The pages' scraping sounds inflamed the ache in Fawn's stomach. She followed Monica onto the patio and gratefully plopped down in a chair at the table Monica ushered her to.

"Nice, huh?" Monica settled in next to Fawn. She gazed around them at the sheltering evergreens and potted flowers blooming in orange. "If we're here long enough, the sun will go down, and the crickets will come out."

Fawn groaned and nestled her purse at her feet.

"What's wrong? Cricket phobia?"

"I want to catch up with you, Mon. I'd love to be here with

you all night. But I get up at four."

Monica's face puckered. "What happened to the five-minute wardrobe and five-minute face?"

"Janet wanted to put me in charge, and I said yes." Fawn folded her arms on the table. "Can't cheat the clock anymore. I try to."

Monica's mouth straightened into a line. "You think you're beating the clock when you eat on the run. You're really cheating yourself."

"It's not so bad." Fawn lowered her arms into her lap. "Today just threw me off my game."

"What happened?"

"Every time I turn around, another stock photo company's cropping up."

"Why's that bad?"

"The media team keeps running in circles, crunching the numbers on the best deal. But some of those sites don't have the human-interest photos we need. They certainly don't have the same quality."

Monica lazed in her chair. "Okay. What else?"

"Demetria agrees with me in her words, but her eyes are always judging me. She does that thing where she shifts her jaw to one side." Fawn slid her jaw askew and back into place. "You know?"

"I've seen her do it in staff meetings."

"And the packaging." Fawn propped her elbows on the table and clasped her hands together. She leaned her forehead against them. "Why are clients still buying physical copies of our products? It's the digital age. Leave the plastic wrap and printed instructional booklets out of it. Buy the videos and download them like everybody else."

The waitress appeared at the corner of the table between Fawn and Monica. She set two glasses of water down. Pulling her magenta pen and notepad from her apron, she brandished them in front of her. "What can I get for you?"

Fawn sighed and picked up her menu. "I totally forgot. I'm sorry."

Monica left her menu on the table. She raised her eyebrows at Fawn. "Share a super-loaded nachos with me?"

A single spot burned in Fawn's stomach. She cringed and shook her head.

"I'll give you a few minutes." The waitress slipped away.

Fawn gripped her stomach and moaned.

Monica grimaced and bent toward her. "Too much jalapeño?"

"Too much... everything." The devouring fire cooled in Fawn's stomach. She braced her forearm against the table's edge. Sweat dotted her forehead. "I lied to you, Mon. Things are terrible. Everything's falling apart."

Monica scooted her chair closer. "Tell me."

"Tara steals my thunder every time I make an advancement in my career, but that's no reason to avoid her and Cal and the boys. I haven't seen my parents in months. They can usually make me laugh and forget this sort of nonsense, but I've been so swamped at work."

"With packaging and picture files."

Fawn nodded. "That's the worst part of it. I love what we do at Better Mind. I believe in taking a snippet of music, a succession of inspiring photos, and merging them with energizing affirmations. I believe in taking the best technology in the world and using it to help people be the smartest, happiest versions of themselves."

Monica gestured to Fawn. "Like the..." She stammered. "...beats and stuff you were telling me about?"

Fawn shook her head. "We used to use binaural beats. I prefer isochronic tones for commercial clients. The managers can play the videos for the whole department or the entire shift. They can run the videos in the breakroom. You have to wear headphones to reap the full benefits of..." Fawn focused on Monica's blank, glassy-eyed expression. "Sorry. I lost you."

"No." Monica rubbed Fawn's arm. "I get it. You have a million choices presented to you every day."

"Demetria makes me feel like an idiot. She claims my decisions and ideas are good, but she moves her jaw. Her eyes glint at me. And I swear she doesn't approve of anything I say."

"That shouldn't matter. Janet wanted you in charge, not Demetria."

"Well, I think Demetria prefers Demetria to be in charge."

Monica tipped her forehead down. "So what's this stomach business?"

Fawn smoothed her hand across her stomach. "I might be forming an ulcer. I'm not sure."

Monica rested back against her chair. "I'd ask, but I'll assume the answer. You haven't seen a doctor."

"No. There's no time." Fawn inched forward to sit on the edge of her seat. "I know how I used to eat. Chicken fingers and Cobb salad and those crazy-good roast beef sandwiches with the salty au jus sauce so delicious, we joked about drinking it."

Monica shared a sly grin. "I might've taken a sip or two when you weren't paying attention."

"How was it?"

"Tasty, but I wouldn't recommend it."

"I used to eat fruit in its natural form, not dehydrated and mashed into a rectangle. I could get through the day on enthusiasm and green tea. Lately, I'm powered by espresso and spirulina. I'm always unwrapping something in bar form, whether it's power, protein, or granola."

"Can you go back to the gym? The elliptical and the spinning seemed to help get some tension out. Not to mention the stair climber."

Fawn splayed her fingers wide. "I don't have the time or the energy." She pinched the stretchy black fabric of her yoga pants. "Don't let these fool you. I haven't worked out in months. They were merely an alternative to the pajama pants I tried on."

The waitress paused beside the two women. "Have we

decided?"

Monica collected the two menus and handed them to the waitress. "Garden salad for my friend. No cheese." She hesitated. "No dressing. Nachos and the Greek pita for me."

"I'll bring your nachos in about ten minutes." The waitress strolled away.

Fawn's chin jerked, and she steadied her teeth against each other to keep her chin from quivering. Her voice vibrated at a quiet volume. "I'm scared, Mon. Things just keep getting worse. This pain in my stomach. The workload at Better Mind. My ties to my family." A tear slid from Fawn's eye, and she wiped it off her cheekbone. "I mean, even Chloe's part of the problem. I love having her as my assistant, but when it comes down to it, she can tow the company line better than I can. I can't find any way out of this tremendous rut I've dug myself into. All I see at the end of this tunnel is total, undeniable burnout. Maybe even dying. I don't know."

Monica carried her chair a few inches closer. "Okay. What *is* working in your life?"

Fawn's eyes widened. "Nothing. I'm not being dramatic. There's not one thing besides your friendship and my SUV that I like in my life right now. My clothes are either for working or sleeping. I have all this furniture in my apartment that nobody sits on because I'm always at the office. I never have anyone over. Half the food in my fridge stampeded past its best-by date and turned disgusting." Fawn pushed her fingers off the metal, scrolled arm of Monica's chair. "Oh, I discovered one piece of clothing that doesn't fit into those categories. It's more for sleeping around."

"How is dating going?"

Acid churned in Fawn's stomach. "I really haven't kept in touch with you very well. Every guy I've chatted with online or gone out with in person has been unbearable."

Monica tipped her head to one side with a deadpan stare.

"No, really." Fawn bounced her feet up and down on the patio stones. "The young guy was boring. The older man was self-centered. The redhead told me I had a screw loose, and the guy with the jet-black man bun couldn't tell the truth to save his life."

Monica shrugged. "It's only been six months since you broke up with Devon."

"*Broke up with* makes me sound empowered and focused, like I took some sort of stand." Fawn released her contracted muscles to let the chair completely support her body. "We were together six years. He lived with me for three of them. We drifted apart until we barely had any reaction to each other at all. It was worse than being roommates. It got to the point where if I showed up to a family party without him, nobody questioned it or bothered to ask about him."

"It took Tara a long time to find Cal."

Fawn fixed Monica with an acerbic, disbelieving glare. "She's two years younger than me, and she's married with two kids in a big house."

"But she wanted to get married when she was in kindergarten. Right? You dreamed about taking the business world by storm."

"I didn't know it was an either-or proposition. I didn't think taking Janet's offer would take over my life and leave me so alone all the time." Fawn reached into her purse for a Kleenex.

The waitress walked over and planted a large plate of mountainous nachos on the table. "About another ten minutes on the salad and pita."

Monica nodded. "Thanks."

The waitress left them, and Monica rubbed Fawn's back. "I'm sorry. Is there any wiggle room you can give yourself at the company?"

Fawn thought about it while she blew her nose. "If it's there, I can't see it. Everybody wants a meeting with me. They treat me like I'm not even human. They waylay me on the way to the bathroom to tell me about another phone call, another criticism, another idea they have. I eat between their grievances and their suggestions. I wedge my entire life into these teeny, intermittent cracks in what everyone else wants from me."

Monica pointed to the nachos, rising off the plate in a heap of melted cheese, ground beef, chunky tomato salsa, and oversized corn chips. "Mind if I dig in?"

"Go for it."

Monica scooted her chair halfway back to its normal position and arranged the nacho plate in front of her. "Have you talked to Janet?"

Defensive energy hit Fawn with a jolt. "No. Hell, no. I can't let her know she placed her baby in the wrong hands."

"You're not the wrong hands." Monica took a chip piled with toppings and forced it to fit into her mouth.

"What am I, then?" Fawn dropped her used Kleenex into her purse. "I'm a wreck. Janet conceived of that company with her husband, and she grew it even after he died. More than twenty years, Better Mind has been around. I have it for two, and I'm ready to throw in the towel."

Monica choked on her food, her eyes alarmed. She took a sip of water. "You want to leave Better Mind?"

"No. Maybe. I don't know." Fawn blew out a breath and ran her hand through her limp tresses. "I don't know what else to do. I love it there. It's the only place I've worked since college. They gave me this great opportunity. Janet basically handed me the keys to the kingdom by mentoring me and asking me to take her place. But I can't just stay there, can I? I can't keep going the same way and expect it to get magically better. If the job's killing me — and not that slowly — don't I have to put my health and sanity first?"

Monica wiped her fingers on a napkin. "Maybe you do."

"I don't know." Fawn crossed her legs and rocked her foot in the air. "What do I do?"

"I think the best course of action might be to relax and figure out how to make everything work together."

"How? I get twenty-four hours in a day. I'm at the office about eleven or twelve of those hours. That's half my day spent at Better

Mind. I can't function on less than six hours of sleep. So that leaves me with six hours in which to first shower and get ready to go to work." Fawn held out one index finger and laid her other one across it. "The remaining hours, so far, have been spent lounging on the couch trying not to drool on myself out of sheer exhaustion and doom."

"You're not doomed."

"I can't keep living the way I have been."

Monica's shoulders fell with sympathy. "No."

"So what do I do?"

Chimes sounded from Fawn's purse. She ducked down to retrieve her phone.

The waitress arrived and set two new plates of food on the table. "Enjoy." She waltzed away.

Fawn sat up with her pink-encased phone lighting up in her hand. "It's hard to enjoy eating when everything hurts," she grumbled.

Monica picked up her pita stuffed with ground lamb, vibrant greens, and creamy tzatziki. She gestured it toward Fawn. "What's blowing up your phone?"

Fawn squinted at the new text. She wrinkled her nose. "Oh, God. It's a badly disguised booty call."

Monica's pitch shot up. "From who?"

"Man bun. The perpetual liar. He claims he misses me." Fawn tapped the screen to send a reply and voiced it to Monica. "Got chlamydia. Sorry." Fawn sent the message and tossed her phone on the table.

Monica laughed. "You're bad."

"He's worse."

Monica glanced at Fawn's untouched salad. "You should eat."

Fawn picked up her fork and fluffed the top spinach leaves.

Monica finished off her pita's first half. "I'm really the only friend you've got left?"

"There are people I could get back in touch with if I cared to.

The good times I had with them seem lifetimes away. I'm not sure we have much in common anymore." Fawn gave in and ate a few bites of salad.

"The ladies down in video production still miss you working with us. They think you're doing a great job with the company. They'd be thrilled if you took us all to lunch or something on a weekend."

Fawn's former coworkers rose up in her mind, smiling and gracious. Some of them grey haired and sharp minded. Others young, exuberant, and fast talking. "Hildegard and Rosa and Yu Su?"

"Yes. Georgia left. Did you know that?"

Fawn helped herself to more lettuce, cherry tomatoes, and roasted pecans. Some of her strength flowed back into her. "I feel like somebody told me that."

"She got a great job at—" Monica stopped herself and stuffed the last big bite of pita into her mouth.

"Georgia was the best cheerleader Better Mind ever had." Fawn let her fork fall into her salad bowl and flopped back against her chair's support. She knotted her arms over her belly. "If Georgia would rather work somewhere else, what am I doing holding onto my loyalty for Janet and her business?"

"What else would you want to do?"

"I have no idea. If I didn't live in the real world, I'd take three years off, travel the world's most tropical islands, and start my own company when I came back."

Monica chortled. "How? You hate flying."

"I know."

"Do you like boats?"

"No. Too many creepy men have either offered or succeeded in getting me onto their boats. I don't do boats anymore."

"Or salad?"

"Georgia's gone." Fawn stretched her legs out and crossed one ankle over the other. "She could recite every affirmation Better Mind had ever included in a video. She even remembered some of the ones that got edited out before the videos went to clients."

Monica pushed her empty pita plate away and returned to her nachos. "And you know every Georgia, Yu Su, and Hildegard working at that company. Maybe you do need a break. Maybe it's not so far-fetched. Take a vacation. Three weeks maximum. See what happens. Find out what it changes for you."

Fawn flexed her top foot up and down. "Part of me is screaming that a vacation won't be enough, and the other part of me is yelling that I'm crazy for not considering it more seriously."

"Three weeks of eating right, walking a sandy beach somewhere, and meeting good men in your same pay grade."

"Where is this place? Because I've never found it."

Monica tapped her temple. "In my mind."

"Right. And what does three weeks away do for my relationship with Tara? Or with you, for that matter?"

"Easy. You take me along, so I'm satisfied. And we never breathe a word of it to Tara, so she's never jealous." Monica polished off the last nacho and stacked her smaller plate on top of the other one. She slid them aside.

Fawn drew her legs back toward her. "What happens if I do meet someone special in a sandy paradise? He could live on the other side of the world."

Monica made a low, thoughtful hum. "That's right. With no way to get to him other than boat or airplane, it narrows your choices to falling for someone local. Less chance of that happening abroad."

Fawn motioned to Monica's plates and outfit. "You've got it all straightened out. You look great. You seem put together."

Monica snatched a crouton from Fawn's salad and munched it. "I don't have it all. I'm out there on the dating apps, too. I've stayed late at Better Mind plenty of nights. Those deadlines for top clients are fierce. I can't imagine what you're going through, but I'm here for you. I'm worried about you, but from where I'm standing — and sitting — there has to be something you can do to break out of this trend."

"When you figure it out, let me know. I'm too exhausted." Fawn speared her fork deep into her salad.

Monica nudged Fawn's arm. "Play it cool, but there is a super-hot guy one table over who keeps glancing over here."

"He's looking at you, Mon." Fawn fit the salad greens into her mouth without caring what impression she gave.

Monica scoffed. "Is not. You're not even paying attention."

"What other leaps of reality can we make?" Fawn stirred her salad around. Croutons clinked against the bowl. "I bet he's unapproachably handsome, loves women in yoga pants, and goes ga-ga over an unfinished salad."

Monica leaned back in her chair. A grin spread over her face, and she twirled a section of her long raven tresses around her index finger. "No, I'm not kidding, Fawn. He's really something."

Fawn sipped water from her glass and rested her fork in her bowl. "All right. Where do I pretend I'm not looking?"

"At the um—" Monica blushed and cleared her throat.

"Wow. He's got you all undone."

"I told you I haven't had the best, most consistent dating, either." Monica cleared her throat with more urgency. "He's to my left. Sort of blond and red hair. Major grin. You can't miss him."

Fawn grunted. "I'm done with redheads, Mon."

"Don't be like that. Just look."

"Okay, here I go. Nice and subtle." Fawn spun her head in an instant and zeroed in on the next table over, offset from their own.

A man sat alone facing Fawn, his hair dyed in bold but muted canary and crimson. The sides were trimmed short, and the several inches of length undulated upward in curves and waves like fire. His skin glowed with a deep, golden tan against his brassy eyebrows. His steely-grey eyes drank her in with a mischievous shine. He rested one elbow in his opposite palm, his empty hand's bent fingers resting against his chin. As Monica had advertised, the man beamed at Fawn with a huge, dazzling grin.

Monica rolled her eyes. "Yeah. Subtle."

Fawn returned to her salad.

Monica's foot prodded Fawn's leg. "Whatcha think?"

"Not my type."

"Based on what?"

"He's immature and self-centered."

Monica held her palm up and swept it through the air in front of her. "Based on what?"

"Too much hair product. Always a sign of self-interest. And the colors look like the kids in high school who dyed their hair with Kool-Aid. Bright and washed out at the same time."

"Okay, I can't explain that. But — I don't know — isn't good grooming a sign he's interested in dating?"

Fawn tapped the tip of her sneaker against Monica's leg. "Why are you pawning him off on me? Why aren't you making your move?"

"Too fancy."

Fawn coughed and slid her empty bowl aside. "I must've missed the top hat and tuxedo."

"His clothes are way too nice for Smuckey's. However much money he makes, it puts me out of the race for his heart."

Fawn wagged her eyebrows at Monica. "Maybe he's slumming it. He's looking for a girl like you."

Monica averted her gaze toward the fiery-haired stranger and lowered it. "Yeah, I don't think so. His shoes look expensive, and his rings flash like solid gold."

Fawn gave Monica a doubtful glance. "They could be plated. Maybe he ran out of money after the shoes."

Monica picked up her purse.

Fawn stiffened straight up in her seat. Her voice escaped her throat low and flat. "Monica, what are you doing?"

Monica pulled out her hefty black wallet. "I'm gonna leave payment for my food and tip. Then, I'm heading to my car. You're going to trade numbers with that gorgeous man — unless he's obviously identifiable as a psycho killer. And you're going to join me at my car to tell me how it went and what his name is. Okay?

Great."

The waitress' black dress and white apron filled Fawn's peripheral vision.

Monica waved to her. "Check, please? Yeah."

The waitress gathered up the used dishes and carted them into the restaurant.

Monica laid several bills on the table and stood up.

Fawn clenched her teeth. "I'm not approaching him."

"You might as well. You have to wait for the waitress to bring the bill. You wouldn't dine and ditch just to avoid a good-looking man, would you?"

"I don't know where you parked."

"Exit the restaurant and turn left. I'm at the end of the row." Monica stepped past Fawn toward the doors to the building.

Fawn shrieked at her. "Mon!"

"Just do it. I'll wait for you. All night if I have to." Monica lifted her keys out of her purse and stuck the ring on her index finger. She whirled it around as she let herself into the restaurant.

Fawn huffed. "Not talking to him." She surveyed the tabletop. With the dishes gone, the waitress had left nothing for Fawn to fiddle with.

She picked up her phone as the chimes struck again. She flicked her eyebrows up and checked the notification. "New message. From man bun." She opened it and read it. "*No worries. Me, too.*" Fawn's skin crawled, and she threw the phone down. "Gross."

The chimes played anew. Fawn turned wary eyes on the phone's screen. "Who is it?" She tilted the phone so she could see the new message's sender. "Thank goodness. Chloe."

Fawn drew the phone toward her and hunched over it. She murmured Chloe's message under her breath. "*Demetria canceled for tomorrow a.m. Slotting in Lars.*"

Fawn tipped her head from one side to the other. "Not a bad idea." She typed in the start of a reply and chuckled to herself. "Mon was right. One less meeting with Demetria, and—"

A hand adorned with two gold rings covered Fawn's phone and carried it out of her grasp.

Fawn sucked in a breath and jerked her eyes up. A sharp, authoritative tone galvanized itself in her throat. "Hey!"

The fiery-haired stranger stood over her, shorter than average. True to Monica's description, he wore an immaculate black button-down shirt accented with navy-blue stripes. And he retained every glimmer of his magnificent grin. He rotated the phone side to side in his hand. "Business or pleasure?" His voice rolled with a thick texture like melting brown sugar.

"Very important business," Fawn retorted. She leapt for the phone.

The man eased back out of her reach and lowered himself into Monica's seat.

Fawn's chest tightened. "You can't sit there. My friend's coming back."

The man shook his head in gentle swivels. "I don't think so. She took her keys out."

"She needs something from her car." Fawn dove across the space between them. Her fingers hit the phone's protective case but failed to close around it.

The man held her phone in front of his shoulder. "If you can name the item she's looking for in less than three seconds without blurting it out in desperation, I'll give you your phone."

Fawn's shoulders drooped. "What do you want?"

"I must admit I heard most of what you and your friend were talking about."

"Big shocker." Fawn lunged for the phone.

The man switched it to his farther hand and sank it low beneath the table's edge. "You're in deeper trouble than missing your phone."

Fawn planted her sneakers on the patio stones and hoisted her purse onto her shoulder. She started to stand up. "I'm getting the manager."

The man held his empty hand out to her. "We can talk this

through just fine without anyone else."

A modicum of understanding made Fawn sigh. Her stomach lining twisted, and she collapsed into her seat. "Look, about what my friend said about me getting your number. If that's what this is about, just type it into my phone and give it back, okay?"

"Sure." The man's grin grew although Fawn wasn't sure how that was possible. He raised her phone in front of him and operated it. "Why do I get the impression you're one of those people who value your devices because your entire life is contained in them?"

The full implications blasted Fawn in the chest. Her heart raced. Who had she just invited to access her phone? Her breath evaded her. "I don't keep that much in my phone."

The man glanced up at her from its glowing screen. "I don't believe you. But I wouldn't look anyway."

"Why not?"

"I can make a point without completely obliterating your privacy."

Fawn held her palm out. "Then you won't mind returning my property."

"In a minute."

"How do I know what you're doing in my phone, then?" Fawn snuck a peek over her shoulder for the manager or even a passing waitress. Only a handful of customers sat at the other patio tables, chatting and laughing. None of them met her gaze.

The man held up Fawn's phone screen for her to see. "I've only done what you asked me to."

Fawn inspected the information he'd entered for a new contact. "Cade, hmm? What, no last name?"

"No need for one."

"And you've marked yourself as VIP. How cute."

Cade grinned and set Fawn's phone on the opposite corner of the table from her. He rested his hand over it. "I know you didn't want my number."

"Ah. You heard that part of the conversation." Fawn twisted

at the waist, searching the patio for the waitress. She peered through the glass panels in the doors to the restaurant.

"And also that you're hurtling toward a wicked burnout."

Fawn faced him. "Are you a doctor? It doesn't matter even if you are. The choice I make about moving forward is mine and no one else's."

Cade bowed his head in a deep nod. "I quite agree."

The patio door thudded shut, and Fawn looked up as the waitress approached her. Fawn dug her wallet out of her purse, fumbling to open it. She collected Monica's bills off the table and added a twenty from her wallet. She tucked the money into the black portfolio the waitress offered her. "Keep the change. All of it. Thanks."

The waitress smiled. "Have a good night. Good night, sir."

Cade answered with a flash of his hand. The waitress disappeared inside the restaurant.

Fawn got to her feet. "Now I can get out of here. Bill paid. Phone number obtained. Phone, please." She pointed to it.

Cade rose up to his full height and sandwiched her phone between his hands. "May I walk with you?"

"You're holding my phone hostage?" Fawn headed for the doors.

"Not hostage. Just holding onto it for you." Cade beat her to the doors and drew one open.

"Rude and polite in the same meeting." Fawn walked inside.

Cade reached her side. "I didn't get a chance to explain why you don't want my phone number. What you really want is to change your life."

Fawn's mouth dropped open at his insight. Then her own words echoed in her head, and she smirked. "That's pretty obvious, isn't it? Nice try."

"You want a solution that's not a compromise."

Clarity and hope balled in Fawn's chest. She wasn't ready to give Cade any credit for his spot-on assessment. Her tone hardened. "You guessed right again."

"You want it all, and you want it now. Is that accurate?"

Fawn passed the dining room tables and stopped in the open entrance area. The last scene she wanted to play out was having Cade accompany her all the way to Monica's car. Fawn planted her hands on her hips. "Let's see. I want my phone. My health. A less demanding job, and a boyfriend who doesn't lie."

Cade leaned toward her. "What if I told you there was a world that could improve everything for you?"

"A whole world, huh?"

Cade's grin and the sparkle in his eyes remained unfazed. "Yes."

"Is this like a clean, family-oriented place like Disneyland, or is this the time of the evening you kidnap me and lock me in your basement?"

"No locks. They're not necessary."

"Okay. So more like Canada."

Cade laughed. "So many jokes. So defensive."

"Do you steal a lot of people's phones? You understand that's illegal, right?"

"I take some. Not a lot. And I always give them back."

"I've yet to see evidence of that." Fawn hadn't felt so irritated and backed into a corner since she'd personally handled Better Mind's biggest clients' worst complaints. Perhaps that was the best angle to use to tackle the ornery Cade. Fawn took a deep breath. She took her hands off her hips and clasped them in front of her. "What can I do for you, Cade?"

He stepped over to the restaurant's front doors and opened one. "Answer me one question. Honestly. Without sarcasm or deflection."

Fawn ambled through the doorway, almost as unsteady on her feet as she felt in her light head. "Okay."

Cade joined her on the sidewalk. "If I could show you a place that could rejuvenate you—"

"Like a vacation?"

"Sort of. A place where you could enjoy yourself and relax

without any of the stress that's plaguing you."

Fawn raised an eyebrow. "Like a date?"

"Together, yes, but as friends." Cade encased her phone in his fingers like a cage. "You could meet the kinds of people you've never mingled with before. Catch up on rest."

Fawn's heart leapt a little. "And sleep?"

Cade nodded.

"Sign me up, but it doesn't exist."

"And you wouldn't have time to go there, isn't that what you'd argue?"

"Do you need me to go over my daily routine again?"

"Would you go?" Cade held her phone out halfway between them.

Fawn laid a hand on her forehead. "Would I have to go with you?"

"That's the only way it works."

"This is still hypothetical, right?"

Cade's eyes twinkled. Fawn stood close enough to him now to see his silver irises were ringed in charcoal grey. A smile still played on Cade's lips as he answered. "Sure."

"Yeah, I'd go." Fawn took hold of her phone.

Cade retained his grip on the other side of her device. "That's a yes?"

"With you as my guide, no time, and at the risk of losing my job, yes, I'd go there if I could."

Cade's finger brushed Fawn's. She blinked, meaning to wrench her phone out of his hand if he didn't let her take it easily.

When Fawn opened her eyes, the only thing in her vision that remained the same was Cade holding the other end of her phone and grinning.

Chapter Two

Fawn's heart threatened to explode. Her grip loosened on her phone as she stared at the changed landscape around them. Smuckey's all-encompassing floodlights no longer defended a parking lot from the intruding dusk. Headlight beams glared into the twilight about three feet off the ground from a dozen ATV's, illuminating grass-blade tips. The restaurant itself was gone, along with the pavement, its vehicles, and the surrounding buildings. Sandy grass cushioned Fawn's sneakers instead of rigid sidewalk. Fawn glanced where Monica had said her car would be waiting. Instead of Fawn's best friend and the lightly rusted sedan they'd ridden in for years, a wide swath of earth sloped down to another patchy field.

A woman's high-pitched squeal snapped Fawn's attention past Cade. People approached from the ATV's behind him, smiling and taking in Fawn with sparkling eyes. A woman with a rich, dark complexion brushed thick dredlocks over her shoulder, bared by a one-sleeved shirt. Another woman fixed her blonde tresses back into a ponytail as she strolled toward Fawn. Beside her sauntered a curvaceous young woman. Purple stripes highlighted her obsidian hair, chopped short at her jaw, while a silver bullring hung from her nose's center wall.

Fawn breathed even faster, her eyes darting at the others. A few umber-skinned men greeted her with polite, excited smiles. Moonlight glowed off the clean-shaven head one of them maintained.

A deeply tanned man of average height reached Cade's side. His medium-dark hair rested around his face, and his honey-toned eyes caressed Fawn's face. He set one hand on Cade's shoulder, rubbing his wide chin with the other. His interested gaze remained on Fawn. "Welcome." His smooth, easy voice dripped with saccharin.

Fawn squeezed the accessible half of her phone. Shock blocked her from feeling the full force of the anger she wanted to spew at Cade. "What the hell is going on? What did you do, Cade?"

The others walked up to flank Cade and his companion. The blonde woman waved. The younger one with the bullring cracked her knuckles.

Fawn's muscles erupted into shakes, her vision boring into Cade. "What'd you do?"

Cade glanced at the man beside him. "Better get moving."

"Right." The smooth-voiced man sent a whistle through his teeth. "Let's ride."

Fawn seized her phone like a vice, but Cade withdrew it from her fingers. The group disassembled, whooping and cheering into the evening half-light. Cade slid Fawn's phone into his pocket and headed for one of the ATV's. She stood frozen in place, her arms convulsing, struggling to swallow.

The smooth-voiced man reappeared in front of Fawn. He popped a dazzling smile and offered his hand. "I'm Jax."

Fawn merely vibrated in place with no move to shake his hand. She tried to introduce herself. "F-F-F-F—"

Jax inched closer and took her hand. "Nice to meet you."

An ATV rolled up next to them. Cade drove it with no helmet on.

Jax leaned over by Fawn's ear. "*Very* nice to meet you." He stepped aside and lifted her by the waist. He set her on the ATV's seat behind Cade. With a wink, Jax patted Cade's arm and moved back a pace.

The ATV's motor gave a surging purr. Fawn let out a muted scream and grabbed onto Cade's waist. All around her, motors sang and revved.

Fawn squinched her eyes shut. Gravity slanted and tugged her forward against Cade's back. She held herself away from him, forcing her eyes open. The blonde, riding on a forest-green vehicle to Fawn's left, greeted her with another wave. The uneven ground bounced Fawn up off the seat, and she tightened her arms around

Cade.

Several more engines zipped along behind Fawn. The group of ATV's curved to the right, racing up the incline they'd just sped down. Fawn clung to Cade. She'd sometimes been forward on a first date, but she'd never been so physical with a near-stranger in her life.

The ATV sprang up over the hill's crest, and Fawn yelped. Jax drew up alongside Cade and Fawn, his hair flapping in the wind. He motioned to Cade, rolling his hand in forward circles. Cade nodded.

All the vehicles accelerated. The grass whizzed by in a blur beneath Fawn's sneakers. She cried out and buried her face against Cade's back.

The ATV veered to the right again, and Fawn let out a yell of terror all the way down the slope. The vehicle bucked over the rough earth as if trying to throw her off. It reached a long stretch of something smoother and slowed to a halt. Every ATV engine cut off at the same moment.

Fawn parted her tensed eyelids and peeked around. Clouds of golden sand drifted through the air. As they settled, they revealed several grassy dunes beyond the twenty-foot-deep beach. On Fawn's other side, the sun sank gradually behind a silver, rippling lake.

Fawn scrambled off the ATV's seat, brushing any potential sand off her clothes. She erupted in breathless anger. "What was that? What do you think you're doing throwing me on the back of that thing without any warning? Or a helmet? Trying to kill me? I don't know you. I don't know where I am or how you got me here so fast."

Sagging exhaustion bent Fawn's knees. She leaned over and supported her hands on her lower thighs. She panted, staring at the ATV's wheel ridges in the sand.

One at a time, five pairs of shoes emerged into Fawn's view. She assumed the black leather dress shoes belonged to Cade. On the left rested two new-looking red, orange, and green sneakers.

On Cade's other side, women's feet lined up in denim slip-on flats, jute wedges, and plum-colored ankle boots.

Fawn craned her head up to look into their faces. Cade and Jax regarded her with calm. The friendly blonde stood next to Cade, her perfectly arched and shaped eyebrows tilted in sympathy. Balanced on the tall wedges, the young woman with the bullring pierced Fawn with disapproving blue-grey eyes. At the end of the line, a tall, full-figured woman towered over Fawn. Her dark hair radiated past her shoulders in great waves, and her eyes glittered emerald. Large, rhinestone-studded hoop earrings nestled amidst her locks. An infinity scarf looped around her neck, and several beaded necklaces rested over its folds.

Fawn gasped for air. "Where's Smuckey's? Where's Monica? She's waiting for me. I don't even know what lake this is."

Cade retrieved Fawn's phone from his pocket. "Don't worry about a thing. I'll make sure she knows you're safe."

"This was a game. A hypothetical. I didn't think…"

Cade gave no answer, his fingertips dancing across her phone screen.

Fawn held her palm up. "If you can't give me an explanation, at least give me my phone."

Cade tossed the device past the nearest two women at his side before Fawn could grab for it. She clutched thin air. The third woman with the thick, wavy hair caught the phone one-handed.

Fawn threw her hands up in aggravation. "I thought you were more mature than this."

Cade sprouted a wide grin. "This is my oldest sister, Rosario. Everybody, this is Fawn." Cade bent into a shallow bow at Fawn. "Maybe you'll find her a little more trustworthy."

A breeze swept around Fawn's back, loosening a strand of her hair and sending it fluttering against her cheek. She tucked the annoyance behind her ear. Her eyes implored Rosario. "Please. I don't really need answers. All I want is to get back to my friend and my own vehicle."

Rosario cradled Fawn's phone between her bejeweled,

manicured hands. "Fawn, everything really is all right. We'll let Monica know you're staying with us for a while."

Fawn slumped over and set her hands above her knees. "What game are you playing? Look, maybe none of you have jobs, but I do. A prestigious one. I worked at it most of the day, and I want to go home. It's pretty simple to understand."

"We'll call your place of employment, too."

A pinch tweaked Fawn's tender stomach lining. She cringed for several seconds of pain. "I'm not staying with you. I don't know you. I don't know where I am. You're not being helpful. I don't find you trustworthy. And I want my damn phone like Cade promised."

Jax and the three women fixed level gazes on Cade.

He shrugged. "*Promised* is a stronger word than what actually happened."

Fawn pushed out a low, ragged breath, trying to get the needling ache under control. "What happened is that you kidnapped me somehow."

Cade folded his arms loosely. "Again, much stronger language than I'd use. Especially considering I asked you at least twice if you'd like a relaxing getaway."

Fawn chuckled with a hard edge. "Relaxing? With the bunch of you flying all over the dunes and this beach?"

Rosario examined the pink case on Fawn's phone. "You get your own room. It's clean."

Fawn spoke through clenched teeth. "I don't exactly have my pajamas, any change of clothes, or even my battery-powered toothbrush."

"Everything will be provided for you."

"Really? Socks. Underwear. Deodorant. A hairbrush. You're prepared to gift me all this for an indeterminate amount of time on a moment's notice? Not to mention, I'm not telling any of you what size I wear in anything. And I haven't seen any buildings around whatsoever, so where's this hotel or grouping of tents you want me to sleep in?"

Rosario paused. "You'll be staying with us."

"You and Cade?" Fawn's temple picked up a hearty throb. "At, like, what? Your *house?*"

All five of the people's jaws lined up in front of Fawn dropped. Their outraged voices overlapped until Cade spread his arms out in front of them and they fell quiet.

He drew in a long, steady breath and lowered his arms. "It's not an ordinary house."

Fawn fumed. "You must think I'm an extraordinary idiot. Do you know who I am?" Fawn strained every muscle in her torso to straighten up and look Cade in the eye. "I'm president and CEO of Better Mind. I'm responsible for more than one hundred employees. I work more than sixty hours a week, and if you don't mind, I have major responsibilities to get back to first thing in the morning."

Rosario took a step toward Fawn and kept her tone gentle. "How about a better mind for you, Fawn?"

Fawn groaned with sarcastic humor. Before she could launch an acerbic comeback, pain shot in five directions through her stomach. Her temple pounded, and Fawn collapsed to her knees. She clamped her palm over the electricity burning across her middle.

Cade sank to his haunches. "You really are safe with us. And you don't appear as if you're in any shape to keep arguing with us or give your friend the details of snagging my number."

Jax howled with romantic intimation. "Whoop! Whoop!"

Cade set his hand on Fawn's shoulder. His manner softened even more. "Okay?"

Fawn found herself nodding. Cade backed up, and Rosario tossed him Fawn's phone. Jax and Rosario braced Fawn while she fought her way to her feet. Cade and most of the others hopped back on their ATV's. Jax and Rosario guided Fawn toward the open seat behind Cade.

Tension gripped her ribs, but Fawn didn't have the strength to struggle. "Not the ATV again."

Jax murmured in her ear. "Don't worry. It's a short ride."

"How would you know? Everyone here's so chummy." Fawn clambered onto the exposed part of the seat and looped her arms around Cade's waist. Her head toppled over, smacking her cheek against his back. She left it there as surrounding motors roared and purred to life.

The ATV she rode on hummed into activity and took off at a slower pace than Fawn expected.

But the last hour of her life hadn't been anything she would've ever expected, and Fawn wasn't sure in her miserable haze if she would ever bother to expect anything specific — or reasonable — again.

~

Silence. Maybe the far-off chatter of energized, happy people. Excited, muffled dog barks. Faint strains of music. Piano?

And a throaty whine.

No. That was what Fawn assumed she heard once she realized the sound issued from her own body.

It was a moan of satisfaction. Comfort. The simple pleasure of a cloud-like mattress and soft, stretchy sheets.

Fawn blinked in the golden glow of morning light floating in through the tall, white gauze curtains along one wall of the room. Hunter- and mint-green stripes gave the wallpaper a timeless, polished feel. She wiped her hand down her face. "What hotel is this?"

The beach. The ATV's. Cade and his entourage taunting her.

Fawn rubbed her eyes. The bases of her thumbs came down clean. "Well, I took my makeup off before I fell asleep. I don't remember coming here at all."

A creepy shiver rattled Fawn's spine from her neck to her tailbone. She jumped out of the bed and its thick-but-light covers. She looked down at herself, still clad in the peasant top and yoga pants. "This seems like a good sign." Fawn reached a finger under her shirt collar and snapped her bra strap against her shoulder.

"Yup, no new funny business to worry about."

She moved her inspection to the room's every aspect. A grand white-linen tufted headboard rose above the bed's messy covers, arched in the middle. On either side of the bed, a black lamp with a white shade sat on a mahogany nightstand. The furniture's edges were carved into cylindrical spirals, and brushed-nickel knobs adorned the drawers.

Fawn turned away from the windows. An oversized mahogany vanity table with exquisite details made her gasp. Its surface supported a wide, three-paneled mirror. Numerous small drawers sported clear-glass faceted knobs that reflected the sunbeams like crystal rainbows. The vanity's matching chair featured a low, padded back and a plumply stuffed seat. Fawn's purse rested on the floor against one of the fluted legs. Beside the vanity, a jewelry armoire called Fawn over to it. She lifted the square lid, its corners decorated in feathers and swirls of gold leaf. Gold, silver, and copper rings glinted at Fawn from royal-blue velvet channels. Gemstones of every color sparkled with every hint of light.

Fawn cried out and dropped the lid. Felt circles kept it from slamming. She covered her mouth with her hands. "This is certainly not a hotel."

Her sneakers sat on the almost-luminescent beige carpeting by a closed door. As she walked to them, the carpet cushioned her every step like a gentle foot massage. Fawn's remaining stress melted, and she pressed her toes deep into the soft fibers. She reached for her shoes.

Tentative knocks on the door caught Fawn unaware. She jumped back from her sneakers and the door. Her heart's pace picked up. "Um, who is it?" Cade still in possession of her phone? The supposedly more-trustworthy-than-Cade Rosario? The winking Jax, or one of the other colorful characters she'd half-met the night before?

A woman's soothing, accented voice slipped through the door. "Caroline Mijada, Miss Fawn. I'm the maid."

"Maid?" Fawn opened the door by its fancy, scrolled handle.

A white apron layered over a short-sleeved blue shirt and chocolate-brown slacks outfitted the petite woman who greeted Fawn. She wore her shiny black hair slicked back and secured except for a wave of bangs gracing one side of her forehead to her eyebrow. The purple gems in her stud earrings complimented her deep-olive complexion. Her large eyes sparkled like cognac above broad cheeks and a narrow chin. Minimal but neat makeup accented her features.

Fawn glanced around Caroline, expecting her to hold a bucket of cleaning supplies or wheel a cart with her.

Caroline pealed with a few light chuckles. "No, there's no one and nothing with me. I'm not here to clean. I came to welcome you to the house."

Fawn peeked past Caroline at the hallway. It ran left and right with a jog a few feet to Fawn's left leading away from her room. No one else lingered within view. Occasional framed paintings and canvases adorned the ivory-gold walls. The art vacillated between modern lines and classic masterpieces. Potted plants and bronze statuettes dotted pristine glass-and-metal tables. Fawn gave a doubtful sigh. "Everyone keeps calling this a house, but..."

Caroline answered with a nod. "It is. Mr. Cade usually calls it a compound."

Like a cult? Fawn convulsed, and her stomach threatened to ache.

"Also, a commune." Caroline folded her hands together. "It's a big house. Lots of people live here."

Fawn laid a hand on her cheek, trying to make sense of the trimmed ivy and far-off laughter. "Nothing adds up about this place. Who are these rich hippie kidnappers?"

Caroline reached her hands out.

Fawn stared at them for a moment. She set her hands in Caroline's.

Caroline held onto them in her warm, gentle grasp. "Miss Fawn, Mr. Cade told me what kind of a life you were living before."

"Before? I need to get back to that life at some point." Fawn almost took her hands back.

"I'm not as good at words as Mr. Cade. Let me try again." Caroline licked her lips. "He told me of your stress. Your long hours. Barely seeing your family and friends. This is true?"

"Yes." Fawn breathed with relief. "That's what you're talking about."

"The habits you want to leave behind, correct?"

"Yes. I haven't made any decisions yet. I'm not even sure how long I'll be staying here. Cade hasn't given me any of the details I've asked for."

"Well." Caroline patted Fawn's hand. "He'll explain everything in due time. Why don't I come in and make your bed for you?"

"I don't know how long I'll be here." Fawn found herself stepping aside anyway.

Caroline waltzed in with a bounce in her stride. "Do you have any questions for me?"

Fawn scratched her arm through her cotton peasant sleeve. "Why would I? I didn't even know you were here or that you were coming."

Caroline shrugged as she approached the bed and fluffed up the pillows. "I've cleaned and straightened for Mr. Cade and his friends and family for many years. I could tell you much about them."

With a renewed shot of energy, Fawn skipped up to Caroline's side. "Okay. What's the deal with all of that? What do you mean when you say *family*?"

Caroline adjusted the snow-white flat sheet over the mattress' fitted sheet. "His parents and his four siblings."

Fawn's eyes popped wide. "Four? I only knew about Rosario."

Caroline pulled up the thick, weightless white comforter from its heap toward the foot of the bed. "There are many people he wants to introduce you to. It's challenging to teach who is who without overwhelming or scaring you."

"I can see that."

Caroline walked around to the bed's other side and repeated her arranging of the covers.

Fawn cemented her hands on her hips. "So Cade has six family members and countless friends. Why do I have to meet them all? Aren't I here for some kind of vacation that resets my brain?"

Caroline brightened into a gracious smile. "The people are part of the respite, Miss Fawn."

Fawn's stomach lining twitched. "People give me ulcers."

"When they expect too much of you, yes." Caroline swept one last wrinkle out of the comforter and breezed over to Fawn. "No one here expects anything from you."

Fawn blew out an exasperated breath and held her hand out toward the open door to the hall. "They expect me to stay here. They expect me to ride all over strange dunes on an ATV with no protection."

Caroline touched Fawn's arm gingerly. "Mr. Cade wants you to make good on your decision to take care of yourself."

Fawn lowered her volume to a hiss. "I thought he was joking."

"You don't want to feel better? To speak with nice people? To eat delicious food?" Caroline bunched the fingertips of one hand close to her lips. She made a kissing noise as she spread her fingers apart from her mouth in an exploding burst.

Fawn curved her palm around the back of her neck. "Yeah, I want that stuff. I just want to know what's going on."

Cade's voice surprised her. "Then, you shall."

Fawn spun towards him as he rapped a few knuckles on the door frame that had held no one seconds before. A jade-green pocket tee and casual navy pants draped over Cade. He sported his characteristic, boundless grin.

Caroline moved to the door. "I'll let you two talk. I'll check on you later, Miss Fawn."

Fawn twisted her lips to one side, watching the nearest

person she had to a friend in this place squeeze past Cade out of the room. "Don't go," Fawn squeaked, almost inaudible.

Cade remained in the doorway. "May I come in?"

Fawn sulked and gestured to the mahogany trappings. "Why not? It's your house."

Cade held up his index finger, encircled with a dazzling black-and-silver ring. "It's your room."

"Not for long. I might've been too exhausted to go home last night, and so far, what I've seen in this house isn't too bad."

Cade broadened his grin.

Fawn smoldered and stuck to her point. "But I really can't spare more than a day or two. I told you about my job at the company."

Cade cleared his throat. "Speaking of which. And, again, might I enter your private space?"

Annoyance constricted Fawn's throat, and she nodded.

Cade strolled in, clasping his hands behind his back. "I took the liberty of calling every person on your phone's contact list. I assured your friends and family you're safe on vacation and can't be reached until you return home."

Fawn pressed her eyes closed. Her stomach pulsed. Cade talking to her parents. Cade dealing with Demetria. Cade telling Monica, who had prompted Fawn to approach him in the first place, that she'd suddenly run off on vacation. Fawn shook her head. "How did that go?"

"Very well, actually."

Fawn groaned, not believing it for a second. "Which of my parents did you talk to? Mom or Dad?"

"Both. We had very pleasant conversations."

Fawn rubbed her creased forehead. "I'm sure you did. They love meeting new people."

"More than you do, I suppose?"

"Under these circumstances, yes."

"I'm sorry. You failed to mention that to Monica last evening at Smuckey's, so I didn't know about that particular trait."

Fawn slowly parted her eyelids and met Cade's humored grin with an icy glare. "What did you tell Demetria? I assume you spoke with her since she's the only one qualified to direct the company in my absence."

Cade's nose crinkled. "I preferred my back-and-forth with Chloe, your assistant."

Fawn laughed with unsettled spurts. "That's your own fault for going through my phone."

Cade rubbed his straight palms against each other in circles. "Nothing a little — or a tremendous — breakfast can't fix."

"Caroline said something about food." Fawn threw a glance at the doorway, but the hall remained empty, dashing her hopes.

Cade offered Fawn the crook of his elbow. "Shall I escort you to the kitchen, then?"

She eyed Cade's arm askance. "Is it that hard to find?"

"Our first-time guests seem to think so."

Fawn's stomach churned and gurgled. "Okay. I didn't eat much last night. And you're not off the hook yet for talking to everybody I know." Fawn hesitated and slipped her hand inside Cade's elbow. "How did Monica take the news?"

"She's thrilled."

Fawn mumbled. "Traitor."

Cade led Fawn to the doorway. "She said it was about time you did something brash and scandalous in the name of your own wellbeing."

Fawn's jaw dropped, and her pitch shot up. "She thinks I ran away with you? To some exotic tourist trap?!"

Cade guided Fawn into the hall and steered her left. "Relax. I explained it was a friendly venture with nothing untoward or *scandalous* going on."

Fawn stumbled and tightened her grip on Cade's elbow. "I'm going to have a lot of messes to clean up when I get home. Did my parents think I abandoned my job for a beachy love nest, too?"

"Not at all. They think you're the luckiest person in the world to meet a new friend who wants to treat you royally at his home.

And they told me how deserving you are of it. They were perfectly lovely."

Fawn gulped. "What about my sister, Tara?"

"I detected a little jealousy, to be honest." Cade flexed his inner elbow around Fawn's hand. "Don't worry. Once she got over it, she was ecstatic for you."

"She'll discover a big way to upstage me after this. Maybe she'll give birth to triplets next year."

Cade frowned. "You're jealous of Tara, too?"

"As soon as our parents applaud me for achieving something, she steals their attention. I know she's younger than me, but at our age, it's pretty immature."

Cade covered Fawn's hand with his over his elbow. "I have four siblings."

"Caroline told me." Fawn bit her lip for a moment. "Did I stick my foot in my mouth? You're not the oldest, are you?"

"I'm the middle," Cade purred. "The younger of the two boys."

"Who's your brother?"

"Jaxon. We call him Jax."

Fawn studied Cade's tanned, relaxed face. "The one who put me on the back of your ATV?"

Cade motioned up ahead.

A kitchen stood open to the intersection of two hallways, the corridor Cade led Fawn down and another to their right. Flat-front cherry wood cabinets provided sections of dense color against the black granite countertops flecked with grey and white. The double-wide refrigerator loomed in reflective, muted black on the far left. Its rectangular panes of glass displayed produce and containers packing its shelves. Its finish matched the stove a few feet away.

Fawn couldn't get a clear glimpse of the stove's details because of the expansive island filling the nearest corner of the kitchen. Its extra counter space stretched out over six stools, four on the near side and two on the left. Silverware rested at each place over folded, lilac cloth napkins. The four people who'd accompanied Cade in coming closest to Fawn on the beach occupied the kitchen, giving her a shuddering sense of déjà vu. Although Cade escorted her and the other four arranged themselves around the island, Fawn felt like her morning had looped back around into the previous night.

Fawn hung back from them, her muscles clenching. "I thought we were having breakfast."

Cade's voice sounded warm and eager. "We are."

"I didn't realize we were eating with other people, or I would've put makeup on."

"Don't be silly. Where's the relaxation in that? All that rushing and hurrying and prepping."

Fawn slipped her hand away from Cade's elbow. "Speaking of looking presentable, am I allowed or expected to wear any of that expensive jewelry you keep in your guest room? I've heard of trusting your guests, but that's over the top."

"Don't worry about it. Wear what you want or leave it alone." Cade set his palm against the small of Fawn's back and eased her forward.

Rosario sat on the far-right stool in a boldly colored kimono robe. She crossed her legs, a minimalist black slipper dangling from each foot. The blonde perched next to her wearing a t-shirt and blue-striped white-cotton sleep pants. The length of her hair had been wrangled into a chic but messy ponytail. On the far-left stool, the younger woman with the bullring hunched over the counter. Her black tank top's spaghetti straps accentuated the sharp rise of her shoulders. Silver stars decorated her hot-pink shorts.

Jax lingered behind the island. Shirtless, his golden tan expressed itself even more now over his face, neck, shaved chest, and chiseled abs. The band of his green drawstring bottoms peeked over the island's counter. Jax planted his strong hands wide apart on the counter and flexed his pecs.

The young woman with the bullring rolled her eyes.

Cade prompted Fawn with a little more pressure on her back. She eked over to the island and sat down on the vacant stool next to the blonde. She kept her gaze lower than Jax's to keep from meeting his.

Cade walked around to the island's other side and stopped at the corner two feet from his brother. "Fawn, this is the gang. Or family, as Caroline calls it. Minus Mom and Dad."

Fawn fought to keep from stammering. "Your parents don't eat breakfast with you?"

Cade grinned. "Meeting several new people at once isn't enough?"

Bubbles shifted along Fawn's stomach lining, and she said nothing.

Cade clapped Jax on the shoulder. "My brother, Jax, you know. Sort of. You might remember Rosario." He pointed to the dark-haired woman in the robe, then aimed his finger at the blonde. "Lisette. Also often considered more trustworthy than me at times."

The siblings laughed, from chuckles to hearty cackles.

Cade pinched the isolated young woman's slender chin. "Our youngest sister, Yoselle. Her bark is worse than her bite, and she dances to the beat of her own drum. Are there any clichés I've missed?"

Rosario raised her hand. "Still waters run deep?"

Yoselle pinned Rosario with her sullen, grey-blue eyes.

Jax slapped his hand against the counter. "A rose by any other name would smell as sweet."

Lisette flattened her palms on the granite slab and leaned over it. "You never understood her, Jax. She's our diamond in the rough."

Yoselle lifted her head and drew her shoulders back. A wry smirk perked up one corner of her full mouth. "I *am* the rough."

Cade clasped his hands together with a loud slap. "All right. That's settled. Breakfast?"

The other siblings nodded.

Fawn murmured. "Yes, please." Another five minutes without food, and she would slump over the granite for support.

Jax leaned across the island and toyed with a lock of Fawn's hair between his thumb and forefinger. "I didn't realize your hair was this color last night. Sort of like caramel. It's making me hungry." His voice rumbled with intent.

Fawn bit the inside of her lip.

Rosario huffed. "*Real* breakfast, Jax."

Cade and Jax stepped over to the counter behind them. They lifted the covers off multiple serving plates and baskets. Almost at once, deep, heady aromas delighted Fawn's nose. Salty bacon and earthy-sweet scrambled eggs. Buttery croissants. Sourdough bagels and spicy sausage.

Fawn's rushing saliva threatened to drown her, and she swallowed. "Who's supposed to eat all this?"

Rosario giggled. "We are."

"The six of us?"

Cade raised his index finger. "We haven't called for coffee yet. Or are you a tea person, Fawn?"

Fawn rested her forearms on the granite. Not sure if that was acceptable or rude, she pulled them off again. "I don't know. Yesterday, I was the go-to-work-on-time-and-be-responsible kind of person. What do you think my beverage of choice should be?" She fixed Cade with her half-serious, half-punishing gaze.

His grin stayed full as he approached a speaker box built into the wall on the other side of the refrigerator. "We'll allow coffee for the day. It's your first morning here. We don't want to change everything at once." Cade pressed a button beneath the speaker. "Gerard? We're ready for the coffee. All six of us. Thank you."

Fawn wanted to keep grilling Cade, but the offerings of food ten feet away called to her. She ran the tip of her tongue over her bottom lip. Instead of challenging Cade, she sounded distracted. "Are you sure you're serving a roast I like? Maybe I only drink light or dark or French?"

Cade beamed with a mischievous twinkle in his grey eyes.

"Oh, I hope it's French you like."

A man rounded the corner with a black beret topping his thin, choppy sandy-blond hair. He rolled a two-level metal cart with mirrored shelves past Rosario to the side of the island. The top held six large, different-colored mugs full of coffee and a red ceramic set of a canister and short pitcher. He raised his faded-blue eyes to the group gathered around the island.

Cade extended his arm around the man's shoulders. "Gerard, this is our house guest, Fawn."

Fawn lowered her feet to the floor and stuck out her hand. "Fawn Claire."

Gerard pattered over to her and kissed the air by both her cheeks. He took her hand in his and smoothed it. His cadence danced with a French accent. "Gerard Bernard. The pleasure is mine. I trust you'll enjoy your breakfast."

"I'm sure I will by the scent of it."

"If there's anything you want I haven't provided, get word to me. I'll prepare it."

"I will."

"The breakfast buffet changes daily, so submit your preferences anytime."

Fawn's heart restricted. "I'm not staying long. I have work to get back to. I'm sorry."

Gerard tilted his head sideways with a hint of a smile. "Is it work you love?"

Fawn tumbled the question and its possible answers in her head. "It's a mission I believe in. It's just a lot of stress."

"Well, you're here now." Gerard pulled away a fraction of an inch.

Fawn stayed close to him. "Do you like what you do?"

"I adore it. You won't find more generous people than this family. Cooking here — baking! — ah. I'm quite content." Gerard rubbed his fingers across Fawn's hand. "I hope you'll decide to elongate your stay. Either way, get some rest. Have fun."

Fawn nodded, and Gerard disappeared around the corner.

Fawn returned to her stool beside Lisette.

Rosario picked up a red mug and handed the purple one to Jax. She passed the green cup to Lisette. Yoselle paced around behind Fawn and her sisters to retrieve the black mug from the cart. She dragged her feet back to her seat. Rosario set the sugar container and milk pitcher on the island.

Cade's eyes sparkled at Fawn. "How do you like our French offering so far?"

Fawn stuck her chin up and refused to let him make her feel too foolish about her words. "Gerard is very nice. An actual French chef? That's impressive."

"We're lucky to have him. The only question left is whether you'd like light or dark roast."

Fawn smirked. "What if I want flavored, like macadamia nut or snickerdoodle?"

Cade bent toward her over the island. "Put in a request with Gerard. You can have your pick of those, Irish cream, gingerbread…" He trailed off.

Rosario blew steam off her coffee. "Pecan pie."

Yoselle grumbled, her hands wrapped around her mug. "Chocolate mint."

Lisette sipped her brew. "Toasted coconut."

Jax lifted his cup. "Crème brûlée."

Cade stepped over to the wall speaker box. "I'd be delighted to inform Gerard what your favorite flavors are."

Fawn replied in a sure, quiet voice. "Dark roast, please."

Cade gravitated back to the island. Rosario moved the cart's last two mugs onto the granite island. Cade slid the blue cup toward Fawn and drank from the yellow one in his hand.

Fawn gulped down a few mouthfuls of coffee. Its richness and continually unraveling depth of flavor made her slow down to savor it.

Cade pushed the canister and pitcher toward her. "Cream? Sugar?"

Fawn shook her head. Her eyes half closed in appreciation.

"Enjoy it. I'm switching you to tea tomorrow."

Fawn pouted and held her beverage closer.

Rosario and Lisette abandoned their cups on the island. They went over to the breakfast lineup and took empty crimson, stoneware plates off a stack on the counter.

Rosario glanced at Fawn over her shoulder. "I'll make you a plate, Fawn, so you don't have to get up. Is there anything you're allergic to?"

Fawn's hurry with downing the coffee needled her stomach. Otherwise, she promised herself, she would've protested the offer. She rested her mug in front of her. "I'd appreciate that. Thank you."

Fawn peeked up and caught Cade watching her. Jax snuck a quick wink at her before wandering to the buffet.

Fawn cleared her throat. "So, if this is your kitchen, how come I didn't smell food when we first walked out? Why's the coffee made somewhere else?"

Cade took a casual sip from his mug. "There's a full chef's kitchen on the other side of the wall behind me."

A stumped sound emerged from Fawn's throat.

"This is what we affectionately call the snack kitchen."

Fawn pointed to the multitude of containers, lush vegetables, and jewel-toned fruits visible through the refrigerator's French doors. "Those are all snacks?"

Cade shrugged a shoulder. "Help yourself whenever you get peckish."

Fawn zeroed in on the refrigerator's counterpart, the wide oven. "Is that a commercial stove? What are those flat burners, induction?"

"It's a combo. Induction and electric."

"With a griddle in the middle."

"Yeah, that flips over so you can cook pancakes on one side and grill vegetables on the other."

"Your snack kitchen really needs a stove with three ovens in it?"

Cade splayed the fingers of one hand at the lowest part of the oven. "That one doesn't cook. It's a warming drawer."

Fawn squinted at the dark metallic finish. "Is that black stainless steel?"

"Yep."

"I thought it was an urban legend. Your snack appliances make my regular kitchen look like it's from the stone age." Fawn scooted forward on her stool. "Okay, do any of you have jobs? Who pays for all this?"

All around Fawn, groans erupted.

Rosario scrunched her nose up as she laid a full plate of steaming breakfast in front of Fawn. "No work talk before lunch."

Jax threw a reply over his muscled shoulder. "Or dinner, as far as I'm concerned."

Rosario headed back to the buffet and took a plate for herself. "I am, however, interested in what you do, Fawn. If you can discuss it without aggravating your ulcer."

Fawn shot Cade a withering look.

Cade spooned a little sugar into his coffee. "I tell my siblings most everything. You don't?" He leveled his gaze at her, belied by his ever-present grin.

Fawn ignored him and took a bite of her croissant. Its light flakiness and buttery smoothness were sweeter and more complex than anything Fawn had ever eaten. She chewed it quickly to answer Rosario's inquiry. "As I said, I'm the boss at Better Mind. We work with different companies to find out their employees' personal needs. What goals they haven't reached. Where their execution is weak. Then we use the best, most-advanced technology in the world to make videos boosting the employees toward success they've never had before."

Lisette placed her full plate of breakfast on the island and sat down beside Fawn. "Videos?"

Fawn hummed in agreement. "It's deceptively simple, right? Who can't watch a few minutes of video?" Fawn ate another bite of croissant, and its tastiness melted the rest of her animosity.

"Gosh, these are good. Anyway, our teams craft carefully worded affirmations. They implant subliminal suggestions into upbeat or calming music. They add in frequencies that help the brain think more clearly, relax faster, or be more alert. Whatever the employees need most. We pair the audio with images of happy, active people. Sometimes, we use video showcasing the same energy and enthusiasm."

Lisette quirked an eyebrow. "And this works?"

"Quite well. A lot of our employees at Better Mind were getting benefits from creating the video components for other companies. I ended up putting a small team together to make a few videos for our team members, as a gift to them."

Rosario carried her breakfast plate back to her seat next to Lisette. "You're a CEO with a sad, outdated kitchen?"

Fawn chewed and nodded. "Too busy working to put my salary to proper use."

Rosario flapped her napkin open. "Okay. Say we're a company, and we've hired you. Gerard is our employee. What would you do?"

"A client manager would start a relationship with you and ask you targeted questions to find out Gerard's strengths and weaknesses."

Rosario sipped her coffee and trailed a fingertip over her croissant's browned edges. "Gerard's creations are delicious and impressively varied. He's mastered the cuisine of many cultures. But he could cook faster."

Jax settled in on the vacant stool to Fawn's left. "And more neatly. He flicked red sauce on my baby-blue shirt last week when I went to check on dinner."

Fawn finished her croissant, silently mourning its passing. "All right. My teams' videos would focus on praising Gerard for his culinary genius and impressive knowledge. This helps break down any barriers Gerard might have to building new skills and puts him in an open, good-feeling mood. My teams would intercut more and more empowering messages about serving food on time easily. He would see and hear affirmations about how effortless it is to prepare food with minimal or no mess at all."

Jax admired Fawn with a bright smile stretched across his face. "How soon can we buy that?"

Yoselle scoffed. "I thought you didn't want to talk about work."

"It was Rosario's question. Don't be rude." Jax shone his smile on Fawn again.

Cade took another drink of his coffee and left the cup on the island. He helped himself to the buffet.

Fawn stretched her neck up to see if any croissants remained in the basket, but she couldn't get a good glimpse inside it. She didn't want Cade to know how much she was enjoying her breakfast. She bit her lip and changed the subject. "Is this a typical breakfast spread for your family?"

They all nodded.

Fawn studied their physiques, baffled. "How do you burn off all the calories?"

Jax devoured her with his golden-honey eyes. "We stay active. *Awfully* active."

Yoselle covered her face with her hands. "Oh, God."

Fawn dug her fork aimlessly into her scrambled eggs. "What's on the agenda for today? I hope you'll leave me out of it. I really need to rest, especially after the unofficial ATV course last night."

Lisette laid her hand on Fawn's arm. "Oh, please come. It's going to be tons of fun. You're our guest."

Fawn could only imagine what their plans were. "For sky diving or parkour or swimming with sharks? No, thank you. Dr. Cade's strict orders."

Cade slathered cream cheese on half a bagel and brought his heaping plate around to the final empty seat by the corner between Yoselle and Jax. "We decided earlier this morning to spend the day lounging at the water park."

Fawn dropped her fist down onto the granite slab. "Damn it. I actually want to do that."

Jax paused his ravenous eating. "Yes? You'll come?"

"I—" Jax's double-entendre dawned on Fawn, and she chose her words selectively. "I'll go."

Rosario and Lisette cheered.

Fawn laid her hand flat on the granite. "I have no suit, though. No towel—"

Yoselle and Cade nodded in unison.

"No sun screen," Yoselle pointed out.

"No sunglasses," Cade drawled. "I assume."

Yoselle pointed at him. "No sandals."

"No hat."

Fawn groaned. "That's not how I sound."

Cade put his hands up. "Either way, we're going to the water park. Caroline will bring you everything you could possibly need."

Fawn eyed him with suspicion. "Without knowing my size?"

"Yep."

"Is she buying me new stuff, or am I borrowing somebody's suit?"

Cade clinked his fork's handle against the granite slab. "Fawn, you worry too much. It's all new."

"I can pay for what I keep."

"It isn't necessary. We like taking care of our guests."

"What about your parents? Your friends?"

"We've invited everybody. Those who want to come will. Some will probably stay here."

Fawn dropped her shoulders. "And nobody has a career to get to on a Tuesday morning?"

Cade shrugged. "I don't know every detail of their lives."

Yoselle gained an ornery tilt to her lips. "Maybe some of them telecommute."

Jax jabbed his fingertip several times onto the granite. "Okay. Officially enough work talk now."

Cade nodded. "Right. We'll finish breakfast. Get dressed. Pack up, and drive to the park."

Fawn nibbled at her eggs, moist and perfectly seasoned.

"What's the name of this park, exactly? Where is it?"

"Fun Splash is about ten or fifteen minutes from here."

"I've never heard of it. How old is it?"

Cade grinned. "We've been going there for years. You're an overworked CEO. I'm not surprised you've missed a few things in the last decade or so."

"Ha, ha. We're not taking the ATV's, are we?"

"No. We usually roll out in a convoy of SUV's."

Fawn flicked her eyebrows up. "The compound goes out in a convoy. Why am I agreeing to this?"

"Because it's sun, splashing, and not having to lift a single finger all day."

Fawn stood up and tucked her stool under the island's overhang. "Where can I find Caroline?"

"I'll page her and send her to your room."

Fawn aimed her finger down the hallway behind her. "It's this way?"

"The green-and-white room."

Fawn headed down the hall. "How much time do I have?"

"As much as you want."

Putting extra speed in her steps, Fawn retraced her earlier path. She peeked through an open door, the familiar green-striped wallpaper and white fabrics relieving her. She walked in and went straight to her purse. Fawn dug her sunglasses out with a satisfied smirk. "I *do* have sunglasses, actually."

Caroline's voice entreated from the doorway. "Miss Fawn?"

"Yes. Cade said you could help me get ready. I'm going to the water park with the others."

Caroline stepped in and lightly took Fawn's sunglasses in her fingers. "You can't wear these. The lenses are too narrow. They won't shade your eyes well enough."

"They're fashionable. They work for driving."

"I'll bring you something better." Caroline handed the sunglasses to Fawn. "You need a suit?"

"Yes. I like a good tankini, but to be honest, I haven't even tried on a bathing suit in a couple years."

"I'll get a variety."

Fawn paused. "You'd do that for me? I've stayed with people before. They never treated me like this."

Caroline beamed. "It's our pleasure."

"I'd like to take a shower, if I can."

Caroline nodded. She led Fawn past a set of double doors to a recessed area of the bedroom punctuated with a half-open single door.

Fawn slowed her stroll. "What's this? What did we just pass?"

"That was the closet. This is the bathroom." Caroline swung the door fully open.

Fawn wandered in. Glossy white tiles covered the floor. Black cabinets with faceted glass knobs supported a long, white marble vanity. Twin silver faucets rose up in high arches to accommodate the green-stone bowl sinks beneath them. Fawn turned to the left, her mouth falling open as she traversed deeper into the bathroom. A two-person jetted tub with inset glass panels filled the left-hand corner. Bending toward the right, Fawn reached the end of her journey. Straight ahead stood the room's final two components. A glass-walled shower occupied the left corner with yellow-green travertine lining the back walls and floor. Complimenting it on the right, a giant white soaker tub rested on four claw-foot legs.

Fawn could only blink in response.

Caroline edged past her to the shower and opened the glass door. "Everything you need is here on the shelf and the organizer. Shampoo. Conditioner. Soap. You have several options already. If you end up staying longer than a day or two, let me know what products you like. You know."

Fawn drifted forward, still in a daze.

Caroline reached into the shower and folded down a teak-wood pallet from the back wall. Its hinge stopped it parallel to the floor. "This is a shower bench if you'd like to sit down." She raised it up against the wall and stepped back. "Towels and wash cloths are hanging here. You'll find more under the sinks."

Fawn pried off her socks. Her bare feet met with subtle but pleasant warmth rather than the chill she expected from the tiles. "Caroline, is this a heated floor?"

"Yes, Miss Fawn. We have heated floors throughout the house and heated driveways as well."

"Drive*ways*? Plural?"

Caroline giggled. "Come on, now. How are you surprised by this?"

"You're right. I hate to ask for anything else."

Caroline set her hands on Fawn's arm. "Please. It's what I'm here for."

"Is there a disposable razor I can use, by any chance?"

"Waiting in the shower for you."

"Someone around here is so detail oriented, I'd like to hire them for one of my teams."

Caroline chuckled into her hands. "Oh, you humor me. You honor me." She waved at her face. "I like taking care of people. You have a nice shower, and I'll have all your choices for bathing suits, sunglasses, and sunscreen waiting on the bed for you. Okay?"

"You can get all that shopping done in half an hour?"

Caroline bobbed her head. "The store's close, and I'm very familiar with it. I go there all the time."

Guilt prodded Fawn for withholding information. "I'm a size—"

"No, no." Caroline held her palms up vertically. "I like to guess. It keeps my mind active. I have three teenagers who aren't always honest what size they need. I've gotten very good at this game."

"Can you guess at shoes, too? I like real sandals. Flats. Not flip-flops. That gum-smacking sound annoys me."

"Miss Fawn, when you see what I've brought for you, you won't believe your eyes. I'll make a believer out of you yet. Just give me a chance." Caroline let herself out of the bathroom and closed the door.

Fawn hesitated and slipped out of yesterday's clothes. "It seems like I've given several people a lot of chances recently," she mumbled. She stepped into the shower and looked for the controls.

A rainfall shower head on a removable wand topped an assortment of body jets. She nibbled a fingernail at the imposing overkill of luxury, her amusement making her feel giddy. "Sometimes, given a chance, you're far from disappointed."

Fawn scoured the walls for a knob or lever with which to activate the water. A two-by-five inch black screen caught her attention beside the upper body jets. In various soothing colors, it offered several illustrated subjects. "Shower. Lighting. Music." Fawn chittered. "You have to be kidding me."

She tapped the blue-droplet icon, and the wide shower head sprinkled a warm rain over her. "Okay, that works." The top of the screen displayed the temperature in large, white numbers. "A little warmer." Fawn searched the display and tapped on a red up arrow in the lower right. The number increased, and the water became even more inviting.

A gleeful grin snaked across Fawn's lips. "Let's see what this does." She selected the yellow light bulb symbol. The overhead lights dimmed in the rest of the bathroom, and a soft, luminescent glow beamed down from above her. "That's pretty nice."

Fawn aimed her fingertip at the pink music note on the screen, eager to find out what tranquil melodies could swell over her. She dropped her hand in admonishment. "Nope. I'm not staying here. Can't fall in love with everything."

~

The last of the shower's soothing, warm water dried off her skin, Fawn wrapped the velvet-soft, oversized towel around her body. She popped the bathroom door open an inch and peeked into the bedroom. "Caroline? Hello?" She waited and heard no answer, not even a quiet footfall on the carpet. "Cade?" she tried. Suspicion crept in. "Jax?" she issued in a wry, flat tone.

Convinced she was alone, Fawn swept out of the bathroom. She glanced at the door to the hallway to make sure Caroline had closed it, and the brightly colored bounty covering the bed stole Fawn's attention immediately. Her eyes darted from classic black to cool turquoise and polka dots to zebra stripes as she giggled in awe. A golden leopard-print bikini took her breath away. She felt the metal beads strung on a white tankini's halter ties and jumped for joy. Her fingers traced the circles cut out of an aqua one-piece's sides. She admired the athletic lines of a hot-pink-and-lime racer-back suit.

A hand-written note rested atop a fuchsia monokini. Fawn picked up the page. *This shade would make those big green eyes of yours really pop, I bet — Caroline.*

Fawn's skepticism melted at the smiley face Caroline had drawn after her name. "How am I gonna pick?"

Bottles of sunscreen and tanning lotion rested on the comforter in different ratings. Caroline had arranged huge sunglasses and several sunhats along one edge of the bed. T-shirts, shorts, and cover-ups filled the rest of the space.

"But where are the...?" Fawn glimpsed by her feet. Eight pairs of sandals stood in two rows on the carpet. Some had practical, simple shapes. Others were gladiator sandals meant to be tied halfway up her shins. Fawn laughed and propped a white straw hat with a wide brim on her head. She waved the note in the air. "I'm never doubting Caroline again. I'll see how things fit, but if she accepts tips, she's welcome to all the cash in my wallet."

~

Midmorning rays blasted into the foyer through floor-to-ceiling windows flanking the giant, white front door. Cade lingered by it, dressed in a navy t-shirt and knee-length trunks emblazoned with dark palm trees. A woven hemp-strand necklace strung with a cowrie shell hung around his neck. His siblings stayed scattered around the room. Jax twirled a pair of sunglasses in the middle of the foyer beneath an unlit chandelier. He wore a bold-yellow tee and baggy cargo shorts. Yoselle lounged in a corner chair between two wide doorways. She deflated with a bored sigh, draped in a black net cover-up hinting at a purple bikini underneath. Rosario and Lisette gossiped close together in another corner, bedecked in maxi dresses flowing from their necks to their ankles.

Fawn strolled into the foyer, confident with the instructions Caroline had given her to reach it on her own. She felt quite at home with her own ensemble. The woven brim of her sunhat flopped up and down with every step. Her sunglasses rode on that brim, tucked amongst realistic fabric flowers. Her purse's emergency liquid eyeliner, bronzer, and rosy lip gloss highlighted some of her best features. A white cover-up shaped like a t-shirt dress hung to her knees. Beneath it, a blue-and-green-foil monokini shimmered in a fierce geometric pattern. Classic brown-leather sandals cushioned her feet, and a squeeze bottle of sunscreen poked out the top of her purse slung over her forearm.

Rosario shrieked and clapped her hands in rapid beats. "Look who's all ready! You're so posh, Fawn. I can hardly deal with it."

Lisette tightened her high ponytail. "Totally."

Fawn met Cade's even gaze. "I'm not too late, am I?"

Jax whistled and plopped his sunglasses on his head. He leaned his forearm on Cade's shoulder. "Well worth the wait, I'd say."

Yoselle grunted with disgust and pushed herself up out of her chair. "Let's go."

Cade gave a single nod to Fawn. "Was everything to your liking?"

Fawn wandered up to him, raising her chin. "*Most* everything. One suit fit a little snug."

A knowing grin invaded Cade's face. "You didn't give her your size, did you? And Caroline still got it right."

Fawn turned her focus to the window and its view. Full sun

spotlighted small evergreens and blooming flowers in the house's landscaping. "Mostly. Like I said, a bit snug."

Cade pried the front door open. "Very well. Small details. Let's go."

Fawn fetched her sunglasses off her hat brim. "Where's everybody else?"

"Already gone, I suppose."

"So no convoy today? I'm sorry." Fawn met Cade with a hyper mix of goading and real apology squirming on her lips.

Cade refreshed his wide grin. "Maybe tomorrow. Somebody's gotten into an impish mood. The body jets of the shower, perhaps? Or the heated floor?" Cade tilted his forehead toward Fawn. "You touched the icon for music, didn't you?"

Fawn shook her head. "I didn't play any music."

Jax swung his arm down, snapping his fingers. "Damn. I thought for sure you would."

Cade opened the screen door. "Did you know, according to informal polling, less than ninety-four percent of our guests enjoy music in the shower on their first morning here?"

Jax ushered Fawn ahead of him with a sweep of his hand.

Fawn hurried outside after Cade. "That's pretty precise, don't you think?"

Cade paused his walking. "Ninety-four point six percent. *That's* precise."

Fawn huffed. Why were they just standing around? She threw a quick glance around her and looked over her surroundings again in earnest. The wooden porch slats and railings were painted a clean, matte white, gently worn. A settee padded with a bright, tropical cushion rested on the other side of the front door's accompanying window. Beyond the porch and its four steps down, a sidewalk wormed its way to a wide semi-circular driveway. Tall, thin evergreens dotted the property along with patches of flowers ringed in pale-grey stones.

Cade started walking again. Every step made a sharp snap.

Fawn glared at his feet. "Are you wearing flip-flops?"

A second series of claps sounded behind her. She glanced at Jax and found flip-flops on his feet as well. "You both are. Did Caroline tell you I hate those noisy things?"

Cade grinned. "She might've mentioned it."

Jax cleared his throat. "Or we might've dragged it out of her."

Fawn stewed in the aggravation tightening her throat. "I'll survive."

Cade motioned to the black SUV idling in the driveway. "Good. I trust this suits your needs. And your tastes."

Fawn's eyes grew into saucers. A fresh coat of wax shone slick and reflective on the spotless black body. The chrome hubcaps flashed sharp cuts of light off their flawless metal shapes. All four doors gaped open, revealing pristine black upholstery on three rows of oversized seats. The spacious interior only seemed larger as Fawn approached the passenger side.

Cade watched her reaction, smug and satisfied. "Never seen anything like this before, have you?"

Fawn could barely enunciate her response. "That's the refrain of every minute I'm in this place."

Cade shared a brief glance with Jax and curved his hand around the edge of the front passenger door. "Why don't you ride up front with me?"

Fawn climbed up into the vehicle before her sarcasm could leak out. She had no desire whatsoever to give up an opportunity like this. "You're driving?" She nestled her purse at her feet.

"I am. Does that bother you?"

Fawn peered through the clear, broad windshield. She hoped to see where the driveway met the road, but evergreens and massive trees blocked her view. "I'm sure you're a good driver. On the road. In an enclosed vehicle. I don't understand how the vehicle got here." She jangled the keys stuck in the ignition. The only keychain held an elaborate, golden letter C. She squinted at it. Was it real gold? Solid gold?

"Hans recovered it from the garage and left it here for us." Cade closed Fawn's door and sauntered around the SUV's glinting hood to the driver's side. He boosted himself up into the seat next to Fawn and clapped his door shut.

Fawn cradled her sunglasses in her lap. "Hans? You have a very international team. Er, employees. What do you call them?"

"Life savers. *Help* in the best sense of the word. But yes, they do come from all over. Caroline's Italian and Puerto Rican."

"I like her very much."

Cade purred. "Everyone does."

Behind them, Yoselle slumped into the left back corner seat. Rosario settled in beside her while Lisette and Jax took the middle row. They pulled the back two doors secure.

Jax tapped Fawn on the shoulder. "I'm right here behind you."

Fawn flashed him a smile and played along. "Perfect."

Jax hummed with pleasure. "Body jets agree with you."

Fawn raised her index finger. "I didn't use those. Just for the record." Her sheer amount of over-sharing dawned on her. "Why am I talking about this?"

The siblings chuckled.

Cade adjusted the shifter into drive. "Because with us, nothing is off-limits. Nothing's taboo."

Yoselle grumbled from the far back. "Except Jax and his flirting."

Cade eased the vehicle forward, gaining speed around a driveway bend leading away from the house. "It's not off-limits, but it's not always appreciated."

Rosario shot a loud whisper at her blonde sister. "Lisette." They leaned toward each other and launched a quiet conversation Fawn couldn't properly hear.

Cade steered the SUV around more displays of flowers and bushes. He directed the group past towering trees, their vast networks of leafy branches passing cool shady spots over the vehicle.

Fawn drew her fingertip across the top line of her sunglasses. "Are your parents joining us?"

Cade dropped his left hand from the steering wheel, letting his right wrist guide them along the path. "No. They're staying in."

Fawn's feathers ruffled in an otherwise pleasing situation. Her back drooped against the seat. "That's disappointing. I was looking forward to meeting them."

Cade shot her an amused expression. "Why?"

Fawn shrugged. "It might be their house, and I've already met the rest of your family as far as I know. I don't want to be rude."

Cade shook his head. "You're not."

"But if it's their house and they worked hard for it, they have a right to know who's staying with them. Is it their house or yours?"

Cade smirked. "Technicalities, Fawn. It really doesn't matter."

"Why not? I'm using hot water. I'm eating your food."

Cade sobered. "Plus, you're still worrying. It's already a commune. What's one more person thrown into the mix at this point?"

Jax applauded. "Here, here!"

Cade patted Fawn's knee with his hand from the wheel, his other hand still languid by the door. "Don't fret. You'll probably meet our parents before you leave."

Fawn grabbed the wheel, her knuckles blanching white. She stared at the foreign driveway bends through the windshield. "Can you keep at least one finger on the steering wheel, please?"

Cade set the tip of his pinky on top of the wheel. Jax guffawed until he snorted. Fawn clenched her teeth and maintained her grip on the wheel.

Rosario spoke up from the back seat in a commanding monotone. "Children, please."

Jax picked at the upholstery, sounding sullen. "You don't even know what we're doing."

"No, but I do know that when Cade does something that makes you snort in amusement, the game's gone too far."

Cade rested his hand completely around the wheel, and

Fawn released it. Jax sat up straighter. Rosario lowered her voice to a whisper with Lisette again.

The road Fawn had been looking for minutes earlier appeared in a T with the driveway. Cade braked and checked for traffic before turning right.

Fawn sat on her hands. "That's one heck of a driveway. Do you include that in your estimate of how long it takes to get to the water park?"

Cade remained casual but courteous. "No. And it's a protracted driveway because large houses require even bigger properties." He pointed to Fawn's window while keeping his eyes on the road.

Fawn gazed out her window. The house's true sprawling, grandiose nature shocked her. How little of the house had she actually seen and walked through? Rounded, terracotta shingles graced the hipped roof atop the building's white stucco walls. Far from being a boring square or compact rectangle, the house stretched out into numerous outlying rooms. Fawn craned her neck to peer at the back of the house, where a large swimming pool sparkled sapphire in the sunshine.

Fawn tapped her fingernail against the window. "Is that a pool? Why can't we swim there? Why do we have to go all the way to the water park?"

From the two rows of seating behind Fawn, Cade's siblings murmured and protested.

Cade held his hand up, and they fell silent. He fielded Fawn's questions. "We'll swim at the house one day soon. Maybe even tomorrow." Cade gave Fawn's leg a brief squeeze just above the knee. "But for today, you're our special guest. And off to Fun Splash we go." His grin popped into play. "Besides, we don't know how short you'll cut your visit with us. Why not get in a trip to the water park before you leave?"

Fawn folded her arms but refused to lose all of her humor. "Ha, ha. Most hosts would be ecstatic to let me use their pool instead of organizing a massive exodus to a public venue."

Jax rubbed his palms together. "Nuh-uh, Fawn. We don't have waterfalls and room for multiple rafts that hold eight people."

Rosario chimed in. "It's a pool, not a high-speed water slide."

Yoselle grumbled. "No private cabana."

Lisette chirped up. "And no lazy river."

Fawn nodded. "You know, you're right. A pool is just a lazy pond. And I'm looking forward to floating around aimlessly on that lazy river."

Cade's grin expanded. "That's what you think."

Fawn put her sunglasses on, reducing Cade's smug confidence to flat sepia tones. "If you think you're bullying me into one of those tall, scary tube-looking rides, you're about to find yourself very mistaken."

Cade said nothing, his attention trained on the road. Fawn scoffed at his immaturity, then made her peace with his lack of response. It was just as well. His non-stop chatter only raised her blood pressure.

Trees and wooden fences flew past Fawn's window. Behind them, verdant fields stretched out to distant lines of more trees. Within minutes, Cade turned off the road into a spacious parking lot.

Fawn studied the amassed cars, SUV's, and trucks. "It's packed. Are we going to get in?"

Cade spoke up with knowing. "We'll find a spot. We always do."

He drove toward the entrance, marked by two wide cylinders topped with pointed, castle-like roofs. At the end of the row, a single open space remained, and Cade took it.

Fawn worked to keep her mouth from falling completely ajar. "That was lucky. I wish that would've happened to me about fifty times in my life."

Jax and Lisette opened the SUV's back doors, and Cade's siblings let themselves out. Cade shut off the engine, and Fawn got out at the same time he did. She surveyed the park's giant footprint, dozens of rides forming a colorful, jumbled scape against the azure sky. A handful of rides rose fifty feet or more, standing out against the drifting clouds.

Fawn frowned. "Those aren't for me. Just the lazy river, please."

Cade chuckled, and Fawn followed him to the rear of the vehicle. He swung up the door to the trunk space. Jax hoisted a big red cooler with a white lid out of the back. He set it on the pavement.

Rosario leaned in and slid a woven basket toward the group. Six terrycloth bundles nestled in it, rolled into perfect spirals. "Everybody take a towel."

Everyone reached in. Fawn clutched air inside the basket, empty by the time she got to it. Jax's smile sparkled at her as he handed her a black-and-magenta towel.

"Thanks." Fawn tucked it under her arm.

Jax grabbed one cooler handle, and Rosario picked up the other. Cade closed the trunk, and the group headed for the miniature castle turrets. They stepped up off the parking lot's pavement onto a wide swath of sidewalk corralling them toward the entrance. They fell into line and moved under the shade of the entry pavilion.

A bright-eyed young woman with wheat-blonde hair greeted them. The name tag on her neon-green polo shirt read *Sandie.* "Welcome to Fun Splash. How many are in your party of fun today?"

Rosario rested the cooler on the ground and dug in her purse. "Six. Five of us have Endless Summer passes." She showed five blue paper squares to Sandie.

The young woman typed in her computer. "Very good. Some frequent fun-seekers, I see. Would you like a summer pass or a day pass for your sixth person?"

"Day."

Rosario's answer came so casually and fluidly, Fawn wasn't sure if she detected a hint of Cade's dramatic sarcasm or not.

Sandie typed a little more and handed Rosario a yellow slip of paper. "Fifty dollars for the day."

Fawn nabbed her wallet from her purse. "I got it."

Rosario counted out five bills and put them in Sandie's hand. "It's on me, Fawn."

Fawn opened her wallet anyway. Jax patted her wrist, and she acquiesced. She secured her wallet closed and dropped it into her purse.

Rosario tucked the yellow day pass in Fawn's bag. "Come on." She lifted her end of the red-and-white cooler.

Sandie smiled and waved. "Have a splashtastic day!"

Jax and Rosario carried the cooler past the pavilion into the sun. Fawn stepped into the brilliant light, and Cade paused at her side.

He showed her a glossy brochure of the park. "This is for you. You're gonna need it."

Fawn took it and folded it open to an illustrated map. "Why?"

"We're here." Cade jabbed his fingertip at the entrance drawn at the bottom. "If you need a locker or an innertube, you can rent them here." He tapped another part of the entry pavilion.

"That's what I need for the lazy river, right?"

Cade hesitated a fraction of a second. "Correct. But I wouldn't go there yet." He pointed out a succession of park areas. "Yoselle's going to be in the Sunset Wave Pool."

"Why?"

"Because that's where she likes to be. Rosario and Jax will take the cooler to the rest area by the waterfalls and the Octo Run."

Fawn shook her head. "I don't know what that means."

"It's what they call the water rapids ride with the eight-person rafts. It has sort of an octopus motif." Cade cleared his throat. "Anyway, I'll be—"

Hoots and hollers stole Fawn's and Cade's attention from the map. A dozen people approached them, smiling, their hair slick with water. Fawn recognized most of them from the ATV adventure the night before. A man with water beads resting on his rich umber skin brushed one of his thick dredlocks over his muscled shoulder. He lifted the fingers on one hand in a subtle wave at his side. Fawn traced his gaze to Yoselle, who relaxed her tense posture and ticked up the corners of her pursed lips.

Some of the arriving friends exchanged complicated handshakes with Jax involving elbow touches and wiggling fingers.

A woman with pink and scarlet streaks in her straight, brunette locks bounced over to Fawn. Her spring-green, almond-shaped eyes captivated above her aquiline nose. She shook Fawn's hand. "I'm Henna."

Fawn noticed crimson stains arranged over the back of Henna's earth-toned hand in a mehndi design like paisley lace. A yin yang with flowers for dots occupied the pattern's center. Fawn marveled at the intricate beauty, trying not to stare too long. "Fawn. I like the decoration on your hand."

Henna beamed.

More quickly than the group had arrived, they swept away from the entry pavilion. The man with the shaved head and the woman with sizable dredlocks moved with them. Henna breezed away, her blue-and-purple cover-up flapping as it dried. The man with dreds lagged behind, and Yoselle trailed at a snail's pace behind him. Jax and Rosario took off with the cooler.

Cade roused Fawn's shoulder with a shake. "See you later. Have a good time."

Fawn erupted, rattling the brochure. "What?"

"Oh, right." Cade raised his index finger and swirled it in the air. "The easiest bathrooms to find are here by the entrance. If you get hungry, find Rosario and Jax by the Octo Run. Otherwise, if you insist on paying for your own food, there are several choices a stone's throw east of here."

"I don't know which direction that is!" Fawn swatted Cade's chest with the open brochure.

He barely flinched. "I'm sure anyone working at the park can help." Cade wandered away with backwards steps. "When in doubt, look for the signs with pizza and ice cream and chili dogs on them." Cade formed a triangle with his fingers. "Or follow your nose." He strolled off after his siblings and their friends.

Only Lisette lingered near Fawn.

Fawn growled with aggravation. She folded the brochure and almost tucked it in her purse. "Can I count on you to stick by me, or should I bribe an employee with some ice cream to shepherd me all day?"

Lisette retrieved a pair of golden sunglasses from her bag and set them on her nose, the one thing around that rivaled her blonde locks. "I can hang with you if you want."

Fawn almost asked Lisette about the man who'd sent a secretive wave to Yoselle, but she thought better of it. Low-key waves were made that way for a reason. No matter how few days Fawn stayed with Cade's family, the last person she wanted to be furious with her was the moody, outspoken Yoselle. Fawn stuck the park brochure in her purse. "Where do we start?"

"It's not where *we* start." Lisette sighed. "It's where *you* start."

"Because it's my first trip to Fun Splash and everything? I can't believe I didn't know this place was here. It's huge."

Fawn let Lisette guide her at an ambling pace deeper into the park, the opposite direction from where the rest of their party had disappeared to. All around them, fellow guests mingled and traversed the grounds. Several young boys shrieked and chased each other.

A red-faced man plodded along far behind them, carrying a limp fourth boy in his arms. "Hey! No running!"

Two grey-haired couples walked the grounds, each pair holding hands and taking in the sights. Groups of curvaceous women chattered and chuckled as they roamed. Teenaged boys pushed one another, jabbering about which ride they wanted to go on next.

Fawn gestured around them. "Is it always this popular?"

"In the summer." Lisette angled her sunglasses down to look around for a few moments before righting them again. "While school is out, I mean. Before and after that, while the heat's here, it's even easier to find a first-place parking spot." She flashed a smile at Fawn.

"Should we go back and rent a locker?"

"We can get one in a bit. I'll hold your stuff for now."

Tense chuckles bubbled up out of Fawn. "Oh, no. Maybe you didn't hear. I'm sticking my innertube in the lazy river and staying there for about the next six hours."

"The river and the tide pool are at the other end of the park."

Fawn's muscles constricted around her bones. "Then where are you taking me?"

She trailed her gaze up a towering ride five stories tall with white metal scaffolding supporting a winding, six-foot-wide orange tube.

Lisette raised Fawn's sun hat off her head. "I'm not asking you to go on the Rain of Thunder or the Kraken's Revenge."

Fawn shook her head. "I'm not going on that."

"Afraid of heights?"

"I'm afraid of lots of things."

Lisette lifted Fawn's sunglasses off her nose and folded the arms with one deft hand. "Well, are you more scared of climbing up all those stairs and sliding down with nothing more than your body — or Cade at the end of the day telling you he was right using nothing but his eyes?"

The answer clenched Fawn's belly. "Damn it. Why do I care what your brother thinks?"

"Because he's funny, and he's putting you up for this impromptu vacation in our house, and he has natural leadership qualities. It's basic psychology."

"Basic psychology…" Fawn slid her purse off her forearm and hung it over Lisette's wrist. "…says it's only fear and stubborn pride that keep me down here on the sidewalk."

Fawn took another long, examining look at the ride. The

angle to its apex reminded her of standing outside her apartment building and eyeing one of her own windows. "I thought I came here to relax. Why does Cade want me to face my fears all of a sudden?"

"I'm not convinced that's why he wants you to do it." Lisette took Fawn's towel. "I'll sit on a bench down here by the exit."

"Is the line long?"

Lisette's elbow nudged Fawn's arm. "Just go. It'll be over in ten minutes tops, and I'll personally vouch for you with Cade."

"And he'll believe you?"

"I've never lied to my brother. Either of them. He trusts my word."

"Then I'm going in." Fawn stripped off her cover-up. "You'll be waiting for me?"

"You can trust me, too. I'll be by the pool the tube drops you into."

A muscle twitched in Fawn's stomach. She strode off for the ride's entrance. With determined steps, Fawn climbed up the bottom slats of the metal staircase bending its way into the sky. She expected to run into the end of the line at any moment, stuck two or three stories off the ground with plenty of time to think about what she was really doing. Instead, Fawn didn't come across any other guests until she ascended to the utmost platform. A park employee in a green polo helped a woman in a zebra-print string bikini start down the tube slide. The woman soon slid down out of sight, screams and laughter echoing up behind her.

Fawn folded her arms and muttered. "I'm not going down like that woman."

The seven guests ahead of Fawn waved her past them.

Fawn wagged her hand in response. "No, that's okay. I'll wait."

A heavyset woman with stringy hair and a skirted black bathing suit giggled and motioned for Fawn again. "We're here as a group. Go ahead. We don't want to hold you up."

Fawn grunted and walked past the applauding group. One of the teenaged boys howled with encouragement directly in her ear, and she winced. The employee guided Fawn straight to the tube's entrance. Clear, cerulean water streamed from hidden jets, splashing and bubbling down the slide.

Fawn's voice shook. "What do I do?"

"Have a seat in the water." The young man indicated the start of the slide with a flat palm. "Cross your legs at the ankle, lie back, and relax."

"Yeah. Sure. Okay." Fawn took a deep breath. "This is just to get Cade off my back." Fawn sat down in the active current. "Lisette will vouch for me." She tossed her right ankle over her left and reclined against the slide. "Now what?"

The employee gave her shoulder a gentle push, and the water's momentum slipped Fawn loose into the tube's half-lit enclosure. A shout leapt out of her mouth. She silenced herself, then realized no one would know what screams came from her versus anyone else in the park. Fawn let out a long, warbling yell of aggravation, relief, and empowerment. The slide zigzagged her left and right on her descent from the top, and its unexpected path drew the laughter out of her. Fawn flew down the slide, floating on water and freedom and fun.

She closed her eyes for a second, and when she opened them, she swore she saw more clearly than she had in years. Every bolt and shadow and soaring water droplet in that tube. In a single moment, Fawn realized she hadn't suffered anything like an ulcer all day hanging out with Cade and his cohorts. Her limbs, lazy and fluid, followed the slide's every whim. A giant smile broke out on her face, and the slide snaked Fawn around one final dogleg.

Fawn dropped off the end of the slide, almost instantly immersed in a turquoise pool. She swam up to the surface, gasping and chuckling. An exit ramp to her left led out of the pool, and she grabbed hold of the metal railing. She emerged from the water, the sun warming her and soft grit sticking to the soles of her feet.

Lisette stood up from a bench fifteen feet away. Fawn wandered over to her. Lisette spread Fawn's towel open, and Fawn wrapped it around her torso under her arms. She tucked the corner in to keep the towel in place.

Lisette regarded Fawn with an enigmatic smile. "How was it?"

"Oh, it was incredible!" Fawn wiped water off her arms. "Have you done it?"

"A hundred times."

"Do you like the body one or the innertube one better?"

"This one."

The sun dried the beads of pool water on Fawn's arms and legs, making her skin feel tight and revitalized. "You win, you know."

Lisette raised her perfectly groomed dark-blonde eyebrows. "Pardon?"

Fawn smiled at the exuberant park guests traipsing past her. "I haven't felt this good in years. To be honest, left to my own devices, I would've floated down the lazy river all day checking work emails on my phone." Fawn stuck her tongue out at her old forces of habit. "If you want me to stay with you longer, I will. If it's okay."

Lisette smiled. "It's fine."

"I know I didn't appreciate this opportunity at first. But anybody who can get me out of my own head that effectively—" Fawn aimed a pointed finger up at the slide's fifty-foot tower. "I have to respect. And say thank you."

"You're welcome." Lisette gathered up the towel and sunhat she'd left on the bench. "What would you like to do next? Do you want to try another ride, or are you ready to dig into Rosario's favorite food here, the funnel cake?"

Fawn took the sunhat and planted it on her head. "You tell me what's available, and I'll do it. I'm tired of not living anymore. Avoiding my death and shirking work isn't enough. I want to experience life to the fullest and figure out what that means."

Chapter Three

A tan band against a white cloud captivated Fawn for a long time. She could hardly believe how one day at Fun Splash had deepened her skin into a healthy amber glow. Fawn stared at her forearm resting on the extra pillow, clueless as to how much time had passed lounging in bed like this. But she had no office to sprint to. No meetings for which to rely on Chloe's assistance in order to arrive on time and prepared. No phone calls to take or return. No messages to listen to. Not a pre-packaged, dehydrated fruit-and-nut bar in sight to snarf down standing up.

Fawn eased herself in a slow roll onto her back. The same silence that had greeted her the morning before sounded sweeter now, not hollow and devoid but rather full and promising. Fawn got out of bed, the short nightgown she'd slept in swirling delicately around her thighs.

Caroline had squealed with delight at Fawn's announcement she planned to extend her stay at the house. Caroline hugged Fawn close. "You'll need so many things. Isn't that what you're thinking? But don't worry, *mija*. I love to go shopping, and I'll bring you everything. You don't have to lift a finger while I'm around."

Fawn swung her hips to watch the nightgown's stretchy black material dance around her legs. By the time she'd stopped chatting about the water park with Cade and his siblings in the snack kitchen and gotten ready for bed, Caroline had filled Fawn's closet with new clothes. Fawn walked to the double doors now and drew them open. She stepped into the deep closet, surrounded by colorful fabrics freshening the white space.

Fawn held her hands out to either side, sweeping her fingers along the countless garments. Thickly woven velvet, feathery chiffon, stiff denim, ridged corduroy, and springy cotton played with her touch. She turned around and selected a silky robe from a hanger near the doors. Large, ornate pale-yellow peonies decorated the cobalt-blue background. Fawn put it on and tied it around her waist as she left the bedroom.

Familiar voices led her down the hall.

Lisette spoke up with a good-natured drawl. "You don't have to be nasty, Jax. It's not even ten."

Rosario chimed in. "You should consider your audience, big brother. We outnumber you naturally, and Fawn isn't even here yet."

Jax responded with charm. "My apologies, ladies."

Lisette scoffed. "Jax isn't happy unless he's crossing some kind of line."

Rosario resounded with two guffaws. "He's not happy if there's any line at all, are you, Jax?"

The snack kitchen came into view, and Fawn found the five siblings hanging around the island in much the same frieze she'd stumbled upon the morning before. Lisette and Rosario perched on the two right-hand stools. Cade and Jax lazed about behind the island, Jax shirtless once again. Yoselle showed the biggest change, drooping over the island's granite slab with languid arms propped on it. Her head rested in one hand, her blue-grey eyes staring off in a dreaming haze. In place of her silver bullring dangled a gold one. A white ceramic carafe and a matching rectangular bowl of paper packets took up the island's center. One of the different-colored mugs graced each place setting.

Fawn rubbed her palms together. "Good morning." She claimed the familiar stool next to Lisette. "What's the order of the day?"

Jax leaned toward her and brandished a gleaming smile. "There is no order. Only chaos."

Lisette rolled her eyes and sighed. "He's in an odd mood, Fawn. You have our full permission to ignore him as much as you like."

Fawn scooted herself right up to the edge of the granite. "What's for breakfast?" She eyed the covered plates and baskets on the counter behind Jax.

He whipped around in a circle, his feet pivoting so he ended up at the counter's edge. He plucked the metal covers off each dish. "It's quite the treat today. Pancakes in blueberry, buttermilk, and chocolate. Belgian waffles."

Fawn pouted in make-believe thought. "Belgian food from a French chef."

"Perfectly delicious. And I made Gerard promise to make us real, traditional crêpes tomorrow if you're still here."

Fawn's hands balled into fists in anticipation of wielding a fork and knife over a plate stacked to the ceiling with fluffy pancakes. "I'm staying, okay? Get used to it."

The other four siblings drew out one united, low-pitched *ooh*. Even Yoselle cracked a grin.

Rosario offered her hand up high, and Fawn met it with her own in a sharp smack. "You're truly ready to be among us. Well done."

Jax held up his index finger. "I'm still enough of a gentleman to fix the lady a plate."

Rosario howled with laughter, slapping the granite. She wiped tears from her eyes. "Cade, correct your brother, please."

A wide, sneaky grin spread across Cade's face while he relished his answer. "The only time Jax has ever actually been a gentleman…" Cade licked his lips.

Fawn giggled along with Cade's sisters. She stuck her elbows on the granite slab and supported her jaw in her hands.

Cade directed his shining gaze at his brother. "…was when he impersonated legendary dancer Fred Astaire in a tux at a costume party."

Rosario screeched with amusement. She kicked the island's wooden base and covered her face with her hands. "It's true! It's so true."

Cade bowed his head to Fawn. "Congratulations again on your breakthrough ride down the body slide and for joining us for the longer term."

Fawn brightened and gave a deep nod. "Thank you, sir."

Cade nudged the carafe and the paper packets toward Fawn. "Hot water. Tea."

Fawn glowered at him.

Rosario sent her a loud whisper. "Try the energy blend."

Fawn sorted through the tea packets, their flavors printed in a variety of colors. "Thanks."

The three sisters vacated their stools and lined up behind Jax at the counter breakfast buffet.

Jax called over his bare, bronzed shoulder. "Fawn, do you like syrup, butter, jam, or something else?"

Fawn picked out a white paper envelope with bright-green writing. "Give me everything. I'll sort it out."

Cade poured steaming, crystal-clear water from the carafe into Fawn's empty mug. She aimed a dirty, unimpressed look at him. She tore the tea bag free of its packaging and immersed it into the water.

Jax slid her plate to her across the island, a stack of pancakes swaying on top of it. "Maybe you can help me out, too." He retrieved a jar of strawberry jam, a cruet of dark syrup, and a butter tray from the counter and arranged them in front of Fawn.

"What with?" Fawn slathered butter on the top blueberry pancake, and the fat melted into the golden dough, making it glisten.

Jax flicked his gaze at Rosario. "You see, my siblings are giving me a hard time when I was merely making a statement of admiration about some of the beauties at the water park yesterday."

Fawn doubted his story in the best of ways. "Uh-*huh*." She drizzled thick syrup over her pancakes. "You've been flirting with me for two days, and you think I'll side with you *why*?" Fawn cut a wedge out of her topmost pancake with her fork.

Jax collapsed at the shoulders in a bright, sheepish grin. "You're right. My apologies."

"I mean, maybe I saw some hunks sparkling with chlorinated dew I want to wax nostalgic about." Fawn ate her first bite, light dough carrying sweet blueberries. The soaking of indulgent butter and powerful syrup soon took over her taste buds. "God, another home run from Gerard."

Rosario carted her plate of Belgian waffles to her stool at the island's end. "Well, go ahead, Fawn. Tell us about these gods among flabby weaklings." She winked at Jax.

Lisette settled in between Fawn and Rosario. "Otherwise, you've only taught our brother half a lesson. And we all want to make sure he gets his full schooling."

Fawn chewed more pancake while she thought. "Okay, did anybody see the lifeguard at the wave pool with the wavy blond hair and the massive pecs? The abs you could count from fifty feet away."

Lisette tittered. "I did."

"And the guy with the earrings and the full back tat of Celtic knots? I'm not usually a fan of nipple rings, but you know, I'll always remember his fondly."

Rosario slumped against the granite's edge, heaving with swells of laughter. Yoselle retook her stool with a smirk and rested her breakfast plate on the island.

Jax combed his fingers through his unruly hair and backed away. "All right. Consider me properly schooled."

Cade patted the granite twice and pointed to Jax. "No new piercings for you, my friend."

Fawn spoke up with her loaded fork halfway to her mouth. "New?"

Lisette sucked her teeth. "An unfortunate incident never to be mentioned again."

Yoselle sneered with light bouncing in her eyes. "Jax thought he could pull off an earring."

Rosario chuckled into her hand. "Until we had to intervene. We tried to literally pull it out for him."

Jax picked up a clean plate off the counter. "*From* me," he corrected with sourness.

Rosario draped a fabric napkin across her lap. "Dear brother, trust me, it was *for* you, completely done on your behalf."

Fawn noticed Cade lingering across from her, the only one without a plate of food. "You still haven't answered my question. What are we doing today?"

Cade interlaced his fingers on the granite and grinned. "Something I think you'll find interesting."

Fawn paused. "Because you assume I'll like it or because you know I'll hate it?"

"We've decided it's the perfect weather for hanging out at the beach."

Fawn smiled.

Cade's palms rode up and down in the air. "Right on the water."

"Yeah?"

"In our boat."

Fawn frowned, and she pinned Cade with her eyes. "You know I despise boats."

Jax brought his plate over to the stool next to Fawn. He reached immediately for the strawberry jam. "Why?"

Fawn maintained eye contact with Cade. "Creepy guys with bad initiatives."

Cade motioned to himself and his siblings. "None of whom are with us today." He reached over the island and lifted Fawn's tea bag out of her mug with a faint smirk.

Fawn smoldered. "Arguably." She stuffed a mouthful of chocolate-chip pancake into her mouth.

Cade deposited the wet tea bag on the edge of Jax's plate. "Be that as it may, we've agreed on the boat we most think you'll appreciate. The pontoon."

Fawn swallowed wrong and coughed. "You thought of me, and you picked an old man's boat. How considerate."

Jax interjected, sawing his jam-soaked pancakes into bite-sized chunks with his knife and fork. "It cost a hundred and fifty-five thousand dollars."

Fawn choked. "Are you kidding me? My grandfather had a

pontoon boat. He used to fish off the back of it in the middle of Lake Maxinkuckee. He got it used, and I think he haggled the guy down to something like five grand. How do you spend that much on a little boat?"

Cade grinned and turned to the breakfast buffet. "When you start with a bigger base and keep adding all the extras that you want."

"For instance?"

Jax answered her. "Reclining chairs. Pillow-top seating." He lowered his tone suggestively. "A beast of an engine."

Yoselle joined in. "There's a little bar with a sink."

Fawn laughed. "Oh, good. Because the five of you should be drinking on open water."

Rosario swept a great wave of her hair back from her face. "The sound system itself cost five thousand."

Fawn hurried her chewing of her next bite. "Okay, I gotta see this boat."

Lisette patted Fawn's shoulder. "Plus, we packed all the under-floor storage into it that we could. So we can bring everything we need for the summer's best picnic and not even crowd ourselves."

Fawn savored a bite of buttermilk pancake. "If this boat's so big, there's room for your parents to join us, right?"

Cade faced Fawn with a short stack of pancakes assembled on his plate. "Room, yes, but not today."

Fawn whined. "Why not?" She stiffened her spine and brought her voice under control. "I know we're not ten years old and meeting each other's parents isn't a prerequisite for spending time together. But come on. I've slept here two nights, and I've met everybody else who lives here. Right?"

Cade popped one shoulder up. "Almost."

Fawn's eyes widened for a moment. "That's how you can afford all this stuff. Everybody chips in. But what's going on with your parents, really? Are they secretly spies or dead or saw me from a distance and don't want to meet me? Is there a separation of generations here?"

Cade speared a waffle onto his plate and came to sit down on the empty stool between Yoselle and Jax. "They have their own lives, Fawn. They don't do every activity we come up with, and they don't have to."

"It's hardly escaped my notice, even with careening down most of the rides at Fun Splash, that for yet another day, none of you seem to have anywhere responsible to go."

Cade grinned. "Neither do our friends."

"Let me guess. You all took the same week off for vacation?"

Cade chuckled with delight. "Yes."

Fawn narrowed her eyes in good-natured disbelief.

Cade steadied himself with an audible breath. "You can't prove or disprove it. Our friends won't be riding on the lake with us, either."

Yoselle dropped her head a little lower over her half-finished pancakes.

Fawn's stomach gave her a sudden signal of movement that she'd stuffed herself past the point of reason. She set her fork down in a sluggish arc. "Can't you invite just a couple of them?"

Jax covered Fawn's hand with his larger one. "And give up valuable time spent with you all to ourselves?"

"Nice try." Fawn slithered her hand away and picked up her mug. Her lip curled at the sight of the yellow-green water instead of black-brown coffee. Her begrudging sip tasted like a smooth punch of spices and herbs, winning her over more than she expected. In case Cade awaited her official change of opinion, she tossed another comment at Jax. "I don't want your mermaid beauties getting jealous of me."

Jax rested his palm high on Fawn's back and heaved a sigh. "I can see that I've lost you, but I aim to win you back."

Fawn raised her eyebrows, prompting him.

"I play guitar. I'll serenade you outside your window. You can't resist that, can you?"

Fawn wrinkled her nose. "Musicians? Every woman sees that

ploy coming from a mile away now. You'll have to do better than that." Fawn caught Cade watching and shared a glimmer of a smile with him.

"All right." Jax slid his plate of chopped pancakes an inch away. "I'll make you breakfast in bed."

Fawn's mouth fell open in amusement. "You want to go head to head with a French chef? I'd let you cook something and eat it just to compare the two."

Jax held his hands up by his shoulders. "Clearly, I can't gain ground because you're not a romantic."

Fawn hummed. "Not a romantic, eh? I believe in honesty and sharing dreams and finding love by any means necessary."

Jax turned his lips into a wicked, daring grin that reached deep into his golden-honey eyes. He spoke low and slow. "I believe in very long walks on very long beaches at sunset and kisses you feel tingling like earthquakes to the tips of your toes."

Burning heat rose up in Fawn's chest. She averted her gaze as blush tinted her cheeks.

The sisters laughed, and Rosario whooped.

Jax sounded satisfied and smug. "Yeah, I got you back. Bring it in." He held his arms out wide.

Fawn leaned over and gave him a quick hug.

Jax's voice rumbled with a barely serious warning. "Be careful, though, not to snag yourself on my nipple ring. But don't worry. I wouldn't sue you because I'd just get our friends to pay for my surgical repair."

Yoselle exhaled with disgust and shoved her plate away.

Rosario stepped down from her stool. "Yeah, enough nipple talk at breakfast to last for a year."

Fawn felt too full to slide off her high seat so soon. "Speaking of those I haven't met around here, I thought I heard a dog barking yesterday morning."

Cade nodded while he chewed his breakfast. "That was probably Axel."

"How many dogs do you have? I haven't seen one paw or one

tuft of fur since I came here."

"There are five dogs, three cats, and whatever Henna's invited in to take care of."

"Can the dogs come to the lake?"

Cade shook his head. "Not the first time you go. It's hard enough to get over your hatred for boats without ten new front paws batting you for attention."

With a snide twist to her lips, Fawn dredged up the strength and willpower to step down off her stool. "I'll just prepare for a day on the lake, then, with *these* ten new front paws." She gave Jax's hand a light slap.

Lisette smirked. "Careful. He likes that."

Yoselle groaned and held her head in her hands.

Rosario waved her youngest sister towards her. "Come on, Yo. We all have a boat to get ready for."

Jax got up as well. "I'll leave you to your own devices, Fawn, and take my perversions with me."

Rosario flitted her fingers at him. "Find a shirt, too, if you can."

Cade met Fawn's gaze. "The only important question left this morning is, can you swim?"

Fawn shifted her robe sleeve up past her bicep and curled her arm up to make it bulge. "I didn't get these muscles sitting behind my desk, okay? I can swim."

Jax lingered beside her, considering her muscles.

Rosario cleared her throat in loud bursts. "Everybody to their rooms, please."

Lisette slipped down to her bare feet. "I know that was a necessary question, Cade, but it's sooo not the most important one." She winked at Fawn and drifted away.

~

Sunshine streamed down on Fawn as she rode in the open-top convertible. Cade relaxed beside her in the driver's seat, his left elbow propped against the door and his right wrist bent over the black leather wheel. The engine rumbled as the car sped along.

Currents of wind kept trying to snatch Fawn's hat. She cackled as she resigned herself to holding her hat's crown in place. "This sure beats the SUV. And the ATV. As nice as they were."

Cade offered her an impish grin. "You appreciate cars?"

"Oh, yeah. I don't know anything about them except putting gas in them and taking them to get the oil changed. But anything that can get me safely from point A to point B in tons of style, I'm a fan of." Fawn glanced behind her at Lisette and Yoselle in the back seat. "Do you think Rosario's mad she lost the coin toss and had to ride with Jax?"

Cade made minimal adjustments to the steering wheel under his tan, limp wrist. "Nah. She corrals him like a mother hen, but she loves him, really."

"Jax could use two mothers."

Cade chuckled and nibbled his thumbnail. "He could at that."

Fawn pressed her shoulder blades back against the seat's cushy white upholstery. "So how far is it to the boat?"

"About twenty minutes from the house."

A cloud shifted past the sun, shooting heated beams down on Fawn's bare arms. She soaked them up with glee. "How did you get so lucky? You're centrally located to all the fun spots."

"Not *all* of them, but we certainly appreciate where we're situated."

Fawn closed her eyes and breathed in the fresh, clean air. "Did you buy the land and build the house, or was the house already here?"

Cade paused. "We picked the spot because it was nice and open. It had that big, flat area to build on. We talked about what each of us wanted, and I made the arrangements to have it constructed."

Fawn turned her head and studied Cade in the billowing light. "That's a lot of responsibility."

Cade's twists and swirls of red-blond hair swayed in the breeze. He breathed out in agreement. "It was."

"Your family must really trust you to get all those plans and details right. My grandparents built a small house after retirement. There's a lot to pick out and make decisions for."

Cade aimed a grin at her. "The same grandpa who fished off his boat?"

Fawn tensed her jaw and pursed her lips, only half annoyed with him. "Yes."

"Did you ever like his boat?"

"I did. It was other people who ruined boating for me."

Cade rested the side of his index finger against his lower lip's bottom edge. "Why did you let them do that?"

Fawn huffed. "Regular pick-up lines are bad enough. You start tossing in nautical ones, it gets old pretty fast. I don't like catcalls on land, where I can walk away. I really don't care to be stranded on a boat with anybody who's pushy, potentially drunk, and got a one-track mind."

"Yet you're boating with us." Cade broadened his grin.

Fawn lightened up a bit. "That's different."

"You wouldn't have said so two days ago. We were kidnappers and phone thieves, remember."

Fawn squeaked with laughter and covered her mouth for a moment. She set her hand on Cade's shoulder. "You know what? I haven't thought about my phone in almost twenty-four hours. That's crazy."

Cade's eyes sparkled silver and steel. "That's a good day at the water park."

Fawn gave his shoulder a single pat of gratitude and pulled her hand away. She drew her shoulders up high and released them. "I'm enjoying this ride. We haven't even reached the boat yet. Do you have your own private boathouse or something?"

Cade retained his grin. "Naw. Nothing like that. We dock it at the marina with all the other boats."

Fawn forced a loud gasp of shock. "That's sacrilege."

"Maybe you'll inspire us to acquire our own boathouse and pier."

Fawn stretched her jaw out in thought. "There's an idea."

Cade beamed.

Fawn admired the verdant foliage lining her side of the rambling road. "You certainly don't have many neighbors out here."

"No, we don't."

Cade turned off the winding road, and they passed under a wide sign advertising Beach Lake Marina. The crisp, white letters popped on a sapphire background rimmed in decorative white lines. He swerved the convertible further to the right, cruising halfway across the crowded parking lot. He cranked the wheel and deftly inserted the car into a narrow spot between two monstrous SUV's.

Cade nodded to the vehicle shading Fawn's side of the convertible. "Does that make you miss yours?"

Fawn gazed up at its gleaming black contours. "No. I'm content with this car for today."

Lisette smacked her palm against the top of the convertible's grey outer rim. "Come on. Let's go."

Cade leaned toward Fawn. "She's one of many wishing they'd make four-door convertibles again."

Lisette let out a puff of impatient air. "Because you're too slow."

Fawn laughed. "What's the rush?" She collected her clear plastic beach bag of things she thought she'd need for the day. She sprung her door open. "I thought we had all the time in the world to goof off and relax." She hopped out of the car.

Lisette pulled the mechanism to fold Fawn's seat forward and give her room to climb out. "There's just such a fun day ahead of us. I don't want to spend all of it jaw-jacking in the parking lot."

Yoselle grabbed her purple-and-black backpack by a strap. She hauled it out of the car through Lisette's route.

Fawn examined the charms swinging from its zippers. Jewels

flashed from simple gold and silver shapes. Two green-and-purple pompoms hung in a pair. "What do you have in there, Yoselle?"

"Magazines," she drawled as she hoisted the backpack's straps onto her shoulders.

"It was nice to hang out with your friends at the water park yesterday."

Yoselle dropped her gaze and nodded absently. "It was okay." A warm light touched her eyes.

Cade got out and closed his door. He came around the car and shut the passenger side as well. "Do we have everything?"

Fawn glanced around them. "Everything but your—"

A sleek, muscle-bound car clad in metallic, lipstick red charged around the corner. Its engine snarled and chugged, crackling and revving. It zipped into a nearby parking space and screeched to an abrupt stop.

Rosario bounced out of the passenger seat, cheering and whipping her sunglasses in a circle beside her head. "Woo-hoo! I do love the Jag." She patted its side.

Fawn rested her hip against the convertible. "Well, I love the Mustang, so it all worked out."

Jax jumped out of the Jaguar's driver seat. "I'm sorry you had to ride with the old lady, Fawn." He pointed at Cade with a daring smirk.

Cade rolled his eyes. "They both have a V-8 engine. And yes, I do make use of it."

Fawn hefted her bag straps up onto her shoulder. "All I know is the higher the number, the more I like the car."

Cade cupped his hand on Fawn's shoulder and whispered in her ear. "Don't tell Jax you know next to nothing about cars. He'll declare it a personal mission to fully educate you."

Fawn shared a conspiratorial smile with Cade. "I'll proceed at my own risk, then. Thanks."

Jax knitted his thick eyebrows together. "What are you saying about me?"

Cade guided Fawn forward. "It wasn't about you, brother.

Sometimes things are about our honored guest."

Fawn looked around the well-used lot, still failing to find a single boat or azure wave. A red-roofed building stood near the parking lot's entrance. A white-clapboard enclosure topped with blue shingles spread low the length of the lot beyond the Jaguar. The outermost edge of the parking lot met with a capping off of thick trees and bubbling water features. Fawn scratched her head through her hat. "Are you sure this is a marina?"

Cade dipped his head. "Quite sure."

"And this lake is really called Beach Lake? Isn't that obvious?"

Cade kept his hand planted on Fawn's shoulder and led her toward the red-roofed building. "You'll forget all about these trivialities when you actually see it."

"But there's no lake here."

Cade steered Fawn across the length of the parking lot.

Fawn gestured to their vehicles. "Isn't there supposed to be a lunch basket for today?"

"Gerard will bring it later. We'll stop off at the marina in about two hours for calls of nature, anyway. It's the one feature our craft doesn't have."

Cade guided Fawn past the parking lot's entrance and the end of the white clapboard building on their right. He rotated her ninety degrees.

Between the two buildings, a cement drive headed straight for a network of piers dotted with a vast array of shiny boats bobbing gently on navy-blue water.

Fawn's heart leapt. "This is where we get to go?!"

Cade grinned with pride. "Yes."

Fawn's finger poked his arm. "Which one's yours?"

"We'll take you to it."

Fawn ambled down the drive with Cade and his siblings surrounding her like a high-energy cloud. "Does it have a name?"

"Yes. You'll see it."

They reached the end of the drive at the water's edge and veered right. Chatter from other boat owners rode on the wind from distant piers.

Fawn almost skipped as she walked. "I'm so excited."

Cade spoke up. "Nobody get pushy, now, and ruin it."

Fawn nudged him with her elbow. She took in the infinite expanse of cornflower-blue sky and its giant, drifting clouds. "It'd take a lot to ruin this day."

They turned onto one of the piers. Its wooden platform stretched out longer than a football field in front of them. Fawn strolled along, noticing all the differences and similarities of the boats they passed. Most of their hulls were clean and white. Some sat low and simple, their noses pointed for speed. A few towered up out of the water, small yachts that looked like mini cruise ships.

Cade released a pleasant sigh. "There she is."

A twenty-five-foot craft waded before them. Its body floated on three aluminum pontoons gleaming silver-white in the sunlight. A black bimini rising on black metal supports lent shade to a small fraction of the boat's interior. The perimeter stood about three feet tall, a swoosh of navy adding an accent to a lighter royal blue. The seating's upholstery invited Fawn toward it with its rich sand color and soft curves.

They walked onto the smaller pier along the boat's port side.

Fawn pointed to the words painted near the back of the boat. "Is that the name of your boat? Grand Mariner?"

Cade grinned. "No. That's the model. This is her name." He gestured to larger gold letters closer to the boat's bow.

"Vanna? Like Vanna White?"

Cade slipped his hands into his shorts pockets. "Vanna like our mother."

Jax popped the integrated door open and stepped onto the boat. "Long live the queen."

Rosario and Lisette boarded behind their brother. Yoselle trailed along behind them.

Fawn's head tilted to one side, incredulous at Cade. "Well, you have to let me meet her now. I can't sail in a boat named after her and not meet her face to face."

"Tomorrow," Cade promised.

"And I want to pet your dogs and cats. Where does everybody else eat breakfast, anyway?"

Cade chuckled. "We'll get it sorted out. Today, we sail."

Fawn followed Cade onto the boat, its flooring reminding her of driftwood slats. On her left, Jax wiggled his butt into a high-backed, luxuriously padded chair. A small table beside it separated it from a matching chair closer to Fawn. Across from Jax curved a padded bench for two or three people. Straight ahead of Fawn, the captain's chair stood tall and over-stuffed at the helm. Directly to her right, a sink graced a small bar. Rosario and Lisette waved to her from the two high stools on the counter's other side. Behind them, more bench seating curved in a graceful L shape. Butted up against it, Yoselle occupied the one last sitting area facing the boat's aft. The gate of aluminum crossbars rested closed between Yoselle's area and the rest of the boat.

Jax grinned and stroked the arm of the vacant chair next to him. "Come sit with me, my lady."

Fawn shook her finger. "Oh, no. Cade's driving again? Isn't there anyone else who can pilot this vessel? I'm not letting Cade dodge all of my questions all afternoon."

Rosario whined, and she drooped over the bar counter. "We need somebody to make us drinks."

Cade offered Jax his hand and pulled his brother up out of his chair. "You steer. I'll pour."

Jax clapped Cade on the back and took up the helm. With the push of a button, an engine murmured, and the floor vibrated under Fawn's sandals.

She gasped. She quickly helped herself to the nearest chair and gripped the armrests. "It's that simple to start a boat?"

Jax purred. "It is when you upgrade to keyless ignition."

Cade jogged off the boat and untied the ropes from their glinting metal cleats fastened to the wooden pier. With the boat untethered, he reboarded and secured the short door behind him. He saluted Jax. "She's all yours, captain."

"Then hold on. I haven't driven this since last summer."

Jax pulled back on the shift lever, and the boat lurched forward away from the jetty. Fawn's body shifted sideways in her seat, and she dug her fingertips into the armrests. She laughed into the wind while Rosario and Lisette applauded from their stools.

Cade hung onto the bar's camel-colored counter. "Can you pick a speed more conducive to tending bar?"

Jax eased the steering wheel to the right, aiming the boat at an opening in the harbor's surrounding land. "Where's the excitement in that?"

Cade shook his head and opened a low door in the bar's under portion. He drew out a bottle of red wine and retrieved two glasses from an adjacent cabinet.

Fawn slid her beach bag off her shoulder and set it at her feet. She pinned a whipping section of her hair back from her face with her hand. "You're brave to introduce red wine on this boat with Jax at the wheel."

Cade shot her a wide grin. "I know. But my sisters don't like white, except for Yoselle."

Rosario puckered her face up. "No flavor."

Cade inserted the glasses into two of the cup holders on the counter's raised shelf in front of Rosario and Lisette. He located a corkscrew and popped the bottle open. Jax gave the shift lever a tug, and the boat's acceleration pitched everyone an inch toward the back.

Rosario fixed him with a glare and lifted one of her two-inch-thick platform sandals. "Jaxon, I swear to you, I will heave this shoe directly at your head."

Jax hid his chuckling mouth partly behind his fingers and adjusted the shift lever. The boat slowed a little, and its speed evened out. It passed through the entrance channel into the broad, sparkling lake.

Rosario fit her sandal back on her foot. "That's better."

Cade tipped the bottle, and scarlet wine flowed into

Rosario's glass, followed by Lisette's. He squeezed the cork into the bottle's mouth and secured it in the fridge. He set his hands on the counter. "Will there be anything else?"

One side of Rosario's lips perked up as she raised her glass out of the cup holder. "No, you may go sit down."

Cade offered a shallow bow and passed Fawn on his way to the padded chair on her left. He settled in, relaxing into its cradling form.

Lisette beamed with mischievous intent above the rim of her wine glass. Her brown eyes shone. "We have some questions for Fawn."

Fawn let out a surprised burst of air. "Me?" She set her fingertips against her chest.

Rosario licked her lips. "Oh, yes. Do you have a boyfriend back home?"

Fawn sat up straighter in her chair, intrigued by Rosario's question. "Are you hinting at how far from home you've taken me?"

Lisette dismissed the inquiry with a snort and wrinkled her nose. "Don't change the subject. Do you have someone?"

Fawn exhaled, not sure whether she bristled with embarrassment, intrusion, or both. She turned her head to the bow of the boat and the sapphire water it sliced through. Her gaze slid sidelong to meet Cade's.

He watched her with enigmatic interest, lazily stroking his chin. A baiting grin hung on his lips, and Fawn couldn't tell how invested he was in her answer.

She turned back to Rosario and Lisette. She threw one knee over the other, crossing her legs as casually as possible with a hint of prickling displeasure. "Well, there's nobody, so…"

The sisters pouted in deep frowns.

Rosario took a prolonged sip of wine. "How long has it been?"

Festering pain stabbed through Fawn's chest. She cleared her throat. "About six months. It was over long before we officially ended it." Fawn took her hat off and rested it with its wide brim in her lap.

Lisette drained more wine from her glass and rested it in its cup holder. "Are you looking?"

Fawn stammered. "I'm just on vacation."

Rosario batted her hand through the air. "Don't mind her. She jumped ahead." Rosario jerked her chin up. "What are you running from? What kind of fuck-up, exactly, was this... What's his name? Or her name?"

Cade resounded with percussive, highly amused laughter.

Fawn kept herself focused away from him on Rosario and Lisette. One of her eyelids twitched. "His name was Devon."

The two sisters winced.

Rosario set her glass in its cup holder. "Honey, nothing good ever came from a man named Devon. You should've saved yourself the trouble from the get-go."

Lisette toyed with her necklace's donut-shaped gemstone. "How long were you together?"

Fawn could barely stutter the words. "Six years."

"You stuck around for some reason. What did he give you that was good?"

Fawn blinked. She tried to search her memories, but they remained elusive behind months of loneliness and hurt. "I don't know."

Lisette offered a sympathetic smile. "Sure you do."

Jax extended his left arm into the aisle between the helm and his sisters seated at the bar. He flexed his muscles. "Was he strong like me?"

The fine sculpture of Jax's mountainous bicep and taut tricep warmed Fawn with a giddy flush. She shook her head. "No."

Rosario's fingertips danced along the side of her glass. "Expressive eyes? Soft hair? Round butt? What? Come on. You can say it here. We're all rooting for you."

Fawn stretched her neck to try to grab a glimpse of Yoselle with her backpack at the rear of the boat. The bar blocked her view.

Rosario spoke up dryly. "Even Yoselle's on Team Fawn."

Fawn rearranged her sundress' cotton folds over her thighs. "Devon had this way of making me feel powerful, invincible. Like I couldn't make a wrong decision. Like I was born to rise through the ranks of Better Mind and take over for Janet."

Lisette raised her face to the sun and closed her eyes. "What did Devon do?"

"He was vice president of safety for a manufacturing plant. Some people thought we were mismatched — and I suppose we were — but not for the reasons they thought." Fawn rubbed her fingers together. "Having two driven, motivated people in a relationship just kills the whole thing. He was passionate about keeping workers safe on the job, and I still believe in boosting employees with the tools they need to feel good while they succeed."

Rosario raised her eyebrows. "But?"

Fawn trailed her gaze over the boat's faux-wood flooring. "I guess he got tired of any number of my habits. Staying at the office past dinner. Detailing my plans and visions for the company for hours at a time. Complaining about missing birthday parties for my nephews and friends. Everything that's only gotten worse since he moved out."

Lisette met Fawn's gaze and shimmied her shoulders. "That's why you're here with us."

"It is."

Cade tapped Fawn's wrist. She turned toward him, and he pointed to the far-off beach hugging the lake's gentle curve. "That's the beach we came to your first night here."

In the sun's full glory, the sand spread out like a blanket with subtle wrinkles and lumps. The granules glowed with warmth. It looked nothing like the tire-track laden birthing ground for conspiracies Fawn had knelt on that night.

She folded one hand over the other in her lap. Frantic panic seized her on that beach and speared white-hot pain through the probable ulcer in her stomach. Now, she sat calm and at ease with the same five people who'd lined up in front of her and tossed her cell phone between them to keep it from her. She drew in a deep breath, considering the same beach from such a different perspective. "Was that really only two days ago? I'm so comfortable with all of you now."

Cade grinned and squared his shoulders. "That's the power of the water park."

His siblings giggled.

Fawn smirked at him. "If you love Fun Splash so much, why don't you date it?"

Rosario and Lisette *oohed* in low tones.

Cade merely maintained his grin.

Fawn gave his reclining arm a playful push. "Huh? What about your last girlfriend? What was she like? And the vast array of wild ones and broken hearts I'm sure Jax has left in his wake?" Fawn flitted her fingers at Rosario and Lisette. "Not to mention the two of you."

Rosario twisted her lips. "Don't forget Yoselle."

"She gets a free pass because she's reading quietly to herself instead of peppering me with the third degree."

Lisette jerked her thumb at Jax. "You'd need a weekend seminar to learn half of Jax's history, and due to its questionable content, you wouldn't want to attend."

Jax's mouth fell open. "Mine?" The incredulous light in his golden eyes gave way to understanding. He wobbled his head from side to side. "Okay, granted, but you've had some *serious* missteps with all kinds of insufferable characters."

Fawn scooted forward in her seat. "What was wrong with them?" She winked at Lisette.

Jax rested against the helm chair's tall back. "Too boring. Overly friendly. Distant. The last one was..." Jax rolled his head against the cushion to meet his sister's warning eyes. "...flaky as sin."

Lisette set her jaw. "Eccentric."

Cade interjected. "He never showed up when he said he would."

Lisette retrieved her glass and rushed several mouthfuls of crimson wine. "He was an artist. He never knew when inspiration would strike."

Jax splayed his fingers wide and shot his hand toward Lisette. "He never once had anything to show for all the time he supposedly spent creating."

Lisette's spine stiffened. "If you added one more bimbo to your list of affairs, I'd need a stronger drink to discuss it."

Jax beamed at her. "Having fun yet? I'm enjoying this. It's good."

Cade chuckled from Fawn's other side.

She marveled at him. "Is this what you do for entertainment? Ride around the lake and rib each other?"

Cade rubbed a fingerprint against the ridge in his chin and hummed in appreciation. "Sometimes."

The subtle wave the family's dredlocked friend gave Yoselle at the water park needled Fawn again. She wanted to ask if the other siblings knew anything about Yoselle's romantic history while their youngest sister sat on the other end of the boat. But if Yoselle overheard or got dragged into the conversation to defend her choices, Fawn would find it hard to forgive her invasion of privacy.

Fawn defaulted to a more general inquiry. "So none of you are dating anyone now?" She still could've kicked herself for sticking so close to her hidden curiosity.

Cade shook his head.

Fawn teased him. "Scared?"

Cade's grin stretched even larger, and his eyes smoldered.

Jax scoffed. "Cade's not afraid of anything."

Fawn's eyebrows flew up. "Nothing?" She studied Cade. "Heights? Dying? Storms? Spiders?"

Cade shook his head through every suggestion.

"Commitment? Being alone? Dentists? Public speaking?"

Cade's voice rumbled to life. "I'd do it all at the same time."

"Get your teeth scraped while speaking on a high platform in a storm as you're dying? That's quite a time."

Jax gave a deep nod. "With a smile on his face."

Fawn articulated her fingers up and down Cade's tanned arm. "With spiders crawling over you and everything?"

Cade held her gaze. "You don't have to be afraid of anything. It's a choice."

"Yeah." Fawn gestured toward the bar without looking. "I proved it at the water park with Lisette."

Cade inhaled a long breath. "Now prove it with everything else."

Fawn settled into the deepest curves of the chair and interlaced her fingers. "With nothing better to do than jaw jack all day with the five of you? That should be easy."

"You wouldn't have said it was easy two days ago." Cade's eyes burned with amusement.

Fawn stuck her tongue out at him.

Jax called over. "Fawn, you want to see the helm? It has a touch screen."

Fawn eased up onto her feet, although the boat skimmed the water with an effortless smoothness. "I'll take a look, but I'm not obsessed with everything that has a touch screen, you know."

Cade asked her an even question. "Do you have a touch screen in your SUV?"

Fawn looked at him over her shoulder. Her heart beat a little faster. "Well, yeah, but I didn't—" She huffed. "I'm not obsessed with them."

Cade and Jax chuckled. Fawn stepped over to stand beside Jax at the helm. She cast her gaze past Rosario and Lisette drinking at the bar for a moment. Yoselle lounged alone on the aft rear-facing seat. She rested her arm on her backpack, no magazines open in her hands or strewn about. Yoselle focused on the beach with distant disinterest glazing her eyes.

A hint of longing, too, Fawn thought. She called out to the

young woman. "How are you doing, Yoselle?"

Yoselle turned her head away and said nothing.

Jax glanced up with sympathy. "Don't worry about her. It's just her way."

A tiny knotted tangle remained in Fawn's belly. Yoselle sat motionless for seconds on end.

Jax injected a little singsong into his voice. "Fawn. We've got two touch screens at the helm."

Lisette exhaled in exasperation. "If you truly want to make this a party, plug your phone into the sound system and let Fawn hear the two subwoofers."

Jax slid his phone out of his deep shorts pocket. "Correction. *Feel* the subwoofers."

Fawn retreated to her chair and gripped the ends of the armrests. She grinned in anticipation.

Rosario raised her near-empty wine glass and whooped. She pointed at Fawn. "You want a party? We'll whip something up for you for this weekend."

Warmth filled Fawn's chest. "I can't wait."

Chapter Four

Fawn paused at Cade's side in the hallway outside her bedroom. She raised her foot and slid off her champagne, sequined ballet flat.

Cade raised an eyebrow. "What's wrong?"

Fawn hopped on her shoed foot. "I can't walk in flats. I should've worn heels. I have to go back and find different shoes."

Cade wrapped one hand around his opposite wrist. "You just explained to me after five minutes in the closet that heels would be too fancy for breakfast."

"That's true, but it's *your* parents." Fawn gestured around them at the grand artwork and exquisite statuettes. "They live *here*." She pulled off her other shoe and retreated through her doorway.

Cade propped his shoulder against the wall with a sigh. "You've been content to dress casually, even in pajamas, around my siblings and me."

Fawn jabbed the toe of a shoe at Cade. "That's different. That was the snack kitchen. This is the dining room with your parents and your friends. I will not be the underdressed house guest who spends all day on the expensive boat but can't bother to look decent for breakfast."

Fawn ducked into the closet and hurried into its deepest depths. She plopped the ballet flats on the carpet and surveyed her high-heel choices lined up on posh wooden shelves suspended three high.

Cade called to her from the doorway ten feet behind her. "What are you looking for? Lost treasure?"

"Something that complements this dress without being too matchy." Fawn swished her full skirt. As soon as she'd seen the dress hanging near the closet's entrance, she knew it was the perfect choice. The short flutter sleeves hung delicately against her upper arms. Like them, the wrap bodice was dyed a striking navy blue. The thin jersey fabric lightened into a kelly green through her waist and hips, only to darken again around her calves. Fawn relaxed her tense eyebrows. "You know what I mean. You dress sharp."

Cade sounded smooth with gratification. "Thank you."

Fawn swept her gaze over the countless pairs of shoes. Black. Brown. Tan. Red. She muttered to herself. "Too tall. Too strappy. It's too early for velvet."

"Shall I call for Caroline?"

Fawn shot Cade a sneer. "I can pick out my own shoes."

"I think the real question is, can you pick out new shoes and still make it to breakfast on time?"

"Shit." Fawn grabbed the first white heels she saw and wriggled her feet into the classic slingbacks. "How come you get to look nice for breakfast, and you're giving me such a hard time?"

She wheeled to face Cade. He stood with widespread feet in the middle of the closet doorway, his thumbs tucked in the pockets of his loose-legged khaki-green pants. A plain, wrinkleless plum-colored t-shirt accentuated his grey eyes.

His tipped his forehead at her. "If you think this is posh, you should see my outfit for Saturday night."

"Yes. The big party Rosario's throwing." Fawn strolled toward Cade. She knocked the side of her shoe against the dark tip of Cade's footwear. "You're more put together than you have been in the snack kitchen."

Cade's eyes sparkled. "These are slippers."

Fawn adjusted her shoulders. "I thought they were shoes."

He shrugged and stepped aside out of the doorway. "An unimportant difference, perhaps."

Fawn strode out of the closet. She sucked in a gasp of false alarm and covered her mouth with one hand. "Can it be you value these dining room meals as well?"

They emerged into the hall.

Cade settled his hands deeper into his pockets. "Why?

Because I'm not as laid-back as my shirtless brother?"

Fawn headed down the familiar left-hand hallway.

Cade tapped her shoulder and redirected her along the jog that shot off to her right. "Dining room's this way. Unless you wanted to stop by the snack kitchen and show off your new ensemble?"

Fawn raised her chin. "Are you insinuating I'd be showing off for Jax?"

"I didn't insinuate anything."

Fawn rearranged the folds of her skirt and swept curls of her hair back over her shoulder. "Rosario and Lisette would appreciate this dress. Maybe Yoselle would, too. I don't know."

"And Jax?"

Fawn eyed Cade sidelong with a smirk. "I didn't realize I needed to announce yesterday on the boat during my dating interrogation that Jax is nowhere near my type."

"He's a far cry from the driven, highly motivated individual you're looking to avoid."

A closed door opened ahead on the right. Caroline wheeled a small, two-tiered cart of cleaning supplies into the corridor. She broke into a bright smile at Fawn and undulated her fingers.

Fawn spread the skirt's fullness wide. "Eh? I clean up good."

Caroline pulled the door shut before Fawn could see inside its room. "You're like a dream, Miss Fawn. I knew that dress would be pretty on you."

Fawn giggled and swished the skirt around her legs as she walked at Cade's side. "See? I don't need a man to compliment me."

Cade bowed his head to her. "I stand corrected."

A sudden thought grabbed Fawn, and she clutched Cade's arm. "What does everyone else wear to breakfast? Am I overdressed?"

Cade enjoyed a hearty laugh from deep in his chest, doubling over. "You're worried about that *now*?"

"Answer me. Should I go back?" Fawn bit her fingernail.

Cade drew her hand away from her mouth with a feather-light grasp and ushered her forward. "Would Caroline lie to you by omission? If she thought you were overdressed, she would've told you."

Fawn's shoulders released their uptight bunching. "That's true. Maybe you should've introduced me to Caroline that first evening on the beach. I might trust her even more than I trust Rosario." She cracked a grin.

Soft voices floated down the hallway.

Fawn's hand seized Cade's. She stopped walking and lowered her voice. "Is that them?"

He held her hand for a moment. His eyes glittered, and his voice became a gentle purr. "They're greatly anticipating your arrival."

"Jesus. I'm like a debutante or something." Fawn retrieved her sweating hand and straightened herself from her posture to her hair and dress. "How do we go in? Do I put my hand around your elbow?"

Cade's mouth twisted with a mysterious grin. "Whatever you like."

"Everybody's going to be there?"

Cade nodded. "My folks and most of my friends. Perhaps all of them. I haven't stopped by for a head count."

Fawn swallowed to moisten her dry throat. She slipped her hand around Cade's elbow. "If I don't look blatantly ridiculous, at least you can help hold me up."

Cade hummed with humor. "You worry too much."

"I want them to like me. I might be here a few weeks." Fawn swept a few of her curls forward over her shoulder to grace her collarbone. "Okay. Let's go."

Cade chuckled and escorted Fawn to the T at the end of the hall. He gestured her to the open double doors ahead on their left. She pulled him with her to the doorway and stepped fully in.

Golden sunlight glowed through the large, rectangular room. At either end, potted palms spread verdant fronds. Colorful birds of paradise lent the space a timeless, tropical atmosphere. A row of floor-to-ceiling windows filled most of the wall across from Fawn. A magnificent ivory-colored chandelier graced the ceiling's center. Beneath it, dark-wood chairs ringed the longest table Fawn had ever seen. Butter-yellow satin covered the padded seat cushions. People filled most of the chairs, plates of aromatic food in front of them. All the people turned toward Fawn.

Fawn was prepared for their welcoming smiles, and she offered a grateful one in return. They erupted into applause, and she hung back a step. She bit her lip and ducked her head. "All I did was show up to breakfast."

The clapping continued, and Fawn picked her head up. Her chest gave up its self-conscious grip on her lungs. "Well, okay. Good morning, everybody."

They stopped applauding.

Cade took his elbow from Fawn's hand and set his fingertips lightly on her back. "This is Fawn Claire. I know some of you have seen her around. She's been staying with us for a couple of days. I apologize there hasn't been a formal introduction until now."

On the far left of the table's other side, a middle-aged woman beamed with an unabashed smile. Thick waves of golden-blonde hair cascaded past her shoulders. Her sea-blue eyes glistened with joy against her deep tan. Her loose sundress, covered with red and yellow flowers, reassured Fawn about her choice of morning attire. Beside the woman, a man's brown hair spiked up off his head. He looked about the same age or slightly older with crooked lines fanning out from his round, walnut-colored eyes. With the top button of his button-up shirt left undone, his collar flared away from his neck. Muscular arms emerged beneath his short, blue-and-yellow plaid sleeves.

The rest of the individuals gathered around the elongated table covered several decades with their ages, although most of them seemed to be in their twenties or thirties. The umber-skinned man and woman with thick dreds sat next to each other. The bold canary yellow of his linen shirt reflected the striking magenta of her dress.

Henna stood out as well, draped in a turquoise shirtdress. Her green jade pendant formed a ring around a Chinese symbol written in gold. Henna offered an enthusiastic wave, which Fawn mirrored at once. Henna issued a loud whisper. "Hey. Good to see you in the dining room."

"Thanks." Fawn spotted the man with the clean-shaven head from riding the ATV's. Some of the others Fawn remembered from the water park, and a few she had not met before under any circumstances. Fawn rocked forward and back in subtle swings. "It really is nice to meet you all."

Cade steered her toward the table's left end. "I'll make sure you get everyone's names later."

The chair at the head of the table and one adjacent to it rested empty, and Fawn assumed Cade was leading her to them. Instead, he gestured beyond them to the middle-aged couple. "Fawn, these are my parents."

Fawn shielded her gaping mouth with her hands. "Oh, my God. Of course. I wouldn't have guessed."

They stood up to greet her before Fawn had a chance to feel completely humiliated by her rambling.

Vanna smiled and folded her hands in front of her vivid sundress. "It's a pleasure having you in our home."

Fawn tried to decipher whether Cade's mother meant that she and her husband ran the house or merely resided in it. Fawn gave up on unraveling that particular family mystery. She shook Vanna's hand. "It's just that you look younger than I pictured you. You look fantastic. This lackadaisical lifestyle really agrees with you."

The woman squeezed Fawn's hand with a knowing smile. "Thank you, dear."

"Mrs…?" Fawn raised her eyebrows.

Cade's mother sent a shiver through her body. "So formal. Just Vanna will do."

"Like the boat," Fawn coached herself.

"Like the boat."

Cade's father extended his hand to Fawn. "Only, my wife likes to go a lot faster than that pontoon is capable of."

Fawn let Cade's father cradle her hand in his big, gentle grip. "With a Jaguar and a Mustang, that must be easy."

He grinned with the same mischief as his son. "Those aren't hers. She drives a Venom GT. You ever hear of that?"

Fawn shook her head.

"It'll terrify you just looking at it. Then it goes from zero to sixty in less than three seconds. It tops out at two-seventy."

Fawn held her eyes closed, struggling to fathom riding in a car speeding that fast. She blinked in disbelief. "Has she topped it out?"

"Oh, yeah. Many times."

Fawn took her hand back. "And I'm to call you…?"

"Rory."

"I hope it hasn't been a problem for me to stay here. Cade said it was all right."

Cade pulled out the chair stationed at the head of the table and rested his hands on top of its back.

Fawn widened her eyes at him in a silent question. "I can't sit there."

Cade flexed his fingers against the carved wood. "You're the guest of honor. You may sit wherever you like."

Fawn helped herself to the chair across from Vanna. Cade settled in at the head of the table, and his parents reclaimed their seats.

Vanna interlaced her fingers on the table's edge, which featured a three-inch wide inlay of a light, red wood around the rest of its dark top. "Our children, like all people, have a strong knack for doing as they please. We encourage that."

"Whatever you're doing, it works. It cured my likely ulcer faster than any doctor could've."

Gerard wheeled his mirrored cart up to the table corner between Fawn and Cade. "*Bonjour.* Good morning." Gerard tipped his beret and lifted two plates off the cart's top shelf. He placed them in front of the new arrivals. "I believe the request from yesterday for this morning's breakfast was my delicious crêpes."

Four thin, sun-gold crêpes lay rolled on each plate, heaped with generous dollops of white whipped cream. Fawn rubbed her palms together. "It certainly was."

"I've prepared some different fillings for you. You'll find lemon, mixed berries, chocolate, and banana. I also use fresh vanilla in my batter."

Fawn searched the table. Some of the plates sat empty, displaying their design of concentric blue flowers on white. The other plates held remnants of unfinished crêpes and smears of cream. "You made crêpes for more than twenty people? That's amazing."

Gerard unfolded Fawn's clay-colored napkin and gracefully swung it across her lap. "What's amazing is the way they taste. *Bon appétit.*" He eased the food cart across the room's large terracotta floor tiles and disappeared into the hallway.

Fawn picked up her knife and fork, licking her lips at the crêpes on her plate.

Cade covered her wrist with his hand. "Before you dive into your breakfast and become practically lost to the physical plane, may I tell you our plans for the rest of the day?"

"Mm-hmm." Fawn cut into a crêpe, exposing a white-yellow filling. "Is this banana or lemon, do you think?"

Cade peered at it. "Banana. Gerard's lemon filling is more yellow than that."

Fawn halved the other three crêpes. Luscious chocolate oozed free. Puréed blueberries, strawberries, and raspberries spilled out onto the plate. Smooth lemon cream shone with a pure hue. "I think I found it."

Cade propped his elbow on the table and touched his first two fingers to his chin. "Fawn?"

"Mmm?" Her mouth watered as she loaded a bite of banana crêpe onto her fork.

"It's usually your first query of the day."

Fawn lowered her fork to her plate's rim. "Sorry. I'll focus."

Cade gazed at her, eyes bright and grin understated. "We're spending the afternoon at the beach. One of the things we didn't tell you about the pontoon is that it can pull people behind it. We thought we'd get some water skiing in."

Fawn looked to Vanna and Rory. "Are you joining us? Please do."

Vanna finished her breakfast and dotted her napkin to her lips. "I can drive so the rest of you can take turns skiing."

Rory planted his hand on the back of his wife's chair. "I'll help with the skis."

Fawn clasped her hands together. "Oh, perfect." She retrieved her fork and took her first bite of the banana crêpe. Sweetness balanced with eggs and flour entranced her taste buds.

Cade sliced into one of his crêpes. "Have you been water skiing, Fawn?" He glanced at his parents. "She hasn't been this excited and easygoing all week."

Fawn devoured a mouthful of the mixed-berry crêpe. Its freshness swam around her tongue, bright and earthy. "These are undoing me."

"So plain cereal tomorrow?"

Fawn met Cade's teasing lilt with a warning, distracted stare. She circled her arm around her plate and pulled the crêpes closer to her. Cade and his parents laughed.

~

Caroline lingered in the hallway outside Fawn's bedroom door.

A beach towel draped around Fawn's shoulders as she approached the maid with tired, wobbly steps after a long, full day. Fawn adjusted the towel around her body, where she'd kept it during the ride home from Beach Lake and through her dinner with Cade and his siblings. Caroline's unexpected presence aroused Fawn's curiosity as much as it could after a rousing, active day in the invigorating sun. Fawn formed a lazy, crooked smile. "What's up?"

Caroline's lips drew into an impish pucker. "I have something to show you."

"Now?" Fawn reached the door and pushed it open. The big, wide bed called to her with nearly audible words. Fawn took one end of the towel and scrunched it around the damp, unkempt locks of her hair.

Caroline wriggled in place and folded her hands against her chest. "It can't wait."

"All right. I don't have to meet anybody, do I?"

"No. It's just this way."

Fawn followed Caroline up the hall from her bedroom, where she hadn't traversed yet. They stopped at a pair of double doors.

Fawn wondered at them. "Whose room is this?" She pulled on the towel's corners to better hide her cover-up and bathing suit.

Caroline's amber-brown eyes gleamed with entertaining secrets she could hardly contain. "It's nobody's room."

"Okay, *what* room is this?" Fawn wiped her eyes, letting a shaky smile shine through again. "I've been falling off skis into the lake all afternoon. Sometimes managing to stand up for a couple of seconds."

"Okay, okay." Caroline rubbed Fawn's arm. "It's not a room, exactly. It's a closet."

Fawn groaned. "This better be the best closet ever. I'm wiped."

"That's why I show it to you now." Caroline grabbed both door handles and swung them into the hallway.

The closet gaped deep and wide. White, wire-rack shelves three high wrapped around the three walls surrounding the doorway. Every inch of every shelf supported pillows, white and mint green and periwinkle.

Fawn's jaw hit the floor as she tiptoed into the closet. "Why are there so many?"

Caroline chuckled. "It's the pillow closet."

Fawn gasped in wonder and pinched a pillow to test its softness. Its light stuffing gave way easily.

Caroline piped up from the doorway. "You can have whatever pillows you want for your room."

"I didn't realize there were so many kinds."

"Pillows are filled with all sorts of materials. Some are firm, some are squishy." Caroline strolled in and pressed her hands into several assorted pillows. Her hand sank in to various depths. "Feathers, foam, tiny beads, buckwheat."

"Buckwheat?"

"Some people like it. The hulls make a gentle crunching noise, and it provides decent neck support if you're looking for that." Caroline hefted an off-white pillow off the shelf.

Fawn pushed her fingertips against it, and the buckwheat inside it shifted. "I like my pillows fluffier, I guess. But not too thin."

Caroline returned the buckwheat sack to its place. "How about three layers of down alternative? Allergy friendly." She moved to the back of the closet and effortlessly lowered a white pillow trimmed in black.

Fawn squeezed it, and its filling caved like a cloud. "Oh, yeah. Let me try this one."

"Of course. You're welcome to anything we have. And if you need something else…"

"I'll let you know." Fawn moseyed out of the closet.

Caroline joined her in the hallway and shut the doors on the amassing of pillows. "Would you like me to put that in your pillow case for you?"

"No, I'll get it." Fawn tested the pillow's give between her palms. It compacted with a hint of resistance that perked her up. "Caroline, do you enjoy what you do?"

Caroline swept her bangs off her forehead. They fell back into place one section at a time. "Cleaning and organizing things? I like it very much. I feel better when there's order, and believe me, they need order in this house."

Fawn traced her finger along the pillow's black edges. "I guess I just noticed you work pretty long hours."

Caroline shook her head. "Don't worry about me, Miss Fawn. I take plenty of breaks to rest and eat. I see my family every morning and every night. Vanna and Rory give me any days off I ask them for. And even some that I don't."

"Is there another maid who cleans when you're not here? Picking up after two dozen people seems challenging to me."

Caroline shrugged and ushered Fawn to her room. "There's only me, but you're all adults in this house. You'd be surprised how little there is left for me to do. Everyone does their part."

Fawn paused in her bedroom doorway. "I find it hard to imagine Cade or Jax taking responsibility. For their clothes. Their wet towels." Fawn shook out the beach towel covering her torso.

Caroline chortled. "They're big boys. And good boys. They don't give me any extra trouble."

Fawn tugged the beach towel off her shoulders. "Either you're better than they deserve or I don't know them very well."

"You'll get to know them. You have the party on Saturday."

"Will you be there?"

"No. It's my day off to be with my family. You have plenty of people to get acquainted with as it is."

Fawn wandered into her room and stashed the beach towel in the hamper. "Do you happen to know what Cade and the others have planned for tomorrow? Any big Friday plans?"

"No, *mija*. They don't consult me for that unless they need my services."

"I was hoping to get a jump on whatever activity they're conspiring about."

Caroline struggled against a burgeoning smile. "There are so many wonderful hobbies you haven't participated in yet."

"Really?"

"Oh, yes. Every season of the year, they do something special." Caroline cut herself off and stepped back from the doorway. "But you're exhausted. I won't keep you awake any longer. Sleep well."

"You, too. Thanks for the pillow."

Fawn closed the door and carried the new pillow over to the bed. She pried the pillow case off the old one and slipped the down alternative inside. She shimmied out of her cover-up and orange tankini. Too tired to concern herself with selecting pajamas from the dresser drawers, Fawn climbed between the sheets. She nestled her head into the pillow's caressing cradle and drifted into slumber.

~

Tying the necklace into place at the nape of her neck, Fawn sashayed back from the jewelry armoire. She beamed with giddy anticipation at seeing her completed ensemble. She flitted over in front of the full-length mirror propped in the corner of the bedroom.

Rosario's emerald eyes had glinted with joy when she gave Fawn her only inklings about the party. "Have Caroline bring you something fancy. What we're eating is, well… don't wear something white unless you want to risk total ruination. Then we're engaging in…" Rosario bit her lower lip as her gaze drifted upward. "…sort of a group activity. And it's just going to be the most marvelous evening ever."

Fawn trailed her gaze over her reflection, mouthing *wow* to herself. She'd kept her hair simple with an updo pinned securely in place, leaving occasional tendrils spiraling down. She'd taken extra care with her makeup to lengthen her lashes, line her eyes with thick liquid black that wouldn't budge, and highlight her lids with begonia-pink shadow. Her cheekbones carried just the right amount of natural blush-colored pigment, and she snatched up the lip gloss tube off the vanity to dot another layer of moist raspberry glaze on her lips. She set the tube aside and recentered herself in the mirror's frame.

Her necklace's dark-cherry beads rested against her collarbone, strung on yellow ribbon. Her dress began with a modest round neckline in fine, cream-colored mesh. Cobalt-blue sequined flowers appliquéd the mesh, floating down from each shoulder and meeting in a V to cascade over the rest of the bodice. A royal-blue pleated sash accentuated her waist. Beneath it, another surge of appliqués burst in asymmetrical spills around her hips. The same royal-blue chiffon formed the voluminous skirt falling in an A-line to Fawn's ankles. She lifted the fabric a few inches to peek at her carnation-pink strappy heels.

Fawn glowed as she collected her lip gloss and a small packet of Kleenex into the quilted bronze clutch Caroline had picked out for her. Fawn sauntered out of her bedroom.

To her surprise, Jax leaned against the wall beside the hallway a small dogleg to the left. He'd wrangled his medium-dark brown hair back from his face, exhibiting the strong lines of his square jaw. Metallic grey accents lightened his black tuxedo. His silver bow tie flashed. Jax straightened up, keeping his hands in his pockets. "I'm here to escort you to my dear sister's illustrious party."

Fawn drew her bedroom door closed. "Is it far?" she joked.

Jax scratched the back of his head. He jerked his thumb down the hall behind him. "Just on the other side of the house."

Fawn approached him, soaring on air. "Are you sure you don't mean *compound*?"

Jax beamed. "You're in a strange mood, aren't you?"

"I've never been to anything this formal."

"Really? You head up a whole company, and they never threw you a proper bash?"

Fawn traipsed up the hall at Jax's side. "There were parties when I took over, one to celebrate Janet's retirement and one to welcome me. I went to prom before I graduated, but none of that was anything like this." Fawn wiggled her fingers, where several of the armoire's large gemstone rings glittered. "You're in a tux, and I look like I robbed a jewelry store."

"You look fantastic, by the way."

"Thank you."

"That color suits you. But you knew that, didn't you?"

Fawn nodded, a little self-conscious about the life she'd fled to stay here. "That knowledge was part of my five-minute wardrobe."

Jax toyed with his cufflinks. "That can't be good. Nothing spectacular ever came out of five minutes."

"I went through this phase where everything about my clothing could get me dressed in five minutes or less. I bought every piece in colors that flatter me. Everything could be worn with five or six other pieces."

"You don't do that anymore?"

Fawn blew out a breath. "I pared my routine down to grab and go. Snatch whatever was clean and in reach, put it on, and rush to work."

"The thirty-second wardrobe?"

"Exactly."

Jax stopped at the T at the end of the hall. "Do you know where you are?" He gestured to the open double doors off to the left. "That's the dining room. We're going this way." He ushered Fawn to the right.

Fawn tested the waters with a faint smile. "Why do you want me to get my bearings? So I can wander the house and do as I please?"

"I want you to feel comfortable." Jax paused by unfamiliar double doors inset with numerous glass panels off center from each other. Outside, lights glimmered against the sunset. "Are you ready?"

"For the party?" Fawn rocked up onto the balls of her feet and dropped her heels back to the floor. "I woke up ready."

Jax pulled the door open and gestured Fawn through the doorway.

She dipped her head in appreciation and strolled out onto a large patio. "Whoa."

Fragrant smoke filled Fawn's nose, streaming into the air from a brick grill off to the left. Gerard manned it, chatting with Rory, both of them in tuxedos. A hefty, square table filled the patio's center, boxed in by twelve chairs. Peach, tan, and goldenrod flagstones formed the patio floor in a variety of generous sizes and natural shapes.

Beyond the table and chairs, Fawn spotted the swimming pool she'd seen from the SUV on the drive to Fun Splash. In the dimming twilight, aided by twinkling bulbs strung from one iron pole to another around the patio's perimeter, the water rested turquoise and serene.

Out of habit, Fawn tucked a tendril of her hair behind her ear. She admonished herself in a whisper. "I'm supposed to be fancy." She rearranged it to hang loose again.

Jax stepped up to her side and shut the door. Lisette and Henna stood off to one side engaged in a low-key conversation, sipping from old-fashioned glasses. Lisette sported a form-fitting, fuchsia racerback dress. Henna's pink-and-scarlet braids snaked through her brunette updo. Red flowers embroidered her forest-green bodice from the high neckline to her thin waist. Fluffy red feathers floated over every inch of her gown's full skirt.

Poolside, Vanna chatted with Yoselle and Kee, the umber-skinned man with thick dreds. When Cade introduced him by the end of breakfast two mornings before, Fawn had been happy to put a name to his face. Vanna radiated vintage glamour in a slate-grey dress with intricate lace forming three-quarter sleeves and covering the bodice with its modest V-neck. The pleated chiffon skirt flowed to her low-heeled black sandals. Yoselle rocked the shortest outfit on the patio, a black satin halter dress that exploded into hot-pink taffeta ruffles just above her knees. Black-and-mesh-striped tights clad her thin but shapely legs above the buckled ankle straps of her chunky black heels. White satin lapels offset the deep black of Kee's tuxedo. His bow tie and leather oxfords matched them.

Cade and Emilian, whom Fawn had also met at the crêpe

breakfast, walked into view on the right side of the patio. Emilian's short, unruly dark-blond hair tufted up around his head. He modeled black from his collared shirt and tie to his tux and shoes.

Cade's unnatural red and blond strands swooped in swells and rose up in points. His baby-blue bow tie made his silver eyes dazzle when they flicked to meet Fawn's. Her heart skipped a beat, and for a minute, she forgot to breathe.

Emilian moved his hands as he talked without stopping. A one-sided grin grew on Cade's face while he gazed at Fawn before he slipped back into his conversation with Emilian.

Jax stirred to life at Fawn's side. "Ah. There's little brother. Now the party can truly start."

Fawn drew a breath and tried to recover herself. "What about Rosario? She's the hostess."

Jax headed off toward Cade and Emilian. Ofelia strode around the house's jutting addition, in no hurry on her four-inch heels to catch up to the men. A bandage dress wrapped her ample curves in sunny yellow, baring her sepia-hued calves.

Rosario appeared several feet behind Ofelia. Small, red fabric roses dotted Rosario's free-flowing hair. Fuchsia flowers and moss-colored greenery decorated the fabric of her deep V neckline. Below the apricot waistband, the flower pattern drifted down on both sides of the apricot skirt. Every other step exposed her left leg through a high slit. She raised her hands in the air and called out in singsong. "Here I am!"

The group applauded, and Fawn joined them. She snuck a peek at Cade in his neat, black wool tux. He laughed heartily at something Emilian said, his fingers lingering on his chin. His confidence and carefree nature rippled a shudder through Fawn. She averted her gaze to Lisette's and Henna's beverages, wishing she had a drink.

Rosario strutted over to stand by the table. She tossed a great wave of her tresses over her shoulder. "Thank you all for coming. I know you didn't have to travel far."

Chuckles shook the group.

"But seriously..." Rosario glanced around. She planted her hands on her wide hips. "Where's the drink cart I ordered?"

Lisette speared her hand up and pointed to the two-shelved metal cart on wheels alongside the house's landscaping.

Rosario flicked pretend sweat off her forehead. "Thank goodness. Well, I had Gerard make one drink for each of us. So help yourselves, pick what you want. Whoever's last takes what's left. Enjoy your drink because one is the limit tonight."

Her siblings and friends whooped.

Rosario lifted her head up regally and scooted a chair back from the table. "This is a formal dinner. But I guess you can't take the informal out of a bunch like us all at once." She flashed an energetic smile at everyone. "Come sit with me, and Gerard will tell you what he's prepared for us this evening."

Fawn took a few tentative steps toward the table, not sure where to sit. Jax, Vanna, and Ofelia drifted over to the drink cart. Fawn veered in its direction as well.

Rosario called out. "Somebody bring me a drink, too."

Fawn grabbed two glasses at random from the cart's top shelf. She passed the orange margarita garnished with a lime wedge to Rosario.

Rosario took a sip and licked her lips. "Please and thank you, Fawn. Why don't you rest yourself next to me?"

Fawn eased into the nearest chair. Lisette and Henna took the chairs on Rosario's other side.

Vanna settled in on Fawn's free side with ice, maraschino cherries, and a twist of lemon peel floating in an amber drink. "How about I sit here next to my new friend?"

Fawn set her clutch under her chair. "That's fine." She drank from the small, stemmed glass in her hand. Its contents reminded her of peach sorbet, but the flavor tantalized her with sweet citrus. The cognac punched Fawn in the tongue, stronger than she'd been looking for. She relegated the glass to the table.

Rory joined his wife, and Jax filled the seat at the end of Fawn's row.

Cade drew the chair out next to Henna, catty-corner from Fawn. Their eyes met for a moment before Fawn returned to her drink for a sip. Emilian lowered himself beside Cade, continuing their conversation. Cade's attention lingered on Fawn and finally swung to his friend.

Ofelia slunk into the corner chair by Jax, armed with a tall glass of cloudy liquid stuffed with mint leaves and lime slices. Yoselle and Kee filled in the two remaining spots between Ofelia and Emilian. Yoselle's spine shot up so stiff, Fawn wondered that she could bend to take her seat. Yoselle drained half her short glass of tawny liquor garnished with half a lemon slice.

Rosario clinked her fork against her margarita glass, silencing the rest of the table. "Leave some liquid in your glasses, please. Fawn is our guest of honor. I think we should all make a toast to her while Gerard finishes up our meal."

Emilian got up and jogged over to the drink cart. He carried back the final two beverages, handing one to Cade as he reclaimed his seat.

Rosario laid her fork down. "I'll begin now that everyone's ready." She aimed a smirk at Cade before focusing on Fawn. "Let's see. I've known you for all of five days. You spent the first sixteen hours or so freaking out."

Her siblings chuckled. Fawn slipped in a quick sip of her sidecar.

Rosario hunched her substantial shoulders forward. "But as I've gotten to know you, I've found a lot more than stress and fear. You have a great sense of humor, you'll dive headfirst into anything without much preparation, and you're tough enough to put up with all of us." Rosario elevated her margarita glass. "Cheers to you."

Vanna wrapped her hand around Fawn's. "I've known you half as long as my children have. But you're delightful company, and I'm so glad you've chosen to stay with us."

Fawn cracked a wry grin. "They told you I fought this, right?"

Vanna offered an easy smile. "Doesn't matter. You're here

now. And we enjoy hosting you."

Rory raised his glass and stretched his other arm around his wife's shoulders. "Here, here."

Rosario exaggerated a frown. "You have to do better than that, Dad."

The family laughed.

Jax stood up, and Fawn tried to keep up with the family's pace.

Rosario tossed her hand up. "There's my brother, the only one to tower over the rest of us as he speaks."

Jax beamed and slid his palm over his slicked-back hair. He extended his glass toward Fawn. "You're all right, Fawn. You're better than all right, and I think you know I think that about you. You bring out the best in us and weather the worst of us. I don't hold it against you that being a guest in our house—"

Cade supplied a different word in an even cadence. "Compound."

Fawn met Cade's sparkling, joking eyes.

Jax cleared his throat. "Yes, excuse me. Compound. It wasn't exactly the first thing you had planned Monday night, but you stuck with it. I don't care how long you stay as long as it's a while." Jax downed part of his drink and sat down.

Ofelia scooted forward in her chair. Her voice danced with the musicality of her Chilean accent. "To Fawn, who has the decency and bravery like me to openly admit Gerard's chocolate crêpes are our favorite. *Salud.*"

Yoselle sat in silence for a prolonged moment, hardly moving. "I like Fawn because she's live and let live. She doesn't judge, and she doesn't pretend to be something she's not."

Lisette chirped up at a low pitch. "Grim, sis."

Cade rubbed his chin and gave a slight wave of his hand. "Leave her be."

Yoselle fixed Lisette with a burning stare. She took a generous gulp of her drink. "I appreciate Fawn being here. That's all I'm trying to say."

Kee spoke up at once. His Jamaican accent wove in and out of his syllables. "It was well said."

Cade nodded.

Kee's glass sat on the table before him, and he turned it deftly in his fingers. "I don't know much about Fawn, but I respect anyone who can fit herself into this group of mismatched ragamuffins. She doesn't try to bellow the loudest, and she doesn't let herself get drowned out by all of our voices. For that, I say, it's total niceness knowing you."

Emilian splayed his fingers. "What can I say? Fawn has style, class, charm, and rugged honesty. Those are the traits we require — no? — to survive any length of time with us. Cheers, indeed."

All eyes fell on Cade. He gazed at Fawn with a gentle, steady grin. He rose to his feet, glass of dark-amber liquid in hand.

Rosario emitted a dramatic huff and rolled her eyes. "Here's my other brother…" she teased with heavy sarcasm.

Cade expanded his grin, keeping his attention on Fawn. "There's more to you than how you hold yourself or the way you dress. I'm sure you'd chalk up most of your current style to Caroline's offerings, wouldn't you?"

Fawn nodded, grateful for a chance to inject some of her own deflective humor into the evening. Appreciation for Caroline's tastes and the family's generosity warmed her to the core. She fiddled with one of her dangling pearl earrings. "It's true."

Cade's wide grin softened. "You're brave. And you're adaptive. The moments where you don't hold your head so high and push forward anyway are the ones that describe you the most." He studied the ice cubes in his glass. "You have substance." He raised his eyes again to meet Fawn's. "You're not a quitter. You know what you want. And you're finally not afraid to enjoy yourself while you chase it."

The others tittered, and Fawn let herself laugh with them. The deep way Cade peered into her eyes made the ten others at the table fade far into the background.

Cade's finger tapped the side of his glass. His grin turned

more impish. "Of course, I must admit Rosario's actions explain more than my words ever could. She's never been moved to throw a last-minute dinner for anybody before. So here's to Fawn."

Cade elevated his glass, and the others at the table followed suit. Fawn burst into a brilliant smile, and her self-consciousness failed to tame it.

Cade's eyes glittered at her. "Bold, humorous, inquisitive. You stand your ground with the best of us. Although I know you will change, try not to change too much."

He sipped his alcohol as he sat down, and the rest of the group joined him. Fawn lingered with her sidecar, Cade's praises whirling and swirling inside her chest. He winked at her and turned his attention to Henna on his left.

Henna's ringed fingers toyed with the stem of her fluted glass half full of fizzy, peach-colored liquor. "Oh, Fawn, I knew from the moment I met you we'd be good friends. No pretenses. No boasting. No whispered asides with me to help you escape the water park." Henna clinked her pink fingernails against her glass. "I'll talk with you anytime about anything. You're one of my new favorite people, and I hope you'll be here a long time."

Lisette stood up at Rosario's side, looking down over her sister's head to address Fawn. "I love it when I'm the last one to toast because I get to pick up all the pieces everybody else left out." Lisette sank her weight into one toned hip. "Fawn, you're fabulous. In every way. You're great company. Level-headed. An open book without spreading around too much information. I respect you, I adore you, I admire you, and I count myself extremely fortunate to call myself your friend."

Rosario chimed in. "You can finish your drinks now."

Lisette led the group in tossing down the remainders of their beverages. The sidecar's luxurious depth of strong flavors made Fawn squinch her eyes shut and shake her head. She giggled at herself as she rested her empty glass on the tabletop.

Rosario's guffawing drowned out everyone else's. "Yeah, we'd better get some dinner over here before we're all passed out on the flagstones in a heap. Gerard! Is it ready?"

Gerard pushed a large cart toward the table. "*Oui.* What I've prepared for you this evening…"

Fawn's gaze drifted to Cade. He returned it with his usual amused mischief. Fawn redirected herself to what Gerard was saying.

The Frenchman set a full plate of fragrant, spicy delicacies in front of Fawn.

The others at the table melted into resounding *oohs.*

Gerard folded his hands together. "No simple, sloppy barbecue for you. This is truly upscale and unique. You'll find lemon-thyme chicken that's crispy on the outside and moist inside. We have shrimp with grilled pineapple on skewers. On the side, I made a salad of grilled vegetables. It combines red bell peppers, summer squash, mushrooms, and zucchini with herbs and a little oil. The corn I glazed in basil butter."

Gerard bent down and retrieved something from the cart's bottom shelf. He set a small, rectangular white ceramic tray by Fawn's plate. It held four bowls of red sauce. "I also mixed four different flavors of barbecue sauce. One is sweet honey. One is Memphis thin and tangy. The third is brown sugar and vinegar. And finally, we have thick sweet molasses."

The mounds of glistening, rack-charred food overwhelmed Fawn. Their amounts and sheer perfection touched her heart. She applauded, and the rest of the group followed her lead.

Gerard patted the air with his palms. "There's no need to celebritize the chef." He raised his index finger. "Until you see dessert!"

Gerard wheeled his cart around the table, setting a full plate of food at each place. Fawn unfolded her yellow cotton napkin, not sure whether to tuck it in her dress' neckline or spread it across her lap.

Rosario chuckled on Fawn's right. "I told you it might get messy, didn't I, Fawn?"

On Fawn's left, Vanna arranged her napkin over her lap.

"That's all right. Caroline's a whiz at getting out stains."

Fawn mirrored Vanna's example and picked up her fork.

Rosario laid her hand on Fawn's arm. "Don't work too hard at being fancy and poised. Most of us are going to use our fingers at some point."

Vanna sipped her ice water. "What kind of barbecue do you prefer, Fawn?"

Fawn refrained from eating just yet while Gerard continued his round of deliveries around the table's opposite corner. "I don't know. I like the sweet sauces, but I also like the hot, smoky ones."

She sought out Cade. Despite the steaming plate of shrimp, chicken, and vegetables before him, he watched Fawn with his elbow propped on the table. Her breath shallowed, and she looked down at her plate before she could blush.

Rosario loaded her fork up with juicy, golden chicken. "Dig right in, Fawn. Mom almost has her meal."

Vanna spoke up in a sweet but firm voice. "If Fawn wants to practice good manners, I support her in that."

Gerard placed the last plate in front of Vanna and added a tray of sauces beside it. "I'll bring the desserts when you're ready. *Bon appétit.*" He wheeled the cart away into the house.

Fawn heard a sound she wasn't used to hearing on the grounds. Everyone was so busy dipping shrimp into their sauces and cutting their quartered chickens, conversation fell away. Fawn spiked several vegetables onto her fork. "It's so quiet."

Rosario smiled at Fawn while she chewed. She hummed in agreement.

Fawn ate with a slow deliberateness she'd missed. She dawdled over the strong herbs and citrus of her chicken. She pulled each shrimp off its skewer and dunked it in a different sauce. Each one delighted and smoldered in its own spicy whirlwind. The grilled pineapple chunks were sweet and tender. The vegetables' mellow, earthy flavors melded together in simple harmony.

In the nick of time, as Fawn and the others pushed their

finished plates away, Gerard reappeared with his cart.

He wagged his eyebrows up and down. "A special occasion such as tonight calls for a special treat as dessert. I hope you saved room in your bellies for pure, unadulterated decadence." Gerard produced a three-inch-high chocolate cake. Raspberry syrup lay drizzled across the top and onto the white plate. He laid it at Fawn's place. "Molten chocolate lava cake."

Fawn wanted to applaud again, but it didn't seem like enough fanfare. She jumped up and hugged Gerard. "Thank you. It really is very special."

His faded-blue eyes watered. "Eat and enjoy."

Fawn settled into her seat, and Gerard served the rest of the cakes to the others around the table. Fawn didn't make herself wait. She sliced her fork right down the cake's middle. Thick, creamy chocolate erupted from inside. By the time Vanna received her cake, Fawn had devoured half of hers, swimming in the dense sponge and gooey richness. The raspberry syrup flew away with the heavier flavors to new heights Fawn had never tasted.

With a moan of indebtedness and a full stomach, Fawn slid her dessert plate away. Half a dozen bites of cake went with it.

Rosario's eyes glowed. "Can't finish it?"

Fawn shook her head.

"Gerard will be so pleased. He'll consider it proof of a job well done."

Most of the others abandoned the remains of their cakes as well. Kee snuck the last bite of Yoselle's cake into his mouth in one quick motion.

Fawn turned the other way toward Rosario and pretended she didn't see it. "You said something about a group activity after dinner." Fawn patted her belly. "How's that physically possible?"

"Have a little faith in me." Rosario stood up and set her fingertips on the table. "Jax, my phone, please."

Three seats to Fawn's left, Jax pulled a bedazzled cell phone from his tuxedo pocket. He slid it across the tabletop to Rosario.

She caught it in her hands. She tapped the screen several

times, and a downtempo, classic love song poured out of unseen speakers. "I have a night of fun, relaxing conversation and dancing planned. We'll start off slow. I made the perfect playlist." Rosario held up her index finger. "No, I will not take your requests. Except from Fawn."

Fawn waved her hand. "I don't have any."

"Then it's settled. I told the rest of the gang they could join us after dinner." Rosario clasped her hands together. "Thank you for being a part of this barbecue. Go mingle." She flung her fingers at her guests. "And dance. I don't want to be the only one cutting a rug. Don't make me push you into the pool for being a bad sport."

Vanna chuckled as she and Rory got up from their seats. "I don't need a threat to have a good time."

Vanna and Rory swayed together in the last threads of sunlight. Jax slipped a lighter out of his pocket and walked the patio's perimeter, lighting tiki torches. Fawn stood up so she'd feel more proactive, although she wasn't sure if she wanted to dance yet or whom she might choose to talk to.

Henna and Emilian leaned toward Cade, distracting him with intense conversation.

Rosario eyed Fawn sidelong. "Come on. We need a dance circle to start things off right."

Lisette leapt up out of her chair, and Fawn accompanied the sisters to a vacant space on the patio. They rolled their shoulders and wound their hips to the slow, steady beat.

The song faded away with gentle cymbal crashes, and Fawn glanced around to see where the other guests had gravitated. Jax and Ofelia slow danced near the other side of the pool. Yoselle and Kee stood over Emilian, listening in to the three-way discussion underway at the table.

Twanging guitars started the next melody, soon joined by bright blasts of trumpets.

Lisette moaned. "Oh, good. I was worried everything was going to come from the seventies. Then you whipped out the eighties."

Fawn struggled to encourage her lethargic body to match the faster rhythm. "I thought you were starting us slow."

Rosario clapped her hands over her head. "I don't want to put everybody to sleep, though, right?" She clapped again and called out. "Where are the rest of my ladies?"

Fawn chuckled. "You're so lucky you don't have close neighbors."

"They're fortunate not to have us."

Vanna danced over, and Fawn made room for her in the circle. Henna dragged a moping Yoselle over by the wrist, and Ofelia bounced up after a minute.

Fawn tried to keep up. "What are the guys doing?"

Rosario glanced around. "Just talking. They'll be all right."

Fast, warping electronic pulses signaled the start of the previous summer's most popular hit.

Lisette cradled her head. She groaned loud enough to be heard over the music and foreign lyrics. "You know I hate myself for liking this song."

Rosario laughed. "What are sisters for?"

The double doors to the house opened, and some of Cade's other friends spilled out onto the patio in their sparkling finery. Kee's sister Jacqui swished her long, elegant mulberry skirt as she sashayed over to the ladies' circle. Her thick dreds jumped and swayed as she moved.

When the tune ended, Fawn stilled her legs, trying to catch her breath. "Is the next one a slow one?"

Rosario nodded.

Fawn blew out a breath. "Thank goodness." A hand alighted on her wrist before she could slink off and plop down in her chair.

Cade's intent eyes kept her from moving in that direction. "If my sister's done enjoying your company, I'll take this dance."

Fawn could barely find her voice. "Yes." She strengthened her timbre. "That's fine."

Cade led her the length of the table to a less crowded spot. He took her gingerly in one arm, folding his other hand around hers. His black titanium ring interrupted their contact for half an inch, flat and warm against the blade of her hand. Fawn rested her left palm in faltering spasms on Cade's shoulder. She inhaled slowly, and her muscles relaxed. Cade guided her in a steady, gradual circle.

Fawn scrambled for something to talk about. "Dinner was delicious. I didn't know barbecue could taste like that."

"Fawn." Cade's faint grin glimmered. "We have deeper things to talk about than well-spiced tomato sauce."

Her eyebrows rose. "We do?"

"How are you holding up after all the toasts?"

"Okay, I guess. I certainly wasn't expecting that."

"I meant what I said. I hope you know how much I admire your resilience and your perseverance."

Fawn trembled and wished it would stop. She could hear the slight tremor in her voice. "Why me, Cade? Anybody at Smuckey's could've been having a rotten day. A tough year. You could've given any of them this opportunity, right?"

Cade shook his head, keeping his gaze deep in Fawn's eyes. "No. Are you having second thoughts now?"

"Not at all. I just..." Fawn swept her tongue between her lips with hesitation. "I'm not always sure where I fit in. There are so many people here. I've never made so many new friends at once, and I've really never been treated so well anywhere."

Cade widened his grin. "So what's the problem?"

Fawn averted her gaze to the others slow dancing on the patio. Rory and Vanna had settled back into their comfortable embrace. Jax spun Jacqui around under his arm. Henna and Emilian put some extra hip and shoulder wiggles into their perfect rhythm. By the pool, apart from the others, Yoselle and Kee lingered close together in a subtle rotation. Yoselle leaned her forehead against Kee's chest for a second before lifting her head and shaking her dark hair back from her face.

Cade bent toward Fawn. "*Is* there a problem?"

Fawn sucked in a breath. "You know, at Better Mind, Janet

came up with four traits that described what she wanted her company to be about. Quality, honesty, creativity, and effectiveness. If I were judging your hospitality skills based on those qualities, I'd have no complaints."

"What are you judging our skills by?"

Fawn blinked. "What?"

Cade brightened his grin to full force. "You said *if* you were judging us as hosts."

"Yes. But I'm not… judging you. I have no right to."

"Of course you do. We've never stopped you from thinking your own thoughts or speaking your mind." Cade adjusted the lay of his fingers around Fawn's.

She bit the inside of her lip, convinced her palms were slick with sweat. "I haven't always known what to think. Around you." Fawn's heart fluttered, slightly uncomfortable. "Around any of you."

Cade's focus dipped to Fawn's lips. "Why do you have to think anything?"

Her fingers gave an involuntary flex around Cade's. "Why wouldn't I?"

Cade responded with a breathy chuckle. "It's called meditation. Clearing your mind."

"On purpose?" Fawn cracked a weak smile at her tenuous joke.

Cade squeezed her hand. "You know about it. A lot of top earners do. Many of them even practice it."

"Oh, really?"

Cade nodded. "It could make you a better CEO."

"I don't even know if I want to stay on as CEO."

"Make you a better friend. Sister. Daughter."

"Well, I'll probably still be those things when I get home."

Cade lowered his voice to a gentle rumble. "What do you want to do with your life?"

Fawn flushed. "I thought I was supposed to be having fun and leaving the work plans behind."

Cade eased even closer to her. "Forget your career. How do you want to spend your days?"

Fawn studied Cade from the swooshes and points of his hair to his groomed dark-blond eyebrows to his softly arched lips. Dancing six inches apart, at a party with her own friends, she would've kissed him. Surrounded by Cade's family and friends, Fawn struggled to swallow. She ducked her chin.

The slow melody trailed off, and a fast Latin drumbeat picked up the pace.

Fawn barely met Cade's eyes when hands cupped one of each of their shoulders.

Jax greeted them with a big smile. "May I cut in?"

Fawn and Cade acquiesced with shallow nods. Cade stepped back, and Jax ushered Fawn aside.

She fought to change gears from one brother to the other. "I don't have the first clue…"

Jax shrugged, already moving his arms and feet. "You don't have to. Just do what feels good. Although…" Jax snatched Fawn's hand and raised it high. "It's always a great time for a spin."

Fawn struggled to think of how to move her body when her thoughts kept drifting to Cade. She pushed him out of her mind and twirled under Jax's arm.

He smiled. "There you go."

Fawn whirled through two more circles to satisfy Jax and prohibit him from prodding for more. She dropped her hand from his and shimmied her way through the rest of the song. When she peeked around for Cade, she spotted him leaning his hands flat on the table, talking to Rosario.

With three horn blasts, the Latin melody made an abrupt transfer into a much more mellow, lighthearted classic.

Fawn met Jax with a wobbly smile. "That was fun." She wiped her palms on her skirt, not certain whether Jax wanted another dance or if she should start concocting a sure-fire escape plan.

A hand on her arm made her heart jump. Was it a savior or another flirtatious invitation?

Rory bowed to her and offered his hand. "May I have the pleasure of this dance?"

"Yes," Fawn assured him, gratitude radiating in her chest. She took a few steps away from Jax and put herself in Rory's practiced, capable hands.

He held her with a light, respectful touch. Vanna waved from ten feet away, where she chatted with Henna and Lisette. Fawn studied Rory with a calm eye, easily finding Jax's strong, square jaw and short forehead. She realized Cade more resembled his mother with her cool-toned irises and Roman nose.

Rory hummed a few bars of the effortless tune. "Nobody else like Sinatra."

Fawn shook her head, appreciative to carry out a more normal conversation. "I have at least six family members who'd agree with that."

"Do you count yourself among them?"

Fawn shrugged. "Why not?"

"What kind of people do you come from? Do they like music? Sports? Volunteering?"

"Fishing, boating, and gardening on my father's side. Animal rescue, reading, and wine tasting on my mother's."

Rory directed Fawn in a suave, casual spin under his arm. "They sound like good people."

"They are."

"From what Cade said, your work keeps you from spending much time with them."

Fawn swallowed. "That's true."

"Well, I hope your time as our guest lets you get back to them refreshed with a new approach to organizing your schedule."

"Thank you."

They swayed to the rest of the tune in silence. As it ended, various other guests gasped, their gazes cast to the dark sky.

Fawn searched the vast panorama of pale pinpoints against

the raven backdrop. "The stars are out."

Rory pointed to the lawn beyond the pool. "You can see them better if you move away from the patio lights."

Fawn gravitated toward the lawn, and many of the others strolled in the same direction. Several small hills rose up sixty feet past the pool's edge, and Fawn stopped before she reached them. Her observations combed the sky, and Cade arrived beside her. His siblings lingered in a half circle behind him, Kee poised at Yoselle's elbow.

Fawn glanced at Cade. "This is beautiful."

He tucked his hands in his pockets. "Are there too many interfering lights where you live?"

"No. Yes. I think so. I've just been too busy for the last several years to really look up there at the right time." Fawn scanned the countless twinkles, feeling a rising wave of warm familiarity. "My dad and I used to hang around outside in the summer. I'd catch fireflies for a while, then we'd scout out constellations together."

Fawn turned in a gradual, steady circle. Her focus shot from star to star. She wrinkled her eyebrows. "I can't spot the Big Dipper or the Little Dipper."

Fawn grunted and rotated again, inspecting the sky. "I don't even see the North Star." Fawn knew she hadn't memorized every star's location, but their spacing and groupings didn't seem right. She locked eyes with Cade, her heart pounding. "What's going on?"

His siblings, Kee, and the others wandered away.

Fawn's arms shook at their retreat. "Cade?"

He held his gaze level with hers. "I have things I haven't told you."

"Why?"

"They might make you uncomfortable."

Fawn set her palm against her packed stomach. Her voice wavered. "I'm not ready to suffer a full-blown ulcer. Will I feel better or worse than I do now if you tell me what you're hiding?"

"I don't know." Cade paused. "You're right if you think you're far from home, Fawn."

She braced herself. "Where am I?"

Cade shifted his arms and shuffled his feet. "That won't make sense to you unless you understand who we are."

Fawn's whole body vibrated. She wrapped her arms around herself. "Do you care to explain that, or is there something else that preempts that information, too?"

Cade shook his head slowly. He reached out to Fawn's elbow but let his hand fall away without touching her. "We're not like you."

"No kidding."

"We're not from where you're from."

"The Midwest? The United States?" Fawn tossed a smirk at the gigantic, illuminated house. "Planet Earth?"

"Your dimension." Cade breathed evenly through his nose for several beats.

Fawn's eyelids fluttered. "What?"

"We're interdimensional beings, Fawn."

"So where are you from? Or is that even the right question to ask?"

"It is." Cade watched Fawn closely. "We're from another dimension. It's fully developed. Heavily inhabited. Rather like your planet in your dimension."

Fawn worked her legs in place to keep her knees from buckling. "You're not even from wherever we are now?"

"No, we're not. The beings — people — where we come from are highly evolved. Some of us more than others."

"Just like Earth."

Cade cracked a smile. "Only in our dimension, the most skilled among us are toying with concepts that are barely comprehended or believed on Earth. Have you heard of the zero point?"

"I don't think so."

"It's the energy tipping point at which our thoughts, hopes, dreams, ideas, and intentions become physical reality." Cade fell quiet.

Fawn's mind whirred faster in some places than in others. She swept her gaze over the house and the figures standing stock still in the light bulb glow and tiki torch flickers. Their silhouettes reminded her of the formal barbecue and dance party they'd all enjoyed five minutes before. Fawn chewed on her lip.

Cade interlaced his fingers and slid them against each other. "Do you understand what I'm saying?"

Fawn backed the conversation up. "Where are we?"

"In a third dimension, one we affectionately call the Playground."

"What do you call your home dimension?"

"Home, I guess. Does yours have a name?"

"Not that anybody told me."

Cade separated his hands and folded them behind his back. "Traveling between dimensions was something else some of us were teaching ourselves."

Fawn blew out a breath. "You make it sound like a hobby. Scrapbooking is a hobby. Bird watching. Cross-country cycling. You don't just jump between dimensions like that."

Cade dropped his hands and graced the palms against one another. "It feels more like a sliding, actually."

Fawn wobbled on her feet and replanted her heels in the grass to stabilize herself. "Which one of you discovered that?"

Cade saluted her loosely with his index finger. "I did."

"And you taught your skills to the others?"

Cade nodded. "As much as I could. They're not nearly as adept as I am. I'm not convinced they use their powers anymore." He skimmed a glance across the sky. "There was nothing here when we got here. It was blackness. It was new."

Fawn stared at him. "And you made planets? You made the sun? The stars? Everything?"

"We didn't make whole planets. Just what we needed to survive and thrive here. Fragments, really."

"Survive?" Fawn scrunched her cheeks up. "If you could slide between dimensions and create matter from nothing, what did you need anything for? What could you possibly *want* for at that point?"

"To live in a physical world, the same as you do. As we once did. To enjoy it. Play in it. Play *with* it. Create. Learn from our mistakes and try again."

Fawn inspected the silhouettes grouped together on the patio. "Who else can do what you do?"

"We all can. My family. My friends. It's just that I became the best at it."

Fawn returned her focus to Cade. He looked at her with candidness instead of hubris, vulnerability instead of humor. "Why did you come to my world?"

Cade swatted his hand through the air. "Dimension. Whatever. Because I can. I get loads of ideas there, and I recreate whatever I like over here."

"So you never paid a hundred and fifty-five thousand dollars for a boat?"

"Paid? No. But when I designed my own pontoon in your dimension, that's how much it cost."

Fawn gestured to the house. "The Mustang? The Jaguar? Your mom's Venom?"

"I created them all."

"With what?"

Cade tapped his temple. "My mind."

Fawn caught her head in her hands. "Shit."

Cade spoke softly. "Are you okay?"

A slight throb pained the side of Fawn's head. "Yeah. I just... It's a little beyond what I deal with in a typical day. You know, I have a hard time telling Monica everything we do at the company. The sound frequencies and how we hide spoken affirmations in the videos' audio tracks. This is miles beyond that."

"But you believe me?"

Fawn managed to nod. "There's so much science I only know about from the farthest edges of its periphery. Theories.

Suppositions. How else would I get from Smuckey's front sidewalk to beach dunes and a crowd of ATV's?"

"You don't want to run home?"

Fawn searched the depths of Cade's unguarded, steady eyes. "How far from home am I? Really?"

Cade snapped his fingers. "A blink away, just like when I brought you here. I can take you wherever you want to go in a fraction of a second."

"With your mind?" Fawn's newfound crush on him slipped away into something untethered and uncertain. She wondered at Cade in genuine awe and breath-taking ignorance.

Cade held his thumb and forefinger half an inch apart. "I might've oversold my part in things. There's energy everywhere — pregnant with possibilities, alive and magnetic. I merely direct it."

"Merely." Fawn lowered her forehead into her palm. "Now you're being modest."

Cade hesitated. "Would you like to go home?"

Fawn took a breath and dropped her hands, fidgeting them together. She rubbed her lips against each other. "I can go home anytime I want?"

"Ask, and I'll take you."

"Not yet. I was making real progress here."

Cade's eyebrows relaxed. "Yes, you were."

"I want this ulcer gone without a trace." Fawn touched her stomach. "I don't want to walk back into my office or my apartment until I know what I plan to do when I get there."

"That sounds wise."

Fawn squinted at Cade. "You can create anything you want?"

"Big or small." Cade's chest rose and fell under his tuxedo jacket with every breath. "I'd love to create something really special for you. Something you'll love."

"For me?"

Cade nodded. "I can make something for you now if you like. Something small. What would make your stay here more comfortable?"

Fawn batted her hand in the air. "I don't lack for anything, Cade, trust me."

His familiar, self-satisfied grin spread across his lips. "I didn't ask if you lacked for anything. I asked you what you wanted."

"On top of the huge house, the cars, and the boat? The water park and the beach that are practically right around the corner?"

Cade folded his arms. "Mm-hmm."

"I don't know." Fawn twirled a tendril of her hair around her finger. She stilled herself. "That's how you do it, though, isn't it? You don't see the need for limits."

Cade's grin tended toward a knowing, enjoying smirk. "There's no need for limits."

"That's what I thought."

Cade held his arms out from his sides. "You want to wake up to birds singing? Crêpes?"

"Chocolate crêpes," Fawn interjected with a teasing smile.

"You got it."

"My own car?" Fawn laid her hand on her head. "No, wait. That's too much. I'll get it."

"Your own boat?"

"What do I want with that?"

"You could sail by yourself. No creeps in sight."

"I like sailing with you and your family. They're still your family, right?"

"Yes."

Fawn smoothed her fingers over her dress' deep-blue chiffon skirt. "I think I need a good night's sleep to process all this."

"Of course." Cade motioned to the house and strolled toward it in step with Fawn. "I'm serious. I'm going to find out what would most make you happy, and I'm going to install it here in your honor."

Fawn flashed him a tired smile. "You don't have to."

"I want to."

Fawn gripped handfuls of her skirt and pinned her eyes on Cade. "Caroline didn't buy this dress."

"No."

"How does that work?"

"I can explain it some other time."

They reached the patio. The others parted to clear a direct path to the double doors leading into the house. They studied Fawn's and Cade's expressions.

Cade set his fingertips on the small of Fawn's back. "She's staying."

The others released their tense shoulders and sighed in relief. A few of them clapped.

A bright smile emerged to light Fawn's face. "See? Why would I leave? Everything I do draws applause, and I don't have to pay for a thing."

Chapter Five

Most of the others seated at the grand dining table had long finished their chocolate crêpes. They lounged in their seats, watching Fawn devour her sugary breakfast while she peppered Cade with question after question. Across from her, Vanna and Rory smiled with pride.

Cade laughed while Fawn sucked a smear of whipped cream off her thumb.

Fawn giggled at herself. "No, I'm only asking because — why is this so funny? Is there anything too small to create? Because when I woke up this morning, there was a cast iron shepherd's crook standing in the landscaping outside my bedroom window with a full feeder hanging from it. One bird after another landed on it. For the entire time I got dressed, did my makeup, and put my hair up."

Cade forced his lips into a straight line. "I don't know what you're talking about."

Fawn swatted his arm. "Yes, you do. I know it was you. Who else was out there putting up a bird feeder between the party last night and me waking up this morning?"

Cade's mouth wobbled. "Jax."

Fawn's eyebrows shot up. "Jax?"

"Yeah." Cade ran his hand over his wily hair. "He decided against serenading you and went with the birds instead."

"You're such a liar." Fawn stuffed the last bite of crêpe into her mouth and set her fork down. She wiped her napkin against her lips while she chewed. "Thank you for the birds, by the way. Their songs were lovely."

Cade grinned and stroked his chin. "You've asked about our pets before."

"Yeah?" Fawn spun in her chair and looked at the doorway to the hall in anticipation. When no dogs came running through, she turned back to Cade.

Yelps and high-pitched barks cut Fawn off from speaking. Paws cascaded over the terracotta tiles, headed straight for Fawn. She scooted her chair back as two dogs rushed up to her side. The short-legged one with black fur running over his back, long ears, snout, and hips propped his front paws up on Fawn's leg. His tapering tail wagged at an urgent pace.

Fawn's heart melted as she ran her hands over his soft fur. "Are you Axel? I heard about you."

The little dog barked and sniffed Fawn's dress.

Cade leaned back in his chair. "Yeah, that's Axel. He's a Doxle. A dachshund-beagle mix."

Fawn glanced at him. "That's a thing?"

"I got it from *your* dimension. Do you think all of us are obsessed with crossing animal breeds?"

Fawn's smile broadened at Axel. "That doesn't matter when you've got a face as cute as this one."

The taller dog, sleek and grey, pushed her snout against Fawn's arm.

She petted the dog's head. "This is a Weimaraner, right?"

Cade nodded.

"Where are your other dogs?"

Cade grinned. "You've already got your hands full. You want more dogs?"

Fawn pushed her lips out at him. "I don't need limits."

Cade's eyes glowed.

In the hallway, barks and thundering paws resounded anew. Three more dogs pattered into the dining room and raced at Fawn. She picked Axel up and supported him on her lap. A shaggy golden retriever sat down beside Fawn's chair, peering up at her and wagging his tail across the terracotta tiles. A grey-and-white Siberian husky rose up on his hind legs to set his front paws on a spare inch of Fawn's seat cushion. His almond-colored eyes laughed while he panted with excitement. The Australian shepherd paced back and forth behind the other dogs. Large black patches dotted his mottled-grey back, and white fur covered his chest above his amber legs.

Cade drummed his fingertips on the table. "Overwhelmed yet?"

Fawn stroked Axel's back. "No. This is amazing."

Axel squirmed toward the table's edge, sniffing Fawn's plate.

She pushed it into the middle of the table. "You can't have chocolate. You'll get sick."

"Axel, yes. Charlie…" Cade ruffled the Australian shepherd's black-and-white head. "…is indestructible. He ate a whole basket of Jax's chocolates once."

"And it didn't kill him? Obviously." Fawn combed Charlie's fur with her fingers.

"He snarfed them down wrappers and all. He didn't even throw up."

Fawn lowered Axel to the floor. "Okay, where are the cats?"

Cade shook his head.

Fawn wiggled her fingers in the air. "You won't call them for me with your mental powers?"

Cade chuckled. "Enough fur for right now."

"Sounds like a limit to me, but all right. I can ask more questions." Fawn crossed her ankles. The dogs settled in around her. "Are you immortal?"

Cade paused. "No more or less than you are."

"So you're not, like, millions of years old or anything?"

"No more or less than you are."

"Jeez. I gotta think of better questions."

The friends at the table got up and ambled out of the dining room. Kee walked out with them.

Henna stopped by Fawn's chair to peck her on the cheek. "It's made my whole week that you're staying."

Fawn chuckled. "Mine, too."

Henna encircled Fawn's shoulders in a hug.

Fawn spotted a new mehndi design of snakes and flowers adorning Henna's hands. "One of these days, I want in on your mehndi parties."

Henna clapped and squealed for joy. "Done." She skipped out into the hallway.

Vanna and Rory stood up.

"We'll see you later, Fawn." Vanna led her husband out of the dining room.

Fawn placed her palm flat on the table. "Here's a good question that usually gets a straight answer. What are we doing today?"

Cade reclined further in his chair. "Whatever you want. The summer's young."

"What does that mean?"

"It means now that you know the truth, I can lay out all your options. The choice can be yours if you like."

Fawn leaned toward Cade. "Caroline said something to me the other night about your family taking full advantage of each season."

Cade grinned. "We do."

"How? I've spent twenty-three hours a day inside for years. The seasons have all but eluded me. They're mostly a changing oddity that makes my commute to work easier or harder."

Cade pushed himself up into a straighter posture. "Well, I will say spending three straight days at the beach agrees with you."

Fawn beamed. She arranged her white shell bracelets over her tan wrist. "Thank you. I think so, too. I could lounge on that sand all day, every day. That water was made for swimming. And water skiing. And the pontoon boat."

Cade rose to his feet. "Might I add some suggestions?"

"Please." Fawn stood up in the small space the dogs had left for her. "Tell me what's possible. What do you guys like to do?"

"Do you really want to know?"

Fawn pressed her palms together and set her fingertips against her chin. "Yes."

Charlie barked once, rounding up the other dogs. He herded them out of the dining room.

Cade slid one palm against the other. "Well, let's see. There's the water park. The pontoon boat. Water skiing. We could have a barbecue out back."

Fawn groaned. "Not the stuff we've already done. New stuff."

"Oh. Right." Cade winked. He clapped a hand over the back of his neck. "We haven't ridden the jet skis yet."

Fawn jumped up and down. "I always wanted to do that."

"I'm not finished." Cade tapped his chin. "If the wind is good, we can go wind surfing."

Fawn tugged on Cade's arm. "You're such a joker. Can't you just make gusts out of thin air?"

"Yeah," Cade admitted. "Or, if you're bored with the lake, there's bungee jumping."

Fawn rolled her eyes. "Next."

"What? It's just like the body slide at Fun Splash, only instead of a snaking tube, they give you a springy rope."

"They're not that similar. Next."

"We do horseback riding up the road. There's a stable and trails."

Fawn smiled. "Yes, please."

"The health club in town has a giant pool with multiple diving boards. They offer lessons."

"Maybe."

Cade clasped his hands together. "We can take one of the boats out at sunset. The view from Beach Lake is inimitable."

"I bet. Because you made it that way." Fawn started for the double doors out of the dining room.

Cade touched her arm to keep her near him. "We can stay at the house for a change and enjoy our own pool."

"Now you're talkin'."

"Stretch out on a pool lounger all day. Have Gerard make us some homemade strawberry ice cream. Or sorbet, if you'd prefer."

Fawn alighted her hands on her hips. "Both. I'm embracing this whole no-limits concept."

"Wonderful, because around here, in the summer, we like to

cap off some of our evenings with an extensive fireworks display."

"That doesn't bother the dogs?"

"No. They just pile up together on the other side of the house. Plus, we have very efficient insulation."

"I'm not surprised." Fawn nibbled her fingernail as she glanced over the bright, colorful dining room. "So I know what my whole summer could look like. What does autumn bring?"

Cade met her with a devilish grin. "Summer preview only. If you want to find out how we spend our fall weather, you'll have to stay here for it."

~

Another red leaf dropped off one of the towering trees extending their branches out over the yard. It tumbled across the grass and swept against the side of Fawn's brown, heeled boot. She barely glanced at it as another gentle breeze took it over her foot and further into the shadow under Jax's lawn chair.

The real show continued in the air, where fireworks exploded in pops of pink and sparkling showers of gold. Fawn applauded with Cade and his siblings, careful not to tip her plate of food off her lap. The zero-gravity chair floated her a foot above the grass blades as if her body rested on nothing. The others fanned out on either side of her, forming a half-moon shape aimed at the colorful light show flashing and sizzling over the house.

Fawn took one of the last remaining bites of her sandwich. Sharp cheddar stung in the best of ways, and mozzarella flowed. Provolone swirled with sweet smoothness. Fawn savored every second of it and hummed in delight. She pointed to the remains of her toasted, triangular sandwich half. "I've said it, and I'll say it again. Best grilled cheese ever. Nobody makes them like this back home."

Cade grinned with spirited enjoyment.

Rosario set the knuckles of her loose fist under her chin. "We know, Fawn. You've said that literally every five minutes since

Gerard brought them out."

Fawn sipped her sweet, tart lemonade and returned the cup to its holder on the side of the chair. "No, you don't understand. This one has three cheeses, and at home, we're lucky to get one. The bacon bits and tomato slices are pure genius. Not to mention—"

Rosario gave a few quick nods. "The bread. We know."

Fawn smiled at her thick sandwich with gleeful greed. "Texas toast instead of some pathetic, skinny excuse for dough? I could eat these every day. And that split-pea soup Gerard made last week. I never would've touched a drop of that at home. It always looked like something that came out of my nephews when they were small, one end or the other. But Gerard packed so many herbs in there, and I still don't know what half of those vegetables were, but I'd devour that again."

Rosario gave in to a half smile. "Get used to it, Fawn. Gerard's quality isn't suddenly going to drop off and go downhill. We eat like this all the time."

Fawn frowned as yellow and aqua explosions mushroomed out in the starry sky. "But this is the last fireworks show for the year?"

Cade spoke up with warmth. "I'm afraid so."

"That's too bad. They're better than any city or beach display I ever saw." Fawn basked in the alternating red and purple blasts firing high above the house. "I'm going to miss this."

Yoselle cleared her throat and stood up from the far-right chair. She tucked her hands in the pockets of her black cotton romper and took them out again. "I'll be back." She strode off toward the house's sliding door. Light streamed out from the hallway inside.

Fawn waited until Yoselle disappeared into the house to say anything. "Is she okay?"

The siblings nodded.

Cade rubbed the side of his finger against his chin. "She skips off sometimes. But she's with the family when it matters most."

Lisette flicked her eyebrows up, seated on Rosario's other side. "Yoselle isn't like Rosario. She doesn't announce all her private business for everybody to hear."

Rosario settled into her chair with a smug purse of her lips. "Well, I certainly don't leave any mystery in my wake, do I?"

The wind stirred with a little more strength, blowing a chill over Fawn's exposed lower legs. Her knee-length cotton dress rippled, and Fawn shivered as she finished her grilled cheese. "I might be going the way of Yoselle."

Rosario raised a dark, dramatic eyebrow. "Leaving us with no clue about where you're going?"

Fawn laid her plate in the grass and stood up. "No, just into the house. I'm getting a shawl. Does anybody need anything?"

Cade tilted his head to meet her eyes. "We have staff for that. Just get what you want."

Fawn did her best Yoselle impression, fidgeting with her dress and flattening her voice into a dry monotone. "I'll be back."

Rosario laughed. "Good one, Fawn."

Fawn rubbed her upper arms through their full-length sleeves as she crossed the lawn. She hurried across the patio and let herself in through the sliding door. She second-guessed which hallway to take across the house to her room. The route flashed into her brain, and she chuckled at herself as she headed along it.

Whispers and the gentle smacking sounds of kissing grabbed Fawn's attention. The den opened up through a doorway on her left, a sunken, cavernous room replete with sectional seating forming a broken rectangle in the middle. Yoselle sat in Kee's lap, their heads bent close together. In a split second, Yoselle jumped to her feet and skittered away from him. She pressed her lips together.

Fawn picked up her pace. After a whole summer with Cade and his family, she felt like the sole witness to Yoselle's almost-secret entanglement with Kee. Those two had cheered each other on during dives off the high board at the health club. They rode their jet skis side by side across Beach Lake, often chasing one another in big loops over the waves. During the family-only boat rides to take in the blazing sherbet-colored sunsets, Yoselle always sought sullen solace by herself in the bow.

Fawn jogged the rest of the way to her room and snatched a weighty, crocheted shawl out of her closet. She slung it around her back and covered her shoulders, its soft frizzy tassels swinging from its two shortest edges. Fawn walked the same corridor back toward the patio and the fireworks. She stopped at the den's open door.

Yoselle perched on one of the sectional cushions, her face buried in her hands.

Fawn didn't see Kee anywhere. She crept into the den and shut the door.

Yoselle snapped up into sitting straight, busying her hands with combing her purple-streaked black hair. She stood up.

Fawn wagged her finger at Yoselle. "Nuh-uh. For three months, I've been privy to whatever's going on with you and Kee. I've kept your secret this entire time. But I'm tired of it. And I don't understand it. Why are you hiding?"

Yoselle sidled around Fawn to the door. "I wouldn't expect you to understand." Yoselle didn't sound bratty or accusing. More like torn and wary.

"Sit with me. I'm sure I'll understand if you explain it."

Yoselle huffed, and her pale shoulders slumped under the inch-wide straps of her romper. "Fine." She slunk over to the couch, and Fawn nestled in beside her. Yoselle tossed her hand. "You weren't here... before... when it started."

"With?"

Yoselle picked at the undersides of her painted black fingernails. "I dated Lucius for six months." She paused. "Anybody mention his name to you?"

Fawn raked her memories. "No."

"And they won't because he's gone." Yoselle pointed at her chest. "Because of me."

Fawn let the shawl slide off her shoulders onto the couch.

"What do you mean *gone*?"

"Back to *our* home, the dimension we came from."

"Just because you dated him?"

Yoselle sighed and flopped back against the overstuffed cushion behind her. "No. The break-up was bad. Like, the worst one in history. *My* history, anyway. We couldn't stand each other anymore. He blamed me, and I blamed him, and we found countless ways of getting back at each other. He fed my favorite shoes to the dogs, and I shaved his intricate facial hair design off his face while he was sleeping." A wicked grin curved Yoselle's lips.

Fawn settled further into her seat as well. "So who sent him away? Or did he leave because he wanted to?"

Yoselle shook her head, her eyes a little wider. "Everybody sent him home. They sided with me. They got sick of the fighting and the pranks. It ended the day they banished Lucius from the Playground."

"How long ago was this?"

"Last year."

Fawn tipped her head to one side. "You're worried that's still fresh in their minds and they'll have a problem with you dating Kee?"

"You don't get it at all." Yoselle moved to push herself up off the couch.

Fawn lifted her boot in front of Yoselle's bare shins. "Make me get it."

Yoselle exhaled in a brief growl. She pinned Fawn with her stare. "I don't have a great track record. None of us do. Mom and Dad have been married forever, and in case you haven't noticed, they're the only ones around here who are. They're happy. They have each other. The rest of us are struggling to figure it out. Until..."

Fawn softened her voice. "Kee?"

Yoselle's hostility melted away. "Yeah."

Fawn set her boot down and clasped her hands over her knees. "Why don't you tell me what you're afraid of so I don't annoy you with more of my wrong guesses?"

Yoselle chipped a flake of black polish off a fingernail tip. "If it doesn't work out — because there are no guarantees — it won't just affect Kee. It'll be too easy for my family to see him as some kind of villain and tell him he has to leave after what happened with Lucius. And Jacqui won't want to stay here with her brother gone. Basically, Kee and I stay together forever, or he and Jacqui get sent home whether they prefer to move or not."

Fawn plucked gingerly at the shawl's soft white-and-grey fringe. "That's a lot of variables to fear, Yoselle."

"I know. Why do you think I haven't been sleeping so well?" Yoselle crossed her legs, bobbing one red-laced black combat boot up and down.

Fawn treaded as lightly as she could. "Why don't you tell your family about your relationship with Kee? Especially if you really connect with him. I've only seen you two get along. You act miserable when he's not around."

"Because I am. Because…" Yoselle studied Fawn for a long moment. "I know my family better than you do." She flipped up the corner of Fawn's shawl. "You think they're all hospitality and clothes and glamour and manners. But they're not. They judge me the most out of everybody in the Playground."

Fawn worked to keep her balking on the inside. "I've seen you gel with Cade at breakfast. Even at the barbecue, during the toasts. He jokes with you. He stands up for you."

"He was the one who first suggested Lucius pack for home. And he wouldn't have had to stand up for me at the barbecue if Lisette didn't knock me."

Fawn began to see Yoselle's point. "True."

Yoselle knotted her arms over her stomach. "If I admit I'm dating Kee, they're gonna gang up on me and tell me all the reasons I should stop. I don't wanna hear it, and I don't want to break up with him."

Fawn laid a hand over her chest. "What if I breach the subject for you?"

Yoselle turned her face away.

Fawn splayed her fingers. "It could work. They don't have the same history with me they have with you. And I don't have the baggage with them that you have. I can talk some sense into them."

Yoselle searched Fawn's eyes. "If it doesn't work, the cat's out of the bag."

A furry orange tail caught Fawn's attention past the end of the couch. She decided not to mention it. "The only alternative is to keep dating in semi-secret, and I gotta tell you. Sooner or later, someone else is going to catch on. You two are subtle, but you're not exactly locked down."

"Then they'd freak out and spread the news like wildfire." Yoselle ran her fingers through her hair. "You're sure you're the right person to speak on my behalf?"

Fawn relaxed into an easy grin. "My company's business is smoothing over less-than-thrilling circumstances."

"I'll wait here. If they riot, let me know to take a vacation somewhere far from home."

Fawn stood up. "I'll sell it to them until they buy it. Okay?"

Yoselle rolled her eyes.

"Great. See you soon." Fawn picked her path out of the couch maze.

One sulking word fell behind her. "Thanks."

"You're welcome." Fawn let herself out of the den and hefted her shawl up around her shoulders.

She reached the patio door and stepped out onto the small side terrace. Strobing silver light illuminated the yard, the six chairs arranged in the grass, and the four people occupying most of them.

Jax beamed. "Fawn's back!" He raised his lemonade.

"Yeah, about that." Fawn came to stand in front of the four siblings, holding the shawl closed around her chest. When all four of her friends looked at her, she found the most natural tone she could. "Yoselle's dating Kee."

"What?" Jax swung his glass hard, arcing the lemonade out of it in a forceful slice that watered the grass. "Damn it! It's Lucius all over again." He shoved the empty glass into its holder.

Rosario rubbed her forehead. "I'm going to get stress creases like last time. I finally plumped them out with that special cream."

Lisette closed her eyes and tapped her fingernails on her plastic chair arms. "Disaster. She's attracted to what's worst for her."

Cade's eyes shone with interest. He ran his fingertips along his jaw line. "What did she say?"

Fawn tugged her shawl further around her. "Well, I think she scripted your reactions pretty accurately." Fawn sank her weight into one hip. "Why are you so tough on her, anyway?"

Lisette opened her eyes, and they flashed in the low light that struck their brown irises. "She makes terrible decisions, Fawn. It's not your fault."

Fawn blew a long, steadying breath through her nostrils. "Why is being with Kee such a bad choice?"

Jax vacillated his hand left and right in the air. "It's not Kee. It's our sister."

Fawn switched her weight to her other hip. "I think you're being awfully unfair."

Rosario, Jax, and Lisette made the starting sounds of protest.

Cade's flat hand cut through the air, and they silenced themselves. The light in his eyes had dimmed to serious. His eyebrows hunkered low, and disapproval set his lips. "Fawn and Yoselle are right. You're harsh with her, and I should've ended it sooner." He got up from his chair.

Jax threw his hands up, his mouth falling ajar. "Do you remember the sadness on Lucius' face when we cast him out? We were friends for a long time."

Lisette's fingers dissected tiny tangles in her thick, blonde waves. "You're not the one who got caught in the middle of their squirt gun wars. The bleach ruined my clothes, not to mention what the hair remover did to my tresses."

Rosario agreed with a deep nod. "We're attempting to create a bit of balance, little brother." She snapped at him with more venom. "If you had your way, Yoselle'd be treated like a *princess.*" She gasped with genuinely wide eyes and covered her mouth with her palm.

The muscle along Cade's jaw pulsed as he moved to Fawn's side. He fixed his siblings with a no-nonsense stare, each in turn. "Yoselle is a princess, and don't you forget it. You pick on her because she's the youngest and she doesn't fight back. She's become quite the easy target for you. No wonder she's been hiding something from us."

Fawn cleared her throat in a few long groans. "For at least the entire summer."

Jax threw a lazy right hook and kicked his feet up. "What?!"

Fawn straightened her posture. "She didn't want to be judged. Things are going well with Kee, it seems." She wondered at the four of them. "Not one of you had any inkling about this? You missed all the little waves they give each other and the smiles and the games they play on the jet skis?"

Cade rested his hand on Fawn's arm over the shawl. "Where's Yoselle now?"

"In the den. She expects a horrible reaction from all of you that will prompt her to flee for some time."

"No." Cade pointed to his siblings. "We're going to show our sister the respect she deserves. No jokes. No flashbacks to Lucius. We all know he wasn't perfect. When he and Yoselle split up, we backed our sister, as we should've. We failed her by wavering in that support after the fact. We'll welcome her out here with loving arms and tell her we accept Kee fully as her boyfriend."

Jax's mouth popped open.

Cade held up his index finger. "You'll pledge your support for Yoselle's choices, or I'll run through all the ways Kee is a better match for her than Lucius ever could've been."

Fawn jerked her chin up. "And I'll tease you mercilessly about your past girlfriends and the way you ogle the ladies at the water park."

Rosario chuckled. "*Girlfriends* is such a forgiving, liberal term when it comes to Jax."

Jax waved for her to quiet, annoyance tilting his dark eyebrows. "All right. I'll behave myself."

Rosario guffawed louder.

Cade patted Fawn's arm. "I'll collect Yoselle and bring her out. Thank you for letting me know."

Fawn's heart fluttered almost imperceptibly. "Of course."

A touch of playfulness ticked up the corners of Cade's mouth. "Good eye, by the way. None of us suspected a thing."

Fawn shrugged. "Weird place, right time, I guess."

Cade strutted into the house. Fawn reclaimed her chair between Jax and Rosario.

Rosario leaned toward her. "What'd you catch them doing in there?"

Fawn rewrapped the shawl around her body. "Nope. Not gossiping. If you ask me again, I'll tell Cade."

Rosario's palm struck her chair's arm. "Damn. I'm the trustworthy one, and you've already given him your allegiance. That's no fun."

"Make a house full of light with high-end appliances and gorgeous clothes, and I'll consider changing my mind."

Rosario cackled. "Point taken."

The foursome watched the succession of firework launches grow, morph, and crackle in the night sky. Some expanded into lemon-colored smiley faces. Others outlined indigo flowers and white stars.

When the patio door slid open, Cade guided Yoselle out of the house ahead of him. Fawn led the siblings in applauding her.

Rosario pushed herself up off her chair and wrapped her arms around Yoselle in a big hug. "I'm sorry. I'll try to be a better sister to you. Of all our friends, I'm glad you're finding happiness with Kee."

Yoselle stood stiff, even as Rosario pulled back.

Cade stretched his arm around Yoselle's shoulders, regarding their siblings with solemn features. "Anyone who has a problem with it has an issue with me."

Yoselle tossed her hair back from her face. "Cade wouldn't tell me what you said."

Fawn walked over to Yoselle, holding the shawl around herself in the chilly breeze. "It doesn't matter."

Cade spoke up. "No, it doesn't. We're treating Kee as we would any of our significant others. He's invited to family get-togethers, and we give him the level of courtesy he deserves."

Yoselle peered at Jax and Lisette in their lawn chairs. "Even from them?"

Cade nodded. "I'll make sure of it."

Jax lowered his gaze for a moment. "We're sorry, kid. We've all made—" He rubbed the back of his neck. "We wish you the best of luck."

Yoselle hesitated and threw her arms around Fawn. "Thank you." She breathed a giddy sigh. "You were right. You did it. I didn't think they'd ever let me date anybody publicly again."

Fawn blinked, stunned, at Yoselle's display of gratitude. "You're welcome."

Yoselle bounced back a step and clapped her hands. "If it's all the same, then, I'd like to spend the rest of the evening with Kee. If everyone's cool with it."

Her siblings, lost in blank stares at her, responded with loose nods. Yoselle grinned and danced through the sliding door into the house.

Rosario gasped, coughing for air. "When was the last time she hugged anyone except Cade? Or Kee, apparently?"

Jax shrugged. "We'll probably see a lot less of her now. But she's happier than I've seen her in months."

Fawn set her hand on her hip. "About three months, Jax?"

Cade laughed. He clamped his hand on Fawn's shoulder. "She's got you there, brother."

Lisette rose gracefully from her chair, her long skirt shifting in the wind. "Thank goodness Fawn was here, looking out for our sister."

Rosario swept Fawn up in a hug. "Yes. We might spend less time with Yoselle, but we'll actually have our sister back in spirit." Rosario brightened and wandered over to her chair.

Crimson and spring-green lights flashed over everything in the yard.

Fawn craned her neck to see the fireworks bursting over the roof. "Have we missed most of them?"

Cade reassured her. "Not a chance."

Fawn stepped toward her chair to join Cade's siblings in the light works' audience.

Cade touched her arm, and she faced him. He ran the tip of his tongue over his lips as he searched her features. "Thank you, genuinely, for what you did."

Fawn ducked her chin. "It was nothing. I just got tired of Yoselle sneaking around and me being the only one who knew her secret."

Cade inched closer, his gaze serious and deep. "No. You stood up for her to all of us. You interfered in the best of ways. Most people wouldn't bother, especially to handle the situation with that much tact and poise."

Fawn met Cade's eyes with a hint of shyness. "If I have tact and poise, it's because of being here with all of you."

Cade shook his head gently. "You had plenty when you came here."

Fawn let her lips curve with a small fraction of Cade's brilliant smile.

Jax called over, cupping his hands around his mouth to amplify his volume. "Hey, you're missing it!"

Cade mouthed a silent *thank you* to Fawn and strolled off the small patio into the grass. Fawn trailed after him and settled into her chair, Jax separating her from Cade once again.

Jax kicked his feet up and tilted his chair back into its full, reclining position. He exhaled with loud relief and stacked his hands under his head. Gold and silver showers fell against the sky, dropping like waterfalls of camera flashes. They faded into darkness. "Isn't this the life, Fawn?"

She pushed her chair back down lower and propped her legs up. She snuggled the soft shawl around her, letting it brush against her jaw like a reassuring touch. "Would I still be here if it weren't?"

~

Brown and rust-colored leaves rustled across the main driveway's semicircle. Fawn braved the crisp wind with the others, bundled up in a quilted down puffer coat the color of champagne. She tugged her off-white knitted beanie a little further down on her forehead.

No one had to point out to her the driveway's current main attraction. A long, wooden wagon sat hitched to a sleek, shiny cherry-red tractor. Squared-off hay bales filled the back of the wagon, leaving an aisle open down the center. The tractor's growling grumble brought the essence of the country straight to the fancy house's door.

Fawn clapped her hands, clad in convertible mittens with the tops off to leave her fingers usable. "I'm so excited!"

Rosario tied her fluffy, scarlet scarf higher against her throat. "Have you ever been on a hayride before?"

"Not since I was eight." Fawn drank in the tractor's exhaust billowing in the brisk air and the wagon's generous size. She waved to Hans perched on the tractor's exposed seat, and he doffed his plaid flat cap to her. Wrapped in a black bomber jacket and grey wool scarf, he sat up with no signs the falling temperatures chilled him.

Jax appeared at Fawn's side. "Where would you like to sit?" He gestured up to the hay bales.

"In the front." Fawn lurched toward the gate-like opening at the back of the wagon. "No, wait. I like to watch off the back, too, at what we're passing." Fawn climbed up the three metal steps into the wagon. She laughed at herself. "I guess I'll ride in the middle." She traversed half the length of the floorboards and plopped down on a bale to her left. She smoothed her coat's length over her thighs. "I'm glad this coat's a long one. The hay won't poke me today."

Jax and Rosario settled in a little distance from Fawn. Vanna and Rory ascended, followed by Lisette. They nestled on bales near the front, behind the tractor. Yoselle and Kee huddled with their arms around each other at the back of the wagon.

Cade bounded up the steps, latching the gate shut behind him. He pulled his cell phone out of his puffy vest's pocket and used it. "Hans, we're ready."

The tractor driver tapped a black device nested in his ear. Cade tucked his phone away and sat next to Fawn. The tractor thundered louder, and Fawn swayed as its engine drew the wagon into motion.

She surveyed Cade's cavalier outfit, a thick vest layered over a cable-knit sweater and jeans. "You're gonna be a snowman out there."

Cade smirked. "I don't get cold easily."

"Oh, yeah?" Fawn knocked her faux-fur-lined knee-high boots against Cade's laced up, tan leather boots. "How come you traded your slippers and flip-flops for outdoorsy footwear, then?"

Cade purred. "Because they go better with the vest."

"You're gonna *freeze.* No self-respecting hayride lasts for less than one full hour."

"Don't expect anything less than two."

"I won't."

Hans slowed the tractor at the end of the driveway and eased it onto the road.

Fawn lifted her exposed cheeks to the sun peeking through the clouds. "What about traffic?"

Cade chuckled. "They'll move over."

"Okay, what about our view?"

"We're only using the road for a few minutes."

The towering oaks and full maples Fawn had enjoyed as the summer's verdant backdrop to her travels had become a fiery spectacle. Sugar maples blazed tangerine and burnt orange. Japanese maples with small, delicate leaves lingered like cranberry shadows here and there. Beeches littered tapering leaves glowing like candle flames.

Hans directed the tractor off the road and between two lengths of wooden fence.

Fawn rocked side to side on her hay bale over the uneven ground. "You know what would make these hayrides of yours absolutely perfect?"

Cade gave her an amused glance. "What?"

"Have a pair of horses pull the wagon instead of the tractor. Does Hans work with horses, too, or just machinery with motors?"

"He can handle horses."

"There you go. A little suggestion from me."

Cade's grin turned sly. "I'll keep it in mind."

Three-story quaking aspens radiated gold sprays atop their white trunks. Sumacs half their height punctuated the landscape in lipstick reds.

Fawn kicked her boot heels back against the hay bale in opposition to each other. "What do you do if one of you does get cold out here? Stop and make a bonfire out of some extra bales?"

Jax laughed, sitting catty-corner to Fawn. "Nah. The hay helps us out in a different way." He patted the bale beside him and flipped its top up like a hinged lid.

Fawn stared at it.

Jax opened a second, stainless steel lid barely recessed within the bale. "Some of these hold hidden compartments."

Fawn bent toward it. "What do you keep in your secret compartments?"

Jax reached inside and raised up a tall, black thermos. "Gerard's hot chocolate, made from scratch."

Fawn nibbled her fingernail in anticipation. "What else?"

Jax pulled out a squat, blue thermos. "Chicken soup broth."

"Also by Gerard?"

"Also from scratch." Jax winked and put the containers away. He closed up the cooler and the hay bale.

"No apple cider?"

Rosario beamed at Fawn from two bales away on her right. "Gerard makes that, too, from the apples we pick every year."

Fawn frowned. "But we haven't been apple picking."

Rosario clucked her tongue. "Yet."

"Yes." Fawn jerked her elbow back in a victory pump at her side. "What else do I have to look forward to before the snow falls?"

Rosario twisted her lips to one side. "I wouldn't say I necessarily look forward to it, but Cade and Jax carry out an epic pumpkin-carving battle that lasts two days."

Jax cocked his head over one shoulder. "It wouldn't be fair to judge our work on less than forty-eight hours of highly detailed precision."

Cade nodded. "That's right."

Lisette shouted to be heard from near the tractor. "The helicopter gives a better view of the trees."

Fawn turned to Cade. "You have your own helicopter?"

He grinned. "No, but I love that you think we do. We rent one, and Hans pilots it."

Fawn rubbed her chin ironically. "Is there anything Hans can't do?"

Cade drew out his single syllable. "No."

"How do you fill the rest of your autumn?"

"Hang gliding. Mom and Lisette bake with Gerard in the chef's kitchen. We all go to this exclusive little shop in town for wine tasting."

Jax folded his hands on the back of his head, his elbows pointing out. "Cade and I build the longest-lasting bonfires, and our father assembles the most decadent s'mores."

Fawn bent her forehead toward Jax. "Even better than

Gerard?"

Cade fielded the question, counting on his fingers. "Gerard sources Swiss chocolate, French gourmet marshmallows, and honey-laden graham crackers crafted in small local batches. It just happened to be Dad who found the most delicious ratio of ingredients to each other."

"Where do you make your bonfires?"

"At home, most of the time."

Fawn feigned surprise with a half-mittened hand over her parted lips. "You don't squeeze a camping trip into your busy autumn?"

Jax guffawed and gripped his stomach as he doubled over. "You'd never catch any of our sisters having anything to do with that C word."

Cade leaned sideways toward Fawn. "We're more the glamping type."

Fawn echoed his smile. "I should've guessed."

"When it gets too frigid for outdoor activities but the snow hasn't blanketed the world yet, Rosario drags us to the opera. The rest of the time, we read to each other and play board games in the den."

Rosario *tsked*. "Don't listen to him, Fawn. He wants you to believe the opera's dreadfully boring while their game playing is quiet and genteel. Just wait 'til you realize you've been watching Cade, Jax, and Dad for their fifth straight hour of a spontaneous darts tournament."

Jax slipped a protruding hay stalk free from the hollow bale and chewed on its end. He wagged his eyebrows up and down. "That's right. And this year, we can wrangle Kee into joining us. Cade's rules."

Rosario scooted over next to Fawn and linked her arm around Fawn's. "Well, this year, I have a good chance at a partner in crime, too."

Fawn laughed. "I'll try my best to sit through one opera, but I've never understood them. I can't make promises."

"There must be something I can rope you into. Do you like walking tours?"

"I did one in Chicago once."

"How was it?"

"Windy and cold and marvelous. I find little shops so interesting."

Cade patted Fawn on the back in slow, rhythmic beats. "Ah, you said the S word. We've lost you to Rosario now."

Rosario pulled Fawn closer to her. "Yes. I want to take you to the fair-trade shop with all the artisans' wares from all over the world. And the bread dipping place that's jam-packed with bread and herbaceous oils. If Yoselle comes with us, we can hit the crazy lady's store where she sells clothes she's destroyed and made whole again." Rosario dropped to a whisper. "She can call it *upcycled* all she wants, but where I come from, it's DIY."

Jax tossed his hay stalk behind him off the wagon and opened up the cooler in the hollowed-out bale. "Who's thirsty? Or shivering?" He eyed Cade with one eyebrow skyward.

Cade folded his arms. "I'm toasty as a roasted marshmallow, thanks."

Fawn raised her hand. "I'll take some hot chocolate, Jax."

Rosario nodded quickly and licked her lips. Jax procured a two-handled stoneware mug and poured into it from the black thermos. He handed the mug to Fawn and filled another one for Rosario.

Yoselle and Kee whipped their heads toward the rich, fragrant steam streaming from the cups.

Jax sighed with dramatic flair. "Yes, I'll get you some, too."

Rory extended his empty hand and called over the tractor's roar. "Um, son? A little parched."

Jax hung his head for a moment. He cast his father a gracious grin. "Of course, pops." He drained the black thermos and withdrew another identical container from the cooler. "Gerard always sends us out with two."

Fawn sipped her piping-hot chocolate, smooth and creamy.

Earthiness and a hint of spice grounded it from being too sweet. She lingered in its childhood delight for a few seconds. "That's nice of Gerard. That way, the last person doesn't end up with chicken broth if they don't want to."

"That's usually me." Jax flowed fresh hot chocolate into mugs for Yoselle and Kee.

Kee kept his balance as he stood up and retrieved the beverages for Yoselle and himself.

Jax filled another pair of mugs and passed them to his father. "I don't know how I became the exclusive beverage king of these hayrides, but I can't remember the last time anyone else poured drinks on one of these."

As Jax made himself a cup, Fawn enjoyed her timeless treat. Cade and Rosario set about restoring Jax's memory about family hayrides to their benefit. Time passed strangely, slow except for the definitive markings of its passage. Somewhere near the gigantic, arcing oaks of yellow and orange, Fawn slurped the last gulp of her drink. Under a particularly bright patch of cerulean sky, Jax and Rory treated the group to a rousing rendition of a traditional tune Fawn had never heard before. The rose and eggplant leaves swayed on the dogwood trees, and Hans aimed the tractor in a new direction.

Disappointment caved Fawn's chest in. "Aw, we're heading to the house, aren't we?"

Rosario chuckled and gestured to the now-dusky sky. "The sun's starting to set. We won't be able to see very well pretty soon."

Fawn pouted. "The colors were beautiful. This route was so good."

Rosario rubbed Fawn's arm. "Don't worry. The night isn't over yet."

Within minutes, the familiar swimming pool gleamed in the dwindling light off to the right. Hans steered the tractor past it and around the side of the property. He cut through the front yard and parked in the driveway where their adventure had taken off.

Fawn marveled at the trail of flattened grass in the wagon's wake. "You don't have Hans drive us back to the road first?"

Cade made low, amused sounds in his throat. "The grass will survive."

Hans cut the engine and shimmied down from the tractor's seat. He popped the two small devices out of his ears. "How was it?"

Cade grinned. "It was fine, Hans. Thank you."

Kee stood up and unfastened the gate's latch at the back of the wagon. Everyone left their used mugs behind on their bales and exited the wagon. They filed up to the porch and gratefully escaped the wind's sharp claws into the foyer.

Fawn snatched her hat off and shrugged out of her coat. Before she could ask what the family had in store for them next, Gerard approached from the right.

He gave a light bow with his hands linked behind him. "Drinks are served."

Cade unzipped his vest an inch. "Thank you."

Gerard swept through one corner of the foyer and headed up the hallway straight ahead.

Jax and Rory collected the others' coats and stowed them in the closet. Fawn moved with the group as it navigated its way deeper into the house and strolled into the den.

The fireplace in the middle of the left-hand wall housed a crackling, lapping blaze. Eight glasses of light-amber liquid sat on coasters around the room, topped off with cinnamon sticks.

Lisette brushed past Fawn and claimed a seat in a high-backed armchair in the corner. She wrapped her hands around the glass on the neighboring end table. She hummed with pleasure. "Hot toddies."

Rosario gave Fawn's arm a brief squeeze before rushing off to settle into a dark, leather pub chair near Lisette. "Fawn, you're not afraid of a little watered-down whiskey, are you?"

Fawn glanced around the den at the various available seats. "Not on a fourth date," she joked. "But there are nine of us and only eight glasses."

Yoselle hugged Kee in the doorway, and he ambled out of sight. Yoselle stepped into the room and eased the door shut.

Fawn's spirits fell. "But I thought Kee was invited now."

Cade gestured Fawn toward him as he reached the center of the room's depth. "Come on."

Yoselle and her parents settled in on the closest L-shaped sofa, facing the far end of the room. Jax nabbed a seat in a papasan chair with a tufted purple suede cushion shaped like a large bowl. Cade retreated to the back of the room and nestled into a boxy chair covered in gold satin that rose into a grand dome above his head.

Fawn crept forward and perched on the vacant sofa cushion next to Yoselle. She picked up the drink waiting on the carved wooden coffee table in front of her. Her voice came out hushed and timid. "What is it we do now?"

Cade grinned and stroked his chin.

Jax stood up, holding his glass high. "We toast, like you haven't seen before." He tried to sit back down, but the papasan's bowl shifted in its frame. Jax half toppled over and planted his butt in the seat with haste. He chuckled at himself.

Cade laughed and pointed at his brother. "You keep choosing that chair, but it's hardly friendly to you when you're sober. You get that drink in you…"

Jax shook his head and sipped his drink. "It hasn't landed me on the carpet yet."

Fawn glanced from face to face in wonder. "Who are we toasting?"

Cade tented his fingers in front of his chest. "Who wants to start?"

Rory started to rise. "I will."

Rosario waved for him to sit even though she was out of his range of sight. "No, Dad, it's not appropriate. I'll start."

Lisette got to her feet, one eyebrow raised in stern annoyance. "Sister, you led the barbecue. It's my turn."

Yoselle and Vanna picked up their glasses. Fawn snuck a sip of her hot toddy, salted caramel and cinnamon swimming around her tongue.

Cade gave a slight nod, his grey eyes twinkling.

Lisette held her drink up toward her father. "To the king. Our figurehead. Our mentor. An example of strength and a steady keel."

The rest of the family intoned, "To the king."

They drank from their glasses, and Fawn hurried to follow suit. Her wide eyes leapt from person to person. Lisette returned to her seat.

Rosario jumped up and adjusted the hem of her sweater around her brown velvet skirt. "Okay, my turn."

The family laughed.

Rosario bowed her head at Vanna. "In honor of the queen. Bringer of beauty. Guiding light and compassionate matron. As insightful as you are approachable. Mother, I thank you."

Fawn caught on fast enough to utter in unison with the family. "To the queen."

Vanna stood up graceful and poised between her husband and her youngest daughter. She lifted her glass toward Jax. "My oldest son, the prince. Full of humor, life, and joy. Charismatic." She tilted her head at him. "Chaotic. But always energized and welcoming."

Fawn recited with the others. "To the prince."

Yoselle sprouted up next to Fawn and turned to Rosario. "The oldest princess, my leader of a sister. Outspoken. Headstrong. But well-meaning and protective. To Rosario."

Fawn spoke with the rest of the family. "To the princess."

Jax slowly rose out of the papasan's soft bowl. He smirked at Lisette. "To the middle princess of the three. The practical. The stalwart. The reliable and direct. The headstrong and athletic."

"To the princess."

Rory succeeded in standing up without anyone prompting him to remain seated. He smiled down at Yoselle resting two cushions away. "My youngest princess, my spitfire. An individual more unique than most. Determined. Bright. Observant. Feisty and truthful."

"To the princess."

Fawn enjoyed another swallow of her sweet, sharp hot toddy. Everyone stayed in their seats, and Fawn searched their enigmatic smiles. She raised her eyes to Cade's. Her heart pounded a little harder, not knowing whether the family would heap adorations on her or Cade next. And if Cade hadn't been counted as a prince behind Jax, what would they call him? Furthermore, Fawn hoped somebody would explain to her whether she sat among real royalty or a family with lofty nicknames.

Cade grinned and blinked.

The accolades came so quickly, the members of his family fired them off one after the other, almost overlapping.

Jax called out. "The greatest entertainer in any dimension."

Lisette spoke up. "Most dedicated, devoted brother."

Rosario whooped and spiked her glass up into the air, splashing amber liquid over the rim. "Brave, bold, happy, and limitless."

Yoselle beamed at Cade. "The most caring, most loving, fairest brother of them all."

Vanna nodded. "So creative, my son."

Rory capped his hand over his wife's knee. "You gave us our freedom with your generosity and your hard work."

Fawn kept quiet, observing the family with shallow, even breaths. She held her hot toddy in her lap.

Jax crowed. "The most inventive."

Rosario leapt to her feet. "Powerful."

Yoselle giggled. "Forgiving. Understanding."

Rory laid his hand over his chest and patted his heart. "You make me extremely proud to call you my son."

Tears glistened in Vanna's sea-blue eyes. "Your love for us is obvious, and we love you, too."

Lisette held her glass higher. "The glue that holds us all

together. Keeps us guessing. Always teaching us something. Making sure we never get a taste of boredom."

The rest of the family joined Rosario in standing up. They raised their drinks toward Cade. "To the jester."

Jax gulped down the caramel and whiskey from his glass. He aimed an unabashed grin at his brother. "The hedonist."

The family continued to launch accolades at Cade and repeat his nicknames to him in raucous joy. "To the jester, the hedonist."

Cade grinned longer than Fawn thought possible without one's jaw aching. He rubbed his chin and wriggled deeper into his chair. His gaze roamed from his brother to his parents to his sisters. His silver eyes met Fawn's, luminous with a far-reaching calm.

His family's toasts devolved into hearty laughter and draining the sweetened alcohol from their mugs. Cade allowed himself more temperate drinks from his glass. As Fawn watched him, she began to understand. Her breath came to her more easily, more naturally. Fulfillment and achievement sparkled in Cade's broad grin. He held nothing back in his creations, and his family reserved none of their adoration. They truly owed their extravagant, exquisite lifestyle to Cade and his abilities. They lavished their gratitude on him, and he soaked up every word of it.

Fawn took timid sips of her hot toddy. Cade was more than a prince to his family. He provided for them, envisioned for them, and labored for them. He both tucked them under his wings and soared to new pinnacles with them.

Fawn downed the rest of her drink. Why Cade was the middle child everyone revolved around and relied on finally clicked into place. He tossed a wink at her, and she smiled back.

Chapter Six

The snowdrifts reached Fawn's knees as she trudged through the heavy white blanket stretching from the parking lot over the three hills a hundred feet away. She groaned, dragging an empty sled behind her by its white rope. The still air chilled her cheeks between her purple fleece beanie and the cardinal-red scarf warming her neck.

Cade grinned at her side, pulling two saucer-shaped sleds. The black inflated one skipped and jumped while the green metal disk glided smoothly across the snow. "It's not that cold."

Fawn shook her body on purpose to make extra heat. "Can't we spend the afternoon in front of a roaring fire in the den reciting poetry? Or can I at least pretend I'm back at the spa getting a hot stone treatment?"

"No. No pretending. You don't need to here in the Playground."

Fawn issued Cade a challenging smile. "Because you can make everything we need?"

Cade beamed at her. "Because I can, and I do."

Jax drew up along Fawn's right side. He held one hand behind him, carrying a handle of the family's white-and-red cooler. An orange beanie covered his head, topped with a sizable pompom. "It's not so bad. One day of sledding and tubing, then we'll retreat inside to play dominoes and heat up the last batch of apple cider."

Fawn pumped a hopeful, triumphant fist in the air. "Yay."

"Or it's just as likely we'll come back to the park for snowboarding or skiing." Jax walked up ahead of Fawn.

Rosario, holding up the cooler's back end, fell into step next to Fawn. "It could be time to rev up the snow mobiles for the first time this season."

Fawn grunted in defeat.

Rosario threw a playful punch to Fawn's arm. "Aw, come on. You came to love those ATV's."

Fawn smirked. "It's amazing how fun things get with the proper gear. And knowing what to expect."

Lisette strolled up by Rosario's other side, bundled in a grey coat and black gloves. "We'd give you the right equipment for our winter sports."

Fawn lifted her boots higher to get through the snow with less effort. "Perfect. With a pair of snow pants, I make mean snow angels."

Cade kicked at the top inch of accumulation. "What a waste of this ideal snow. It's not delicate and powdery. It's wet enough to pack without feeling like you're lifting weights." Cade transferred one of the saucers' ropes into his other hand. He bent over and scooped up a generous handful of white.

Fawn backed up a few paces and shielded her face with her palm. "If you're slinging that at Jax, I'm not getting caught in the middle."

Lisette shook her head. "They'll save it for the yard at home. More trees and building corners to hide behind."

Jax pretended to dodge incoming snowballs. "We're gonna get all tactical and shit."

Fawn rapped her knuckles on the cooler. "What's in here this time? Hot chocolate? More of that spiced punch? Mulled wine with an orange-zest garnish?"

Jax lifted the lid. "A few hot beverages, yes. The other half of the chest is filled with other kinds of supplies like goggles, pocket warmers, and gauze."

Fawn spotted the white packages in the cooler printed with blue letters. "Gauze?"

"Yeah, ever since we collided a few years ago."

Rosario huffed and rolled her eyes. "Doing something stupid. Might as well tell Fawn the whole story."

Jax brightened into a self-satisfied smile. "Half the story. Cade and I sledded down at the same time—"

Rosario marked off air quotes with her free hand. "Jousting, they called it."

"—and we ran into each other, oddly enough. My head broke a cut open on Cade's face. So now, we come prepared."

Rosario closed the cooler. "You could just grow up and use your brains first."

Lisette snickered. "It was using their so-called brains that sent them down the hill at the same time in the first place."

The group reached the nearest hill. The other two mounds rose toward the sun further off to the right. Fawn glanced back to see if Yoselle and Kee still followed the rest of them. She hadn't heard a peep from them since the ride over. They navigated the snow as one, an arm wrapped around each other's waist. Their outside hands trailed sleds behind them.

Fawn climbed the hill, her sled scraping along the crest of the snow. The others ascended with her to the nearly flat apex, a long kidney-bean shape. An errant gust blasted Fawn in the eyes, and she blinked against its dryness. "It's still not too late to kick back on the couch with a hazelnut chai and a book. You're all so good with reading and delivering what you've memorized, even the stuff that evaded me in high school makes sense."

Cade clapped Fawn on the back of her puffer coat. "Nice try. Another day. A colder day."

Fawn grumbled. "It *is* cold."

"That's how the snow got here." Cade abandoned the green disk on the ground and plopped into the inflated black tube. With a casual salute, he pushed himself over the slope's edge across from where they'd scaled the hill. He laughed the whole way down the bank, and his siblings cheered him on as the tube sped across the level snow.

Rosario and Jax propped the cooler on the gently rounded hilltop. Kee passed Jax the rope to his red plastic sled.

Fawn ran two quick counts in her head. "We don't even have enough sleds."

Jax maneuvered the red sled to the top of the slope. He

motioned Rosario to its waiting, vacant rectangle. "Sister?"

Rosario hopped in the front, and Jax sat down behind her, propping his knees up with his boots nestled against Rosario's hips. Kee settled into the back of the orange sled, and Yoselle snuggled into the front with her back against his chest. Cade popped up from his finally still tube and spiked his fists in the air. The others hollered and cheered as they pushed off down the hill.

Lisette perched on the cooler's lid. She folded her gloved hands over her thigh. "Go ahead, Fawn."

Fawn moved toward the hill's popular decline. "You're not sledding?"

"I prefer beverage and equipment detail. If your hands get frosty, come see me. Otherwise, enjoy yourself."

Fawn situated herself in her yellow sled with her legs out straight. With a few nudges, her plastic vehicle slipped down onto the slope and picked up momentum. She whooped as the icy wind glided across her cheeks. She felt grounded and weightless, secure and soaring. She gained more speed by the bottom and careened along the snow, nearly flying. Some distance from the hill, the sled eased into a gradual stop.

Cade gathered the rope to his black tube and wandered over to Fawn. "You forgot how fun this was, didn't you?"

"I did." Fawn jumped up and snatched her sled's rope. "That's okay. I remember now."

Cade walked with her toward the hill. "You might not understand our constant drive for self-indulgence."

"No, I do." Fawn met Cade's eyes, her gaze as solemn and assuring as her voice.

The muscles around his eyes relaxed.

Rosario's loud outburst shattered their peaceful moment from halfway up the incline. "You're going to *die*, Jax!"

Fawn looked up.

Jax stood tall in the red sled at the slope's crest. He splayed his hands apart, one in front and one in back of him to steady himself. His wild grin widened. "It hasn't killed me yet, and I haven't succeeded, either. I'll get it this time."

Kee shouted up at him, bringing the orange sled back with Yoselle at his side. "Do it, man!"

Yodeling tribal-like sounds, Jax pitched forward over his right foot. He zipped past Rosario trekking up the hillside. Jax yelled in victory, and his sled bounced off a jutting piece of snow. The sled left the ground and twisted. Jax flew through the air, his call changing from a *woo* to an *ahh*. He landed face first in a deep patch of snow while his unmanned sled whizzed off by itself.

Rosario threw her hands up. "Jax, you idiot, are you okay?"

A magenta-and-black glove emerged from the snowbank. Within seconds, Jax lifted his head with a smile lighting his bronze face. "What did I hit? A rock?"

Rosario growled and hiked the last few feet to the hilltop. "Whatever it was, it isn't half as hard as your head."

Jax chuckled as he struggled to get up from the packed and shifted snow. "Lucky thing, too. Mine's still intact." He knocked his knuckles against his hat and rattled the pompom.

Fawn and Cade tramped up the slope. She glanced at Jax jogging after the runaway sled. "What you could use here is a chairlift."

Cade grinned, a little brighter than usual. "You're full of suggestions, aren't you? We thought about it, but we like sledding best when it's simple."

Fawn shrugged. "What's difficult or complicated about an entire ski lodge? Plenty of hills, tall and short. And you don't have to fight your way uphill in two feet of snow."

"You want a real battle?" Cade plodded to the hill's plateau. He discarded his black inner tube and picked up the green saucer. "This monstrosity is completely out of control."

Fawn gave it a skeptical once-over. "It doesn't look that challenging."

Cade clucked his tongue as he laid the saucer at the decline's apex. "Go ahead. Underestimate it. It only increases its power."

"Who said I was looking for a fight?"

"Don't tell me you're chicken." Cade's eyes glinted in the clear winter light. He rested himself inside the saucer's green edge.

Fawn threw her sled's rope down. "I might not be as fearless as you or Jax, but I'm not backing away from a perfectly harmless disk." She planted herself at the saucer's front and folded her legs in tight.

Cade put his hands on her waist and pulled her back toward him. "You gotta consider your center of gravity."

Fawn bristled at the implications. "I was. Don't I want to sit close to the front to balance you out? Not to mention, when did you ever let a silly little concept like *thinking* interrupt your fun?"

"You're right."

Cade shoved off in one brisk motion, and Fawn gripped the rope handles on either side of her. The saucer raced down the bank, forging an effortless path through the snow. Cade grabbed the handles, too, and the saucer rotated as it slid onto the level white terrain. Fawn closed her eyes as the revolution sped up, pulling her body sideways. She let loose a cry of exhilaration and uncertainty. Cade laughed behind her.

Fawn popped her eyes open. The saucer completed a full spin, traveling further than her yellow sled had from the same starting point. It aimed its passengers straight toward a twelve-foot evergreen. Scraggly branches covered its lower trunk. Fawn could only see them as signs of past accidents and collisions.

Fawn yelled over the racing wind. "We have to turn it!"

Cade stuck his head next to hers. "Can't."

Fawn tugged on the right-hand rope.

Cade shook his head. "What part of *out of control* don't you understand?"

Fawn exhaled a desperate huff and yanked harder on the handle. Six feet from the evergreen's pointed needles, Cade let go of the ropes. He slung one arm around Fawn and tackled her to the left. She tumbled off the disk with his weight behind her. Together, they hit the snow, its thick depth absorbing most of the impact. Fawn's whole body jolted. She blinked, lying in an indent compacted to her exact, sprawling shape. The green metal disk thumped against the tree trunk. Fawn sighed with relief, her muscles quivering.

The park rested still and silent. They'd averted crisis. Snowflakes melted into wet patches on her cheeks. From deep in her belly, Fawn laughed at the absurdity. Nothing hurt. The sunlight shimmered, uninhibited, off the scattered trees and continuous pure-white folds. Fawn guffawed, accepting her fate in the cradling snow. Cade's arm lingered over her, one of his legs a weight on her calf. He laughed with her, reclined past her left shoulder.

Rosario called out, breathless as her voice grew nearer. "Are you two okay?"

Jax sprinted at them from Fawn's peripheral vision, abandoning his sled. "Is this a gauze moment or a narrow scrape?"

Fawn laid her forehead on her wrist and cackled. Cade didn't make any moves to get up, either, his limbs entangled with hers.

Rosario's pink snow pants swished into view as she surveyed the scene. "Are you all right? That was a wicked jettison."

Fawn nodded. She wanted to get to her feet and collect the green saucer. She meant to answer Rosario's and Jax's concerned questions with real, verbal answers. But she snuck one peek at Cade's hysterical enjoyment and broke into even goofier howls at their misadventure.

When Fawn finally did compose herself just enough to peer up at Rosario, she expected to see shared humor or distant disdain. Instead, Rosario folded her arms. She held Fawn's gaze steadily, her emerald eyes glowing with a smug, suggestive knowing. She made a purposeful glance at Fawn's position in the snow up against Cade. Fawn found nothing romantic about crashing into the elements and could scarcely believe Rosario would read *romance* into their graceless predicament.

Cade pulled away from Fawn and extended his arms under him, raising himself out of the frigid landscape. Fawn rolled the other way and sat up. Jax extended his hands to her, and she let him hoist her up.

Jax offered Cade a fist bump. "You got incredible distance."

Fawn measured the length of their saucer trail with her eyes and brushed at her coat's slick exterior. Rosario shifted her knotted arms and watched Cade and Fawn, her mouth twisted awry, her eyes glinting.

~

The foyer chandelier's bright lights reflected off its dangling golden crystals. Fawn retrieved her thin chenille gloves from her coat pockets and put them on.

Almost no sound reached her from the rest of the large house. Voices trickled from the dining room and the den. Cade pried the front door open to the black, moonless night.

Fawn tucked her scarf ends under her coat to better insulate herself against the chill seeping into the room. "The others aren't coming?"

Cade's lips perked up in a gentle smile. "Come on."

He held the door open, and Fawn walked out ahead of him toward the dark driveway. As he secured the door shut behind them, a few outdoor lights flicked on, illuminating a grey-speckled frost-white horse. The bell-laden black harness hitched the horse to a sleek, vintage white sleigh upholstered in tufted red velvet. Black swirls and wispy loop-de-loops curled along the two-passenger sleigh's side.

Its unexpected beauty stopped Fawn's breathing. "I thought the others were joining us."

Cade answered quietly. "No. This is something special I planned just for you."

Hans strolled around the horse into the cool light and rested his hand on the harness.

Cade planted his palm on Fawn's back. "When you said at the hayride we should use horses to pull the wagon…"

Fawn shook her head and drew a breath. "I didn't mean…"

"Well." Cade gestured Fawn toward the sleigh. "It put this idea in my head. I'm sorry it comes three months later."

"That's okay." Fawn gravitated to the sleigh's single seat, her movements slow like in a dream. She propped her boot on a short metal step extended on two metal curves fixed under the sleigh's body. She boosted herself up and hesitated to sit down.

Cade strode over to Hans and shook his hand. "We're taking it. Thanks again."

Hans nodded. He produced something from his pocket and tucked two black pieces into his ears. Cade climbed up into the sleigh with Fawn. Hans scaled the other step up into the driver's seat, simpler and higher than the passengers' bench.

Fawn ran her gloved fingers over the ribbed top of the full back cushion. "It's so fancy. I bet this velvet is really soft."

"I thought you'd be used to fancy by now." Cade eased himself onto the seat.

"I would've thought so, too. This is different." Fawn claimed the vacant half of the bench to keep from looking rude or ungrateful.

Cade reached forward enough to tap Hans on the shoulder.

The driver held the reins in his firm fingers. "Walk."

The horse stepped forward, the sleigh skating along the semi-circular driveway.

Cade paused, turned slightly toward Fawn. "Hans can't hear anything we say."

"What are those things he uses?"

"Wireless earbuds. He listens to music, and if I call him, he takes my call."

Fawn's heart picked up its pace. "Why is it important he can't hear us talking?"

Cade still sounded more tense than his usual, casual self. "Maybe it's not. I just didn't want you to hold anything back, believing this wasn't a private conversation."

Fawn looked past Cade at the yard's passing, shadowed

trees. "Are we heading to the road? Is that good for the sleigh?"

"They didn't plow it today after yesterday's snow. We can use it."

"When you said…" Fawn licked her lips. "…for me to get my coat, I thought it was going to be a whole-family outing. Like the hayride. This is so elegant."

"Do you like it?"

"Very much."

Hans drove the sleigh onto the road's clean, unstirred snow.

Cade opened a compartment in the back of the driver's seat and withdrew a thick, folded fleece blanket. "In case you get chilled."

Fawn helped him spread the blanket over their legs. "Freezing temperatures seriously don't affect you?"

"They do, but not much. I don't see the enjoyment in that."

Fawn tucked the blanket's corner around her hip. "Everything really is about happiness and pleasure with you."

Cade's carefree grin popped into place. "Why not?"

"It's the opposite of how most people live. How we're taught to structure our lives."

"And does that make for a pleasant time?"

Fawn allowed a dry chuckle. "No, it's miserable."

"But you've learned so much here with us."

"I might be stubborn, but even I can learn a few new tricks in six months." Fawn's eyes widened. "It's okay that I'm still a guest here, isn't it?"

Cade replied easily. "Definitely."

Fawn relaxed against the tufted cushion with a sigh, relief comforting her chest.

Cade's fingers fidgeted on top of the blanket. "This isn't a goodbye ride, Fawn. It's to give you something you wanted, an experience you asked for."

"A gift?"

"Exactly."

Snow lined each wooden post and rail of the fence running

along the roadside. Beyond it, white patches dotted grey rocks and collected in bushes' bare branches. Silvery white sparkled, highlighting the straight lines and crooked forms of trees reaching to the dusky sky.

Fawn inhaled the cool, pure air. "You could make it snow right now, couldn't you?"

Cade tilted his head. "I could, but I wouldn't do that to you."

Fawn studied Cade as she hadn't in months, the faded-yet-bold colors of his swooping hair. The earnest, enigmatic intelligence shining in his charcoal-and-titanium eyes. The lips she had thought about kissing at the barbecue. She lowered her gaze to her own hands resting in her lap. "It hasn't always been easy and joyous here, though, right? It sucked to kick Lucius out and send him home."

Cade took a deep, steadying breath. "It did. We don't often think or talk about it."

"Because it's painful?"

Cade leaned an inch toward Fawn. "It doesn't do anyone any good. Does shame grow trees? Does guilt sprinkle snow on the hills? Do regret and self-punishment assist anybody in any way?"

Cade's earnestness and passion touched Fawn. She closed the space between them and gave Cade a long, firm kiss. She held his face in her gloved hands. His arms wrapped around her back, and Fawn pulled away enough to look at him. She hummed a low note of understanding. "This is why you said Hans is in his own private world. At the sled hill, Rosario knew there might be something more to us."

Cade enjoyed a barely audible chuckle. "Would you have come with me if I told you this might be a date?"

"I don't know. I'd like to think so, but the words might've scared me."

Cade kissed her cheek. "Why?"

Fawn focused on him with a prompting stare. "You can't imagine why I'd be a little reluctant to even go on one date with you? I mean, for starters, if it crashes and burns, it'd get pretty awkward with me staying at your house."

Cade tapped his fingertip against her chin. "We'd survive."

"Or I'd go home, which I am *not* ready to do for several reasons."

Cade grinned. "One of them being that you like me, or you wouldn't have kissed me."

Fawn wrestled with showing a genuine smile or a wry twist. "Okay, I can't hide from that. But you can see why I might be a bit intimidated or overwhelmed or insecure about letting myself become romantically involved with you?"

Cade ignored her protest and nuzzled the side of her neck. His breath felt warm against her skin as he spoke. "It's only daunting or disconcerting if you let it."

Fawn tipped her head to the other side, her eyelids drifting closed. Her uncertainty spiked, and she fluttered them open again. "Um, you're a maker of worlds and a traveler between dimensions. Your entire family toasts you just to say thanks. I—"

Cade set his index finger to her lips and leaned back. He took her hand. "Don't you think I've already realized all that and decided it doesn't matter? I don't care where you came from, what you think you're capable or incapable of, or what you'd like to say to discredit yourself. You're here with me now. I know who you are. And you kissed me, so… what are you trying to do? Take it back?"

"No, I'd never—" Fawn took in more of the still, silent beauty beyond the sleigh and its trotting horse. The stars in their foreign assortment hardly bothered her anymore. She slid her gloves off and laid her bare hands over Cade's. "You're not a prince or a king to your family, but you are to me. You've done nicer things for me as a new friend than my VP or Devon or any of the other guys I dated."

"Does that scare you?"

Fawn bit her lip. "Not in the usual way. It's more like, am I good enough for you on a cosmic scale? I'm worried I know more about what I'm getting myself into than you do. I've spent half a year in your house with your friends and family, learning your philosophies on life. What you've seen from me…"

Cade shook his head. "Shh. Shh, shh."

"The fear, the stress, the resistance."

"And after all this time, that's how you choose to define yourself?"

"Not on a normal day. But this is not a normal day."

Cade propped three fingertips of one hand against his chin. "Would you care to expound on that?" His grin baited her.

Fawn's mouth relaxed toward a smile. "You know how different it is. We've rarely spent any time alone. There are usually at least four other people around us." Fawn basked in the warmth of Cade's hand under hers. "But I don't want something that's convenient or rushed or shallow. That's why I'm reminding you I come with baggage."

"So do I. Did you not know how to look for it?"

"You mean your family? They're the best, brightest baggage I ever met."

Cade grew solemn but kept his voice soft. "My responsibility to my family is great and something I take very seriously."

"I know."

Cade picked up Fawn's hand. "But if you think I put them first in all things or would consistently remind you of their importance to me, you're mistaken." He kissed the backs of her fingers and laid her palm over his heart, where she felt the soft wool of his thin coat.

Fawn whispered. "Am I enough for you, Cade? Over weeks or months, am I going to be the woman you plucked from another world so you could help turn my life around? Or am I someone you're interested in for my determination and my strength?" She pressed her palm against his chest. "Do we stop this now, or am I enough?"

Cade held her hand in place on his coat and kissed her. "How could you not be? You spin through your universe riding on your planet the same way we all do."

Fawn balked. "That's a major simplification, and you still haven't answered me."

Cade lifted his free hand and teased Fawn's hat off her head. He dropped it in his lap and wiggled his fingers deep into Fawn's hair. He brushed his lips against hers several times before his mouth molded hers into an open shape. His tongue slid across hers, entwining and intoxicating. His other hand flexed around hers by the time he broke the kiss, staying so close his mouth almost touched Fawn's when he spoke. "Yes."

Heat burned through Fawn's body. She unfastened the top snaps holding her coat's extra flap secured over its zipper and slid the zipper pull down a couple inches. "That kiss kind of did your answering for you."

"I wanted you to have all the confirmation you wanted."

"You're not scared I want more than some scramble of an affair? I don't mind messy. Hard, I can do. As long as I know you're there and you care. I just can't be alone inside the illusion that I'm with someone."

"You shouldn't have to. And you wouldn't, not with me."

A lazy smile lit Fawn's face, and she placed a light, lingering kiss on Cade's lips. "I wanted to do that since I saw you walk onto the patio at the barbecue. That tux was made for you. Or you for it."

Cade shrugged. "It was custom tailored, of course." In a gentle movement, his finger traced a lock of Fawn's hair down from her temple and hooked it behind her ear.

Fawn leaned her cheek into Cade's hand. "When you told me about dimension hopping and creating everything I've seen, I almost forgot about being close to you. Dancing with you made me confused about what I'm truly after and why I'm here. It's a very attractive life you offer your guests."

Cade's eyebrows rose a fraction. "And?"

Fawn smirked. "I didn't know if I would or should make a move on you. I don't know how you fit into my life. I only know I like having you in it."

Cade pecked her lips. "I fell for you on the drive to the marina."

"Which one?"

"The first trip. We took the Mustang to introduce you to the pontoon boat."

"That was around my second full day here."

Cade brought Fawn's hand to his lips and kissed it. He still carried her other hand near his heart. "It was exactly your second full day here."

"You fall fast."

"I fall honestly. I don't judge whether it's fast or not."

Fawn's mouth gaped open. "That day in the car, we were just talking."

"I like talking with you."

"I didn't share anything brilliant."

"You're funny. Forthcoming. You like cars, and you play well with my family. What was I not supposed to like?"

Fawn took a breath, sure she could come up with a few points. Cade headed her off from speaking with a long kiss. She chuckled. "What were we talking about?"

Cade squeezed her hand. "We can talk as little or as much as you desire."

Fawn picked her hat up and pulled it on her head. She snuggled up to Cade and shared more lingering kisses with him. She curled up against him with his arm around her and watched the timeless scenery crawl by the sleigh.

In time, Cade pressed her closer and kissed her forehead. "Are you ready to go home?"

Fawn nodded.

Cade produced his phone from his coat pocket and operated it with his free hand. He set it to his ear. "Hans? Take us home."

The driver directed the horse off the road into an open field and made a wide turn in the untouched snow. He drove the horse onto the road in the opposite direction.

Fawn shifted her cheek against Cade's shoulder. He left his

phone on the blanket beside him and arranged more of the fleece over Fawn's upper body. They rode in silence all the way back to the house. Hans stopped the horse in the driveway. Cade draped the blanket on the seat next to Fawn. He helped her down from the sleigh and gave a thumbs-up to Hans. The driver waved, and Cade accompanied Fawn to the front door, his arm firm around her waist.

Fawn clutched his coat collar to get closer to him, his sweet, woodsy cologne tickling her nose. "Okay. Best date ever."

Cade pushed the door open. "For me, too."

They hurried in out of the cold, dim night. Cade locked the door, and they took off their coats. Cade hung them up, and they left their wet boots on the mat by the door. Cade strolled with Fawn up the nearest hallway.

Fawn marveled at the house's lack of sound, even quieter than it had been when they took off. "Is anybody here?"

"They might've gone to bed early."

"Did you tell them to do that?"

"I don't control everything." Cade guided Fawn past the snack kitchen. "Hungry?"

"No. Gerard doesn't skimp on dinner. And I always finish my plate."

"Tired?"

"Just really relaxed."

Cade led Fawn to her bedroom door. "Well, I can leave you here and bid you good night. Or you're welcome to join me in my room." Cade brushed his fingers against Fawn's hand. "Much like my kiss in the sleigh, I will let your actions speak for you. I'm going to my room, and you may follow me or not as you wish. It's up to you." Cade pressed his lips to the back of Fawn's hand. His eyes smoldered into hers. "But I had a fantastic ride with you."

Fawn's body fluttered in at least three places. Cade walked away, and Fawn stood like a statue in the hall outside her door. She'd never seen any room in the house she thought might've belonged to Cade. No one, not even Cade or Caroline, had pointed it out to her.

Fawn popped her door open. Her pulse thumped. Cade turned a corner, and Fawn nibbled a fingernail. If she lost track of him, she'd never find his room in this maze of doors and hallways. She took a half step into the doorway, toward her own bed. Its white comforter and three different pillows promised her the indulgent luxury she'd grown used to.

In an instant, Fawn pulled the door shut and jogged down the hall after Cade. She rounded the corner where he'd disappeared. He stood halfway up the long hall outside a closed door. Fawn slowed to a listless walk as she approached him.

Cade conjured up half his normal grin. "I knew you'd come."

"How?"

Cade's eyes glittered. "How could you not? After everything we've said, everything I've taught you?"

Fawn gestured behind her. "It was either lie awake in my room frustrated or be with you."

Cade swung the door ajar into the room, giving her a sly gaze. "Who says we're not making progress?" He flipped the light on.

Fawn rubbed her fingertips together. "I don't usually do this on a first date."

"Are you suggesting I do?"

Fawn fiddled with her shirt's ruffled collar. "No. You're just suave. You say all the right things. I haven't done this—" She pointed into the bedroom. "—in over a year."

Cade kissed her forehead. "Relax. Neither have I."

Fawn joked with him. "Too busy snowboarding and skiing and swimming…"

A flourish of Cade's hand ushered her into the room. Fawn stepped in, expecting an eclectic mix of chaotically colored knickknacks and mismatched furniture. Or perhaps sleek, modern pieces and high technology.

A black chandelier streamed light through a hundred round, faceted crystals arranged in a bowl shape. A metal, stemmed flower capped it at the bottom. To the left, the king-sized bed's rectangular headboard stretched flat and white halfway up the wall. Two cream leather pub chairs dotted opposite ends of the windowed back wall, angled toward the room's center. A rich sandalwood dresser and valet stand in a vintage French style with drooping, curved drawer pulls graced the right-hand wall. Between the two pieces of furniture hung a framed abstract, broken skyline of dark on aqua and white. A white, alpaca-wool rug covered most of the cornflower-blue carpeting.

Fawn looked over the room again, the bed's end tables matching its minimalist, smooth style. The lamps arranged on each table dangled crystals beneath their cylindrical, grey linen shades. "It's not at all like I thought it'd be."

Cade clicked the door shut. "So you've thought about my bedroom?"

"Not a lot. Not much at all." Fawn let Cade take her in his arms. "Are you going to turn everything I say into a flirtatious joke?"

"Why not?" Cade tightened his embrace around her. "See, you're looking at it only from your point of view. You say, 'A man from another dimension slipped into mine, took me home with him, and I fell for him.' But I say, 'I went searching for sources of joy, and I rescued a woman from herself, and I fell in love with her.'"

Fawn held onto Cade's arms. "I guess I didn't realize this could be special for you, too."

Cade touched his nose to Fawn's. "Couldn't it?"

Fawn's eyelids flitted closed. "I don't know."

Cade kissed her with a passion he'd reserved in the sleigh. It swept Fawn up in its breathless tangle of swoons and sighs.

When Cade broke the kiss, Fawn leaned her forehead against his chin. "I guess it is."

Cade picked her up in his arms and carried her to the bed. He laid her down on its thick royal-blue comforter, even more downy and plush than her own.

Fawn patted one hand against the comforter. "I thought your

bed would be bigger."

Cade leaned over her and grinned. "Shh. For the first time since you've been here, you talk too much."

Fawn played with his pointed, plaid collar sticking out from his thin navy sweater. "You said you like talking to me."

"Did you come to my room for conversation? I could've sat you in one of my pub chairs."

"Right." Fawn guided Cade's lips down to meet hers.

Cade stroked her cheek. "Are you still nervous? You're stalling."

Fawn took a deep breath. "It's the whole interdimensional angle. I imagine you having all kinds of unbridled experiences in places I've never been remotely close to."

Cade studied her lips. "Let's see if we can't replace those unfounded fears with something a little more physical and immediate."

His hand slid along the inside of Fawn's thigh over her fitted jeans. She held his face in her hands and kissed him. He climbed on the bed, and she tugged his sweater off. He set his chest against hers and kissed her deeper, interlacing his fingers with hers. Fawn choked back a moan.

Cade laid kisses along her jaw and whispered in her ear. "Don't hold back. There's more soundproofing around this room than the theater room."

Fawn sighed. "How come you get to talk and I—"

Cade's hand made contact directly between her legs.

The electric bolt through her body made Fawn arch her back. Her breath hitched. "Shutting up now."

Cade unfastened her jeans and glided them off her legs. He slipped her socks off and kneeled beside her. He passed his hand over his hair. Fawn rose up enough to circle her arms around his neck and weigh him down toward her. She undid the first buttons on his shirt, and he helped release the bottom ones. He pried the shirt off, and Fawn ran her palms up his muscled chest. Her fingers danced across his toned abs, extracting a long exhale of awe and desire.

Cade pulled her shirt off and tucked his first two fingers under her underwear band.

Fawn leaned her head back, whispering. "Yeah. Yeah, yeah."

The stretchy satin slid the length of her bare legs. Cade's hands dove under her back and unhooked her bra. Fawn sat up to let him take it off her.

He shook his head with a trembling chuckle. "You're so beautiful."

She frowned at his jeans. "You're way too dressed."

Cade smirked and reclined on his elbows. "Come fix it."

Fawn kissed him while she unfastened his pants. She wrenched them off and plucked his socks off his feet.

He flicked his eyebrows up, left looking like an underwear model at a photo shoot. "Still too dressed for you?"

"Not for long."

Cade's eyes glowed. He cradled Fawn's cheek and kissed her. Fawn pulled his underwear off and pressed adoring kisses over his chest. He tackled her onto her back and enveloped her in his arms. She matched all of his kisses, hot and wet and continuous. His hand alighted between her legs again, and she moaned. Fawn nodded, and Cade slid into her so gradually, her mind went blank at every sensation. She squeezed her fingers around his taut biceps.

Cade kissed her temple. "Do you want it fast or slow?"

Fawn wrapped her arms around his neck. "I just want you."

Cade's mouth devoured hers, and he thrust more deeply. Fawn loosened every sound stuck in her throat. Cade leaned them on their sides, where they writhed, plastered to each other, until they came. Cade kissed her without stopping for several minutes, caressing her hair and her back and her side.

Fawn panted, her legs once again entwined with Cade's. "I've never been loved like that."

Cade left a gentle kiss on her shoulder. "There's more. This isn't going away."

Fawn admired every shade of grey in Cade's irises, the perfect gold of his well-earned tan, and the chestnut hairs of his few-day stubble. "I could listen to you say that all day, every day."

Cade shared a long, soft kiss with her. "Stay in this bed with me, and I'll tell you whatever you want to hear."

Fawn laughed. "Let me guess. You have a micro kitchen hidden behind the painting."

"The snack kitchen's not that far away. As you've noticed, it's fully stocked."

Fawn giggled.

Cade made a guess. "Too many kitchens?"

"No. You have the right idea." Fawn poked a cranberry swirl of Cade's hair, and it moved. She combed her fingers through an entire section of it, flexible and feathery. "I always assumed your hair was stiff and tacky with two tons of product."

"I remember, from the restaurant."

"This is what you use your creative powers on? Your hair?"

"Why not?" Cade scooted up the bed and launched the decorative throw pillows onto the floor.

"Why those colors?" Fawn propped herself up on an elbow. "It looks like you dyed your hair in leftover Fruit Loops milk."

Cade grinned. "I like it. It brings me joy, and it makes me stand out."

"You like being the center of attention."

"In all the dimensions I visit."

Fawn clicked her fingernails against each other. "Do you have a last name at all because of where you come from?"

"No. We never needed one, especially here." Cade rested against the remaining pillows and the tall headboard. "Does it make me too mysterious?"

"Not a chance. What kind of a name is Cade, though?"

"I always thought it was a good one. What sort of name is Fawn?"

"It sounds youthful and perky." Fawn inched toward Cade and laid her hand on his thigh. "Can I tell you something if you promise not to laugh?"

Cade trailed his fingertips through Fawn's hair. "I'll try to hold it in. What's weighing on you?"

"I was scared to have sex with you. I pictured you having some bed that would dwarf a California king. The sex swing. The sex wedge."

Cade chuckled. "When I need them to have a good time, I'll make them."

"You're actually kind of *normal*, you know that?"

"I do."

Fawn trailed her fingertips along his cut abs. "I have another confession I'm less proud of."

"Mmm?" Cade swept Fawn's tresses off her neck.

"When I first came here, for a long time, I was convinced you were the laziest person I'd ever met. Irresponsible. Dangerous. After I learned who you are and what you do — for this place, for your family — I think you work harder than I do. You take on so much responsibility. You work diligently every day you're alive, whether it appears that way or not."

Cade slid down and lay face to face with Fawn. He took her hand. "One day, I swear, I will make you something special and magnificent. Something that moves you. Something you'll treasure. Something that shows you how much your being here means to me."

"I thought the sleigh ride was a gift for me."

Cade nodded. "It was. This would be bigger and better."

"Just two more questions."

Cade pressed a lingering kiss against Fawn's hand.

She hesitated. "What about Jax? He's hit on me pretty much every day I've been in this dimension."

"I'll take care of it."

Fawn nestled closer to Cade. "Should I go back to my room? I don't want to cause problems or have people looking for me."

Cade slapped his palm against the comforter. "You've been with us six months, and you're concerned about appearances?

How are you still so uptight?"

"It's nobody's business what we did or what we're doing."

Cade eased himself off the bed and retrieved his phone from a gold, two-tiered mid-century beverage cart by the door. He tapped the screen a few times and set the phone to his ear. He rubbed the back of his neck. "Yes, Caroline, it's Cade. I wanted to let you know Fawn won't be using her bedroom this evening and not to fret. I'll see you in the morning. Maybe. Thanks." Cade hung up and flopped his phone down on the cart.

Fawn gasped and pointed at the phone in horror. "You disturbed Caroline for this?"

Cade shrugged. "I left her a message. I didn't disturb anyone." He came over and sat on the bed.

Fawn grazed her hand up and down his arm. "Do you think they'll approve of me being with you? Your friends and family and the people working for you?"

Cade's voice warmed. "They'll approve."

"Because you'll make them?"

"Because they like you. If they don't approve, I can banish them from this dimension until they do." He spared her a brief kiss. "But I doubt it'll devolve to that."

~

Golden morning sunlight poured into Cade's bedroom. Fawn stood by the floor-to-ceiling windows filling the back wall, serene with reassurance and peace. The streaming beams left silver shadows across the snow from the naked trees and thicker evergreens. From the open door to Fawn's left, the hair dryer whooshed.

Her mouth curved in an easy smile. She directed her gaze further out, to the woods at the edge of the property.

Out of nowhere, a figure moved into Fawn's peripheral vision right outside the window. She shrieked and jumped back, covering herself as best she could. Emilian glanced in at her, bundled up in a hat, scarf, and coat. He offered a distracted but polite wave. His steps followed the clear stone-paved path running alongside the house. He shoved his hands into his pockets and passed out of sight.

The hair dryer silenced. Cade wandered out of the bathroom, his canary-and-strawberry hair hanging down in waves.

Fawn motioned out the window, still hiding behind her other hand. Her pulse raced. "Emilian just saw me... in my natural state."

Cade hummed. "That's why we don't linger right next to the windows at certain times of the morning unless we don't mind that sort of run-in. Are you okay?"

"I guess. He just kept walking. It's not my number one choice for how to jumpstart my day." Fawn gestured around the undressed windows. "Why don't you have curtains? Isn't that more to the point than keeping a distance from the windows?"

Cade shrugged. "I don't like the way curtains look in here. I like the sun." Cade stood behind Fawn and wrapped his arms around her waist. "If you decide to spend most of your nights in my room, we can have Caroline transfer your robes and other clothes into my closets."

Fawn closed her eyes. "Of course you have more than one. But what about your clothes?"

"I'll get rid of some. I don't wear all of them, anyway." Cade kissed her cheek.

Fawn opened her eyes and turned to face him. "What's the best way to break the news about us to your family?"

"Start small." Cade crossed the bedroom to a speaker panel in the wall by the door. He pushed a button. "Jax? Sibling breakfast in the snack kitchen. Tell the others for me." Cade came back to Fawn, styling locks of his hair at whim with absent fingers. Each one stayed perfectly in place.

Fawn planted her hands on her hips. "That's starting small around here? Telling four people we hang out with every day?"

Cade offered a small grin. "They also happen to be my best

friends who want the best for me. I thought you'd find it less intimidating than telling my parents."

Fawn twisted one of her tresses, and her heart slowed. "Oh, your parents."

Cade's shoulders slumped. "I thought we'd chased all the fear out of you."

"I've only been in two dimensions, and…"

Cade patted her hand. "They adore you. So do my siblings. We should get dressed unless we want to make this really awkward." Cade went to the closet beside the bathroom. "Let me get you something I haven't worn yet."

"You're sure you'll have something that can fit me?" Fawn ruffled her hair and rolled her eyes. "Of course you're sure."

Cade emerged carrying a white terrycloth robe, grey t-shirt, and drawstring pants. "Good enough?"

Fawn felt the thick, lavish terrycloth. "This is hotel-spa quality. It's wonderful."

She dressed quickly while Cade threw on a dusky t-shirt and striped periwinkle-and-navy sleep pants. He tucked her arm around his elbow and led her out of the room.

Fawn glanced both ways at the empty hallway. "I have no idea how to get to the snack kitchen from here."

"Did you forget how you got to my room last night?" Cade winked and guided her to the left.

Fawn bounced her shoulder off Cade's. "Some of it might be a blur, but most of it isn't."

They turned a corner and strolled past Fawn's room.

She freed her arm from Cade's. "I don't want to give the secret away right off the bat."

Cade snuck a kiss to her cheek. They meandered up to the snack kitchen's granite island. Yoselle sat up on her usual stool, kicking her feet in opposition to each other. Jax stood shirtless behind the island, and the other two sisters perched on their counter-height seats.

Yoselle groaned and shifted her shoulders. "Why do we have

to eat in here instead of the dining room? I'm missing out on priceless Kee time."

Fawn reclaimed her stool next to Lisette.

Cade rounded the island and clapped a hand on Jax's shoulder. "I have an important announcement."

Rosario straightened up and rubbed her palms together. "This oughtta be a good one. You know I despise bad news before I die."

"For me, it's good, and I hope you'll be happy for me. For us. Fawn and I are dating now."

The three sisters gasped, their completely different emotions combining into a single complex sound. Stunned shock mixed with high-pitched glee and excited hope.

Cade squeezed Jax's shoulder. "The flirtation game's over for you, my friend."

Jax slapped Cade on the back. "Hey, that's great. I didn't mean anything by it."

Fawn smirked. "Yeah, you did."

Jax splayed his fingers. "Okay, I did. But that stops now. I promise. That's really cool."

Rosario squealed with delight. "I can forgive a late breakfast for this. Thank goodness. Does this mean Jax comes fully dressed to morning meals?"

Yoselle reached over and grabbed Fawn's hand. She'd changed her gold bullring back to the silver one, and her full smile dazzled. "Fawn, does that mean you're staying even longer?"

Fawn faked a pout. "How come everyone thinks I'm leaving sometime soon? I'm not going anywhere."

"Yes! It's almost like having another sister." Yoselle held her hands up. "*Almost.* No pressure."

Jax leaned on the island and shot Yoselle an amused grin. "Man, you've changed."

Yoselle stuck her tongue out. "I don't have to hide my relationship, thanks to Fawn. Now she doesn't, either."

Lisette cleared her throat and sipped her orange juice.

"Congratulations."

Fawn smiled up at Cade. "Thanks."

Cade glanced at the empty counter tops and then at Jax. "Where's breakfast?"

Jax drummed his index fingers on the granite. "Gerard's bringing it in a few minutes. He has to cart it over from the dining room."

Rosario propped her forearms on the island's edge. "Have you told Mom and Dad yet? You know they'll want to know as soon as possible. They're gonna freak out."

Fawn raised her eyebrows. "Is that good or bad?"

Cade retained his cool. "It's good."

Rosario nodded. "I know for a fact our mother wants to get to know you better, Fawn. She told me herself."

Yoselle bobbed her head up and down. "Yeah, it's gonna be fine."

Fawn grumbled. "Easy for you to say. Did you ever meet Kee's parents?"

Yoselle shook with a self-satisfied giggle. "Nope, they're a few dimensions away."

Cade smacked his palm on the island, grabbing everyone's attention. "We're telling Mom and Dad after we eat. And it's going to be phenomenal."

Chapter Seven

Thin, shallow patches of dirt-tinged snow littered the verdant grass. Fawn sat in one of the oversized lawn chairs on the pool's patio, staring off at the dwindling signs of winter. The dogs bounded and yelped across the lawn beyond the patio. Henna leapt with them, bundled in a cable-knit sweater, jeggings, and suede boots. She teased the dogs with a high-pitched squeeze toy shaped like a hot dog. She threw it as far as she could, and the dogs raced off after it. Fawn and Henna shared a chuckle before Henna ran off to join the animals.

Fawn swept her fingers lightly over the back of her left hand, where Henna's handiwork had stained dark ruby in a mehndi pattern of threaded beads. The dainty design curved three strands of complementary lengths from the base of her pinky down, over, and up where they encircled her index finger like a ring. The pigments had barely started to fade.

One of the double doors whisked open, and Cade came to rest himself in the chair next to Fawn.

She gestured at the poor excuses for snowdrifts. "I'm actually sorry to see the snow go. The sledding. Movie nights in the theater room huddled under blankets with the cats nestled up to us. Even the opera. Especially the sleigh rides and the hot stone treatments at the spa."

Cade rubbed Fawn's knee over her light-blue, fitted jeans. "Every season carries its gifts and its bothers."

Fawn twisted her mouth into a thoughtful frown. "I won't miss falling over so much on those hills, though. Sledding, I can do. Snowboarding and skiing aren't natural to me."

"That's what memories are for. And next winter."

Fawn gave in to a smile. "I'll always remember putting the top up on the Mustang and riding around to look at all the holiday lights with you. Leaning my head on your arm and holding your hand."

Cade lit up his smile as well. "Spring might not bring hot stones, but we do enjoy the hot springs. We pack picnics to eat in the park. We go white-water rafting. We ride bicycles all over the countryside, down by the beach, and over to this general store with vintage candy."

Fawn hummed in appreciation, feeling the new season's warmth already. "Sounds wonderful."

"And..." Cade dipped his hand into his army-green jacket pocket. He held up two tickets. "...I got us in to see the outdoor concert tonight in town."

Fawn threw her arms around him, her heart singing. "Do we get to dress up and everything?"

Cade leaned his head against hers. "We can if you want."

"I do. I don't care if we're the fanciest people there." She planted a long kiss on his neck. "You're already the best boyfriend, you know. You can stop trying to outdo yourself."

Cade shook his head. "That's not my way. If you're really excited about spring, maybe my mother will take you for a hair-raising spin in her Venom."

Fawn's laugh trembled. "I'm not sure I'm brave enough for that. I did look at it, though, in your parents' garage. Your mom let me sit in it."

"I know. You raved about it for an hour."

After dinner, Fawn adorned herself in a long, shell-pink satin gown. Caroline helped her pick out aquamarine and peridot rings for her fingers.

Caroline couldn't stop beaming.

Fawn checked her chandelier earrings to make sure the bead drops hung straight down. Her mouth curled in a self-conscious grin. "What?"

"I'm so happy to see you two together."

Fawn let Caroline clasp a dainty, silver bracelet around her wrist. "We've been dating a couple months. You treat it like it's brand new."

"I treat it like the sweet celebration it is." Caroline's brown eyes gleamed. "And I know you're hiding behind that vague figure."

Fawn acquiesced with an exhale. "A hundred and seven days."

"That's more like it. I'm thrilled for both of you. You're nice people, and you complement each other well."

Fawn sat down on the vanity bench and strapped her opalescent high heels on.

Caroline shut the jewelry armoire's open drawers and lid. She lifted a silver rope chain from her apron pocket. "I want you to have something. It would honor me if you would take it and wear it tonight." Caroline showed Fawn the pendant, a carnelian oval so dark, it was more burgundy than fiery orange. "It'd look so striking against your dress. It was passed down through my family. My mother entrusted it to me when I turned sixteen."

Fawn's mouth hung ajar. She almost couldn't find her words. "Caroline, I can't accept it. Don't you want to hand it down to your daughter?"

"I have plenty to bequeath to her. Dishes, linens, a drawer full of my mother's and my grandmothers' jewelry. Please, *mija*. It would make me so happy to see you wear it."

Fawn nodded.

Caroline fastened it at the nape of Fawn's neck. The housekeeper clapped when she saw the pendant in place. "*Perfecto.* Mr. Cade will like it, too."

Fawn hugged Caroline before she waltzed out of her bedroom, which became less familiar by the day.

Cade waited for her in the foyer, holding her magenta trench coat. He greeted her with a kiss. "Flawless."

Fawn danced her fingers over the carnelian pendant. "Caroline gifted me her family heirloom."

Cade slipped Fawn's coat over her arms to her shoulders. "That was kind of her."

Fawn stole another kiss, and Cade escorted her out the front door to the Mustang idling in the driveway. The concert music washed over Fawn for two hours like an exciting dream. Sometimes, the orchestra bowed so fast, the split-second notes made her pulse race. On the smooth, slow songs, Fawn took flight, feeling Cade's arm ever around her.

Fawn rode home humming tunes she'd forgotten the titles and composers of. She fell across the bottom half of Cade's bed, her legs dangling over the edge. He hovered over her, steadying himself on one hand. One kiss led to more and capping the night off with a tangle in the sheets. Fawn fell asleep with her back nestled against Cade's chest, satiated and at ease.

In the morning, Fawn threw a tropical-patterned silk robe on and crept out of Cade's room. Three doors away, at the corridor's end, a latch clicked.

Fawn met Jax's gaze, surprised to see it turn guarded and sheepish. She smiled at the sense of mystery he didn't often display.

Jax straightened the button-down shirt he'd worn the night before. He whispered. "Where are you going?"

Fawn pointed down the left-hand end of the corridor. "To my room. I wanted to get something." She aimed her finger at the door Jax had just emerged from. "Whose room is that?"

Jax wiped his palms on his khakis and allowed himself a brighter, honest grin. "Ofelia's."

"Ahh." Fawn nodded. "I thought she liked you."

"Well, unlike you, what I'm doing is on the down-low for now. So…" Jax winked. He grunted in displeasure and swiped his hands through the air. "Not a flirty wink. A secretive gesture."

Fawn cracked a smile. "It's okay. I got it. Lips are sealed."

"Thanks." Jax strode away up the hallway across from him.

Fawn continued to her room, warmed by all the romances taking place within the house's many walls. She let herself into her old bedroom, finding it almost foreign to her. She collected her lip gloss from her purse and wandered back to Cade's room.

They showered together in the double-wide stall, tiled in tan-

and-green travertine and finished with glass-panel walls. They dressed simply and casually in muted hues before striking off hand in hand for the dining room. They laughed at Vanna's and Rory's jokes. They appreciated Yoselle and Kee's absence from the table, off sharing a private meal somewhere. Lisette bent her head close to Emilian's in quiet, solemn conversation. Fawn said nothing about Jax and Ofelia's innocent squabbles over their favorite breakfast foods. When two cats showed up beside the table, Fawn giggled uncontrollably while Henna gave in and squeezed both their furry bodies onto her lap. Gerard introduced fresh maple syrup for the breakfast's banana-walnut pancakes, and Fawn embraced it with the hearty applause the rest of the diners received it with. Cade fed Fawn her first bite soaked in syrup, and the group banged on the table with raucous cheers. Fawn savored the different levels of sweetness on her tongue and bowed over the table to her rowdy audience.

~

Fawn walked with a bounce in her step. Pop music stuck in her head, making her feel light and floaty at Cade's side. Trading her ruffled dress for her silky robe hadn't dimmed her glowing mood. She tried to keep her excitable voice down, traversing the halls from Cade's room to the snack kitchen. She turned a sly grin on him. "This party was almost as good as the barbecue. Except maybe better because I got to dance with you almost the whole night."

Cade beamed like the cat who ate the canary. "Glad to hear that ranks higher on your list than stumbling our way through one song's strained conversation."

"It wasn't that bad. I still enjoyed it." Fawn veered around the corner. She approached the snack kitchen's island and rested her elbow on it. "What's stocked in here tonight?"

Cade pulled a cheese plate from the fridge and produced a jar of chocolate-covered macadamia nuts from a cabinet.

Fawn straightened up from the granite and bounced up and down. "You're so bad, you're amazing. Those look great."

Cade stashed them on the counter and searched the fridge some more.

The song in Fawn's head reached a crescendo. Fawn moved her body in subtle, rhythmic increments in the hallway light. "Dancing outside in the spring feels so different from doing it in the summer. Lighter. And the flowers around the patio are gorgeous."

Cade set a bowl of cherries on the counter. "None of them hold a candle to you."

Fawn's nose scrunched up. "I don't think you can really compare me to a peony or a hyacinth."

"Specifically, no, but you are beautiful. You were absolutely enchanting tonight."

Fawn hummed a few of the notes sailing through her head. "Nobody puts a playlist together like Rosario."

Cade folded his lower lip down. "I compliment you, and you praise my sister?"

"Her picks are stubbornly sticky." Fawn held her fingertip to her chin, teasing Cade in return. "Jax looked dashing, but then he'd have to in order to impress Ofelia."

Cade chuckled wryly. "Don't leave out Yoselle and Lisette."

Fawn's shoulders collapsed, and she faked a tired sigh. "But then I'd have to run through all our friends, and that would take hours. I guess I can skip to lauding you."

Cade broadened his grin and tipped his head toward Fawn. "Or you can show me what you thought of me." Cade eased himself behind Fawn and turned her toward the island counter with gentle fingers. He kissed the back of her neck. "Dancing under the stars. Swaying so close to me." He breathed in her sensual perfume. "The tux."

The pop song faded away, and Fawn released a smooth exhale. "I do like that tux. And you in it."

Cade nibbled her ear. "How much do you like it?"

"A lot."

Cade slid his hand up Fawn's thigh, raising the hem of her short robe.

Fawn pushed against his hand with a sharp gasp. "Are you crazy? Two major hallways converge here. Somebody could see us."

Cade lowered his voice. "Nobody leaves their rooms at night."

"We did." Fawn gestured to the snacks on the counter.

"You don't think they're sleeping or otherwise occupied?" Cade's lips grazed the edge of Fawn's ear. "Hmm?"

She shivered from her neck to her feet and recalculated the amount of light reaching them from the hallway. "You've expanded my comfort zone beyond the point of reason, sir."

Cade purred. "Isn't that where the most fun is to be had?"

"Finally, we've narrowed your entire philosophy down to a mantra."

Cade turned Fawn's head and kissed her. He bent her a few inches over the granite, one hand hiking up the side of her robe.

Fawn reached her hand back and glided it down the flannel leg of Cade's sleep pants. "We're gonna get caught."

"We won't."

Cade clenched her robe collar in his teeth and tugged it away from Fawn's neck. He kissed the top of her bared shoulder, and she melted. He patted the underside of her bottom, and when he pressed himself against her, she grabbed his pant leg to pull him toward her. Cade leaned his chest against her back, and she felt his heat radiating through her thin robe. He entered her, and Fawn's other hand clutched the granite's edge. She pressed her lips together to keep from making a sound. Cade ran his palm over her stomach, smoothing and bunching her robe's material.

Fawn dropped her head back, Cade's temple touching her own. They finished in a dozen hard strokes, panting and sweating. Fawn slumped herself in a dramatic heave over the island. Cade kissed her cheek and withdrew himself. He straightened his pants.

Fawn arranged her robe over herself. She glanced around as if seeing with new eyes both alert and relaxed. Her mind had gone completely blank. "What did we come here for?"

Cade stepped over and picked up some of the snacks.

"Gotcha."

"Get more food if you want it."

Fawn held a hand to her head to make it focus more sharply. She shook away the calm, fuzzy feeling and walked over to the cabinets. She retrieved a jar of pretzel sticks. On second thought, she also snatched a canister of Gerard's homemade peanut biscotti. She giggled at herself as she and Cade walked back to his room. He laughed with her softly.

When the sun rose in the morning and glinted off the flower leaves' dewdrops, Fawn gravitated toward the huge windows. The ample light bathed her body in yellow tones and welcoming heat.

Emilian stumbled into view, jostled off-balance by the five dogs darting and leaping around his legs. He caught Fawn's eye and waved. Fawn returned the gesture, and Emilian directed the dogs further up the path past the windows.

Fawn drew in a lengthy breath and released it. She sought out the butterfly garden straight back and to the right. Sunset-orange monarchs and bright-yellow swallowtails flitted about the trees and daylilies. Birds serenaded and chirruped from the crystalline water collected in the stone birdbath off to Fawn's left.

Cade padded up behind her and wrapped her in his arms. "What are we looking at?"

"Everything." Fawn laid her hands over Cade's. The serene satisfaction that filled her must have been the same kind the sun felt as it shone down and toasted the air. "I don't think any life could feel better than this."

~

The wooden platform wrapped around the colossal oak's wide trunk twenty feet above the ground. Fawn maintained a loose grip on the safety line connecting her harness to the rope between this tree and another one encircled by a similar platform fifty feet away. Rosario's forceful screams and laughter radiated through the open spaces while she rode the zipline to the next ledge. Her wavy dark hair fluttered in the breeze and threatened to spring loose from its cage of bobby pins.

Lisette stood next to Fawn in barely amused silence with Yoselle on her other side.

Yoselle's pink camouflage t-shirt and black yoga pants kept her conspicuous amongst the brown branches and countless shades of green leaves. She cupped her hands around her mouth. "Go, Rosario!"

Rosario howled in answer.

Fawn inhaled the aromas of rich, heady earth and sweet, clean leaves surrounding them. "I wish Jacqui and Henna could've come with us."

Lisette chirped up in an even tone. "Sisters and you only today."

The nearby guide in her red helmet gestured to Yoselle. "Are you ready?"

Yoselle bucked her chin up. "Born ready."

The guide's focused eyes sparkled above her freckled nose. She transferred Yoselle's snaphook from the rope attached around the tree to the zipline. She checked to make sure Rosario had landed on her feet at the other end and cleared out of Yoselle's way. "You're good to go."

"You bet your ass I am." Yoselle jumped off the platform's edge, hanging in a smooth glide through the woods' airspace.

Rosario beckoned to her, hollering. "Come on, sis!"

Yoselle snickered. "Straight atcha!"

Fawn laughed with them, enjoying her adventure but glad to wait her turn.

Lisette eyed Fawn sidelong. "How are you holding up?"

Fawn tugged on the legs of her knee-length shorts, but the straps hugging her thighs wouldn't let the fabric budge. "I'm awake and unscathed. My old fear of heights doesn't really bother me anymore. Quite a change from the water park last year, huh?"

Lisette filled her chest with a deep breath. "Yeah," she said, her voice clipped. "After an hour and a half of this, you're going strong?"

"Yeah." Fawn glanced at the empty place on the platform by the guide. "Do you want to go, or should I?"

The guide inched toward the snaphooks fastened to the tree's safety rope.

Lisette waved the guide back, her attention staying on Fawn. "Summer's just about here again."

Fawn beamed, crawling with enthusiasm over the plans she'd made for herself. "I know. Another week or two, and I'll be back at Fun Splash. I think I'm gonna conquer it this year. I'll have the whole summer, including the precious time before school lets out. It'll be less crowded, and I can go on every single ride. I'm gonna nail down what my favorites are this year."

"Is that right?"

"Yeah."

Lisette clucked her tongue several times. "You know, we wouldn't even have the water park if it weren't for Evan."

Fawn bunched her eyebrows up and chuckled. "What's that mean? Is he the owner or something?"

Lisette looked Fawn dead in the eye. "He inspired it."

Fawn exhaled, her humor draining away. No play lurked in Lisette's glinting brown irises. "What do you mean? What kind of an answer is that?"

"The truth."

The guide stepped around to where the two patrons could see her. "Are you ladies sliding to the next station soon?"

Lisette ground her teeth together. "You'll give us a minute. We paid for our time here, and I won't be rushed just because we got the group rate."

The guide disappeared around the other side of the tree.

Fawn studied the frustrated grooves in Lisette's forehead and the purse of her lips. "Lisette, what's going on?"

Lisette took her ponytail holder out and made quick work of tying her blonde locks back again, high and tight. "Look. I'm doing you a favor bringing this up and staying on this platform with you to discuss it through. I could just as easily zipline ahead of you for the remaining hour and a half, keeping you behind me, guessing and worrying."

Fawn's breakfast of waffles and strawberry crêpes rippled in her stomach. "About what?"

"This isn't my place, but it needs to be said. Has my brother — has Cade — told you he'll create something special for you?"

Fawn's heart cringed. "Yes."

"Of course he has."

"Why is that bad?"

Lisette tapped the toe of her boot against the wooden platform and folded her arms. "We didn't used to have a water park. Evan was a guest in our house, and before he left for home, Cade made Fun Splash because Evan wished we had more summer activities than just the lake."

Fawn stared at Lisette, her brain waiting and foggy.

Lisette huffed. "Okay. Marjorie. When she was about to move out of the guest room, Cade gave us all skis and forged that cross-country trail through the other side of the park. Because Marjorie lived in Canada, and she missed some of her favorite pastimes."

Unease made Fawn's muscles twitch. "Guests from where?"

Lisette propped her hand against the oak's stiff bark. "Jeremiah stayed with us for a few months. He was an interesting character. Half British, half Filipino. He's the reason we have a restaurant in town that serves authentic fish and chips alongside sinigang and cassava cake. A restaurant, by the way, my brother created."

Fawn gulped. "With his mind or magic or whatever."

"Yeah."

Fawn swallowed again, overly conscious of the tickle of saliva dispatching down her throat. "I'm not the only guest you've had."

Lisette leaned closer to Fawn's face. "Bingo."

Long-forgotten scraps of Cade's conversation fought to become coherent strings of words instead of remaining elusive, broken threads. "I think I knew that. I might've gotten that impression somehow."

"Cade might've mentioned it at Smuckey's."

Fawn blinked at Lisette in confusion.

Lisette's nostrils flared. "The restaurant in your dimension that an actual business owner conceived of, planned for, set up, opened, and was operating a year ago when you met my brother there."

A privacy fence of evergreens had surrounded the patio where Monica gushed over Cade. Fawn had walked out Smuckey's front doors with Cade, letting his nonsensical claims go over her head. They didn't seem vital then. Fawn slapped her forehead now. "The others Cade brought to the house from other dimensions."

Lisette smirked. "Now you're getting it."

Fawn lunged a half-step at Lisette. "Stop toying with me and tell me whatever you think is so damn important."

Lisette's lip curled a little as she surveyed Fawn from her hair to her sneakers. "You're not here to become one of us. You're here for rehab because you were running your life back home off the rails."

Fawn snorted. "So what? I'm allowed to stay here as long as I want. I've been dating Cade for six months. I don't even use my—" She caught her word choice and cleared her throat. "The guest room anymore. You or Cade or anybody else can invite whomever you want to fill it."

Lisette shook her head. "One at a time, Fawn. That's the rule. It's a good rule. Sometimes, my brother needs to be kept in check or guided."

Fire burned in Fawn. "Cade doesn't need you or anyone else to tell him what to do."

"You're wrong. He does." Lisette scanned the treetops

underlining the infinite, cerulean sky. "He's a master of creation. I'll give him that. We all will. He's a master of himself most of the time."

"You're not his mother, and he's not a child."

Lisette patted the tree bark. "Our mother dotes on him, as she should. That's fine. If it falls to me to be the practical one, the one who remembers what's at stake, so be it. And often, it does."

Fawn pierced Lisette with a challenging gaze. "What's at stake, Lisette?"

"You wouldn't understand. You can't do what we do. You haven't trained yourself."

Fawn squared her sneakers to Lisette's boots. "I've lived here for a year, spending hours every single day with at least one of you. I know things by now. I understand more than you give me credit for."

Lisette hung her arms at her sides. "Dozens, Fawn. My brother's ferried almost a hundred people into our dimension and set them up as guests in our home."

Fawn's chest stung, but she refused to wince in front of Lisette. "Are you jealous I'm taking Cade's attention and time away from you?"

Lisette counted on her fingers. "We used to have our own boat launch until Cade built the marina to impress Marisol. He thought it'd be more fun to have countless vessels in the water instead of just ours. Cade made the planetarium for Antony, the vineyard for Kiki, the old-timey barbershop for Kelvin, and the sleigh for Patricia. She was an antiques dealer convinced she'd been born in the wrong century."

Reeling, Fawn grabbed hold of her safety line. "What does any of this have to do with me?"

Lisette scoffed. "You know I'm not naive enough to believe you don't get it by now."

Fawn glared at her.

Lisette motioned for the guide. "I won't tell you any more. You'll have to go to my brother for that."

"I plan to."

"Good." Lisette zeroed in on Fawn's double grip around the safety line. "Would you prefer to be assisted down from this point, or are you steady enough to finish the course in the air?"

Fawn lowered her hands, her tone steely. "I'll zipline it."

"Great." Lisette disengaged her snaphook from the tree's rope and secured it to the zipline. She addressed the guide. "Be a doll and help Fawn."

Lisette leapt off the platform, speeding away from the oak. Fawn stared after her, only seeing half the details in blotchy, different-colored smudges. Rosario and Yoselle had already moved on out of sight. Fawn felt a thousand miles away from the guide a foot to her left. For the first moment in almost twelve months, Fawn suffered alone.

~

Several minutes after Rosario, Lisette, and Yoselle entered the house, Fawn skulked out of the SUV. She marched across the driveway and mounted the stairs to the front porch. She tore the door open and rushed into the foyer, slamming the door in her haste. Fawn strode up the right-hand hall past the guest room, which she growled at in fury. She rounded a corner and speed-walked the rest of the way to the bedroom she shared with Cade.

She stormed inside it, looking for him. "Cade?" She pried her sneakers off and dumped them on the carpet. Her anger shook her, and she pulled off the rest of her clothes. She checked the bathroom for him before throwing on a plain yellow polo shirt and jeans. Fawn kicked her sneakers into the corner behind Cade's valet stand and tied on a pair of outdoor boots from the closet. She tried to push the ire out of her with her outbreaths, but the majority of it clung to her sinews and her lungs.

Cade strolled into the doorway and knocked on the jamb. "Here you are. How was your afternoon with my sisters?"

Fawn approached him with slow, stiff steps. "Can I talk to

you?"

"Sure."

"In private."

Cade moved to close the bedroom door.

Fawn stopped its swinging with a smack of her flat palm. "Not here. How about in the garden, where there's fresh air? No one's out there, are they?"

"Not to my knowledge." Cade kept his tone casual, but a concern in his eyes belied it. "Everybody else is out shopping, walking the beach, or holed up in the den, waiting for dinner."

Fawn nodded. With a grim set to her lips, she led Cade down the hall to the nearest outer door. They took the paved walkway around part of the house to the start of the garden path. They walked under the entry trellis covered in pink clematis and snow-white jasmine. The flowers filled Fawn's nose with intoxicating, romantic scents that only fueled her outrage.

Cade raised his golden face to the sun's glow. "Perfect weather today."

Fawn controlled her temper enough to prevent herself from snapping at him. "I had a talk with Lisette while we were on the course."

Cade glanced away at soft clumps of purple wisteria hanging from a sturdy iron pergola. A cushioned rattan loveseat and a pair of matching chairs sat in the shade beneath it. He braved Fawn's gaze, the corners of his mouth weighed down. "What kind of conversation?"

"I'm glad you're taking this seriously because it wasn't pleasant."

Cade halted his trek through the garden and laid his hand on Fawn's forearm. "Why wouldn't I treat it seriously? You're practically vibrating with rage."

Fawn lowered her arm from Cade's touch. The garden spread out around them, blocking the sound and view of the rest of the grounds. "She told me how many people have been here, how many guests you've hosted from other dimensions."

Cade's eyes sank closed. He buried his fingers in his two-tone hair. "That wasn't her place."

"So she said."

"What else did she mention?"

Fawn barked his name. "Cade."

His eyes flew open.

"You hid things from me, and that's all you can say?" Fawn's voice almost failed her. "You knew... You knew — fully — when you invited me into this dimension other men had lied to me and wedged a distance between themselves and me. And I hated that." She screamed at him. "Lisette told me she wasn't even letting me know the whole story."

A sob filled Fawn's throat, and she crumbled to her knees. She cried, not even caring if Cade saw it. "This entire year has been a lie, hasn't it?"

"No." Cade dropped onto one knee, meeting Fawn with a rigid jaw. "Lisette overstepped her boundaries, and I'll deal with her. But I'm not losing you because of this."

Frustrated laughter bubbled out of Fawn. "I was never supposed to *be* with you. Don't you get it? Lisette made it pretty clear you brought me here to let me rest and unwind all the damage I did to myself before you took an interest in me."

Cade lightened his sternness. "I brought you here to give you a chance you weren't going to get where you came from. You didn't know how to help yourself. You couldn't carve out time in your schedule in which to figure out if you wanted to keep working the job that was killing you."

"Did you whisk me here to rehab me or to date me? To be a counselor or my friend?"

Cade answered solemnly. "You're here to get your feet back under you. To catch a break and settle everything that had balled up into an unhealthy mess."

"Answer my questions."

Cade observed her for a moment. "I let people rehab themselves. I had no other intentions when I transported you here."

Fawn narrowed her eyes. "Not even to befriend me?"

Cade shrugged. "I allow life to take its wandering path. I forge close friendships with most of the people I entertain. I don't have to seek it out."

Fawn wiped tears off her cheeks in curt motions with the base of her thumb. "What about dating? Did you have romantic relationships with anyone else you invited into your house?" Her stomach clenched, and she shook her head. "You don't need to respond to that. I sound stupid just asking it."

Cade laid his hand over Fawn's knee, barely connecting with it. "I had brief affairs with three of them. Jax romanced more of them than I did."

"You repeatedly told me I could stay here. I told you I wanted an honest relationship."

"I'm sorry. Everything I relayed to you was true."

Fawn slipped sideways onto her butt in the grass, away from Cade's outstretched hand. "Don't act like lies by omission are supposed to make me feel secure in what we had."

Cade cringed and recovered his composure. "I would've told you more. I should've. That was my responsibility to you as my guest, not only in my house, but in my dimension. I brought you here, and I owed you a fuller explanation."

Fawn caught her breath. "Which is?"

Cade sat on the ground and interlaced his fingers. "My name is Cade. I have no last name. I traveled here from another dimension, into the nothing, into its raw potential, into its dormant energy. I used my abilities to work with it, shape it, play with it, dance with it. I directed the formation of the ground we rest on, the expanse of the sky, the stars that twinkle out of place for you."

Fawn said nothing and didn't take her eyes off him.

Cade's fingers fidgeted against blades of grass. "I built this house and this garden. I gave us the seasons. Anything our guests enjoyed that I hadn't already supplied for my friends and family, I installed here."

"As parting gifts?"

"In a manner of speaking." Cade ran his tongue across his lips. "That's not to say my promises to you were hollow. I took pleasure in making you happy. I still do."

"What's the rest of what you're hiding?"

Cade plucked at the grass, breaking some of the blades. "I let my closest friends and family accompany me to this dimension to enjoy what I could create here. Everyone else—" Cade hummed in displeasure. He wiped his palms against each other, trembling. "I constructed the town."

Fawn stared deeper into his darting eyes. "What are you saying?"

"Only my family and friends are... real. They're the only ones who came with me. Everyone else is a product of my imagination. They're like programs that run on their own. Their personalities change and grow, but they don't have their own consciousness."

Fawn let her numbness hide her other emotions and got to her feet. "How was that so difficult to admit?"

Cade pushed himself to standing. "Fawn—"

She exploded. "Caroline was the first person I befriended here. She comforted me before I trusted the rest of you. I worried about how much work she was putting in for you. She gave me a necklace she said had been passed down through her family. She has no family."

"She's very generous."

"She's not real. She supported us dating. She claimed she could guess my clothing sizes — even my shoes — because of her children. How can she possibly be Italian and Latina if you made her up? And Gerard be French?" Fawn put her hand on her chest. "I've spent months convinced Kee and Jacqui were from Jamaica."

Cade softened. "Our dimension might not be a perfect mirror to yours, but we have similar equivalents. The rest we learned from your world, and it helped me assigned certain traits to the helpers I created."

"If everyone at the water park is fake, how come Jax was ogling the women?"

"Because he sometimes forgets — or chooses to forget. I think he believes if he hits on them enough, I'll bring more people from our dimension into the Playground. That's not likely to happen."

Fawn wrapped her arms around her belly. "But why would you make people up that are that convincing, even to your own brother?"

Cade held his palms out. "This is going to sound insidious because of how long I've taken to fill you in. But you must believe me, I had all my guests' best interests at heart." He hesitated. "It *is* to put you at ease. It's to help you find your balance here and get situated in a world like the one you just left."

Fawn nodded. "It's to trick me and deceive me. You fooled me into thinking I had an ally in this place named Caroline who's Italian and Hispanic. You paraded your fake French chef around for three meals a day, cooking and baking my requests." She swept her arm out. "You had Hans drive the sleigh even though you could've controlled every movement of that horse yourself."

"Would you have wanted to stay if there were no one else here besides my family and friends? If there were no town, no employees, no staff doing jobs around the house?"

"No wonder Caroline can shop for clothes so quickly. No wonder Gerard could cook up any meal with no notice."

"Wouldn't it have been strange and lonely without them?"

Fawn rubbed her arms. "Try living a lie for almost a year in a dimension that's not your own. That's lonely."

"The longer I waited to tell you, the harder it got."

Fawn uttered a sarcastic chuckle. "You know what's hilarious? I was daydreaming about returning to Fun Splash this year. I wondered if Sandie was working there this summer. Sandie, who doesn't exist. I bet she's still sitting at the entrance, right? She was efficient, chipper. She wasn't in danger of getting fake fired by her fake boss."

Cade's voice dropped to a breathy monotone. "Don't do this."

"What?"

"Make judgments in anger that can't be taken back. I've said all I can say. I'm sorry."

Fawn brushed at her jeans to fling off any clinging dirt. "You said at the barbecue that anytime I chose to go home, you'd take me."

Cade's eyes pleaded with her. "Please, don't go."

"In the blink of an eye, you told me."

Cade shook his head and sniffled. "I said it because I will."

"I want to go home now."

"I'll take you wherever you want." He rotated his simple copper bracelet around his wrist. "Will you do me the favor of waiting until tomorrow night?"

Fawn huffed. "Sure. It'll give me a chance to say goodbye."

"You're free to pack any of your belongings and take them with you. They're yours."

Fawn tucked her thumbs in her belt loops. "I don't want it. I'm going home in my peasant shirt and yoga pants like I came here in. With my purse and my phone."

Cade hung his head. "We owe you that."

Fawn had never witnessed him humble and broken. It did little if anything to soften her tough exterior. "I don't even care enough to ask you what Lisette meant about there being stakes to all of this. If hosting me for so long puts something big and crucial at risk, maybe it's high time I go home."

Cade parted his lips but didn't form a sound.

Fawn stepped away from him toward the garden entrance. "You can't make the effort to explain it to me anyway, can you?"

Cade reached for her hand.

Fawn scampered a few paces away. "We're done. I'm sleeping in my own room. And it's way too late to worry about saying bitter words that can't be erased. Lisette started that trend."

Fawn spun on her boot sole and struck off toward the house. Her strides swished through the grass, unmatched by any other noise. She was glad Cade stayed planted where he stood and didn't chase after her. Her vacation in the Playground was over and so was her association with Cade.

~

The cotton peasant top felt scratchy and ill-fitting after all the perfect cuts Caroline had provided. Fawn plucked at the fabric over her chest again, where it seemed to both balloon and cling over her figure.

The foyer's grand chandelier hung above her head, shocking the square room into bright, cold light. Yoselle and Caroline hung on each other, crying and not bothering to hide their watering eyes. Jax looked on with a glum, solemn expression setting his eyebrows and mouth. Rosario stood tall and rigid at his side, her arms tied in a tight knot over her stomach. Vanna's arm hooked around Rory's, their eyes sad and wide with longing. Gerard lingered in the doorway across from Fawn, wiping tears from under his eyes.

Fawn ignored Lisette, who'd relegated herself to a corner chair where Fawn could barely see her behind her parents.

Cade hovered behind Fawn at the front door.

Yoselle launched herself forward and slung her arms around Fawn. "It was great to know you, Fawn. I appreciate that you came and got to know us."

Fawn nodded and patted Yoselle's back. Yoselle backed away, and Fawn hugged Rosario and Jax in turn.

Vanna stepped forward and gripped Fawn's hand. "It was an honor having you as our guest. Thank you for being here."

Rory shook Fawn's other hand. "Best of fortune to you. You deserve it."

Lisette's sulking left a silent pause through the room.

Caroline wrapped Fawn in a tight squeeze, and Gerard added his arms around the two women.

You're not real, Fawn repeated in her head. *Your love's not real.*

She pulled apart from them and moved to the door. She lifted her purse off the floor. "Let's go."

Cade swung the door open, and Fawn strutted out into the night. Cade shut the door and jogged past Fawn down the porch stairs. The Mustang rumbled in the driveway, its headlights cutting two beams through the darkness.

Hans waited beside the passenger side, and he opened the door for Fawn. "*Auf wiedersehen.* It was lovely meeting you."

Fawn grumbled as she climbed into the car. "You're not real, either."

Cade spoke curt and low to Hans. "Thank you." He clapped Fawn's door shut and got in behind the wheel.

She marveled at him with dry disdain. "You really buy into the illusion, don't you? That there are more living beings in the Playground than you, your family, and your friends."

Cade clenched his jaw and put the car in drive. "I enjoy the comfort of kind, helpful people." He pressed on the gas and steered the accelerating Mustang toward the road.

Fawn gazed out the windshield to avoid the scenery she'd so often admired out the window. "Don't think I haven't noticed you've chosen to drive me away in my favorite car. It won't win me back."

Cade cleared his throat. "I assumed you'd notice. I hoped you'd savor one last ride in it." He gazed at her like he had more to say pressing just behind his irises, but he diverted his attention to the driveway.

He turned the Mustang onto the country road, barely slowing down.

Fawn crossed her legs away from him. "Where are we going, exactly?"

"Another place I hoped you'd delight in seeing again."

"Why leave the house at all? With that expansive property you own?"

Cade set his index finger against the dip in his chin and shook his head. His voice bent under the weight of his emotions. "I can't take you out of this dimension from there. Not after everything that's happened."

"Is it a long trip?" Fawn rolled her eyes. "Of course it isn't. Nothing here is."

Cade sped the car up and raced alongside the quaint wooden fences almost the color of shadows in the dim light. After five or ten minutes Fawn lost track of, Cade directed the car into a deserted parking lot. Its surrounding trees and painted sign of rules clued Fawn in immediately.

She pursed her lips. "The park where we went jogging and had picnics. Where we went sledding down the hill together." She paused a beat. "It won't help you—"

"Get you back. I know." Cade gestured through the windshield. "It's also the best place to show you what I've made for you."

"Classy."

Fawn jumped out of the car, and Cade walked with her through the grass. The barest sliver of moon let the stars bathe the three hills in their hazy glow.

She watched him, his expression difficult to gauge. "That's it? You're not going to fight for me?"

Cade pressed his lips together and shook his head.

Fawn made a thoughtful, sarcastic hum. "You put up a bigger struggle coaxing me here."

Cade strode faster, and Fawn kept pace at his side. They mounted the first hill they arrived at.

Fawn blinked away images of sledding and picnics. "Where is this big to-do?"

Cade pointed upward. Fawn craned her neck. In an instant, she wondered if he had already guided her home. The North Star burned bright straight ahead. All the others greeted her from more familiar positions.

Nostalgia washed over her, and she steadied herself. "There's no depth to them." Fawn motioned to the twinkling pinpricks. "Stars back home aren't suspended in a flat plane. Some are further away than others."

Cade slipped his hands into the pockets of his loose linen pants. "I did what I could in the time I had to study your galaxy. I reordered the stars for you, and that's all you can say?"

"Two days ago, if you'd brought me here and displayed this for me, I would've had sex with you." Fawn patted the grass with her shoe. "It would've been touching. Really. If you hadn't lied. If you hadn't hidden behind your secrets. You don't get to betray me, Cade, and expect an outpouring of gratitude when you do what you naturally do. It looks nice, but it's not worth as much to me as honesty."

Cade worked his mouth for several seconds before he found his voice. "Stay."

"No. This completes the dance, doesn't it? You discovered me, rescued me, and gave me a gift I don't get to take with me. This was just an experiment to help me make over my life back home. I was never meant to build a life in the Playground, with or without you."

Cade blew out a shaky breath. "What location would you prefer I transport you to? Your SUV is parked at your apartment complex. We didn't leave it in the Smuckey's parking lot very long."

Fawn dried a forming tear from her lower eyelid. "My apartment, then. No sense in having you drop me off on the Smuckey's front sidewalk where we left from."

Cade produced Fawn's phone from his pocket and gave it to her.

"Finally." Fawn buried her phone in her purse.

"We just have to…" Cade wiggled his finger in the air. "We have to touch a little. That's how it works."

Fawn sighed and held out her hand.

Cade crossed her index finger with his. "Blink."

Fawn batted her eyes closed for a split second.

The glaring outside lights of her apartment building speared in around the edges of her curtains in the long, dark room.

Fawn stood with her back to it, Cade's finger overlapping hers. She dropped her hand away. "I guess that's it, then."

Cade almost hid in the room's cave-like haze. One cheekbone and the same side of his jaw illuminated in the faint glow that reached him. "You have everything you asked me for. Did you want to check on your vehicle before I leave?"

"No, I'm sure it's there. All that's left is the leaving."

In an instant, Cade popped out of Fawn's sight. She remained as unmoving as a statue for a full minute before she swept her hand through the air where Cade had been. Finding nothing but shadows, Fawn fumbled her way to the switches by the door and flipped on the overhead lights.

Their beams stung her eyes, and Fawn took her time blinking to get used to them. When her vision cleared, what she witnessed haunted her.

Instead of thousands of meticulously cared-for square feet, her outdated, ignored eight hundred stared back at her. The cream couches had no special touches, details, or history. Fawn pattered past them. She nearly glanced into the bathroom but gulped and kept walking.

The hefty pine table looked like something a high schooler made in shop class, and it shocked her. The chairs looked almost as simple and unrefined, their seats covered by uninspired tie-on cushions. Fawn entered her bedroom.

The queen-sized bed drowned in messy sheets and a thin, pink blanket. One of her clear plastic storage boxes poked out from under the frame. Fawn yelled out and gave it a fueled kick that sent it back under the bed and made her foot throb. Her closet door yawned open. Her high school t-shirt lay on the floor next to her patterned cotton sleep pants. Fawn abandoned her purse on the dresser and pulled out her phone. She sat down with it on the mattress' edge. Its springs creaked and barely compressed for her in an uneven slope.

Fawn's hands quivered where she rested them on either side of her. "This is a nightmare. Why did he show me all the things I don't have and drop me back in this dump? Curse you, Cade. I almost wish I never met you. You were supposed to make my life easier to navigate, not intolerable."

She coached herself through a long inhale and left her phone on the bed. Slowly, deliberately, Fawn stood up and stripped off the clothes that now seemed like a dimension-traveling uniform. She hauled all of them out to the kitchen and dropped them in the garbage. She returned to her room and tugged on the old t-shirt and rainbow-themed pajama pants.

Fawn carried her phone into the kitchen and opened the fridge. Not one item filled it. She found the freezer similarly empty, as well as her food-storing cabinets. She placed a quick call to order a pizza from her contacts list.

With a snack on the way, Fawn conjured up her voice mail. "There's probably a million of them."

The chipper, electronic female voice assured Fawn, "You have no new messages."

Fawn hung up. "Either someone deleted them or nobody tried to call me while I was on that *vacation*. I use that term rather loosely."

She consulted the round, cheap clock ticking on the wall. She drummed her fingers on the counter. "Ten's almost too late, but I think they'll forgive me."

Fawn reopened her saved contacts and dialed her parents. Every ring chirruped for what felt like minutes. She rapped her knuckles on the counter in an impatient rhythm.

Finally, a click. "Hello?"

Her mother's high, crisp voice stunned Fawn. Her throat constricted. "Mom? It's me, Fawn."

"Oh, Fawn! Goodness, gracious. I have to tell your father." Muffled and farther away, Donna called out. "Tan? Tanner? Get on the other phone. It's Fawn. Yes."

A second click, and Tanner's marginally deeper, gruffer greeting emerged from Fawn's phone. "Hello? Fawn, are you all right?"

Fawn heaved several breaths in and out, almost breaking down. She held it back. "I'm okay. I just got home. I thought you should be the first to know."

Donna let out a pleasant sigh. "Well, we're dying to hear all about your adventures and what you did on this trip."

Tanner broke in. "Did you swim with the dolphins?"

Fawn braced her hip against the counter's edge. "No, Dad. There was a lake but no ocean."

"How about boating? Was there a boat?"

Grief grabbed Fawn's neck, and she squinched her eyes shut as tears rippled in them. "Yes."

"No chance of it being a pontoon, eh?"

Fawn stomped her foot on the scuffed white linoleum. "Yeah. It was."

"Hey! That's great."

Donna eked back in. "Fawn? Honey, what about your new friend? Wasn't that considerate of him to put you up in his house and let you get some rest?"

Fawn clamped her palm over her mouth while a war battled inside her chest. At last, she lowered her hand. "Yes, awfully nice."

"Do you think you'll vacation with him again? Or invite him to stay with you in your apartment?"

"No." The lump in Fawn's throat shrank away. "We, um, had a falling out. We're no longer speaking."

"Oh. I'm so sorry to hear that, my love. I know we're glad to have you back. Monica will be, too, I'm sure. And Tara, of course, and Cal and the boys. I bet your company's been lost without you."

Fawn rubbed her eyes with her fingers. "With Demetria at the helm, I assume they're peachy."

Donna hummed a bright note. "That's a good attitude to

take. You sound more grounded, Fawn, if not a little weary."

Fawn fiddled with the cabinet knob that had been loose for years. "It's a bit jarring to be in my apartment again, in the life I left."

"I understand. Are you going to take another week off work to get situated?"

Fawn's jaw firmed. "No, I'll go in as soon as I can."

"It's Saturday. That gives you a whole day tomorrow to get re-acclimated. Whenever you've got a minute free, me and your dad would love to hear whatever stories you wanna tell."

A tear slipped free from the corner of Fawn's eye. "Yeah. It all feels like a dream now."

"A fun dream, I hope."

"Most of it was."

Tanner butted in. "It's only getting later, gabby gooses."

Fawn wandered out of the kitchen into her bedroom. "Good night, you two. I'll keep in touch."

Donna chuckled. "Get some restful sleep. We'll see you soon. Welcome home, Fawn."

Fawn hung up and tossed her phone on the bed. She rubbed spare material of her t-shirt and sleep pants between her fingertips, finding it rough and common. "This might be worse than I've gotten used to, but I will make this life work."

~

A horn blasted from Fawn's left, and she swerved back into her lane. Grogginess slowed her thought processes and her movements. She made a clumsy grab for the coffee in her center console cup holder. Some black liquid splashed into the neighboring round space, and Fawn slurped a mouthful down, greedy for the caffeine to kick in.

The bitter taste choked her. She wiped tiny granules off her tongue onto the roof of her mouth. "It tastes like a tire fire." She powered her window down and sloshed the rest of the coffee into the street. She tossed the cup onto the passenger-side foot mat.

Fawn turned the CD player on. Loud thumping pop spewed out, and Fawn bared her teeth in disgust. "I guess I don't like this anymore." She ejected the disc and threw it over her shoulder into the back seat. "Get a better producer."

With a few more turns through the city streets, the tan-stone office building slid into view. Its height overshadowed all the buildings around it, and Fawn's heart didn't know whether to calm down or speed up. She pulled into the parking lot and automatically steered her SUV toward the space reserved with a plaque reading *CEO Only.* A flash of cherry red made Fawn slam on the brakes.

When she focused on what was in her way, she recognized Demetria's two-door sportster. The vice president's spot beside it stretched empty. Fawn grunted and parked in Demetria's space.

Fawn grabbed her purse and stumbled toward the building's entrance. She groaned at her pinching, wobbling high heels. "Put some comfort foam in these, would you?"

The doorman bowed his head and swung one of the glass doors open. Fawn breezed into the lobby and hurried for the elevator. She hid in the back corner, packed in with ten other people.

With a ding, the elevator doors whooshed together. Fawn watched the digital number climb above the panel of buttons. She patted her purse in a random tattoo. Floor by floor, the rest of the elevator's occupants emptied out.

At last, Fawn reached over and pressed the button for the fifteenth floor. She tugged her knee-length skirt down and adjusted the fit of her turquoise blouse around her shoulders. "I gained too much muscle swimming and riding that mountain bike for these clothes."

A chime rang through the elevator, and Fawn stopped fidgeting. The doors parted.

A young woman stood in tall black heels, blue patterned leggings, a short pleated skirt, and a black-and-white pinstriped blouse unbuttoned halfway down her chest. She held a notepad in one hand with a glittery pen clipped to it. Her short, bobbed locks radiated a pale, yellow blonde. Her eyebrows flew up as she focused on Fawn and gasped. "It *is* you!"

Fawn found a detail she'd missed before. A pair of black plastic glasses lined with reddish pink hung from the young woman's blouse. "C-Chloe?"

Chloe giggled. "Yeah, I know, I changed my hair. I've changed a lot of things while you were gone."

Fawn's head spun, and she clung to the familiar. "Same glasses, I see. Same style of pen."

"Those are surface ripples, Fawn." Chloe darted away toward the offices. She paused and looked over her shoulder. "Are you coming? I scheduled a meeting with Demetria first thing."

"Right." Fawn caught up to Chloe's side.

Chloe flipped her hair back. "I don't have to wear my glasses as much. Demetria introduced me to her vitamin guy, and my eyesight's been much better."

Vitamin guy? A weird feeling tensed in the back of Fawn's throat. "That sounds great." She passed a boardroom's closed door, and her stomach chittered.

"I got engaged."

"What?" Fawn looked for Chloe's left hand to find a ring.

Chloe shrugged. "Then I broke it off because Demetria said he wasn't good for my career."

Fawn blinked several times. "Demetria said?"

"Mm-hmm. She's been a real mentor to me."

"And she was referring to your career as a what?"

"This." Chloe separated her pen from her pad. "The best, highest-paid assistant at Better Mind. She wants to turn me into the best, highest-paid assistant in the whole city. What do you think about that?"

"That sounds great."

Chloe gave a rueful chuckle and rubbed Fawn's arm. "You'll get used to it."

Fawn tipped her head to one side. "What?"

"Being at work again. That was a long vacation you had. You're still kind of…" Chloe whirled the pen in a circle next to her head. "…up in the clouds."

Fawn straightened her spine. "I'll come down soon."

"I'm sure you will."

Demetria's red car being parked in the CEO spot ruffled Fawn anew. "Demetria's expecting me?"

"Just as you requested, I informed her you'd be in today as soon as we got off the phone yesterday."

Fawn nodded and braced herself for a fight.

Chloe arrived at Demetria's door. Through the internal glass windows, Fawn zeroed in on Demetria rifling through papers on her massive desk. Chloe reached for the door handle.

Fawn laid her hand over Chloe's wrist to stall her. "Between you and me, before we talk to Demetria, how has the company been?"

"Good. Demetria's had meetings with all the right people, all the right departments. She took my notes on the way you orchestrated things."

Fawn nodded. "Go ahead."

Chloe pushed the door open and knocked on the jamb as she entered. "Demetria, Fawn's here."

Fawn strolled in just behind Chloe, and once the assistant stepped aside, Fawn met Demetria's eyes directly.

For a woman with a solid, mature air, not one wrinkle graced Demetria's face constructed of large, sharp, angular bones. Her sleeveless, grey-and-orange color-block dress showed off her muscular arms. Only the shrewd purse of her lips and a few glints of silver amongst her shorn, black locks hinted at her age.

Instantly, the disapproving twist of her mouth lifted into a brilliant smile. "Welcome back. How was it?"

Fawn lowered herself into one of the upholstered chairs facing Demetria's desk. "Fine."

Chloe remained standing over Fawn's left shoulder and set

the tip of her pen to page.

Demetria intertwined her fingers. "Good. And you're eager to return to your routine and duties here at Better Mind?"

Fawn squinted at Demetria as if it could help her see, even metaphorically, the vice president's true insinuations. "My vacation was about hitting the reset button on everything that was wrong in my life. I'm back now, and I have every intention of raising the bar for this company and myself."

Demetria flashed an enigmatic grin. "That must've been quite the vacation."

"It was."

"You deserved it." Demetria motioned to Chloe. "All right. So you'll regain Chloe as your assistant. I assume that's what you want."

"Yes."

"I'll tell you up front I didn't make any major changes to anything in your absence. It wasn't my place. I knew you'd be back."

"Any hiccups you should notify me of?"

Demetria scrunched her face up and shook her head. "No real problems this year. What did we make decisions on, Chloe?"

Chloe pointed her pen at Demetria. "We changed the packaging on the physical product."

"Right. It's streamlined, easy open, and environmentally friendly. The press ate it up."

Fawn's lips fell open. "You got coverage for that?"

Demetria nearly smirked. "I merely suggested to the local station they do a short series on businesses taking their environmental impact into consideration. I gave an interview. It was nothing."

Chloe chortled. "We saw a nice bump in interest for our videos, though."

Demetria snickered.

Fawn flexed her foot up off the floor. "Any other changes?"

Chloe flipped through her notes. "We started a program for

employees with photography skills. If they can submit high-quality, high-resolution images we can use in our videos, we pay them a flat rate. No royalties moving forward."

Fawn flicked her eyebrows up. "That's a pretty smart idea."

Demetria shifted some of the papers on her desk. "Someone had to find the solution to the image problems." Demetria stifled a cough. "It was going to be you or me, Fawn. You just happened to be on a beach somewhere."

Fawn gazed at Demetria askew, taken aback.

"Your tan gives it away."

Chloe beamed. "You look great, Fawn."

Fawn got to her feet. "If there's nothing else urgent to discuss, I'll go to my office now. I haven't been in there yet."

Demetria put on a dazzling smile. "We're so happy to have you back."

Fawn reached the doorway and pinned Demetria with a focused stare. "You knew I'd come in this morning. Why did you park in my spot?"

Demetria hummed a note of understanding. "*Mea culpa.* It was an oversight. I'll park in my place tomorrow."

Fawn headed to her office. Scurrying footsteps behind her startled her.

Chloe jogged up to her side. "It's wonderful to have you back. When I got your call out of the blue, I was over the moon."

Fawn strutted into her office. Its cold colors shook a shiver up her spine. "See if we can get some paint samples. I'd like to redecorate."

On her right, her laptop rested beside a trio of silver picture frames with their backs to her. Fawn rapped her knuckles on the metal desk's glass top. "Look into wooden desks with bigger drawer capacity. Maybe painted spring green or something fun. See if any local artists or antique dealers have a vintage desk in good shape. Keep the same height."

Fawn frowned at the blinding orange of her plush desk chair.

Before she could speak, Chloe made a dry scoff. "You're

kidding, right? We have meetings all day. Demetria wants to throw you a welcome-back party, so she needs to know what kind of cake you want."

Fawn waved her hand at the office around her. "New paint. New chair and desk. Warmer artwork. Something beachy works for me. Nothing with boats, please." Fawn dropped her purse off in a half-used filing cabinet drawer behind her desk.

Chloe gawked at Fawn.

Fawn nodded at the pad of paper in Chloe's hand. "Write it down. I'm serious."

Chloe turned to a fresh page and scribbled for several lines. "There's a lot to do, Fawn."

"I know."

"It's not like being on vacation where you feel like you have plenty of time to accomplish everything you want."

Fawn ignored her and wandered across the room to the windows. "Have maintenance remove these curtains. Take the rods down, too. Fill in the holes."

She surveyed the street over a hundred and sixty feet below her. Rust patches rode by on dusty trucks and small sedans. The restaurant across from her building had its curtains closed. "For lunch, can you see if that place has a take-out menu online?"

Chloe sputtered. "Lunch?"

"Yeah. See if they have a soup and sandwich to go or something."

Chloe rushed up to Fawn. "We don't have time for soup and sandwich." She flipped to another page. "There's a dozen decisions that waited a year for you to get back and make them. I called Janet, too, and I—"

"Janet?" Fawn lingered at the window and its grand view. Two robins flew by, soaring above the restaurant's roof. "What did she say?"

"She wants a meeting with you, of course. This week, if we can squeeze it in. She's very intrigued by your holiday."

"And you think I should pack my schedule even tighter to

speak with her?"

Chloe's eyes rounded into saucers. "A strange man did call her from your phone to tell her you'd be away and couldn't be reached. Then we heard nothing for almost a year. You know how important this company is to her."

Fawn licked her lips. "Next week."

Chloe made the uncertain, beginning sound of a word.

Fawn flared her nostrils. "Next week."

Chloe wrote something down.

Fawn started off at a jog across her office.

"Wait! Where are you going?" Chloe chased her. "The letterhead and the website have only gotten a year older. They're more outdated than they were when you left. And Lars loves the changes Demetria made to the packaging, but he wants to discuss bumping up the price so customers will feel pulled toward the digital-download option. It would decrease the amount of shipping we need to do."

Fawn patted the door frame. "Find out if Demetria would be willing to handle that detail."

"What?"

"I've been gone for a long time, and I have to see someone."

"Who?"

Fawn raced to the elevator as fast as she could without twisting an ankle. She summoned the elevator and rode it down to the fourteenth floor. She scurried past droves of unfamiliar faces in the tan corridor before she spotted a figure trailing long black hair behind it.

Fawn sped up to Monica's side and touched her arm to get her attention. "Mon? It's me. I'm back."

Monica's jaw clenched until one of its muscles pulsated. She glared straight ahead, getting passed by coworkers for several seconds. Her shoulders stiffened under her short-sleeved blouse, and she met Fawn's gaze with stony grey eyes. "Congratulations. I'm thrilled for you."

Fawn's confidence crumbled. "Mon?"

Monica took off, and Fawn followed her just as quickly. Monica darted into the ladies' restroom, and Fawn ran in after her.

Monica whirled to face her. "What do you want from me? What do you expect? Huh?"

Fawn leaned her back against the closed restroom door. "I'm sorry. I didn't have my phone the entire time I was gone."

Monica knotted her arms together over her belly. "So I gathered. I told you to get his number, Fawn, not abandon me without any kind of heads-up."

"I tried to get my phone back. He wouldn't give it to me."

"And all of a sudden, the woman powerful enough to run a complex organization can't retrieve her own phone or come home without it."

Fawn threw her hands up. "I wasn't anywhere around here. I didn't have my SUV. I literally left with my purse and the clothes I was wearing."

Monica's upper lip curled. "You ran off with him, just like that?"

"It wasn't like that. He wanted to help me get my health back."

Monica yipped. "Woo! That's a line. A real charmer."

"I ate home-cooked meals for a change. I spent days boating on the lake with no computers or cell phones in sight. He did what he promised he'd do."

Monica tightened her folded arms. "So you became friends."

"Yeah."

Monica tossed her arms down. "Bullshit!" She pointed in Fawn's face. "Nobody disappears for that long because of a *friend*. I told you I'd wait for you in my car all night if I had to for you to snag his number. That doesn't mean I wanted to wait three hundred and sixty-five of them like an idiot!"

Fawn raised her index finger. "I was gone for fifty-one weeks. *Not* a full year."

"Forgive me if that negligible bit of information strikes me as completely asinine."

The door thumped against Fawn's back. She pressed it closed. "Occupied! Try the other one." Fawn picked up the rubber doorstop from the corner of the checkered floor and rammed it under the door. She held her hands out from her sides to try to appeal to Monica. "Look, I understand you're pissed. I'm sorry. It was never my intent to desert you. I wasn't even interested in him like that, if you remember."

"But you got interested."

"I did. I admit it."

Monica kicked at the floor. "How'd he win you over?"

"First, there was a barbecue with dancing and formalwear. Then, in the winter, he took me out for a sleigh ride."

Monica shifted her jaw from side to side. "Romantic and creative, I'll give him that."

Fawn slashed her flat hand through the air. "But it's over. He lied to me. I didn't know everything I was getting into."

"The only reason you scurried back home was because he was dishonest?" Monica's eyes glinted hard. "That's not very flattering."

Fawn scratched her head, some of her hair loosening from its plastic clip. "I got caught up, okay? In the food, the freedom, meeting all the people around him."

"How many?"

"People?"

Monica nodded.

"Let's see…" Fawn rested her eyes closed. Did she count those Cade had created or not? "Um… he had four siblings. His parents. I don't know how many friends. Plus three people working for him."

"Spoiled rich boy."

Fawn shrugged. "Not so spoiled. He works really hard. He doesn't have anything handed to him."

Monica shifted her weight from one foot to the other. "He was a hypocrite, then? A workaholic who whisked you off to some sort of paradise."

"Not addicted to his work. Trust me. He loafs around plenty."

"But you don't deny wherever he took you was a paradise?"

Fawn smacked her palm against her thigh. "What do you want me to say? There were cool cars and scrumptious meals and fireworks going off all summer. We went glamping and hang gliding and horseback riding. I even ziplined and bungee jumped. That's how far out of my comfort zone he helped me get." Fawn pressed a fingertip to her aching temple. "Why am I defending him?"

Monica pushed the nearest green stall door open. "I guess you still have the feels for Mr. McRomance."

"No, I don't. I regret that my healing and adventures hurt our friendship. Being able to talk to you and rely on you was the best thing I had going in my life before I left."

"And now?"

"It's something I want again. I need to talk to you, Mon." Fawn advanced a step and lowered her tremulous voice. "It's been three days since I found out what he was hiding and broke up with him. I know I'm here at work. I'm dressed the part, but I'm hurting. I spent every day with Cade, and being away from him, even by choice, is surreal. I can't sleep. My mattress is a joke. My clothes suck. My furniture is hideous."

Monica sneered. "Sorry it's so terrible being back."

"You're not going to help me with any of it? Give me any advice or stories to get me through this?"

"No."

Fawn staggered back a step. Her hair clip slipped a half inch. She took it out and threw it in the garbage, cursing its weak hinge. She tucked a lock of her hair behind her ear and decided to strike back where it hurt. "Are you dating anybody?"

"No."

"How serious was your last relationship?"

Monica cocked her hip. "Not very. I'm picky."

Fawn's mouth curved in an ironic grin. "Still spinning that lie? Okay. Let me tell you something straight to your face. You're not, objectively, my best choice for a shoulder to cry on when my relationships self-destruct. You're too big of a coward to admit you like your relationships fast, fun, and shallow. It's the same reason you're working the same job down here on fourteenth while I rose to CEO."

Monica jerked her chin up, and it shook. "You have *no* idea why I stay in this job."

"Enlighten me."

"There's so much you don't know."

"That goes both ways." Fawn sat down in a wobbly aluminum chair by the door. She slid her feet free of her shoes and rubbed one sore heel. "You relish your short, hot affairs. You don't have to reveal who you really are. You cut them off before they get complicated and you make yourself vulnerable. You break up with them before they can find a reason to walk away from you."

Monica sniffed. "What's your point?"

"You're trying to judge what happened between Cade and me. You had all kinds of wisdom and criticism and suggestions about Devon and what I should do to get over him. You don't have experience with long-term, dedicated relationships."

Monica tapped her foot once. "Are you done? 'Cuz I've been holding my tongue to spare your feelings, too."

Fawn waved toward herself. "Bring it. Get it all out."

"*You* blame your problems finding boyfriends on the low quality of men you meet. Liars and bores and lazy-asses."

Fawn massaged her other foot. "They are. They expect too much and don't want to listen as much as they talk."

"The truth is you'll never be happy with anybody." Monica clicked one high heel against the floor. "You won't let yourself. You're not satisfied with the men employed at Better Mind because that could get awkward. You don't respect the men who don't work here because they can't understand what you do. You're a perfectionist, Fawn, as a part of this company and when you date. You want a man who's already perfect when he gets to you, and that's not gonna happen."

Fawn shoved her feet into her shoes. "That's not true."

"You're jealous of me. I have minimal responsibilities. No ex-boyfriend baggage to cry about." Monica poked a fingertip against her chest. "I can do whatever I want, and nobody cares. Nothing I do is gonna end up in the newspaper with *CEO* printed after my name."

Fawn leapt to her feet. "You've always envied me. I got love. I attracted mentors. I have a huge office with windows and my own assistant."

Monica sidestepped into the stall's doorway. "Get out. I still have to pee. Or do I have to wait until my lunch break so I don't go on company time?"

Fawn ripped the hall door open and strode out of the bathroom. She marched to the elevator and rode it up a floor. She sauntered into her office, grateful to find it empty.

Guilt clawed at her heart, making her anger ebb. She ran her fingers through her hair and went to the filing cabinet behind her desk. She retrieved her cell phone from her purse. Pulling up her contacts, Fawn dialed the phone at Monica's desk. It rang and rang until Fawn gave up and ended the attempted connection. "Damn it."

Chloe strutted into the office. "Oh, you're in here. Good. I've got an update. Demetria will head up the pricing of physical product versus digital downloads."

Fawn plunked into her desk chair, everything about it making her cringe. "Any updates on redecorating?"

"I'll speak with purchasing by the end of the day."

Fawn laid her phone on the desk's spotless glass top and reconsidered it. "Is Demetria in her office or a meeting?"

"Office. I just left her."

Fawn snatched her phone up and dialed Demetria. "Hey. You had some great ideas while I was gone, like contacting the press about going green with our packaging. Do you have any other suggestions for company improvements?"

Demetria's voice slunk with unknown intentions. "Sure, I do."

"Now that I'm back, I'd like to go over them and give them my honest appraisal. Would you compile them for me?"

Demetria hesitated. "I'll have them on your desk in the morning."

~

Fawn set her travel cup of coffee next to her laptop. It was the highest-rated flavor in the city, organic, fair trade, and gourmet. It still paled in comparison to any beverages Gerard served in the Playground, but Fawn could stomach it, so she considered its purchase a resounding success.

What stole Fawn's attention now was the plastic portfolio resting in the middle of her desk. Fawn sat down in the obnoxious orange chair. "Come on," she muttered. "Give me something I can work with."

Fawn flipped to the first page. The company letterhead with its green, blue, and magenta swirls put a bad taste in her mouth. "Yeah, we're gonna update that A-sap."

Fawn scanned the computer-printed suggestions. *Add more product bundle levels. Supply clients with additional, proven ideas of effective ways of using our videos. Assemble a think-tank team to tackle long-standing issues. Reach out to local businesses with a free trial period.*

The next two pages introduced no better options. The final page only contained two items that hadn't fit on the previous papers. Fawn stared at the lists. Extra space stretched around the margins and between each line of text. "This is fluff." Fawn slapped the portfolio closed and shoved it off her desk. It fluttered in wild acrobatics and warping sounds before it hit the carpet.

Fawn covered her eyes. "None of this is any good. It's tired, regurgitated at best. Shallow, boring, pathetic." She moved her hands to press against her temples. "I thought she cared about whether this company went under or rose up again."

She jolted upright, looking through her office's inner window toward Demetria's. "She loves Better Mind. She just hates me." Fawn sucked a mouthful of coffee into her system. "She doesn't want to arm me with any ideas that could benefit me or make me look good."

Fawn pushed herself up and walked over to the windows above the street. She folded her arms and tapped her fingers against her upper arm. "Not just *good*. Competent. She parked in my spot on *accident*." Fawn scoffed and tossed her hair off her forehead. "If this is the game she wants to play, she can go for it. I'm not the pushover I was last summer. I can come up with my own ideas. Janet gave me this position, and I'll be damned if I'm gonna let Demetria shoulder her way into my job."

~

Chloe bolted into Fawn's office, scribbling on her notepad.

Fawn raised her attention from typing into her laptop. "How's that new furniture coming?"

"Uh…" Chloe put her glasses on and rustled through her elongated pages. "I found some options to show you."

"When is the artwork arriving?"

"Um…" Chloe ruffled the pages again. "Friday."

"Great. Have maintenance put them up right away."

"And that takes precedence over…"

Fawn's tone fell flat. "Chloe."

The assistant peeked up from her notes with wide, glassy eyes.

"Hanging five paintings isn't going to take long. There are already nails or screws in the walls."

Chloe turned to her freshest page, her breath fast and wheezing.

Fawn allowed herself half a grin. "Take a real breath, Chloe. It's okay." She lowered her laptop screen against the keyboard. She relaxed her shoulders and folded her hands in her lap.

Chloe pulled in a rasping inhale. "Okay, I got Lars to agree to give me his questions instead of tying you up in an hour-long meeting."

"Excellent."

"The letterhead redesigns will be here..." Chloe consulted the previous page. "Tomorrow. And Demetria's too busy with the new pricing structure to keep her appointment with you this afternoon."

"Perfect." Fawn leaned forward, lifting her eyebrows at Chloe. "Take a break. Take a long lunch or something."

Chloe shook her head. "I can't—"

"You can. Your boss, the CEO, just said so."

"Maybe later. I'm still trying to move your meeting back with video requisitions. Sally says it's urgent."

Fawn smirked and opened her laptop. "It's not, no matter how many times she claims it is. Push her back to next week. If she balks, tell her at least she's on my radar at all."

Chloe made a note. "Will do. Do you want anything while I'm gone?"

"No. Oh, did those dry fruit things get replaced with real fruit yet?"

Chloe sighed with relief. "Yes."

"With recurring deliveries, right?"

"Yeah."

"Good. I want everything easy and effortless."

Chloe made light, tense chuckles. "Demetria's going to fight you on that."

"Let that be my problem."

Fawn pulled her laptop closer, and Chloe whisked out of the office.

Alone, Fawn's confidence melted as she read over the half-dozen company improvement ideas she'd typed up. "I have to do better than this."

Fawn ignored the thin attempts for now. She opened her email, bracing herself for more barely polite backlash and requests for face-to-face conversations. Her eyes settled on a sender name she didn't recognize. "Birdie Lidell. Looks like she works at the company." Fawn clicked on the email.

Dear Ms. Claire,

We've never met. I started working at Better Mind only a few weeks before you took your big vacation. I hope it was a good one. I wanted to say, welcome back!

Well, I don't know how to word this. I know I've only been at the company little more than a year. I'm not your assistant or one of your high-tier managers. I work in sound down on fourteenth.

But I want you to know I took this job because I was already using sound to improve my mood. I was doing affirmations for myself and being picky about my music. Why listen to sad or angry messages all the time, right?

Anyway, after I started choosing songs and hiding audio extras in Better Mind videos, I saw some areas where they could be stronger. Don't get me wrong, Ms. Claire! I love Better Mind. This is the greatest, most fulfilling job I've ever had. And it comes to me naturally. There are so many pluses about working here, but the longer I've been here, the more suggestions I've developed on more we could do. I never shared them before because I knew you were the official CEO and Ms. Barnes was just filling in for you. Now that you're back — welcome back! — I wanted to reach out and see if you were interested in what I've come up with.

I don't want to waste your time. People have told me how swamped your calendar is. So I'll include a few of my ideas here so you can see if they're worth following up with:

Fawn closed her eyes and laid her hand on her pumping heart. She delved into Birdie's insights.

1. Selling directly to businesses is smart, and I understand that's how the company's always functioned. But what about catering and selling straight to regular people? A lot of people are looking to improve themselves, like I was. I don't think this addition to our repertoire would change too much about the video creation itself, but I could be underestimating that. (And the company name still makes sense! Ha.)

Fawn's pulse sped up, and she read faster.

2. We could introduce more diversity to our teams, which would turn into putting more diversity into our videos. By that, I mean the images, music, and affirmations. This would (I think) help Better Mind's sales team be more effective reaching out to ethnically diverse companies and other women-run businesses. Like ours. :)

Fawn smiled.

3. Have you considered a really tiny product package for small businesses? I have a friend — I'll keep this short — who owns a music store. She has a few employees, and they're sometimes lethargic and uninterested in their work even though she only hires people who love music as much as we do. I talked to her about Better Mind videos, but the packages are too extensive for her needs. The profit might not be huge, but it would improve people's lives and help save small businesses like hers.

Fawn dried her sweaty palms on her skirt. She murmured. "So far, so good."

4. I know Better Mind has always specialized in videos, but what about audio-only files? If we made them without any subliminals or mood-altering tones, they'd be safe to listen to while driving. That way, employees — here and at our clients' companies — could hear affirmations and helpful music to or from work. Putting them into an app would make it effortless to access. Just a thought.

Fawn gasped and scrambled up out of her chair. She clamped her hands over her mouth. Her body danced up and down with excess energy. She bent down to read the rest of the email.

Those are pretty much the best suggestions I have. I didn't want to sit on them any longer if they could be of use to you. I hope it's not too much to put on your plate right after your vacation!

Fawn shook her head.

You probably get people's dreams and sketches for new

products all the time.

Fawn huffed with humor.

Sorry this got so long! Welcome back, these are my ideas, and I hope to hear from you. If not, I'll assume…

Fawn picked up her cell phone and dialed Chloe.

The assistant answered on the first ring. "You need something?" Liquid streaming echoed in the background.

Fawn winced. "First of all, if you're in the bathroom, you don't have to take my call so fast. Second thing, I need you to get in touch with an employee in sound. Her name is Birdie Lidell. I want an appointment with her as soon as she has time."

The splashing stopped. "*She* has time? What about your time?"

"I want my time to accommodate her time. Do it and let me know when to expect her. Any part of the day is fine."

Fawn hung up and let her phone clatter to her desk. She walked around it and eased her office door closed. She swung victorious fists high into the air. "Yes!"

She welcomed a deep breath into the bottoms of her lungs. "This could change everything." Fawn strolled toward the windows but paced back toward the door. "I can't let myself get too carried away with this, can I?" She pattered toward the windows and their view of cornflower-blue sky. "Yes, I can. I definitely can."

Fawn strode up to the windows, laughing. "Demetria wants my job. I want something easier than Better Mind can possibly give me for as long as I want it, which is the rest of my life. With Birdie's brilliance, I could give this place incredible leverage. I could feel good about leaving it, even in Demetria's greedy hands, and know Janet's vision is well taken care of."

Fawn tittered at the city laid out at her feet. "I could do anything I wanted. No guilt. No shame. No looking back, and no regrets. I don't know who you are, Birdie, but I'm about to. Everything's about to change."

Chapter Eight

Pale-grey mannequins with post-modern, exaggerated angles posed in the big shop windows. A flowered dress of red on white draped over one form while others sported a polka-dot blouse and a see-through robe with leopard-print trim.

Fawn opened the glass door and strolled into the bright, clean space. Warm, golden light illuminated bronze racks of colorful clothes. The stone floor imitated marble, supporting a blue-and-beige geometric rug in the entryway topped with a round metal table and a ceramic vase filled with a generous cloud of real, pink roses.

High-heel clicks announced a woman with flowing midnight-brown hair and tawny skin. Her genuine, confident smile reached her almond-shaped russet eyes. She shook Fawn's hand. "I'm Ray. Are you Fawn?"

Fawn nodded.

"Nice to meet you. Welcome to Maven Boutique." Ray aimed a pointed finger along one wall of garment racks. "Like I said on the phone, we are full service. Whatever you need, we can provide for you or get you vetted references for. I've been in business eight years. I know the best salons, the most valuable spas. I'll make sure you get what you want and are totally satisfied."

"Perfect."

Ray ushered Fawn to a pair of purple damask armchairs, and they sat down. Ray crossed her ankles. "You said you were interested in building a new wardrobe from the bottom up?"

Fawn rested her purse by her feet. "Completely. I saw myself in my old high school t-shirt and pajama pants with my hair in a slouching ponytail, and I said, 'I am *not* that girl.' I donated everything I'm not wearing on my way to this appointment."

Ray stroked her dimpled chin. "I like that. It shows you're serious."

Fawn tugged on the excess material of her baggy tank top. "This isn't me. The bad fit. The jeans that squeeze my thighs but never touch my ankles."

"How are you for shoes?" Ray glanced at Fawn's feet.

"I need well-made ones. It's been a long week of hobbling around on pinching, unsteady heels, and it's only Thursday."

"You need clothes for work?" Ray tipped her head to one side. "What kind?"

"Comfortable because I work long hours. Or I used to. My schedule has recently been truncated. I don't know how long it'll be before it changes again."

"Do you care about style and trends, or no?"

Fawn linked her fingers together. "I like timeless. Classic but unique."

Ray bobbed her head. "I'm digging that vibe. Yeah. We can make that work for you. What else do you need to dress for in your life?"

Fawn breathed in the roses and fabrics and Ray's sweet, potent perfume. "I got out of a five-and-a-half month relationship less than a week ago. I'll be hitting the dating scene pretty soon."

Ray's lips ticked down at the corners. "I'm sorry to hear that. We'll find you the right clothes that make you look and feel better than you ever have. That'll boost your confidence and move you forward to new possibilities."

"Thank you." Fawn looked over the back half of the boutique's offerings. "I'm also getting more involved with my family. I'm having them over for dinner tomorrow night."

"So, casual." Ray brightened her smile. "Upgraded casual."

"Exactly."

"What's your budget? A general ballpark is fine."

Fawn waved her hand. "As much as it takes. I haven't treated myself in ages. I want the wardrobe more than I want the money."

"My favorite kind of client. Even when the sky's the limit, I still aim for real value. Are there any styles or looks that are unappealing to you?"

Fawn tented her fingers. "I want to look like I own this town. Anything else has to go."

Ray stood up. "Nothing frumpy or outdated or distressed or ill-fitting. I gotcha. Tell me if I'm close or if I'm way off base." Ray crossed the narrow store to a rack and lifted off a black denim dress with tied shoulder straps. "I see you in this for date night. The jean material is familiar and classic, so it doesn't seem too formal or suggestive. The ties are youthful and fun but can still cover up your bra straps so you can be comfortable."

Fawn walked over for a closer look. "I had a denim dress. It wasn't as classy as this. I love it."

"Let me show you…" Ray carried the dress with her to a rack nearer the front windows. She snatched up a black-striped cream-colored blazer. "This for the office. One-button closure. No fuss. It's modern with clean lines and will definitely shine a spotlight on you."

"What's it made of?"

"Crepe, so it's super light. That's gonna increase how much you can wear it throughout the year."

"I'll take that, too."

Ray held up a finger and rushed to the boutique's opposite front corner. "I'll also want to set you up with work-to-evening pieces in case you have to run from work to a dinner date." She isolated a copper-sequined tank top.

"That's awesome."

Ray laughed. "We'll replace the one you have on." She collected the three pieces of clothing in a large mesh shopping bag. "I'd love to have you try on a lavender blouse or jacket with tan plaid pants. It'd be chic and versatile."

"Sounds great. And if the denim dress does its job, I'll be hunting something in this vein." Fawn pointed to the red robe on the mannequin.

"That's the goal. We'll pick out some jewelry and shoes and leggings for you."

Fawn drew her shoulders up in a prolonged shrug. "I'm a

blank canvas."

Ray crinkled her nose. "That's my favorite kind."

~

Fawn clinked her fork against the side of her half-filled glass of white wine. Standing at the head of the table, she grinned as she surveyed her family seated around the rest of the wooden surface.

Across from Fawn, Tara leaned toward the son fidgeting and singing within reach on her right. "Casper, you need to be quiet now. Aunt Fawn has something to say." Tara's blonde highlights glinted amongst her light-brown locks falling past her shoulders.

Casper looked up with large eyes in his tanned face under his combed sandy hair. Donna and Tanner picked up their wine glasses, their eyes sparkling with uncertainty and pride.

Fawn allowed the same emotions to uplift the corners of her mouth. "Okay, this isn't exactly the way I would've planned it. I gave away most of the art from the walls. We're stuck with the same designless table and uninteresting chairs. And thank you, Tara, by the way, for volunteering to sit in the seventh chair I bought from a neighbor this morning in the hallway."

Their parents laughed. Cal cackled from Fawn's left. He pushed his glasses up his short nose and snuck a peek at his wife's reaction down the table.

Tara's posture slumped but remained tense beneath the faded, wide-neck shirt slipping halfway off her round shoulder. "You're welcome."

Fawn twirled her glass in her fingers. "My apartment's not fancy, but it will be. Or I'll move into a new one that is. I haven't decided." The bare walls didn't seem so much abandoned now as buzzing with refreshed potential.

Donna gasped. "Fawn, that's wonderful! You're overdue."

Tanner batted the air. "Don't worry about what it looks like and what's on the walls or not there. Fawny, we just appreciate being invited."

Donna's grey eyes watered. "We love you so much. I'm overjoyed this vacation has done you such good. You look fantastic."

Fawn snaked her arm out from her side. The long fringe hanging from her lilac shirt danced and swayed.

Donna widened her eyes in expectation at Xavier and Casper. "What do you think of your aunt's new look, boys?"

Xavier wrinkled his full cheeks. "She's covered in purple snakes."

Casper slapped the tabletop with both palms. "It looks like gross spaghetti!"

Tara laid her hand over Casper's and hushed her voice. "That's enough."

Fawn set her glass down. She sauntered past Cal to her nephews, shimmying to make her fringe jump and gyrate. "That's okay. I'm gonna give each of you a high five. You know why?" Her palm met with Xavier's and Casper's in turn. "Because what you did is called honesty. Honesty should be rewarded, and it is in my apartment."

Xavier whined, his eyebrows pinched together. "You can't move, then!"

Fawn returned to stand behind her chair and sipped her wine. "It'll still be true no matter where I live." She relegated her glass to the table once again. "Now, I didn't make the food. I haven't found a cooking class with a seat open yet that fits my schedule. It's the best restaurant take-out I could find."

Tara turned her cute little nose up half an inch. She patted her left hand against the table, catching flashes of rainbows from the cheap chandelier lights in her wedding ring's diamond.

Fawn set her forearm on top of the back of her chair. "You think I got watered-down minestrone and wilted salad with cold chicken chunks, don't you? There's a massive bowl of Caesar salad in the kitchen that could feed a horse. Mashed red potatoes with mushroom gravy. I got macaroni and cheese for…"

Donna grinned and gestured at Casper and Xavier. "The

boys?"

"For *everybody!*" Fawn motioned in a sweeping circle. "It has five cheeses and bits of lobster in it. Oh, what's supposed to be an appetizer that I forgot to put out." Fawn whipped her flat hand back an inch above her head and chuckled at herself.

Tanner offered a reassuring smile and nodded. "That's all right."

Fawn giggled. "It's a creamy spinach-and-artichoke dip we eat with grilled flatbread."

Donna rubbed her palms together. "Cut to dessert, Fawn. I'm dying to try all this already."

"I got two things because I know our tastes run a little differently from each other in this family." Fawn gestured to Tara and the left side of the table. "The plains." Fawn bowed to her parents on her right. "And the heap-it-ons, especially if it's chocolate and nuts."

Tanner shook an excited fist. "Hey! We're represented."

Fawn turned to Cal and the boys. "I got a plain, rich cheesecake for Tara and her crew. Plus a pizookie for the rest of us. That's a cross between a pizza and a cookie for those of you who weren't in the know. It's not piping-hot in its intended iron skillet, but it still looks like a delicious way to die. So, Mom should be happy."

Donna beamed and shook a finger at Fawn. "You know us so well!"

Tara started to get up with a wry frown. "If that's the whole menu, I'll help you carry it to the table."

Fawn waved for Tara to sit down. She lifted her stemmed glass toward the ceiling. "Before we eat, I want to make a toast to my younger sister."

Tara stared at her and shifted in repeated, uneasy movements in her seat.

Fawn took a sip of wine. "Tara has never gotten the recognition she deserves. She's been my constant supporter since we were kids. She has two amazing kids of her own, as rambunctious and free-spirited as they are. And I think Tara should win some sort of medal for dating in this crazy world until she reached the finish line. Tara and Cal, you're my heroes. Mom, Dad, you're my original heroes from the start. I think we all deserve major credit for the work we've done, the relationships we forged, and being ourselves through the whole d— um, *darn*, I was going to say *darn* — thing."

Fawn drained the rest of her wine, sweet and light and smooth. She set her empty glass on the table and blew out an amused, happy breath.

Donna chuckled as she returned her glass to the table with an inch of wine still inside. She nodded at Fawn's glass. "Is drinking before dinner something you picked up on vacation, Fawn?"

"Yes. Along with eating immediately after. Tara, I'll accept that offer of help if you're willing."

Tara stood up on shaky legs and lumbered around the table. She slung her arms around Fawn, shaking with tears. Tara shook her head against Fawn's. "I haven't always been the best sister." She sobbed in Fawn's ear.

Fawn patted Tara's back. "Neither have I. Would you do me a huge favor, sis, and get me some recent photos of the boys? I have the world's oldest pictures of all of you in my office. I'd love to trade them out for something newer."

Tara sniffled, hanging on Fawn's sturdy stance. "You got it."

"You, Cal, and the boys are gonna see a lot more of me from now on. If it's okay."

Tara nodded. "That'd be great." She hung onto Fawn with, Fawn thought, no hints of letting go.

Fawn shared a gentle smile with Cal. "I have a potentially extensive project in the works at Better Mind, but I'm hoping to play my cards right and carve out a lot more family time moving forward."

Tara tightened her hold and lowered her voice. "I didn't mean to try to outdo you. It's not a goddamn contest. Sometimes I forget that. You always went big or went home."

Fawn stilled her head against her sister's. "Now I'm doing both at the same time. And you're winning at things I haven't begun to figure out yet."

"You will."

Fawn glanced at her parents, watching with glowing admiration. "If all it takes is a killer wardrobe, I've got it in the bag."

Tara pulled back and wiped tears from her broad cheeks. "No, I'm serious. You'll get it all worked out."

~

Chloe stepped back another few paces on her towering heels. "Smile naturally. You don't want to look desperate." She raised her cell phone, checking the screen and changing its angle in relation to Fawn. "Which is ridiculous advice, because most of the people on Bonfire *are* totally desperate."

Fawn brushed a fuzzy speck of lint off her pink satin blouse. "I'm choosing not to take offense to that because you're using it, too."

"Helping you rub two sticks together since, well, earlier this year."

Fawn clucked her tongue and spared a glance at the windows between her office and the hallway. "Yeah, I saw the slogan on the website. Not sure if I'm crazy about it."

Chloe tapped her phone screen several times. "Can you look slightly toward the door again? The light from the windows made your tan luminescent."

Fawn rotated her head an inch away from the sunbeams streaming in through the bare windows.

"Yeah, like that." Chloe gushed. "You look like a goddess." Chloe touched her screen and moved the phone. "You look super relaxed, too. That vacation did you all kinds of favors."

Fawn clenched her teeth in exaggeration. "Can I stop smiling and start blinking now?"

Chloe swiped through the recent photos on her phone. "Yes, we're using this one. I'll email it to you, and we'll upload it."

Fawn took a seat in her forest-green upholstered desk chair. "My bio doesn't sound too lofty?"

Chloe wobbled her head in uppity nonchalance and finished with her phone. "What do you expect? You run a big company. I think you seem accomplished, not snooty."

Fawn found the attached picture in her email and uploaded it to her Bonfire bio page. "Good idea taking it in my office. I was worried I'd look married to my job."

"Eh. The deep tan and fresh-from-vacation smile make up for that. You look like a hard worker who's ready for some real fun."

"So I just launch my profile, right?"

Chloe adjusted her glasses and squinted at the laptop screen. "Yeah. You filled in your likes, dislikes, hobbies, what you're looking for, what you hope to God to avoid. You're done."

Fawn hesitated and clicked *submit.* She rubbed her sweaty palms on her lavender-grey skirt. "Let's see how long it takes me to get some hugs or winks or emails or whatever."

"On Bonfire, they're called sparks. Someone flicks a spark at you, and you get to decide if you want to spark them back or grow that spark into an ember."

"I thought this site was supposed to make dating easier." Fawn caught the time in the bottom corner of the laptop screen. "Shoot. I have an errand to run."

Chloe pocketed her phone. "Is there anything I can do for you?"

"No, it's a personal one." Fawn grabbed a gold-and-blue envelope from her lime-green desk's top drawer. "You're free to leave. Go home. Get some rest."

"When are you heading out?"

"Soon." Fawn hurried out of her office and took the stairs down a floor. She speed-walked through the corridors to the spacious office Monica shared with three other video compilers.

Monica, striding on her way out, almost slammed into Fawn. She sucked in a shocked inhale and backed up. She narrowed her focus on Fawn, and a smirk wrenched her mouth. Monica clutched her purse strap high up on her thin shoulder. "I was just going, so…"

Fawn worked to maintain her level mood. "This'll only take a minute. It's not official."

Monica almost sneered. "Too bad. I don't want to do personal with you anymore."

Fawn gripped the door frame farthest from her to block Monica's exit. She held up the envelope. "I have a gift for you."

"I don't—"

"I know you don't want it. I saw you dodge me Friday. You were in such a hurry, you ducked into the men's room."

Monica shifted her big, black leather purse to hang parallel to the floor. "Yeah. One guy screamed, 'Whoa!' The other guy leered at me and said, 'Heyyy.'"

"I heard them. Man number one was calmed down with a gift card to the café. Man number two was summarily fired."

"It's not exactly overkill. He's—" Monica blocked out fierce air quotes with her fingers. "—*accidentally* walked into the ladies' room at least twice in the past few months."

Fawn extended the envelope. "Take it."

"Why? You already sacked the pervert. What more do I need?"

Fawn opened the envelope and handed the contents to Monica.

Monica huffed. "What's this? A brochure?"

"Yeah. For a vacation package, actually."

Monica's eyes grew into big grey circles. "Are you for real? It's for real." Her breath hitched as she held up a ticket tucked into the brochure. "With airfare?"

Fawn let out a tense exhale. "It's been hell without you, Mon. I hate what I said to you last week. I hate that you work so hard and didn't get a no-expense-barred getaway. So I bought you one.

You'll have beaches, massages, five-star meals, and everything else included. You can experience the best of what I had and not pay a penny for it."

Wild giggles bubbled up out of Monica. She covered her mouth, her eyes sparkling. "I can't let you give this to me. I was tremendously — okay — *slightly* unfair. You didn't mean to run off with Cade. Of course you didn't. You didn't even want his lousy number, for Pete's sake."

Fawn relaxed against the doorjamb and let a half smile slide into place. "Friendship salvaged?"

"Consider it one hundred percent saved." Monica rubbed Fawn's arm. "I can't believe I was gonna let that fiery-haired fiend erase how close we were."

"It's my fault. I lost track of who I was and what I had here." Fawn stopped herself from mentioning circumstances she didn't want to explain or lie about. She pointed to the floor. "I have Better Mind and you and my family."

Monica swiped her bangs to one side. "Yeah. I know what you mean. Can we do dinner sometime, or is your schedule a monster after your time away?"

Fawn dropped the envelope into the nearby office trashcan. "I've got a strong lead on new directions for the company. If it pans out, I can do whatever I like with my schedule."

Monica whispered. "Are you leaving Better Mind?"

Fawn glanced over her shoulder at the vacant hallway. "If I do, it won't be for a while."

Monica raised her eyebrows. "But you're thinking about it?"

Fawn pressed her fingertips into her stomach. "I don't want another ulcer, Mon. I kept pushing myself so hard, hoping a break would finally open up for me." She pointed at herself. "But it turns out, I'm the break. I'm deciding enough is enough. And I can position all of this — everybody involved — so that we all get a resolution that works for us. Me, Demetria, Janet. Maybe even Chloe and Birdie."

Monica's brows ticked. "Who's Birdie?"

"The woman with all the ideas we never saw coming." Fawn patted Monica's shoulder. "I'll tell you everything when I know more."

"You better."

Fawn nudged Monica with a playful elbow. "Quit hiding from me."

Monica grinned. "Agreed."

"I have a little work to do before I go home. I'll get to it and let you leave."

Monica pressed a long, loud smooch on Fawn's cheek. "You're the best, Fawn, once again. No more running off."

"Nope. Not even if Chloe's dating site hooks me a real catch."

Monica hummed in disapproval. "Definitely don't rush into any vacations with those losers."

Fawn scratched the back of her head. "Some of them have degrees and are kind of hot."

Monica scoffed. "I take back what I said in the bathroom. *You're* not looking for someone who's perfect, but I certainly *want* you to find someone matching that description."

"Well, we'll see who the site matches me up with, anyway."

~

Fawn beamed over the wine glass' rim at the man across the table.

Nico's sandy-blond hair curved in an asymmetrical wave above one eyebrow, the sides more relaxed. His eyes, the color of soft gingerbread, reflected the flickers of the candle's dancing flame in the middle of the table. The top button of his indigo button-down left his collar resting casually open. Nico laughed and spread his hands out from his sides. "I don't take an issue with it. I'm just surprised, that's all. Most women I've met won't drink on the first date because they don't want to make a wrong impression."

Fawn enjoyed a long drink and put the glass on the table. "I like the nice things in life. That's my message. I'm not going without something because it could mean something particular to somebody else."

Nico chuckled. "I'd drink to that, but unlike you, I decided not to order any."

Fawn wrinkled her nose flirtatiously. "I wouldn't think any less of you."

"Where's our waiter when we need him?" Nico peered around at the nearby tables.

The only visible staff members hustled some distance away.

Fawn sized up the entrées she and Nico had barely started eating. "My guess would be that the waiter shows up in time to offer us dessert."

Nico flashed a winning smile. "Don't tell me you do dessert and wine at the same meal?"

Fawn answered in exaggerated nods.

"All on a first date, too. Wow, you're brave. How'd you end up on Bonfire?" Nico scooped up a bite of his pasta.

Fawn's fork clinked inside her shallow bowl. "My assistant at work suggested I try it. She's been using it for months."

"Successfully?"

Fawn chewed a bite of spanakopita, earthy spinach mixing with tangy feta cheese under an umbrella of flaky phyllo dough. "I don't know. Chloe's younger than me. I'm not sure she's looking for the same things. And she broke off an engagement within the last year, so I'm not up-to-date on her relationship priorities."

Nico smoothed his plain black tie. "You have to know what a stand-out you are. When I saw your picture on Bonfire, I thought you were a knockout. Every time you smile, I need sunglasses."

Fawn warmed.

Nico straightened his tie and left it alone. "For the last time, I hope it wasn't too forward or weird of me to ask you out for a Thursday night. I was afraid you'd be taken if I waited until Friday."

"No. It was a pleasant surprise to get your, um, spark." Fawn directed her fingernail across an annoying itch on the back of her neck. "It's hard to find someone I might have something in common with who's also at a high level in their career."

"I understand, trust me. Being a VP of sales doesn't always make me the popular guy. One woman told me she'd rather date a dentist."

Fawn flicked one eyebrow up. "She'd have white teeth for the rest of her life if that worked out."

"That's fine for them. But what about me?"

Fawn motioned to their meal and the restaurant around them. "You're eating with me. I don't think you're a shark dressed as a vacuum hawker. I have a sales team. It takes guts and determination and a cool head to sell anything."

Nico rested his large hands on the table, taking a pause from his dinner. "Could my company borrow that for the department slogan? We'd get a lot more respect."

"Sure."

"Enough about work, though. It's tough, isn't it? You work all day, it gets in your head, and it's a challenge to switch gears when you're back on your own time."

Fawn finished a forkful of spanakopita. "Speaking of gears, I do like cars."

Nico tapped his fingertip on the table. "I remember that from your profile. What cars are you into?"

"Expensive ones."

Nico guffawed. "Who isn't?" He ate some more pasta. "It's funny. I wanted to be a race car driver when I was a kid."

"Did you? How'd you make the historically difficult transition from that into sales?"

"Can I just tell you I love your sense of humor?" Nico rushed a sip of ice water. "Okay. I was on board with the speed, the pit crews, the danger. The only problem was my reaction time. Too slow for driving two hundred miles an hour. It turned out, though, my brain works at the right speed for answering questions and suggesting the perfect product."

Fawn leaned over and whispered above the surrounding hubbub. "It seems to me the world needs more good salespeople than it does race car drivers."

Nico sighed. "If I had a glass of wine, I'd toast you."

Fawn shrugged and frowned, her heart hardening. "I don't need toasting anymore."

"No?"

Fawn shook her head. "Do you at least drive a fast car? Or did you put all those dreams behind you?"

"I drive a German car most Americans haven't heard of."

"You're a trendsetter."

"Trying to set a good example."

Fawn used her fork to cut another bite of spanakopita. "What's the engine like? V-what?"

"Six."

Fawn loaded up her fork. "I rode in a Venom GT once. The only V-8 I've ever experienced."

Nico hummed low in disapproval. "V-6 is faster. It's more powerful."

"Not necessarily."

Nico laid his fork down and fought off a superior grin. "I did a lot of research on this before I bought my car." He squared the fork to the table's edge and met Fawn's gaze. "Smaller numbers mean faster speeds. Do you know wire gauges? It's sort of like measuring those where bigger numbers relate to smaller sizes. Not everybody knows that."

Fawn pursed her lips, and her excitement cooled into tepid despising in her chest. She set her fork on the maroon tablecloth as well. "You're a smooth liar, aren't you?" She wiped her mouth with her cotton napkin and draped it on the table.

Nico's square jaw constricted. "I'm not. What are you talking about?"

Fawn collected her purse from the tiled floor. "The V corresponds to the engine's number of cylinders. Each number has its strengths and drawbacks. And they have nothing to do with getting bigger or smaller like wire gauges."

Fawn got up and lingered at Nico's side. "You thought I was a bimbo who liked expensive cars because they're pretty and cost a lot. Well, your German car — if it exists — can step aside to let my knowledge through because it was a German or an Austrian who shared it with me." Fawn forgave Hans for being a figment of someone's imagination if his lessons rescued her from an unsuitable date. "Did you even want to race cars as a kid, or did it just sound good?"

Nico glared at the candle flickering in its holder.

Fawn pulled her keys out of her purse. "Don't message me. Don't call me. Don't spark me. And learn to lie better or — wild suggestion — give it up and tell the truth. I assume you were paying?"

She drew her posture up straight and strode out of the restaurant. She climbed into her SUV and tore out of the parking lot. At the first red light that hindered her progress in getting home, Fawn freed her phone from her purse. She opened Bonfire's app and switched her profile status from *looking to ignite* to *looking for friends*.

~

Birdie erupted in another fit of giggles. Her dyed-orange hair lay in a classic pixie undercut with buzzed sides. Her large, chunky silver hoop earrings swung with her amusement. She showed her teeth and gums in a bright smile against her pink-toned, rosewood skin.

Fawn and Chloe rippled with Birdie's full-hearted enthusiasm. Fawn rested in the comfort of her new desk chair, comfortable once again with Chloe's standing presence hovering over one shoulder.

Fawn gave Birdie a few reassuring nods. "It's all right, Birdie."

Birdie wiped her fingertips along her lower lash lines. "I never dreamed anything like this would happen to me."

Fawn pulled a box of Kleenex from her middle desk drawer.

"Well, you're keen on what's working and what doesn't. You see gaps in our products the rest of us didn't notice."

Birdie shook her head at the Kleenex. "I'm all right. I wasn't trying to do anything special. I was just being me."

Fawn put the tissues away. "That's what always turns out for the best. Now." Fawn planted her palm over the half-inch thick portfolio on her desk. "How was collaborating with everyone? The managers and the different department heads?"

Birdie waved her splayed hands. "They were great. Everybody was nice and listened to all of my ideas."

"And you think everything's in here I need to look over to make the final decisions on turning your suggestions into reality?"

"Yes. We looked it over really thoroughly. We didn't want to leave anything out."

Fawn stood up and scurried around her desk. "I'd shake your hand, but what I really want to do is give you a hug, if that's okay."

Birdie laughed. "Oh, sure."

Fawn hugged Birdie briefly. "What I want to do even more than that is add my own plan to what you have in the proposal. They're your ideas, and I'd consider it only fair to promote you to serving on a brand-new team I'm calling Company Improvement. How does that sound?"

Birdie's chin quivered, and she stilled it, looking Fawn straight in the eye. "I'd be honored, Ms. Claire. I accept."

Fawn smiled. "Good. First, the committee will implement the changes in your proposal. When those are running smoothly, the focus will be on finding other areas we can reform or create."

Birdie fluttered her hand toward Fawn's desk. "That's a lot of planning around a report you haven't even read yet."

"I'll get through the whole thing this afternoon."

"You let me know if there's something that doesn't make sense."

"I'm sure it's impeccable. I'll let you know within the next few days what my reaction is."

Birdie raised a thin eyebrow. "Could you give me that news

before I get off work for the weekend? I don't want to worry about it for two extra days."

"I'll let you know tomorrow."

"Thank you for everything. This opportunity..."

Fawn leaned toward Birdie. "You made this opportunity. You're observant and smart. You spoke up about what you thought should be done differently. And it's going to make a world of difference for a lot of people. We'll hire more employees. Not only will the company make more money, but you will, and the whole community will get an uplift."

Birdie beamed her unabashed smile. "That's what I wanted."

"You got it. Email me or call me if I can do anything else for you."

"And if I get any more ideas."

Fawn dipped her head in a smooth nod. "Sure. These will keep us busy for at least six months to a year, but I'm always ready for fresh options."

Birdie stepped toward the door. "Nice talking to you ladies. I'll be waiting for that reaction from you, Ms. Claire." Birdie breezed out into the hallway and skipped past the inner windows.

Chloe propped her hand on the corner of Fawn's desk. "She has a ton of energy. No wonder she was more alert to these glaring holes in Better Mind than the rest of us."

"Yeah." Fawn returned to her chair. "Okay. I'm literally taking the rest of the afternoon to sift through this proposal. I don't want to rush through it and miss anything."

Chloe retrieved her notepad and pen from the top of the filing cabinet behind Fawn. "Gotcha. I'll hold your calls."

Fawn slid the portfolio toward herself. "Can you bring me a cup of water about every hour? And a snack at three."

Chloe jotted down a note. "Fresh fruit and organic sandwich crackers incoming."

"We'll want to do something for Birdie's department, too, to commemorate her leaving."

Chloe wrote some more. "Party for Birdie."

"Something lovely and lively."

"Noted." Chloe strode to the doorway. "Text or call if there's anything that crops up."

Fawn darkened at a peripheral constriction in her chest. She glanced over her shoulder at the windows showing her the hallway extending toward her vice president's office. "I doubt Demetria will try to talk to me yet, but if you happen to find she plans to interrupt me, can you block her?"

"Like a fullback after the half-time show. My ex-fiancé was a football nut." Chloe shut the door on her way out.

Fawn opened the portfolio and dug a pen out of her top desk drawer. She let Birdie's proposal unfold, straightforward, energetic, and inclusive. Fawn intended to identify potential challenges and time frames for execution. More often, she marked passages she wanted to remember for their inspiration and accurate description.

After an hour, she carted the portfolio across her office to the sitting area and studied it on the deep, off-white canvas padding of a faux-wicker sofa. She pored over another section in a chair she dragged closer to the sunny windows. Fawn found herself in her desk chair once more as she brought the project to a close.

A bright grin stretched across Fawn's face and wouldn't stop. She soared, her mind drifting through the possibilities. A more profitable Better Mind. A recognized, listened-to Birdie. Maybe even an appeased Demetria. Fewer unemployed in the city.

Fawn stood up and paced her office floor. The future that spoke the most to her unveiled itself. A free Fawn. Awash in options. Walking away from the job that once held her hostage and carving out a new life for herself. Hopefully, a pleased and supportive Janet.

Knocks rattled the glass door. Chloe waited on the other side, and Fawn motioned her in.

Chloe swung the door open. "Do you want another cup of water, or are you done?"

"It's finished." Fawn rubbed her forehead, concentrating on a light crease. "It's good. Solid. Actionable." *Depending on how many people implement these plans and who I have working on them, I could be out of Better Mind forever in a year, two max.*

Chloe raised her dark eyebrows. "So no water, then?"

"No."

Demetria paused outside the door, arranging her suit jacket over her forearm and carrying her red-leather tote bag.

Fawn wandered toward her. "Heading home already?"

Demetria smirked. "You've been holding bankers' hours. My oldest has a recital I'm expected to attend."

"Sounds cute."

Demetria rolled her eyes, which were imperceptibly puffy. "Dreadful. Did you get the proposal?"

Fawn perched on the nearest armrest of a chair matching her sofa. "Birdie delivered it right on time. I read the whole thing. There's nothing left out or skimmed over. The next six to twelve months of our working lives are in that portfolio."

Demetria grunted and skulked away.

Chloe issued a dismissive hiss through her teeth and lowered her voice. "She pissed off her vitamin guy, and he won't sell to her anymore. She gets super cranky when she's malnourished." Chloe walked up to Fawn. "I think what you're doing for Birdie is great, and I'm stoked to work for a company that listens to good ideas, even when they don't come from the inner circle. Who knows? Maybe I could be the next Birdie."

Fawn crossed one ankle over the other. "I'd love to see that for you, Chloe. You're a dedicated, hard worker. I bet you can do anything you set your mind to."

Chloe tittered and took a hop toward the door. "Are you leaving soon, too?"

"Probably. I'll just jot a few notes down about the proposal."

"I can find a hole in your schedule for you to speak with Birdie."

Fawn pushed herself up from the chair arm. "Tomorrow. If upper management can keep bankers' hours, so can you."

Chloe smiled and scampered out of the office.

Fawn relocated to her desk chair and stared at the portfolio's muted red cover. Were there any notes left to make? She sat back in the chair, her fingers fidgeting but not moving to grasp her pen on the desk.

To the portfolio's left, Fawn's laptop rested closed and silent. Beside it, three new photographs filled the familiar silver frames. The old pictures had been blown up and inserted in wide, grandiose frames decorating her office walls. The replacements on her desk showed her parents wide-eyed at the Mall of America the previous summer. The twins posed with their backpacks on their most recent first day of school, and Fawn's six family members crowded together in her parents' living room. Fawn gazed at the image's details without picking it up to study it closer. Tara and Cal's ruddy cheeks held clues to how loud and uncontrollable their twins had behaved that day. Donna and Tanner smiled with easy pride. Xavier and Casper shot their faces toward the camera with massive smiles, holding an arm around each other's shoulders.

A hint of guilt dampened Fawn's spirits. *I wasn't there.* Fawn guessed at places she could've fit into the picture had she been present. She could've squeezed onto the couch with the adults or knelt on the floor with the boys.

Did they miss me? Fawn didn't expect them to. She didn't demand their eyes cast downward with traces of sadness or their smiles falter with regret over her absence. At the same instant a phone or camera captured that photo, Fawn had romped through another dimension, thinking less and less about that same family.

Fawn covered her face with her hands and stomped her feet. "I have a chance to get it right, now. To be present. To stay healthy. Be happy. Give them the daughter, the sister, the aunt they deserve."

She took a Kleenex out of the drawer and dotted it to the corners of her watering eyes. She tossed it into the white ceramic trashcan beside her desk.

A dark figure caught her attention just outside her office doorway.

Cade stood there, his cherry-and-canary hair swooping toward the ceiling. His golden arms showed beneath the short sleeves of his navy button-down. Black pants draped over the rest of him to his brown leather sandals.

Fawn felt pulled to him as if by a magnet in her chest. She wasn't sure whether to blame remnants of their past relationship or his natural presence. She sniffled and cleared a small frog from her throat. "You may come in if you're so inclined." Fawn shut her pen away in her drawer.

Cade took slow, deliberate steps three feet into her office, not quite up to Fawn's desk. He sunk his hands into his pockets and gazed around. "Your office has a more peaceful vibe."

Fawn scooted her chair to sit squarely with the desk. "I just redid it."

Cade took in the pictures of the boys and the large prints of bright, far-reaching beaches. "I got selfish with you." Cade's eyes maintained a distance from Fawn, braced against the moment and their past. Swirling to the surface rose his yearning and torment only to submerge again. "I've never been that selfish with anyone, a guest from your dimension or someone I knew from my own."

Fawn swallowed and said nothing.

Cade held himself back from her. "I liked you and your company, so I failed to tell you certain things when I normally would have."

Fawn guessed at what Lisette might've added. "If I'd been another guest."

"Yes."

Fawn inspected her fingernails, natural and rounded.

Cade's voice became firmer and clearer. "I build a complex world, Fawn, but I adore purity above all things. Pure joy, freedom, self-expression, pleasure."

Fawn kept her focus off Cade, directing it past him at one of the padded armchairs. "You like things simple, and we left off in a very rugged place."

Cade eased toward her a few inches. "It's not about purity this time. It's about you."

Fawn shifted in her seat, almost wishing he hadn't come.

Cade licked his lips. "What was at stake for us was our family life. A carefully practiced and balanced order. Nothing more than the status quo."

Fawn drummed her nails on the desk. "Lisette thought it was important and worth protecting."

Cade made a strong pace forward. "Lisette didn't love you. She gave her loyalty to a fine-tuned system that didn't include you or allow for any deviation in our plans."

Fawn's eyes trailed up to meet Cade's. "What plans were those, exactly?"

"To continue enjoying an endless procession of guests, giving them respite and receiving ideas for improving our world in return."

Fawn laid Birdie's proposal off to the side on her laptop. "I tried to date again after you. It didn't work very well."

Cade touched his fingertips to his chest. "I ache because of the way I hurt you. I was uncharacteristically private about what I do and why you were there. I slid by to check on you, to see… if nothing else… that your time with us wasn't completely wasted."

Fawn turned her trio of silver frames around to show Cade the new photographs. "I have everything I didn't when I met you. My health. New prospects that can make Better Mind profitable enough that I can walk away. I toasted my sister at a family dinner I hosted in my apartment. She cried. This is the closest Tara and I have been in fifteen years."

Cade took a long pause and kept himself steady. "Congratulations."

Fawn nibbled her nail while something with equally real teeth bit at her insides. She shook her head. "Something's not right, and I know that. Then you show up."

Cade watched her, silent.

Fawn gestured to the picture frames on her desk. "Everything I wanted is right in front of me. Within my reach if not already in my hands." She got to her feet and smoothed her cotton skirt. "But no matter how easy it is, I'm still trying. Something isn't lined up. Something's off." Her heart hurt for Cade as she looked at him. "Missing."

Cade slipped his hands from his pockets.

"I didn't have to try with you. I didn't have to win over your family or your friends. I didn't have to give them gifts or grand speeches to convince them I wanted them around."

Cade hesitated half a second. "Your office looks great. *You* look great."

Fawn leaned her hip against the desk's corner. "It was effortless in the Playground. Not because Gerard fed me instead of a restaurant." Fawn rubbed her skirt's ruffled peplum between her fingertips. "Not because Caroline brought me made-up clothes as opposed to buying them from Ray at Maven. I could just be myself without expectations or judgments or rules or supposed-to's. There were no what-if's that weren't joyous."

She moved a partial step closer to Cade and sat down on the desk's front corner. She laid her palm flat on the neon-green surface. "I should be more comfortable and natural here, but I'm not. I'm living the embodiment of everything I learned from you in the Playground, but it's not..." Fawn's voice squeaked, and the wall around her heart cracked. "I miss you like I've never missed anyone. And nobody wants to hear about it because to them, you're the guy who kept me away for a year and broke my heart."

Cade's answer rumbled to life. "It wasn't a whole year."

Fawn nodded. "That's what I tried to explain. They find it moot."

Cade gravitated toward her more slowly than he'd ever moved. "My family's admiration and praise used to be enough to make my sacrifices worthwhile. This time, it hasn't been. It might never be again. It's been eighteen days since you left."

"I know."

"It turns out the most cloud-like mattress and the vastest array of down pillows don't matter when you miss someone this much."

Fawn whispered. "You miss me?"

Cade blinked. "Like crazy."

A tear leapt from Fawn's eye, and she dried it off her cheek. "You know, it's really disappointing to hunt for a new boyfriend after you. It's downright daunting."

"Yeah?"

Fawn shrugged. "Well, you reordered the stars for me."

Cade snorted. "You pointed out the faults in my arrangement."

"I was being mean." Fawn sighed. "I'll always remember the first time Caroline opened up that pillow closet for me." Laughter struck Fawn without warning, and she set a hand to her head. "I mean, there's another item I can hardly discuss with my family and Monica. A walk-in closet for pillows. They'd be out of their minds with jealousy if they even believed me."

Cade drew in a solemn breath. "Fawn, everything about the way my family operates is designed to draw our guests in. It's to put you at ease, make you comfortable with each member of our group, and give you enough that's familiar to encourage you to stay with us."

Fawn recognized the speech. "I know that."

Cade's hands fidgeted. "Down to every day's activities. Whisking you off on an ATV to wear you out and throw you off balance so we can talk you into spending the night. Letting you hang out with my siblings instead of me alone so you're making multiple points of contact with our world. Giving you restful days at the beach so you can get your bearings in a strange place. Even the six stools at the snack-kitchen counter so we can seat all five of us siblings and one guest." He held up his index finger for emphasis.

"I don't care." Fawn jumped up from the desk and laid a kiss on Cade's lips. When he didn't pull away, she dared to run her fingers over the day's coarse stubble on his cheeks. She could hardly believe she was touching him again. Compassion she hadn't allowed herself to think through before came rushing out. "I understand you never meant to hurt me. The only secrets you kept were about your dimension, not about yourself."

Cade lowered his chin and closed his eyes for a moment. His voice dragged with regret, and his irises flashed with determination. "I still hate that I mishandled my feelings for you and my duties to you as your friend. It would never happen again. There are no secrets like that left to hide."

Fawn kissed him, wanting to kiss him for as long as he would let her. He trailed his fingers down her arms, eliciting familiar shivers. Her longing ebbed away, making her more comfortable than she'd been in weeks. Fawn caught her breath and leaned her forehead against Cade's jaw. The warm contact soothed her further and reminded her of old times. Happy ones that brought a slight but unmistakable smile to her face. Her fingertips toyed with his sleeve. "If you asked me back to the Playground, I'd go instantly."

Cade cradled Fawn's face in his hands and kissed her. "Would you?"

Fawn hummed in agreement. "If I'm not being too forward."

Cade whispered, his lips lightly grazing hers. "You're perfect."

"Do you forgive—"

Cade pressed his finger against Fawn's lips to quiet her. "Do you forgive me?" He removed his hand.

"Yes," she breathed.

Cade smirked with precocious intent. "Would you like to get back together?"

Fawn closed her eyes in a prolonged, serene blink. "Yes."

Cade interlaced his fingers with hers. "Would you like to return to the Playground with me?"

"More than anything in the world."

Cade brushed his lips against Fawn's. "I'm glad you're so

impressed with my placement of the stars. Maybe that'll buy me some much-wanted relationship security."

Fawn chuckled. "With everything else you have going for you, I don't think you need it. Is Jax still with Ofelia?"

"No. They ended their affair amicably. Neither one of them could ever stay with one person for very long."

Fawn lifted her eyebrows. "Yoselle and Kee?"

"Together and strong."

"Good."

Cade nestled his forehead against Fawn's. "What about your people?"

Fawn examined her heart and her belly, both of them calm and relaxed. "I have no qualms about going with you. I'll figure out the rest of the details once I'm settled in the Playground."

"All your jewelry, all your clothes, all your favorite pillows and slippers are waiting for you."

Fawn exhaled with peace and delight. She withdrew herself from her embrace with Cade and retrieved her purse from its filing cabinet drawer. She walked halfway around the desk and paused. Fawn pulled her cell phone out and stuffed her purse in the bottom desk drawer. She strolled up to Cade, ready to go.

One final impulse tugged at Fawn, and she set her phone on the desk at arm's length.

Cade's hands alighted in the curves of her sides, well fitting and intimate. "Are you sure you want to do that?"

"Why not? It didn't do me much good last time. I don't know what to say to them or how long I'll be gone. It might as well stay here until someone reaches out to my — what did you call them? — people."

Cade gave Fawn's sides a gentle squeeze and peered around her office. "Is there anything else you want to bring or leave behind?"

Fawn took hold of Cade's arms. "I have everything I need."

He gazed back at her steadily. "It wasn't what you wanted originally."

"It's what I want now."

"Then only good things and wild adventures await you."

Fawn leaned up. "Without me even having to ask."

Cade kissed her, and Fawn blinked. When she opened her eyes, a different room spread itself around them, and her office several dimensions away stood empty.

About the Author

Cassandra Leuthold's hilarious fantasy adventure, *The Corundum Conundrum*, won recognition as a New Apple Book Awards official selection. Writing hooked her at age seven, and she never really stopped.

She loves playing with ideas most people think of as opposites: the magical and the everyday, the modern and the vintage, the darkest nights and brightest lights. Even while delving into fictional worlds, she remains a tea aficionado, DIY crafter, and unapologetic music junkie.

Cassandra stretches out in front of the TV with her writer husband and their cats. She wields a Bachelor's in Liberal Studies and a Master's in English.

Find freebies and more book fun at her website, cassandraleuthold.com.

www.ingramcontent.com/pod-product-compliance
Lightning Source LLC
Chambersburg PA
CBHW021231250626
47155CB00008B/2959